Hertfordshire

Leona Deakin started her career as a psychologist with the West Yorkshire Police. She is now an occupational psychologist and lives with her family in Leeds. She has written three novels in the acclaimed Dr Augusta Bloom series: *Gone*, *Lost* and *Hunt*.

www.penguin.co.uk

Also by Leona Deakin and published by Black Swan

Gone

Lost

Hunt

LEONA DEAKIN

BLACK SWAN

TRANSWORLD PUBLISHERS
Penguin Random House, One Embassy Gardens,
8 Viaduct Gardens, London SW11 7BW
www.penguin.co.uk

Transworld is part of the Penguin Random House group of companies
whose addresses can be found at global.penguinrandomhouse.com

First published in Great Britain in 2021 by Black Swan
an imprint of Transworld Publishers

A CIP catalogue record for this book is available from the British Library.

ISBNS
9781784165505 (pb)
9781473578647 (digital edition)

Typeset in 12.5/14.75 pt Garamond MT Std by Jouve (UK), Milton Keynes
Printed and bound in Great Britain by Clays Ltd, Elcograf S.p.A.

The authorized representative in the EEA is Penguin Random House Ireland,
Morrison Chambers, 32 Nassau Street, Dublin D02 YH68.

Penguin Random House is committed to a sustainable
future for our business, our readers and our planet. This book
is made from Forest Stewardship Council® certified paper.

For my parents, Jillian and Norman.
Thank you for raising three strong women and always encouraging us to follow our dreams.

How easy it is to make people believe a lie,
and how hard it is to undo that work again!

Mark Twain

I

She knew what she had to do. She had planned it meticulously, silently, over the past week. No one suspected a thing. They never paid her enough attention to notice.

They were all so much more than she was. She was weak and pathetic and overly reliant on the men in her life. Men who would use her and control her. Men like her father and her brother. She had tried so hard to take advantage of the chance she had been given; the chance to live a better life, but she had failed time and time again.

She parked the car in a deserted car park and climbed out. It was still dark. Swinging the rucksack on to her back, she secured the straps tightly around her shoulders and waist. It was heavy, and when she stooped to check the laces of her walking shoes she had to be careful that it didn't tip her off her feet. As she stood, the wind felt icy against her cheeks, and she pulled the sleeves of her jacket over her hands before setting off up the hill.

The path wound upwards through bracken and rocky outcrops. Ahead she could see the top of the sun breaching the horizon. Everything was silent. There were no birds to herald the dawn or wildlife to welcome its warmth. It had been a particularly cold January. Snow had fallen across the UK, and she passed a few icy white patches lingering at the side of the path.

If she were in a better state of mind, she would have thought it beautiful. But she was not. The self-loathing had become so bad that she had not been able to face her reflection in the mirror for months now. She managed to style her hair by touch and had stopped wearing any make-up. Others had congratulated her, misinterpreting her actions as a statement of liberation. But it was nothing more than self-hatred.

As she neared the top of the hill she twisted the thick elastic band on her left wrist in a figure of eight and looped it around her right wrist so that her hands were tethered in front of her. The elastic dug into her skin and her shoulders ached from the weight on her back. She might be determined but she also knew she was weak. There was every chance that at the last moment she would panic and chicken out; she had to be sure changing her mind would make no difference. That was why she had filled the rucksack with stones.

Paula would understand in the end. She would be better off without her. Stronger.

The ridge above the loch was exposed and the gusts even colder. She leaned into the wind, picking up pace and widening her stride, one foot in front of the other, until without pausing she stepped off the edge and plunged feet first into the freezing water below.

2

Day 1

Gerald Porter sat upright at the small table. The mop of red hair he usually wore long and a little unkempt was today brushed back from his face. With no press or public to see, there was no need to cultivate his trademark 'man of the people' image. The glass of water in front of him remained untouched and the seat opposite empty. He knew they were leaving him to stew; expecting that the longer he spent in this windowless room alone, the more desperate he would become to speak and escape. But Porter was stronger than they knew.

An hour and forty minutes later the door opened and a smartly dressed Asian woman entered. Her black hair was secured neatly at the nape of her neck and her dark eyes studied him, not with the awe and respect he was used to but with curiosity and a touch of impatience. She was accompanied by an older man. The one who had brought him to this room earlier today. What was his name again? It had been a town, Chester or Lincoln maybe?

'Mr Porter, I am Detective Chief Inspector Mirza. I believe you've met Detective Inspector Bristol.'

Bristol. His first wife had been from Bristol. He should

have remembered that. He did not respond to their introductions. There was no need. They knew who he was.

DCI Mirza sat in the chair opposite. 'I understand you are having some trouble recalling your whereabouts from 8am on Wednesday 24th January until midday on Friday 26th?'

Porter smiled. She got straight to the point. You had to like that.

When he did not respond she continued. 'Your PA informs us you had not booked any leave and that you claimed your last-minute trip was urgent. She also told us that having no details of your whereabouts in your diary for this amount of time is rare, if not unprecedented. So, where were you?'

'Why do you want to know?'

'You know why.'

'Explain it to me.'

Mirza placed her hands together on the table and leaned towards him. 'A serious accusation has been made against you, Mr Porter. It would be in your best interest to cooperate.'

Porter sat back in his chair and placed his hands behind his head. 'It's not my responsibility to prove my innocence. It's your responsibility to prove my guilt.'

'But surely it's in your *interest* to prove your innocence. This will be less painful if you do. Now, why don't you tell me who you met and why?'

Porter returned to his previous position with his hands on his thighs and his back straight.

'Did you take a charter flight out of Luton airport to Dubai on Wednesday 24th January?'

Porter said nothing.

'Who did you meet with out there, Mr Porter? Was it someone you don't want us to know about? Is that why you're hiding it from your own government?'

For the next twenty minutes, the DCI asked her questions and did her very best to tease and then goad him into replying. She was good, too. He could see why she'd made it so far in the police. Her ability to switch from helpful advisor to powerful threat was skilful, elegant almost. But he said nothing.

'Mr Porter, as you are unwilling to cooperate, I have no choice but to detain you for longer.'

'Good.'

Mirza's eyebrows rose at his response.

'Hold me under the Terrorism Act. That gives you fourteen days to interrogate.'

'Are you confessing to working with terrorists, sir?'

He waved his hand to communicate that her need to know was irrelevant. 'You have no idea what you're dealing with here, Detective Chief Inspector. So, detain me for fourteen days. No charges, no bail and I will speak to only one person about this matter.'

'And who might that be?' The policewoman straightened her graceful neck.

'Dr Augusta Bloom. And I suggest you get her here ASAP.'

3

Augusta Bloom let the others stride ahead as they reached the summit of Ingleborough mountain in the Yorkshire Dales. She wanted to take in the view. It was the kind of crisp cold winter's day that provided clear skies as far as the eye could see, from the snow-capped peak of Whernside to the north, then across the valley towards her childhood home of Harrogate. Following her mother's move into a care facility, Bloom had recently bought a small cottage just outside the town with the proceeds from the sale of her family home. She needed a base for when she visited from London; she enjoyed the escape to the fresh air and hills.

The walking group she had joined today was new to her. The people were nice enough, although the pace was a little slow for her taste. She had made the mistake of mentioning she was a psychologist to the older man with the walking poles and flat cap, and found herself deluged with details of his wife's battle with depression. She repeated that she was not a clinical psychologist, so had little insight into mental health, but the man was in transmit mode. Sometimes it was better to say she worked in research.

Her phone was on silent but she felt it vibrate in her jacket pocket. She was surprised she had signal up here.

The number was blocked, which usually meant the police were calling.

'Dr Bloom, this is DI Bristol of Westminster Police. Can I ask if you've ever had any professional dealings with Gerald Porter?'

She stepped away from the group. 'As in the Foreign Secretary?'

'Yes. He's asking to speak to you and we would like to know why.'

Bloom had no idea. She had only ever seen the man on the news. And why were the police calling? 'Is he in custody?'

'What makes you ask that?'

'I assume you're not in the habit of managing a Cabinet minister's diary, Detective Inspector.'

'He is refusing to speak to anyone but you. Why would that be?'

'I don't know. I've never met him. What is he accused of?'

'I'm afraid that's classified.'

'I see. So what do you want me to do?'

There was a pause before the DI said, 'How quickly can you get into central London?'

Bloom hung up after agreeing to make her way to the capital by early evening. It meant she would have to dip out of the walking group and start heading there immediately. She had intended to stay in Yorkshire for a week and have a well-deserved break. It had been a rough year. An old client, Seraphine Walker, had resurfaced, intent on impressing Bloom with an elaborate game she had designed to recruit fellow psychopaths. Bloom's closest friend and business partner Marcus Jameson had been caught in the crossfire and their relationship had been changed for ever – a fact that brought her great sadness.

Several hours later, Bloom arrived at the Ministry of Defence's Whitehall building in London as instructed. Once she had passed through security she was met by DI Bristol and escorted to the lifts. He selected LG4 and they descended into the basement. She knew this building was reported to have as many floors below ground as above. It contained Churchill's war rooms, where he and his advisors had worked during the Blitz.

Once out of the lift, the detective inspector followed signs to zone seven and eventually came to a stop outside room thirty-one. He made small talk along the way about the cold winter they were having but gave no details of what she should expect behind the door and so she did not ask.

Foreign Secretary Gerald Porter sat at a small table in a windowless room with a smartly dressed woman who introduced herself as Detective Chief Inspector Mirza.

'Mr Porter. I'm Dr Bloom,' she said, holding out her hand.

'Thank you for coming,' he said, taking her hand in both of his as if there was a long-standing affection between them. His trademark red hair was brushed back neatly from his face and his green eyes held her gaze for a second or two longer than was polite.

'I'm not sure how I can help,' she said to both Porter and Mirza as she took the seat next to the DCI.

'That makes two of us,' said Mirza. 'So, Mr Porter, you have what you wanted. Shall we begin?'

'Indeed we shall, once you and Bristol here kindly step outside.' Porter smiled at the policewoman with a warmth that did not reach his eyes.

'That's not happening,' the DCI said immediately.

'I said I would speak to one person and one person alone.' His gaze moved back to Bloom.

Mirza continued to protest and explain that it was critical she hear his explanation personally, but Porter simply stared at Bloom and in turn she stared back. This was all very odd.

Eventually Mirza nodded to DI Bristol, who opened the door for them both. 'I will be standing outside,' she said in a final attempt to exert her power, but it was clear the Foreign Secretary had won that battle of wills.

When they were alone, Porter relaxed his posture and averted his gaze.

'Your reputation precedes you, Dr Bloom. I appreciate your swift response.'

'What reputation would that be?'

Porter ran his hands through his hair and ruffled away the neatness. 'I have heard good things from influential people.'

'Which people exactly?' Bloom was unsure how a senior politician would have come across someone like her. They hardly moved in the same professional or personal circles.

'I need your help with something of a sensitive nature.'

'Is this to do with why the police wish to speak to you?'

Porter raised his eyebrows. 'No, I would not trouble you with such mediocrity,' he said. 'But I am prepared to offer the Detective Chief Inspector a deal. If you can meet my request, I shall respond to hers.'

'I don't think she will go for that.' Bloom had not missed the policewoman's tone of impatience. She was not a woman used to being batted away, Bloom guessed.

'Don't you worry about that. It is all in hand. What I need from you is help with a personal family matter. My older sister, Greta, has been tormented for years because of her daughter Scarlett. She has begged for my help but the timing has never been right. Politically.' He met her eyes again. 'You understand.'

Bloom knew family scandals could be kryptonite to political ambitions. 'How old is Scarlett?'

'Twenty-nine.'

'Has she been in trouble?'

'Not that I know of.' Porter smiled but did not expand. He looked like he was enjoying himself.

Bloom considered the options. 'She has contrary politics?'

'I expect so but that's not the issue.'

'OK.' Bloom waited.

'Have you heard of Artemis?'

Bloom looked at him blankly. 'The Greek goddess?'

'The organization dedicated to furthering women's rights.'

'Unfortunately not.'

'Greta tells me Scarlett has had some involvement with them over the years.'

'And you view that as a bad thing?'

Porter's lips twisted into a now condescending smile. 'I'm not a misogynist, Dr Bloom. I have no problem with women who earn their place in the world.'

Bloom chose not to take issue with the concept of a woman having to earn her place. This was not the time. 'I still don't understand why you need my help.'

'Scarlett is my sister's only child. Greta raised her alone. They spent all their spare time together until Scarlett went to university, and then everything changed. Over the course of that year Greta had less and less contact with her, and it has now been nearly ten years since they last spoke.'

Bloom raised her eyebrows. It wasn't unusual for the relationship between parents and children to change when the latter left for university, but this was a bit different. Bloom wondered at the nature of the mother–daughter relationship. Was their apparent closeness healthy, or was there something Scarlett might feel aggrieved about, enough to cut all family ties?

'You want me to reconcile your sister and your niece?'

'I hear you are something of an expert when it comes to uncovering why people go missing. Scarlett not only fell out of contact with her family but also all of her friends.'

'Have you asked Scarlett yourself? Perhaps there was a good reason she chose to cut ties with her past.'

'I received one email from her about five years ago, saying she wanted to make her own way in the world and Artemis was her family now.'

'How did you feel about that?'

'I didn't have a problem with it but I now understand that no one in the family has been able to reach her for a number of years. Her phone and email are all defunct. You think it lax of me not to have helped sooner?' he said in response to Bloom's silence. 'In my defence, Greta can be somewhat drawn to the dramatic and we have not always seen eye to eye. But the time comes when you face the kind of thing that leads you to make amends.'

Bloom wondered if this was whatever DCI Mirza was so keen to talk to the minister about.

'Have you or Greta spoken to the police?'

Porter narrowed his eyes. 'I made it clear. No police. Police mean press. That's why you're here. I want this investigated quietly. Scarlett's father passed away when she was a child, but he was a wealthy man and he left her a cool £2 million to be accessed at the age of twenty-one. Greta tells me this is no longer in the trust-fund account. Can you believe she never bloody checked the money was still there until I told her to? In all these years of bleating on about Scarlett.'

'When was it moved?'

'Not long after her twenty-first.'

'Could she have simply placed it in a personal account?'

'Of course, that's possible – but if this group has defrauded my niece I can't afford for that to become common knowledge. Am I making myself clear?'

Bloom nodded. She could see how this might prove embarrassing for a politician with a history in corporate finance. 'What's Scarlett's surname?'

'Marshall.'

Bloom wrote it down. 'How worried are you?'

Porter rolled his eyes as if this was nothing more than a favour he was doing for his dramatic sister, but Bloom caught the tension around his mouth. The whole thing angered him.

'If Scarlett's motives are rational, I have no concerns.'

'But you suspect they may not be?'

'That is where you come in. I need a spy and you are exactly the kind of woman Artemis wants in their ranks.'

4

Detective Chief Inspector Mirza was waiting for Bloom when she emerged from the room.

'What did he tell you?'

'He asked me to do him a personal favour and said in return he would answer your questions. What exactly has he done? The basement of MOD Main Building isn't the usual place to question someone.'

'Well, Gerald Porter is not just anyone. We have a PR nightmare on our hands if this isn't handled right. What favour has he asked for?'

Bloom looked down the brightly lit corridor and couldn't help wondering what was beyond each of the closed doors. 'I asked first.'

'I'm afraid I can't tell you that.'

Bloom studied the DCI. She was attractive, with flawless skin and large brown eyes alert with intelligence. On the train to London, Bloom had emailed one of her trusted contacts in the Met to ask if they knew DI Bristol of Westminster Police. They had confirmed that Bristol worked for Mirza, who had been promoted six months earlier to an undisclosed posting with the Ministry of Defence. Bloom's police contact had no idea what the secondment related to. It was as tightly zipped as any undercover operation, he had said. Based on who Mirza had in custody, Bloom guessed the DCI was tasked with handling any criminal activity perpetrated by Members of Parliament or the government itself. If this was true Mirza and her team were to keep in line the very people who funded and managed the police service. They would need to be squeaky clean, tight on process and highly sensitive to the fallout of any investigation they undertook.

'But he could have told me everything in there. So you'd already accepted the risk of my finding out by inviting me here and then leaving me alone with him.'

Mirza pursed her lips into a tight ball. 'I did my research before we called you and the bosses spoke highly of you. They even recommended I attend your course.'

'Well, it's coming up soon. I'm sure we could squeeze you in.' Bloom taught an annual module on the psychology of crime to senior leaders at the College of Policing's Harrogate site.

'If Mr Porter told you nothing of value then there is little point briefing you myself. He is clearly stalling for some reason.'

'I can't tell you if he said anything of value if I don't know what the information you need is. You can trust my discretion, Detective Chief Inspector, as I'm sure your bosses also told you.'

Mirza took a long breath in, then sighed. 'We received an anonymous tip that Porter has been selling secrets.'

Bloom frowned. 'He's the Foreign Secretary, why would he take a risk like that?'

'The money or the power. I tend to find it's one or the

other. Plus he has the opportunity: lots of meetings behind closed doors with bigwigs from around the world. I suspect someone knew what he was doing and waited for him to trip up. Last month he took an off-the-books trip to Dubai to meet someone he doesn't want us to know about.'

'Well, he mentioned nothing about any of that to me. He simply asked me to try and reconcile his sister and his niece, who've been estranged for a number of years.' She was careful with her words, aware that Porter had said he wanted no police involvement in his family situation. It would not serve her well to break his trust now, before she knew what all this was about. 'He said if I can do this, he'll answer your questions.'

'He's buying time. I wonder why. Did you agree?' When Bloom indicated she had, Mirza said, 'Thank you. You had every right to decline.'

'Reuniting people is what my partner and I specialize in, and when the police call I make it my business to do whatever I can to help.'

'Can you do it in fourteen days?'

'You're holding him under the Terrorism Act?' She knew that was the only condition under which a suspect could be detained for so long.

'Can you?' Mirza repeated.

'I shall do my very best.'

5

Day 2

The website for Artemis was slick and minimalist. Its home page simply stated its purpose as a force for positive change through the empowerment of women. The other three pages were labelled Testimonials, Membership Details and About Our Founder. Bloom clicked on the latter. The group's founder and CEO, Paula Kunis, was described as a vocal champion of women's rights. Her biography listed the many international conferences she had addressed and boasted that she had shared the stage with the likes of human rights lawyer and wife of Hollywood royalty Amal Clooney, and former prime minister's wife and barrister Cherie Blair.

On the testimonials page she watched a short video in which a range of Artemis members from different professions and corporations congratulated the group on its inspirational message and collaborative network. Then she checked out the membership page and saw there were various levels of involvement women could have, from paying a small monthly fee to gain access to online resources and discounted events through to full corporate membership listed as 'price on application'. It also included a number of forthcoming seminars Artemis was running in the city. There was no mention of Scarlett Marshall anywhere. Given the organization's clear efforts at self-promotion Bloom was surprised they were not capitalizing on one of their members' links to government.

'G'day, g'day,' said her business partner Marcus Jameson as he came to look over her shoulder at what she was reading. 'How was the Foreign Secretary?'

Bloom smiled at him. It was a source of huge relief that he had reverted to his cheery morning greetings again after their recent troubles. She was under no illusion that her perceived transgressions were forgotten but at least he was trying to behave like normal.

'Put it this way, I told the DCI to tread carefully and watch his tendency to use verbal trickery to dodge her questions.' Bloom took note of the contact details for Artemis. Their HQ was located in Edinburgh.

'Typical politician.' Jameson took his seat and opened up his laptop.

'Hmmm,' said Bloom. That was not what she'd meant but if the cap fits . . .

'What did he want you for?'

'He wants me to further the cause for women's rights.'

Jameson choked a little on his coffee. 'Gerald Porter is interested in women's rights? I thought the guy was one step away from Trump in his views.'

'His niece is a member of Artemis, a women's networking group-cum-campaign. He thinks there's something odd about it.'

'Course he does. It isn't populated by the plummy-accented public-school boys of the establishment.'

She pursed her lips. 'He wants to pay me to spy on them for him. He blames them for Scarlett becoming estranged from her family and he wants us to find her and reunite them.'

'Be careful. This group might be a problem for him in some way. It could be nothing to do with his niece, just politics. Don't be his pawn.'

'I haven't accepted yet. I told him I would speak to his niece and then take a view as to whether we can help in any way.' She turned to face him. 'The police are holding him under the Terrorism Act in the MOD's Whitehall building.'

Jameson's eyes widened. 'Blimey. What's he done?'

'I was sworn to secrecy but in short they think he may have betrayed us in some way.'

'Us, as in . . . ?' Jameson gestured with his hands to indicate *all of us.*

She nodded. 'But more importantly I don't trust this "find my niece" story. He must have all manner of people who could do that. Why me, a stranger to him?'

'You think Artemis is linked to whatever he's done?'

'I think there's a very strong chance.' She turned back to her screen and signed up to attend an Artemis seminar running in three days' time called Pursuing Gender Equality. She wanted to see for herself what the group was about.

Jameson sighed. 'Why don't we get simple missing person cases any more? Why do we have to get involved in large-scale cover-ups?'

Bloom smiled at her ex-MI6 partner. 'You love it.'

'I'm not sure that's true. Speaking of which, your friend's preliminary court hearing is coming up. Are you planning on going?'

Bloom's old client Seraphine Walker was facing trial for inciting the murder of a Bristol optician, among other crimes.

'I expect so. You?'

He scowled. 'If I never see that woman's face again, it won't be a day too soon.'

6

Greta Marshall's home was a modest detached house on a sprawling estate near to Milton Keynes. She opened the door on its chain and peered out, as if expecting a genuine threat to be waiting on her porch.

'Mrs Marshall, my name is Augusta Bloom and this is my colleague Marcus Jameson. Your brother Gerald has asked if we can provide some help with your daughter Scarlett. I left a message on your answering machine to say we would call by. Did you get that?' Bloom had spent the morning calling Greta Marshall with no joy, and so they had decided to take a drive out this afternoon.

Greta narrowed her eyes but nodded. She still held the door on its chain and showed no intention of releasing it.

'Could we have a quick chat, please? We'd like to find out if we can be of help to you and your daughter.' There had been no luck locating Scarlett via Artemis. Bloom had called the number listed on their website, posing as an old school friend attempting to trace fellow pupils for a reunion, and been told in no uncertain terms that they did not share details of their members. They would neither confirm nor deny that Scarlett was part of their group.

'Gerald sent you?'

'That's right, yes.'

Greta stared out at her with a mixture of suspicion and fear. Her hair was neatly styled in a helmet of large curls and she wore a string of pearls over her cream blouse. Bloom resisted the urge to glance at Jameson.

A moment later Greta closed the door. Bloom and Jameson waited to see if she would release the chain. When nothing happened, Jameson knocked again.

'Mrs Marshall? We are here to help. Genuinely,' he said.

'Leave it, Marcus. She's not going to let us in.'

'How do you know that? Maybe if we pitch it differently. Tell her what we do and the successes we've had.'

Bloom was already walking back down the path. 'That look on her face when she asked if Gerald had sent us? I don't think she trusts him. She's possibly even scared of him. And by extension she doesn't trust us.'

Jameson came to her side with a sigh. 'I see your point. She does look like something of a mouse.'

They reached his car; the Audi estate was new, a little treat he had bought himself for Christmas. Bloom guessed it was a reward for the trials of the past year.

'Let's look into the extended family. See if there's someone we can go through who Greta trusts,' Bloom said. 'Did you make any progress with Scarlett's whereabouts?'

'She has no social media presence that I could find. She's on the council records as living at her mother's house but she's never registered to vote, here or anywhere else. I've asked Lucas to dig deeper.' Lucas George was the freelance technical wizard they employed for any online research.

Jameson paused, then tilted his head in the direction of the house next door to Greta's. 'Twitcher. Two o'clock.'

Bloom did not look in the direction Jameson had indicated. 'Do you want to go or should I?' They both knew a neighbour who hovered at the curtains could be a useful asset.

'It's a man, so you go. Use those feminine charms.'

Bloom gave him a withering look then walked up the adjacent path and knocked on the curtain twitcher's door. A man in his seventies answered. He had white hair that grew in a halo around a large shiny bald patch.

'Good afternoon. I wonder if you can help me? I'm trying to trace Scarlett Marshall, Greta's daughter. I knocked next door but didn't have any luck.' She wasn't entirely sure whether this man would have been able to see Greta open her door a crack. She assumed probably not but chose her words carefully anyway. 'You'd be doing me a huge favour if you could tell me whether she still lives here.' She often found that a plea for help coupled with a direct question had people answering before they thought better of it. On this occasion, however, she need not have worried.

'We haven't seen Scarlett for many a year. She seems to have abandoned her poor mother. She's not well, is Greta. Something of a recluse. I said to Marjorie before she passed, God rest her soul, that girl should be here looking after her mum, doing her shopping and the like.'

'Does she ever visit, as far as you know?'

The man shook his head. 'I like to make sure Greta has fresh milk and bread so I get some for her every week when I go to Tesco's. It's not far away. One of those twenty-four-hour superstores.'

'I'm sure we could all do with a neighbour like you looking out for us.'

The compliment clearly pleased him and he opened the door a little wider. 'It's icy out there. Why don't you step in, and I'll tell you about Scarlett.'

Twenty minutes later Bloom climbed into the passenger seat of Jameson's car. It was lovely and warm and he was listening to Radio 2. As she closed the door and put on her seatbelt, he said 'Radiohead. *The Bends*' in response to a competition question.

'Any joy?' He turned down the radio.

'Peter was a chatterbox. Filled me in on all the local gossip. Seems Scarlett has not been seen since Christmas eight or nine years ago and her mother hasn't heard from her for almost all of that time. Greta herself never leaves the house and relies on the likes of Peter to bring her food and supplies. Seems like the neighbourhood has a nice little care network going.'

'She's a recluse then?'

Bloom nodded. 'Sounds like agoraphobia. The last time anyone saw her outdoors was a few years ago when she sat on the step in the sun.'

'So could Scarlett be similarly reclusive? Is that why she's not been around?'

'Agoraphobia doesn't tend to be hereditary, as far as I know. It's often caused by a culmination of life events that heighten a person's anxiety. They could certainly both be anxious in temperament, however. That's often a shared characteristic in families.'

'A worried parent raises a worried child?'

'Something like that, yes. Peter told me Scarlett was a happy girl, always popping in for tea and cake with his late wife. They lived next door throughout her childhood. Apparently she was a keen gymnast in her youth but gave it up in her early teens, probably because her mother couldn't take her to the various events. I asked if Greta and Scarlett were close and he concurred with Gerald Porter, saying they spent a great deal of time together and always seemed happy in each other's company. He had no explanation for Scarlett's absence, only that perhaps there had been an argument but he and his wife felt it would be rude to ask.'

'The overly polite Brits strike again. How many times do we hear that people don't ask the important questions because they're worried it would cause offence?'

Bloom couldn't disagree. They had dealt with many a case of missing family members who had been mistreated or abused under the noses of neighbours who felt they shouldn't intrude.

'I called Lucas while you were in there. He's found little trace of Scarlett online. She has a Facebook account but hasn't used it in a decade. He did find a few school friends who had discussed her absence on their Facebook pages and appealed for her to get in touch. But this was years ago.'

'There's no such thing as a private conversation these days.'

'True. I chose a good time to leave the espionage business. It's hard to spy when anyone with computer skills can track your every movement.'

'Are you telling me you left because you couldn't hack it any more, old man?'

Bloom expected a smirk. Her partner usually enjoyed her attempts at humour but instead he flashed her a look of irritation and changed the subject.

'I'll ask Lucas to send me the contact details of Scarlett's friends. See what they can tell us.'

Jameson had left his job with MI6 a number of years ago, opting to work on more rewarding investigations with Bloom. He had never revealed why he chose to walk away from his career and start over, but Bloom suspected something traumatic may have triggered it. For all his charm and humour, Jameson could be easily angered and was often overprotective of vulnerable clients, particularly women.

She said, 'Something is definitely amiss here. This should be simple. Porter said his niece was estranged from her family but otherwise had told him she was happy living her own life. So why can't we find her? Why is she a ghost?'

'Maybe she's dead.' He shrugged. 'You must have considered it. Her uncle said the last contact he had was five years ago and she's not been to see her mother for even longer.'

'If her mum was ill she may simply have run away. Some children can't cope with a sick parent.'

'They don't have to be ill. My father drives me and Claire crazy and he's perfectly fit and healthy.'

Bloom smiled. She could relate to that. Her heart surgeon mother had been a formidable character before the dementia set in. She could chastise Bloom with nothing more than a look. It had been a relief to escape to university.

'We should probably talk about that, by the way.'

'What? My mother?'

'Your decision to leave the spy game.'

Jameson started the car. 'Nothing to say.'

'It'll be a quick chat then.'

His jaw twitched and he turned the radio back up.

7

Nine years earlier

Scarlett joined the meeting as late as she dared and took the last seat on the back row. It was no surprise to find most of the people there had chosen to sit on the three rows at the rear, leaving the front two pretty much free. It was a session on improving assertiveness after all. The tall girl next to her wore a pretty green sundress buttoned up the front and gladiator sandals. Scarlett crossed her thin cardigan over the vest top that was past its best and had started to shed bits of cotton at the seams.

'Hi,' said the girl, flashing Scarlett a look from under her fringe. She had thick blonde hair. The kind that hung neatly in the style it was supposed to, which in this girl's case was a chin-length bob.

Scarlett smiled but didn't speak, as the woman at the front had already started. Politeness was important. It was one of the few things she remembered her father telling her and so she clung to it, as if living by his rules might somehow keep him alive.

She listened to the talk with predictable dismay. She didn't want to work at her assertiveness, or to push herself to train her mental muscles, or to face the cringing embarrassment of standing in front of strangers like one poor volunteer was doing and being brave enough to 'have a go'. She wanted a download or an upgrade, something instant and metamorphic. If she could have taken a pill and crawled into a chrysalis to emerge the next day as an assertive new version of herself, she would have taken it. Who cared whether it had been fully tested, or approved by some medical advisory board; she would swallow it without hesitation.

She had always been a people pleaser. From as young as she could remember she had delighted in a *wow* or a *well done* from her parents. After her father died, she grabbed the opportunity to help her mum cope, feeling less empty with every *Thank you, sweetheart* and *Isn't she a good girl?* But by the time she reached secondary school she realized trying to please everyone was a handicap. She never felt able to say what she wanted or what she thought or even just no. It left her feeling like she wasn't really there. Her friends asserted their personalities and their preferences with pride. They bravely announced who they fancied or what music they liked while she just nodded and went along with the majority, scared to say something wrong or ridiculous.

'I could never get up there like that,' said the blonde girl as the meeting ended. She nodded towards the volunteer who'd 'had a go' and was now receiving pats on the back from a small group of older students at the front of the room.

'Me neither,' said Scarlett, desperate to escape before anyone asked her to be brave.

'I'm Melanie.'

'Scarlett.'

'I like your necklace.'

'Oh, thanks.' Scarlett touched the thin gold chain with a heart pendant that her friend Tracey had bought her for her last birthday.

'I used to have one similar that my nan gave me but I lost it. I'm such a scatterbrain. What are you studying?' she added, because this was one of the mandatory three questions you asked as a new student, along with *Where are you from?* and *What A levels did you do?*

'Accounting and Finance. First year.'

'Nice. I'm doing Geography. First year too. I'm not sure I like it though. I might try to change.'

'What to?' Scarlett was intrigued. She didn't know changing your degree subject was an option.

'Oh I don't know. I'm also really indecisive.' Melanie giggled and her cheeks reddened a touch. 'Maybe I should try Accounting and Finance.'

They walked out side by side. Scarlett tried to think of something interesting to ask her.

Melanie waved to a group of girls already in the hallway. It was midday on Saturday so the student union was fairly quiet, most of its population either nursing hangovers or playing sports.

'A few of us are going to Albert Dock for a milkshake. A new parlour's opened up. Do you want to come along?'

'Oh no, sorry, but thanks.'

'Please, it's always nice to have new people to talk to. And they make milkshakes out of Mars Bars. How cool is that?'

Scarlett smiled. That did sound cool. She had no plans and it was a sunny day. Plus Melanie looked so keen for her to go along and she did need to make friends.

'Sure. OK. If you're sure the others won't mind.'

'Of course they won't.' Melanie linked arms with her. 'The more the merrier. Come on.'

8

Day 3

Lucas George came into the office first thing to meet Bloom and Jameson as arranged. He was a short guy of stocky build, with rosy cheeks and blond hair cropped close to his scalp. When Bloom first met him she had found his crumpled shirt and scuffed trainers concerning. But her worry was unfounded. Despite appearances, he was sharp, organized and efficient in all manner of digital investigation work and had quickly become an essential part of their team.

'Lucas, my man,' said Jameson, patting George on the back. 'How the devil are you?'

Once the men had swapped a few pleasantries, Bloom took her seat and kicked off the discussion.

'So far we haven't had any luck finding out where Scarlett is or how we can get in touch with her. Artemis won't release any membership details over the phone, which is fair enough, but I understand she has no digital footprint to speak of either, Lucas?'

'Only a shell persona. As I told Marcus, she is registered to vote at her childhood home but never has, she has an old Facebook account without any recent activity, and she isn't on Instagram, Twitter or LinkedIn. I checked some of the old platforms such as Friends Reunited and MySpace but again nothing.'

'That's unusual for someone of her generation, isn't it? Can we learn anything from her Facebook page?'

'It looks fairly standard for a young girl in her late teens at the time. She didn't post much – mainly pictures of her with her friends and the odd cheesy inspirational quote.' He brought up Scarlett's page and scrolled through the images on his iPad so Bloom and Jameson could see. The quotes she had posted included: 'When you think about quitting, think about why you started', 'No one can make you feel inferior without your consent' and 'Use your smile to change the world. Don't let the world change your smile.' Then there were a handful of pictures of girls with arms around each other, smiling into the camera.

'Scarlett is the red-head on the left in this picture.'

Bloom took the iPad and enlarged the photograph. Scarlett was the kind of girl it would be hard to describe. She was of average height, with straight shoulder-length auburn hair; not as pretty or glamorous as her friends; neither skinny nor curvy. 'The quotes might imply she was feeling disillusioned with things but she seems happy enough in the photos. Anything further?'

'Only that she doesn't appear to have an email address or mobile phone registered in her name. I found a Hotmail account she'd had around the time she emailed her uncle but it's no longer active. I can dig a little deeper to see if I can get into the Artemis membership database or look for bank accounts, loans and the like?'

'Hold fire for a bit,' said Jameson, knowing that this next level of investigation was not entirely legal. 'There's nothing to suggest Scarlett is in trouble. She may just be one of the few who choose to stay off grid. What about the Artemis group? What do we know about them?'

Bloom answered. 'Their website describes them as a women's networking group and campaign. Their founder and CEO, a woman called Paula Kunis, is building quite the reputation as an influencer. She has spoken at over twenty international conferences on improving gender diversity in businesses and even did a TED Talk in 2017 in light of the Me Too movement.'

'Was it any good?' said Jameson. 'I take it you watched it?'

'She was impressive. She's clearly a lady who's good on her hind legs, as my father would have said.'

'She also has over thirty thousand Twitter followers,' said Lucas, looking up from his iPad.

Bloom continued: 'She was born in America. Came over in the early two thousands according to her bio and worked for a large hotel chain on reception. After a short while she started an in-house support group for the women with low-income jobs she saw as being unfairly treated, such as cleaners and waitresses. She then convinced senior management to rewrite their policies to ensure equality for all and give women access to professional and managerial careers.'

'Surely most companies were doing that by then anyway?' said Jameson.

'You'd be surprised,' said Bloom. 'There's a lot of unconscious bias influencing how companies operate.'

'It's commendable, I suppose, but isn't it more of a marketing message now rather than a genuine fight for equality? We've had two female prime ministers, we have female soldiers on the front line and women at the highest level in all professions. Look at your own mother the heart surgeon. Artemis smacks of a female PR engine to me.'

'So speaks the voice of white male privilege.' Bloom felt her hackles rising.

'Oh, come on, that's not fair. Compared to lots of other countries, you have to admit in the UK men and women are pretty equal.'

'No, I don't have to admit that. I'll laugh at it if you like.'

He looked at her appraisingly. 'Seriously, you feel that strongly?'

'Marcus, there's no comparison between my experience and yours. From the start of my career with the police I was a woman in a man's world; I had to think about how I dressed, what I said and how I reacted, in a way men simply don't need to.'

'OK, but you chose to work for a pseudo-military organization that was established to uphold the law and is thus predominantly populated by men. If that environment has some inequality in it, it's for a legitimate historical reason.'

'Is it? You said yourself we have female soldiers on the front line, so the idea that men are the only ones strong enough to fight and defend is flawed, isn't it?'

Bloom saw Lucas shuffle in his seat. He was not comfortable with the tension in the room.

'You have a valid point, though,' she went on, 'and it's exactly why things can't be equal. Men do tend to be physically stronger, which means you two can walk down any street at any time of the day and feel safe. That's just not the case for a woman. I can walk down a street at 5pm on a sunny summer evening and still feel concern at the footsteps behind me, still feel relief when I find they belong to a woman.'

Jameson's jaw twitched as he hunted for a counter argument, but if he thought of one he chose not to share it. 'You like what Artemis stands for, don't you?' he said instead.

'Absolutely. I applaud them in fact. If things are ever to change, groups like this are crucial for raising awareness.'

'Well, I looked into how long they have been going,' said Jameson, his tone one of appeasement. 'According to Porter, his niece joined ten years ago but Artemis only registered as an official organization with Companies House eight years ago, designating itself as a charity. The registered address was originally in London but transferred to Edinburgh in 2014.'

'That's an interesting move,' said Lucas.

'For an organization so focused on influencing big business, moving out of the capital is unusual,' said Bloom.

'Property is cheaper up there. Maybe it was a budgetary decision,' said Jameson.

'So head for the commuter zones or somewhere like Leeds or Manchester with a direct train line into the city,' said Bloom.

Jameson shrugged. 'Remember she's an American. Our

country is tiny to them. Edinburgh to London would be within one state in many cases.'

Bloom nodded. It was a fair point. 'So Artemis appears to be legitimate and fairly successful. Do we have any idea what Scarlett might do for them?'

Both men shook their heads.

'We have a limited amount of time to find her, due to circumstances outside of our control,' Bloom said. DCI Mirza's fourteen-day deadline was already down to twelve. 'Marcus and I are meeting one of the friends you found on her Facebook profile this afternoon, Lucas. She told me she has had no recent contact with Scarlett but was happy to talk to us about her. And she may be able to help us speak to Scarlett's mother, Greta,' she added. 'I'm also attending an Artemis event on Monday to see if I can make contact that way with someone who may put us in touch with Scarlett. But in case neither of those things work, could you put us together a strategy for what could be done next digitally, Lucas? Then Marcus and I will formulate a plan.'

Once Lucas had said his goodbyes and left, Jameson said, 'And so to Porter. I've confidentially sounded out a number of contacts on whether there are any scandals bubbling within government and so far there have been no hits. Whatever he's involved in is very hush-hush. I don't want to dig too much deeper in the old guard as it may raise alarm bells, and I know you promised DCI Mirza we'd stay low key.'

'Good thinking,' said Bloom. 'Did the Foreign Secretary come up in any of the Artemis research?'

'Not as far as I could see,' said Jameson. 'I didn't find any links between Gerald Porter and Artemis and they're certainly not his bag. The organizations that support him are things like the fox-hunting association and a number of pseudo-right-wing groups. But I didn't find any conflict between them, either. There is nothing to suggest they have come to his attention politically.'

'OK, well, our remit is simply to find Scarlett and see if she can be reunited with her family. Let's not get dragged into other things unless absolutely necessary,' said Bloom, with a horrible feeling it was already too late.

9

Bloom and Jameson met Scarlett's school friend, Tracey Jepson, in the small kitchen at the rear of the beautician's she managed in the centre of Milton Keynes. The raven-haired thirty-year-old looked significantly younger than her years; a testament to her profession.

'Are you sure I can't get you anything?' The shelves around them housed a mixture of tea, coffee and cereal boxes alongside packs of nail varnish and large dispensers of cleansers and moisturisers.

Bloom and Jameson both declined.

'When did you last hear from Scarlett?' asked Jameson.

'Gosh. I can't even remember now. It was years ago. A few of us kept in touch after school and she was part of that for a while and then she just stopped calling and coming along. It was weird.'

'Lots of friendships drift after school, I expect,' said Bloom.

'I know, but Scarlett dropped all of us at the same time. It was like we'd done something to upset her but we could never get her to respond and tell us what. She even stopped speaking to her cousin, and they were always really close.'

'What's her cousin's name?'

'Harris. Harris Marshall. He was really hurt when she

shut him out. You should speak to him too. I'm friends with him on Facebook, I could message him for you?'

Bloom thanked her. 'What was Scarlett like back then?'

Tracey folded her tanned arms across her turquoise tunic. 'She was a bit quieter than the rest of us. She had a tough time at home. Her mum was always ill with something. It would have driven me nuts, but Scarlett never complained.'

'Might that have contributed to her absence?'

'If it did, none of us would have blamed her. But she was close to her mum, she always said she owed her so much for raising her alone after her dad died. I can't imagine that would change. If you want to find Scarlett, her mum would be the best person to ask.'

'Greta hasn't heard from Scarlett for nearly a decade,' said Jameson gently.

Tracey looked visibly shocked.

'You weren't aware of that?' asked Bloom.

'No! I often thought if I really wanted to contact Scarlett again I could just call her mum, but I figured if she didn't want to be friends she didn't want to be friends, you know? Is that why Mrs Marshall has hired you? Does she think something happened to Scarlett?'

'The family simply want to reconnect,' said Bloom, keeping her response suitably vague and non-dramatic. 'Did Scarlett ever mention a group called Artemis to you?'

Tracey frowned and shook her head.

Bloom opened up the browser on her phone and showed Tracey the Artemis website. 'Her uncle Gerald said she was heavily involved in their women's rights movement.' She couldn't be completely sure but it looked like Tracey shuddered a touch at the mention of Scarlett's uncle. 'Did you ever meet Gerald Porter?'

Tracey took the phone and looked at the website. 'A few times when we were younger. He wasn't a politician then.' She scrolled down the page. 'Are these the assertiveness people?'

'How do you mean?' said Bloom.

'Scarlett told me someone had offered to help her with her confidence, that she was going to some assertiveness classes. I thought it was with the uni but . . .'

'You think it may have been Artemis? They do offer workshops on improving confidence and the like. Which university did she go to?'

'Liverpool Hope. She was studying Accounting and Finance but I don't think she ever finished it.'

'And when did she do the assertiveness classes?'

'Now you come to mention it, it was just before she ghosted us.' Tracey looked up with wide eyes. 'You don't think someone at the classes told her to dump us, like to stand up for herself or something?'

'No one else went with her to these groups or classes as far as you know?' said Bloom, taking back her phone.

Tracey shook her head. 'She was the only one who went to Liverpool and the rest of us probably have enough assertiveness to go around, if I'm honest.'

One of Tracey's colleagues put her head around the door to say Tracey's next client had arrived. Bloom thanked Tracey for her time and the beautician showed them out via the salon, which was full of activity and chatter due to the arrival of a hen party complete with bride-to-be in a cheap veil. As they reached the door Tracey said, 'I've just remembered. I did see Scarlett again, a year or so after we lost touch. She was in Boots in town. It was odd.'

'Odd how?' said Bloom.

'She was with this other woman who didn't speak, she just stood smiling while we talked. And Scarlett was overly friendly in a kind of fake way. I assumed it was because she felt bad about cutting me off and I remember thinking I wouldn't be friends with her if we'd only just met.' Tracey's eyes moved away from the window where she had been staring and back to Bloom. 'That's sad, isn't it? When people change so much you can't remember why you were friends.'

When they were out on the street, Jameson said, 'Seems like Scarlett got in with a new crowd and dumped her old mates. That can't be unusual when people go off to university. The question is, were her new mates kosher or were they using her for her money and her contacts to the government? And what happened to her next? Why did she go off grid?'

'She didn't have strong links to the government back then, I don't think. Porter wasn't much more than a local MP.'

'So money then? Did this Artemis group know she had a trust fund and see her as a source of cash?'

'Cutting her off from her friends and family so they

couldn't talk sense to her?' said Bloom. 'What?' she added in response to Jameson's raised eyebrows.

'I recognize that tone. You've got a hunch.'

Bloom frowned and shook her head. Jameson's penchant for hunches and gut feelings made her nervous. She relied on evidence and fact; until she knew more, voicing her suspicion wouldn't help anyone.

10

Day 4

The morning sun was a bonus; the weather report had predicted rain. Lori had dressed appropriately in her Ronhill waterproof jacket and peaked cap. She never let the weather disrupt her daily run. It would be stupid to, living in the north of Scotland. People up here lived by the rule that there's no such thing as poor weather, only poor clothing.

There was no pavement alongside the field wall but the road was quiet – she could see it was clear ahead and she had turned the music in her headphones down low so she could hear any traffic. Cyclists were the worst. They could appear out of nowhere in big groups that could swallow up a lone runner. Not that she saw many on these early-morning runs.

She felt surprisingly good today. The blisters she had gained in her last 20k trail race had healed and her muscles felt flexible and strong. She loved this type of run; the feeling of freedom and strength as she lengthened her stride and swung her arms to take her up the largest of the three hills she had to conquer.

As the gradient increased, the lactic acid built in her legs and her breath began to feel heavy in her chest. At the top she would pause and take in the view. The sun rising over the Highlands was a thing of beauty you had to see to believe.

At first, she thought the sound of the car was in her music, perhaps because it didn't sound like a normal car. The driver had failed to change up a gear and the engine protested with a high-pitched whine. As she rounded a sharp left turn she realized the sound was behind her. She just had time to glance back and see the white vehicle make the turn and then lose traction on the road. The tyres screeched on the tarmac, drowning out the music in her ears and flooding her body with adrenaline. There was no time to think. She instinctively jumped in the air in an attempt to vault the field wall or land on the car bonnet but the impact catapulted her over the wall and into the field. She rolled three or four times in a spiralling somersault, barely noticing the shrubland tear into the skin on her legs and rip her jacket. On the second or third roll, she heard her arm break as it landed awkwardly below her.

Lori came to a stop face down, her heart pounding in her chest. It took a moment for her brain to catch up, like a rebooting computer. The first thing she noticed was the smell of grass filling her nostrils and the sound of a bird cawing above her, and then she tasted the metallic tang of blood. How bad was it? She could feel her legs. That was good. She wriggled her feet and to her relief they moved painlessly. Her torso felt fine, her breathing didn't hurt, but as she shifted position a searing pain took over. Lori lifted her head and her eyes immediately moved to her broken arm. The bone protruded through the skin just below her elbow. The sight filled her mouth with bile. She looked away and took a deep breath.

Calm down, calm down, calm down.

She had her phone. She needed to call for help.

Carefully, she rolled on to her good arm and used it to push herself into a sitting position. Her bad arm ended up in her lap and she could feel the wetness of her blood soaking into her shorts. Gritting her teeth against the pain, she fished her phone out of the holder attached to her good arm and checked the reception. One bar. *Please let that be enough.* She dialled 999. The line crackled but she heard the operator answer.

'There's been a car accident. I need an ambulance. I don't have much reception.'

As the operator patched her through to the ambulance service, Lori glanced to her left. The white car sat in the field, its bonnet crumpled from the impact against the wall. She could not see the person in the front, thanks to the glare from the morning sun on the passenger window, but what she could see in the back brought her to her feet.

Forgetting the pain in her arm, she began to run towards the car. The child looking out watched her with wide eyes. She continued to talk into the phone. 'A car hit me and a wall. There's a child in there.' She didn't know if the road had a name or number so she described its location as best she could from the village where she lived. 'We're about two miles up the hill on the left.'

She reached the car and could now see a woman in the

driver's seat. Her head lolled to one side and she was not moving. Lori tried the back door but it was locked. The child was a boy about five years old. He had started to cry. Lori looked around to see if there was anything she could use to open the door and that's when she saw the flames.

She took a couple of steps back and watched in horror as the orange wisps flickered against the front of the car.

'Hello. Can you hear me? An ambulance is on the way,' said the voice at the end of the line.

'There's a fire. Oh God! The car is on fire, and there's a child in the back. He's trapped.' The stones from the wall had scattered around the car and Lori realized she would have to use one to smash the window.

'Send a fire engine,' she shouted before throwing the phone backwards into the field and away from the car. Hopefully it would stay connected and act as a beacon for help.

The flames had doubled in number. Lori picked up the nearest stone and threw it at the front passenger window. It cracked but didn't break. She tried again and this time the rock broke through and hit the driver on the arm. The woman did not react. Lori pulled the sleeve of her jacket over her good hand, keeping her broken arm close to her body. Then she pushed the glass inwards and reached in to open the door.

'Hello? Are you OK?' she shouted to the driver. There was no response. 'I'm going to get your little boy out then I'll come and help you.' She looked over the seat at the boy. He was crying in loud sobs now and calling out for his mummy. 'You're OK, honey. Can you undo your seatbelt and climb over to me?' The boy didn't move. He reached out his little arms for his unresponsive mother.

Lori knew she couldn't climb over to him, not with her broken arm. She had to open his door. With her body flat against the outside of the car she extended her right arm along the top of the seat and reached for the door handle. It was just out of reach. She pushed her body closer into the door frame and tried again. She could feel the heat from the flames now. Her hand found the handle and she managed to curl the ends of her middle and index finger around the lever but when she tried to move it her fingers simply slid off. She swore under her breath and tried again.

'Mummy, Mummy,' whimpered the boy, his sobs catching in his throat.

On the third attempt the lever snapped outwards and the door opened a touch. Lori reached for it again and this time it worked. The driver stirred in her seat and made a low murmuring sound.

Lori quickly moved to the rear of the car. By the heat and the smell, she knew time was running out. She yanked the door open and reached over the boy to release his seatbelt. A moment later she was lifting him out of the car. Afterwards, she would not know how she did this with a bone sticking out of one arm, but she did. He clung to her neck with his right hand and reached back to his mother with his left.

The young woman was clearly alive but Lori wanted to carry the boy far enough away to be safe. She made it to the unbroken section of wall, intending to tell him to stay there while she went back for his mother, but then an explosion cracked the air with a deafening bang and Lori stumbled forward a few steps. The little boy screamed in her ear and she instinctively turned him away from the sight and hugged him closer to her.

11

Bloom spent Sunday afternoon reading up on Gerald Porter and the women's rights movement. Her research into Porter revealed he had enjoyed a successful career in City finance before moving into politics. He had a degree in Maths from Cambridge and an MBA from Harvard. At the time of the 2008 financial crisis he was on the board of a private equity firm that received negative headlines relating to suspected fraudulent investments and a company culture that staff described as toxic and rife with bullying. In the end, the firm and all its executives were cleared of any wrongdoing, but less than a year later Porter quit his lucrative position and announced he would be moving into politics. The timing struck Bloom as a little suspicious, as did his decision to radically change career. Had he been encouraged to leave because of his role in the scandals revealed in the press, she wondered; perhaps he'd received a payoff in agreement that he would not trade competitively against his former firm.

She also found it a depressing reality that men such as Porter are attracted to politics. People need politicians to be motivated to make a difference with a strong focus on public service, but all too often those who gravitate to that career do so for other reasons: the power, the status, the ability to influence things to their own advantage.

Porter had been elected as the Conservative MP for Windsor in 2011, and appointed to Foreign Secretary a year ago, after the previous incumbent resigned following a scandal around allegedly racist remarks made on social media during the Brexit campaign.

Despite the rumours of wrongdoing in his earlier career, Porter's role as a politician appeared to be unblemished until now. Could he really be selling British secrets? He wasn't a young man, but at fifty-two he was not exactly retirement age either. Then again, people of wealth view such life stages differently. Maybe he was looking for a nest egg that could give him and his current wife a life of luxury in the sun.

Bloom looked up from her laptop screen and watched the rain fall outside her kitchen window. Porter had given her the impression he was in some kind of danger. His talk of finally responding to his sister's calls for help regarding Scarlett made her think he was trying to make amends before something bad happened to him. But the worst the British justice system might do would be to put him in jail, so who else might he have betrayed?

And did any of this have anything to do with Artemis?

She turned her attention to women's rights. Following the first wave of feminism that focused on the right to vote in the early twentieth century, the second wave was described by the *Encyclopaedia Britannica* as based largely in the United States in the sixties and seventies where women were seeking equal rights and greater personal freedoms. The whole thing made for depressing reading. Bloom had grown up with an accomplished heart surgeon for a mother so had never questioned that any career was open to her, but women had been prevented from earning a medical degree as recently as 1873 – less than one hundred and fifty years ago. In fact until the First World War, and the need for women to step into the jobs of the men who went to fight, women had struggled to gain access to any professional career, including teaching and nursing.

Bloom remembered one of her university lecturers telling them the riddle of a young boy who had been involved in a car accident that killed his father but, when taken to hospital and rushed into surgery, the surgeon took one look and said, 'I can't operate on this boy, he's my son.' How is that possible, her lecturer had asked the group, and a moment of confused silence had passed over the student body until a small voice from the back said, 'Is the surgeon his stepdad?' Bloom remembered the lecturer smiling and telling the group, 'This is the power of stereotyping. Why would none of you conclude the surgeon is obviously the boy's mother?' Bloom remembered feeling ashamed to have missed that, especially given her mother's job, but that had only served to make the lecturer's point so much clearer. Stereotyping helps us to make sense of the world quickly, he had told them, it is a clever and efficient tactic of the human brain but it is not without its consequences or its flaws. We pigeonhole people to help us to understand others, but those pigeonholes can become cages.

Women's efforts to break free of their particular cage had included fights not just for political and career equality but for the right to not be discriminated against simply because of their gender. It was a sad truth that a group that makes up half of the human population found it necessary for laws to be passed in order to be treated fairly. And even in recent years petitions and pressure groups had still had to fight for the likes of abortion rights, the criminalization of forced marriages, the removal of topless Page 3 girls from UK newspapers, and equal pay. Groups like Artemis were not only a support network for women, they were necessary for making progress.

So maybe Artemis were working in opposition to Gerald Porter or his government in some way. That could be why he hadn't minded his niece cutting ties. Her involvement could be embarrassing for him.

Bloom knew she needed to tread carefully. When she had called Artemis enquiring about Scarlett Marshall she had been told they did not reveal membership details, and that was probably for good reason. If these women were activists pushing for change they would have enemies. She needed to approach them with care and earn their trust if she had any hope of them leading her to Scarlett.

12

Day 5

The Artemis seminar was held in the lower-level business centre of a well-known hotel chain. Bloom took a seat at the back of the room in a vacant row. There were around twenty other women present; a few were wearing casual clothes but most were dressed in business-type workwear. It was due to start at 1.30pm – well timed for professional women to attend during their lunch break. Most attendees appeared to be on their own, as suggested by the quiet in the room and the fact most of them were looking at their phones or the small Artemis pamphlet that had been left on the seats.

Bloom looked through the pamphlet herself. It listed various other seminars and courses the group offered, including ones titled Increasing Assertiveness and Enhancing Executive Presence. On the back page it had pictures of an Artemis-owned exclusive spa retreat where women were invited to relax, reflect and reinvent themselves in luxurious surroundings. Bloom expected that might set you back a fair few pounds.

When a woman moved to stand at the front of the room, Bloom placed the pamphlet in her handbag and looked up. The speaker was in her fifties with wispy dark hair that rested on her shoulders. She wore a deep-green pencil skirt with a bright white blouse that washed out her pale skin. She introduced herself as Margaret Lowe and briefly described how, with the help of Paula Kunis and Artemis, she had risen from a secretary in the financial sector to the Head of Procurement. Becoming a member of Artemis had changed her life and her prospects, she said, mainly because it changed her view of herself and what she was truly capable of.

It was a strong opening and Margaret spoke eloquently. She went on to address the issue of gender equality in the workplace, which for Bloom contained a few too many sweeping generalizations – like no woman is paid what she deserves – but on the whole presented a powerful case for change.

'If you recognize any of the things I'm talking about from your experiences,' Margaret said as she closed, 'please do consider supporting us, either through membership or by spreading the word about Artemis. Thank you.'

The group clapped in a polite British manner.

Outside the room a range of pastries, cookies and muffins was now on offer along with large flasks of hot water and coffee. Many of the women rushed out, presumably heading back to work, but a handful including Bloom stayed. She wanted to see what else she could find out about the group and maybe even ask about Scarlett.

Before she had finished making herself a green tea she was joined by two Artemis members wearing branded name badges. The older of the two, a woman in her mid-thirties, wore the same style of pencil skirt and white blouse with dark-green piping around the collar and cuffs. She introduced herself as Victoria and asked if Bloom had enjoyed the session. The other woman was younger, early twenties at the most, wearing a tailored green dress that looked too old for her. Her badge announced her as Amber and she looked at Bloom with an intense gaze.

'It was thought-provoking,' said Bloom.

'Wasn't it?' said Victoria, placing a hand on Bloom's upper left arm. 'Margaret is one of our best, a truly inspirational speaker. Have you attended any of our other events?'

'No, this is my first.' She flashed a glance in the direction of the younger woman, who still gazed at Bloom with a wide smile. It brought to mind Tracey's description of the silent, smiling woman she had seen with Scarlett in Boots.

Victoria's voice took on a syrupy tone. 'Well, we are truly honoured to have you. Every woman is welcome at Artemis. Do you work?'

'In research. Not very interesting, I'm afraid.' She had decided in advance to keep her true profession quiet. Not only could announcing yourself as a psychologist be distracting but until she knew more about this group she preferred to keep her counsel.

'And not very well renumerated. I bet your male colleagues are paid better. Which university?'

Bloom considered making an institution up but decided it was safer to stick close to the truth. 'I'm freelance at present.'

At that moment they were joined by the petite young

woman who had welcomed Bloom when she arrived. She wore a badge announcing her name as Natasha and she carried a clipboard. 'Can I take your contact details, please? We like to follow up with some complementary documentation.'

Bloom noted this woman had the same green colour in her outfit. She wore a dark-green blouse tucked into cigarette pants. Was it a uniform of some kind? A way of showing allegiance to the Artemis brand? On first glance the Artemis logo on their name badges looked to be written in purple lettering, but on closer inspection Bloom could see that there was a green border around the word. Purple and green on a white background felt like a familiar combination. And then she remembered: it had been the colours of the suffragette movement. Their green had been brighter but no doubt the influence was there. She recalled reading that they had chosen white to reflect purity and green for hope but she couldn't remember what the purple had stood for.

The three women smiled at Bloom as Natasha awaited her contact details. Their attention struck Bloom as a little unusual. At other business or academic events, networking sessions such as this were typified by people constantly looking out for their next target – or in Bloom's case, the quickest escape route. She took the clipboard from Natasha and wrote Ms Augusta Webb in the name section. She occasionally used her mother's maiden name when she didn't want people googling her and this felt like one of those times. She completed the section for contact number with the Pay As You Go phone she and

Marcus used when necessary and then put a line through the email box and handed the board back.

'Do you have an email address?' said Natasha.

'Only a work one. And I prefer to talk to people, if I'm honest.' She added an embarrassed kind of laugh to the statement for effect.

Natasha mirrored Bloom's laugh with a warm one of her own. 'Don't worry at all, Ms Webb. We prefer talking to people too. It's lovely to have you here, thank you so much for coming.' She also briefly touched Bloom's upper arm before walking away. It was clearly an Artemis thing. Bloom wondered if these people had studied something like neuro-linguistic programming, a training in influencing techniques that was popular with sales professionals and the like.

Victoria turned to Bloom. 'I work freelance too. I advise companies on how to ensure their in-house communications are gender representative. You'd be amazed how many company magazines are filled with pictures of suited men.'

'And white middle-class men in the main, I expect,' said Bloom.

Victoria looked delighted at that, throwing her arms wide. 'Oh my goodness, yes. You see it too. The unfairness, the prejudice, the unconscious bias. It's everywhere. That needs to change, don't you agree?' She glanced at her younger colleague. 'Amber and I are some of the many doing something about it and it's' – she paused, looking up at the ceiling before saying in a breathless voice – 'empowering.'

'Empowering,' repeated Amber, her smile still firmly in place.

Bloom suspected the whole speech was rehearsed including the dramatic pause and gaze up to the heavens. She decided to test the robustness of their sales pitch.

'Women alone can't change the gender imbalance, surely? Doesn't it require men to think and behave differently?'

'Never doubt that a small group of thoughtful, committed citizens can change the world; indeed, it's the only thing that ever has.' Victoria's response was passionate and emphatic. The volume of her voice rose and a few people standing around looked over.

Bloom recognized the quote often attributed to American anthropologist Margaret Mead. She had found it genuinely inspiring when she first heard it, until she discovered no one could prove Mead had ever said it.

'But' – Bloom shuffled her feet and avoided eye contact; she didn't want to come over too confrontational – 'don't some of that small group still need to be male?'

'Your question is valid. Of course it is. Questioning everything is core to all we do at Artemis. We don't just welcome women with questions, we positively seek them out because we need them.' Victoria's hand went to Bloom's arm again. 'We need women like you. You should join us for one of our weekend retreats. If you liked today you would love that. It's full of interesting speakers, exciting debates and practical planning. It's your chance to really start making a difference.'

'I do want to effect some social change. That sounds

appealing,' said Bloom truthfully, 'but a weekend would be difficult. I have a sick mother.' She wanted to tread the line between showing enough interest to maintain contact while avoiding signing up to anything for now.

Victoria made some sympathetic noises about Bloom's mother and then proceeded to talk about how wonderful the retreat was again. Bloom checked her watch and made her apologies, saying she needed to rush off for another appointment. She expected some resistance but Victoria simply thanked her for coming and said she hoped to see her at another event.

Walking away from the hotel, Bloom called Jameson.

'What did you find out?' he said on answering.

'I didn't ask about Scarlett.'

'What? Why? Wasn't that the point of going?'

'Marcus . . .' She knew he was savvier than that remark implied.

'You do remember we're working against the clock here.'

'Gerald Porter's request was not simply to find his niece but to establish the nature of Artemis and what hold they might have over her. I need to tread carefully. I don't want them closing ranks. I need to earn their trust.'

'I thought you said you weren't going to be his spy.'

'I'm not spying. I'm investigating. Trust me. I know what I'm doing.'

'Do you think something's off about this group then?'

'I'm not sure.'

'But you've got a feeling?'

She knew this was Jameson having a little dig. He

trusted his gut feelings implicitly and found her reluctance to do the same amusing. Bloom smiled to herself; if he was making fun of her that was good. That's how they used to be before Seraphine.

'I have another call coming in. I'll ring you back.'

'Charming,' she heard him say as she ended his call and accepted the unknown number that was calling the Pay As You Go phone. It was Victoria. She said she was so impressed and intrigued by Bloom's observations that she had mentioned them to the head of Artemis in London and that both women would like to invite Bloom to drinks that evening. Victoria made sure to stress that a meeting with her senior colleague was an incredible honour and only possible because the woman in question had a rare free evening. Apparently, she was in great demand and hard to get an audience with.

Bloom hung up, having agreed to travel to Canary Wharf to meet Victoria and her senior colleague, Melanie. She had taken Victoria's flattery with a healthy dose of scepticism. The invitation to meet a more senior member was no doubt the next step in the Artemis recruitment process. It was an effective sales tactic; nothing quite beats the high of 'somebody really likes me'. How many of the other women who had stayed behind were receiving similar calls? Most of them, she suspected. A group like Artemis could only survive by finding new members to fund their activities. And although she didn't want to be pressured into buying a membership or booking one of their costly retreats, she couldn't afford to play hard to get. DCI Mirza had only given her fourteen days and it often took much longer to find those who did not want to be found. She had to take every opportunity that came her way. The more she could uncover about the group and its activities, the quicker they could find Scarlett.

13

Lori awoke from surgery feeling groggy and nauseous, to find her parents and her partner Suzi waiting at her bedside. Her broken arm was in a large bandage from her wrist to her shoulder. The consultant had explained earlier that they had needed to pin the bone back in place and she was looking at a twelve-week recovery. So that put paid to the race in spring.

Suzi kissed her forehead and passed her a glass of water as Lori shuffled to a sitting position.

'Feeling OK?' Suzi said as she perched on the bed.

Lori nodded, sipping the water slowly. She'd had surgery once before as a child and suffered awful sickness on coming round.

'You're a local celebrity after yesterday,' said her father in his thick Glaswegian accent.

'Oh God. What have you done?' Her parents could be proud to the point of embarrassment. They never tired of showing her off to anyone who would listen with stories of how well she was doing.

'It's only the local paper,' said Suzi with a knowing smile. She knew how awkward Lori's parents could make her feel.

'Up to now,' said her dad and Lori's mum nodded, as if a special feature in the national press was a given.

'Stop them,' Lori said, squeezing Suzi's hand and closing her eyes. 'Please.'

Suzi laughed.

'How's the little boy?' When no one answered, Lori opened her eyes. 'Did you check?'

'His family collected him. His mama passed away.' Lori's mum shook her head at the fact and Lori closed her eyes again. She knew the young woman could not have survived but still it was hard to hear.

When Lori's parents had tired of singing her praises and headed off to do the weekly supermarket shop, Lori asked a nurse if she could speak to the little boy's family and pass on her condolences.

'I'm afraid not,' said the nurse as she placed Lori's painkillers on the side table next to her water. 'From what I heard, the aunt arrived about ten minutes after the ambulance reached the hospital and took the boy away. They thought she'd taken him to the family room but apparently she'd left, so we still don't know who the little fella and his poor mum are.'

'How did she get here so quick?' Lori looked at both of them. 'We were up in the hills, miles away from anywhere.'

'They'll have ID'd the car and contacted the owner,' said Suzi.

Lori shook her head. 'There's no way they'd be able to read that number plate and I didn't think to check it before . . .' She fell silent as the fiery images intruded on her thoughts.

Suzi frowned and looked at the nurse. 'You're sure the woman was related and not some nutjob?'

The nurse didn't comment as she moved on to deliver pain relief to the next patient. When she had completed her ward round she paused by Lori's bed again.

'The hospital is putting out an appeal and hoping the article in the paper will encourage someone to get in touch. I'll be sure to let you know if we hear anything.'

Lori cringed again at the thought of the newspaper article – but if it could be of help, perhaps it wasn't so bad after all.

14

Bloom waited in the impressive glass lobby of a financial services business in Canary Wharf. Victoria had explained that as well as heading up Artemis in the city, Melanie Coombs was the brand manager for Mercury Finance.

Bloom watched Victoria cross the lobby, accompanied by a tall woman of slim build with shortly cropped white-blonde hair. In contrast to Victoria's conservative skirt and blouse, Melanie wore a fitted mustard-coloured dress that stood out from the black and grey suits milling about.

'Ms Webb, how lovely to meet you.' Melanie approached with her hand outstretched and a friendly smile.

'Please, call me Augusta. This is an impressive building.' Bloom shook the woman's hand, or rather her fingers, which is all she had really offered.

'Wonderful, isn't it? We only moved here last year and it's a delight. Victoria said you attended our gender inequality seminar. How did you find it?' She gestured for Bloom to move to the rather swanky independent café located within the lobby area. 'I heard it went really well. Margaret is just fabulous. One of our favourite speakers.'

Bloom watched Melanie as she moved around the space and selected a table for them. Her language was expressive and positive but her slightly hunched posture and rapid speech suggested a woman conscious of her height and a touch uncomfortable in her own skin.

'Artemis is a wonderful organization. It changed my life. If you're looking for purpose and truth you've come to the right place. We will not disappoint.'

Her words reminded Bloom of something but she couldn't quite place the memory. 'I find that working as a woman in a man's world can be a lonely affair. I meet some impressive individuals but the ratio of male to female at senior levels is disappointing.' She had read the mission statement on Artemis's website. She knew they were intent on challenging such things.

'Yes, I see. That must be tough for you.' Melanie's focus on Bloom was a touch overdone, like a bad actress trying to convey sincerity.

'It can't be too different for you in the financial sector. It's very male dominated, isn't it?'

'Ha ha. Yes. Totally. They're a law unto themselves as well. They don't like taking advice from a woman.'

Especially one dressed like a model, Bloom suspected. She totally agreed with the principle that a woman should be able to wear whatever she wanted but she also knew in practice she could fall foul of people's natural tendency to make judgements on the basis of appearance. A fact that was just as true for any man.

As Melanie and Bloom chatted about a woman's place in the working world, Victoria took on the role that Amber had taken at the seminar, a passive observer, her smile fixed and permanent. The whole thing was, in the words of Scarlett's friend Tracey, a bit odd.

'How long have you both been associated with Artemis?' Bloom asked.

'Oh many years,' said Melanie. 'I met Paula very soon after she arrived in the UK. She's an American by birth but, luckily for us, she has chosen the UK to be her home. She is an inspirational individual, a visionary. She's challenging perceptions like no one I've ever come across and I believe she will absolutely change the world.'

'Change it how?'

Melanie glanced at Victoria and smiled. 'That is all to be revealed.'

'To you, or to me?'

Melanie looked momentarily uncomfortable. 'We are all on a journey to learn about the future, don't you think?'

'I suppose, yes.'

'Victoria is right, Augusta, you seem like a real Artemis person. She did right to introduce us. I'm so pleased I was able to free up the time. It is quite unusual at such late notice. Perhaps it was meant to be?'

'In what way am I an Artemis person, do you think?' Bloom made sure to smile. She didn't want her enquiries to sound too investigative, only interested. Something told her these women could be easily spooked.

Melanie brightened at the question, leaning forward and speaking in an animated way. 'Your observations are insightful and your questions thought-provoking. You are bright and curious and above all motivated to make a better world for yourself and others. Why else would you have come to our seminar and then made the effort to meet me? There is still so much to do, so many battles to face, and we need committed, courageous women to join us. So you are exactly the kind of woman we need.'

Melanie's praise was making Bloom feel good, inspired even, until the near repetition of Gerald Porter's words sent a small shiver down her spine. *You are exactly the kind of woman Artemis wants in their ranks.*

Walking back to Canary Wharf tube station, Bloom reflected on her first experience of Artemis. She liked what they stood for very much and their members were clearly well placed in the business world. Under other circumstances it would be a group she would genuinely consider joining, except for one thing: her sense that their interaction with her was a little off.

She called Lucas.

'I think Artemis may google me tonight and I could do without them finding my real name. Is that something you can help with?'

'What name did you give them?'

'Ms Augusta Webb. I used my mother's maiden name.'

'OK, that shouldn't be a problem.' Bloom could hear Lucas tapping away at his keyboard. 'I can put up a fake profile and make sure they reach that instead of anything else. What should I say you do?'

'I told them I'm in research, freelance.'

'As a psychologist?'

'I didn't specify. Perhaps go for something else. Something less threatening.' She thought about what she could realistically pull off if quizzed. 'How about behavioural insights? Lots of businesses now look for such things for their marketing and media activities.'

'Fine. Leave it with me. I can temporarily remove anything to do with your investigative work with Jameson too. Might be safest.'

'Not sure that needs to be temporary, Lucas. I think both Marcus and I are comfortable with anonymity. The people who need us tend to find us.'

'Gotcha. Give me five. I'll set up the dummy profile now and do a brief LinkedIn page. There are some behavioural insights roles advertised on Glassdoor. I'll use them for inspiration.'

'Brief is good. I told them I'm a technophobe with only a work email address.'

Lucas laughed. 'Perfect. I'll set one of those up too. Thanks.'

Bloom hung up and took the escalator underground, deep in thought. What was it Melanie had said? *If you're looking for purpose and truth you've come to the right place.* Why had that jumped out at her? There was nothing wrong with the actual words; they just didn't sound like something a business might say, or even a political group. What they sounded like were the promises of a religion. Is that why Artemis felt off, because the business-orientated, politically motivated PR was a facade? If so, it was elaborately done and executed well. You had to give Paula Kunis and her team kudos for that.

15

Day 6

Bloom sat in the gallery of the courtroom, waiting for proceedings to begin. This was only the Plea and Trial Preparation Hearing to determine that there was enough evidence to proceed. The trial itself would start next month.

While she waited for things to begin, she set to reviewing a request to take on a new juvenile client for counselling. She dedicated one day a week to work with youngsters caught up in the justice system. This latest young man had allegedly participated in the fatal stabbing of a boy from a neighbouring school. It was important work for Bloom, a way to atone for the mistakes she had made early in her career with the very woman on trial here today.

It was no use, she couldn't concentrate on the request notes; she powered down her iPad and placed it on her lap. The courtroom was quiet. Only a few staff milled about while the Crown Prosecution's legal team chatted casually around their table. There were a handful of other people in the gallery, none of whom Bloom recognized. She assumed they were press. The social media activity instigated by Bloom and Jameson's police contact, PC Lyle, exposing the activities of Seraphine Walker had drawn a good deal of attention. A psychopath collecting psychopaths was the sort of irresistible story that had journalists from the red tops salivating, especially when one of the psychopaths chose to kill her optician husband in an attempt to win Seraphine's 'game'. Bloom expected that the trial would be something of a media circus.

Seraphine Walker had been a teenage client of Bloom's who had faked her own death aged fourteen but then turned up alive and well last year as the mastermind of an elaborate game that she dared a select group of individuals to play. The purpose of her game was to assess the functional psychopaths that live amongst us in order to recruit the most intelligent for her own nefarious activities. Bloom and Jameson had managed to halt the game, hence today's trial, but Seraphine's subsequent interference in their investigation into the abduction and memory loss of Captain Harry Peterson, an officer in the Royal Navy, indicated her activities were far from over.

The door to the courtroom opened and Seraphine entered with her defence team. She had hired one of the top barristers in Leeds; a grey-haired gent with an air of confidence that bordered on arrogance.

Seraphine wore a cheap-looking black suit with a crumpled white shirt, and her hair hung lank and greasy over her shoulders. Bloom sat forward in her seat and studied her nemesis more closely. The woman's flat black shoes were nothing like the footwear Seraphine normally wore. She was the tailored, glamorous type. Her outfits were always figure-enhancing and her heels high.

It was one of her many weapons, and Bloom wondered why she might have chosen not to employ it today.

Twenty minutes later, standing outside Leeds Crown Court, Bloom had her answer. The case had been dismissed for an abuse of process; evidence had apparently been lost and Seraphine had walked free. Bloom watched her now standing with her barrister as he made a statement to the press. She looked small and broken; a woman whose life had been destroyed by a false accusation. But most importantly, Seraphine Walker looked like a nobody. Something she certainly was not. Bloom was relieved that Jameson had chosen not to join her. The whole thing would have made him furious. He had suffered more than most at the hands of Seraphine's twisted mind games.

'My client has asserted her innocence from the start. This has been a trial by social media. The scourge of society today. Words spoken in private and in jest were taken and twisted and turned into something they were not. True justice has prevailed today as the court here saw fit to treat the charges against Dr Mendax with the contempt they deserved.' The barrister held his hand up as the few press in attendance fired questions at Seraphine. 'My client will answer no questions but she does wish for me to make a statement on her behalf. As a world-renowned psychiatrist, she has a wealth of insight into the minds of those who are different, but this does not make her a manipulative psychopath. Thank you.'

Dr Sarah Mendax was the alternative identity Seraphine

Walker had created for herself after faking her own death in her teens. But she would always be Seraphine to Bloom. The barrister walked off with a protective hand on Seraphine's back. During the whole proceedings Seraphine had never once looked Bloom's way. But Bloom had no doubt the other woman knew she was there.

'I expect you predicted this outcome,' said Assistant Chief Constable Steve Barker as he came to her side. He was PC Lyle's boss and had also worked closely with Bloom and Jameson to expose the game. He would be as disappointed as she was today.

'Not exactly. But I can't say I'm entirely surprised now it's happened. I expect Seraphine has friends in the CPS. People who can manipulate things in her favour.'

'Well, take some comfort in the toll it has taken. She looked rough today.'

'Broken,' said Bloom.

'That's something, isn't it? Enough to stop her playing silly buggers again.'

Bloom smiled at Barker. He was one of her favourite police contacts. A lion of a man with a strong moral compass and a good brain. 'Don't underestimate her, Steve.'

'You think she'll bounce back?'

'I don't think she needs to.' Bloom was momentarily distracted by a familiar-looking woman emerging from the court. 'I think today was a ruse. Look, can we catch up later? I need to say hello to someone.'

Barker agreed and headed off in the direction of the city centre. Bloom made her way to where the woman stood typing on her phone. Her fingers shook a little as she texted. She wore a smart blue trouser suit, her hair was styled neatly in a chin-length bob and her nails were professionally done; but she looked older than her years.

'Penny?' said Bloom.

Seraphine's mother looked up and showed no surprise at seeing Bloom. 'Hello, love.' Her Yorkshire accent was still strong. 'I was sorry to hear about your mum. How's she doing?'

'She's oblivious enough not to care too much,' replied Bloom. Her mother's early onset dementia had meant a move to a home was the only option in the end. Bloom still felt it was a tragic end to her accomplished career.

Penny nodded. 'That's something then.' The lines around her eyes were deep and many. Years of grieving for the daughter she thought she had lost, Bloom expected.

'When did you find out about Seraphine? I wasn't sure if I should try to track you down, but . . .' The truth was, Bloom had never forgotten the venom of Penny's hatred all those years ago. She had blamed Bloom for her innocent child apparently taking her own life.

'They put her in the paper, didn't they. Couldn't miss that. I knew before I even read a word. You know your own child.'

'I'm sorry.'

'What 'ave you to be sorry about? Turns out you did nothing wrong.'

'I don't know about that . . .'

Penny reached a shaky hand out and squeezed Bloom's arm. 'It's I should be apologizing.'

'Not at all. You were grieving. I completely understand.'

Penny looked back at her phone and sighed. She was the same age as Bloom's mother. They had been school friends but somehow Penny looked even frailer. It was jarring to see. Bloom's mother had succumbed to a cruel illness at too young an age but until that point she had been happy and productive. What had Penny's life been like?

'Have you spoken to her about it?' said Bloom.

'She says speaking to me would be a waste of time apparently. Her solicitor asked me not to contact her or speak to the press. Seraphine doesn't want anyone to know about me. They were quite . . . strong on that.'

'Did they threaten you?'

Penny placed her phone in her handbag, folded the flap and took her time fastening the clasp.

'Penny, are you OK?' Bloom felt suddenly protective of the first real victim of Seraphine's psychopathic games.

'I'm fine, love. You must be busy. I hear you've done very well for yourself. You get yourself off.' She looked up and attempted a reassuring smile.

Bloom took one of her business cards out of her bag and handed it over. 'If you need anything, please call. I do understand and I'd like to help if I can.'

Penny asked for details of where Bloom's mother now lived and promised to call in on her. It was unlikely Sylvia Bloom would remember her old friend but you never knew what comfort a familiar face or voice might provide.

Bloom repeated that Penny could call anytime and the women said their goodbyes.

Bloom stood for a moment and watched the residents of Leeds walking by. She should feel relief at Penny's renewed view of her. So why did she feel so empty?

16

Under the watchful eye of the press, Seraphine thanked her barrister and climbed into the taxi he had hailed for her. It had gone well. Not that she ever doubted it would. There was real advantage in seeding as many organizations as you could with your own people, the justice system included.

As they drove away from Leeds city centre she took a hairbrush and set of grips from her handbag and tied her hair in a bun. She had seen Augusta watching from above. It was nice to know she cared enough to come, even nicer to see the look on her face when the case was thrown out. She didn't look furious; frustrated was a closer description. Most likely she had anticipated it.

Mother had been there too. What a pathetic waste of fresh air she continued to be. She had tried to reconnect on discovering Seraphine was very much alive. Not having to deal with such interference had been a real advantage of being dead. What the woman thought either of them had to gain was a mystery. You could not find two more different beasts. Penny was a tangled web of turbulent emotion. She could never begin to understand what made Seraphine tick.

Perhaps that's why she had such a connection to Augusta. Dr Bloom had been the only adult to 'get' her teenage self. How different life might have been if she'd had a mother more like that.

Not that she was complaining. Things had turned out well enough.

Out of the window she watched as they turned into a vacant parking lot and pulled up next to the only other vehicle: a Range Rover with blacked-out windows.

She paid the taxi driver and removed the disgusting suit jacket she'd worn for court as she walked to the other car. Forty-five minutes later she climbed out of the Range Rover in the Brasserie car park of the Devonshire Arms Hotel & Spa, wearing a cashmere coat and Jimmy Choo boots.

'The bag, ma'am?' the driver said, looking at the hold-all on the back seat that now contained her courtroom suit.

'Dispose of it, would you? I won't be requiring it again.'

On the cobbled area in front of the Brasserie a wedding party were having their photographs taken. Seraphine felt every pair of eyes on her as she crossed the immaculate lawn. She would be the talking point of the event, she knew. Who was the glamorous woman walking to the helicopter? A model? A millionaire's wife? A movie star? Never would they guess the truth. A fact that made her smile as she greeted the pilot who held open the door for her.

'Flying conditions are good, ma'am. So relax and enjoy the hospitality. Oh and congratulations.'

'Thank you, George.'

Inside, no expense had been spared. The seats were

leather, the headphones Bose and the tea, coffee and biscuits from Fortnum & Mason.

Seraphine watched her home county pass below her in a patchwork of never-ending fields and forests. It had felt strangely nice to come home but even better to be leaving; business was bad and needed her full attention.

By the time Hyde Park came into view, Seraphine had been fully briefed over the phone by her assistant Joshua. He was waiting for her on the helipad of their Knightsbridge building, a stone's throw from the world-famous department store Harrods.

'Welcome back, ma'am.' He was a young man only two months into the role, but he was bright – and, more importantly, ambitious. She had high hopes for him. He wasn't one of them; he'd never make it to senior management but she needed a normal for an assistant, someone who had the capacity for loyalty.

They walked to the lift and took it one floor down to her executive suite.

'I expect there'll be a few nerves waiting for you in here,' said Joshua as he handed her the briefing pack he had prepared.

'You don't know us all that well yet, do you, Josh? But thank you. Well done.' Seraphine smiled back at him as she stepped out of the lift.

The lift door closed, taking Joshua away, and Seraphine placed her hand flat on the biometrics scanner and faced the screen. Once her identity was confirmed the door to her inner sanctum opened and she walked through. It was the whole top floor of the building and the intelligence hub of her operation. The technology was cutting-edge and globally enabled; the data analytics ran continually and she could see what was going on everywhere she had an interest.

And then there was the view. On one side it looked across Hyde Park and the Serpentine, and on the other down Constitution Hill to Buckingham Palace.

'Did you find him?' she said on entering the boardroom and removing her coat. She hung it on the coat rack then walked to the large oval table but remained standing.

'It's odd. He's disappeared.'

It was Clive Llewellyn who answered. He had been one of her first UK appointments, a corporate lawyer with clients in the City's top firms. He was a broad-shouldered bear of a man whose ability to blend in was second only to his intellect.

She looked around the table. There were nine chairs; three now left vacant. The remaining five could not be entirely trusted, she knew. It was not in the nature of psychopaths to group together, no matter how high-functioning they might be. It was incumbent on her to ensure the cause was compelling and the consequences of betrayal clear. Which was why she needed to find Gerald Porter.

'People can't disappear. Not from us.'

'He has,' said Stuart Lord. Stuart had been one of the psychopaths she had recruited via the game investigated by Bloom and Jameson – the very investigation that had resulted in this morning's court appearance. Unlike Faye Graham, the player who had lost control and stabbed her husband to death, Stuart had been an impressive player: calm, calculating and ruthlessly competitive. Although it was true to say Bloom would never have got the better of Seraphine without some thoughtless texting on Stuart's part, she was not about to ignore the man's potential. Stuart was a rising star and quickly becoming her go-to guy for the more unsavoury elements of their work. He had a history in petty crime and drug dealing that made him particularly good at working those angles.

'Gentlemen,' she said to Llewellyn and Lord. 'I gave you one simple job to do. Find Porter. Would you like to explain yourselves?'

'We checked with our people in the cabinet office, the secret service, the police, the military – and nothing,' said Lord.

'What about the Freemasons, the Round Table, the gentlemen's clubs? They will shield one of their own and Porter knows who to avoid.'

'I checked,' said Llewellyn. 'We looked under every rock, but this bug has either bugged out or hidden somewhere clever.'

Seraphine walked to the window and looked at Buckingham Palace. The flag was up. The queen was in residence.

'He wouldn't have bugged out. He's too close to the prize, or so he thinks.' Porter was after her crown, he had absorbed every detail of her plan and decided to take it for himself. And he'd made good progress before she spotted what he was up to. She walked back to the table and took her seat. 'I rooted every single one of you out from under your rocks for good reason. No one gets to climb back under.' She sat back. 'Is it me or is this metaphor irritating?'

There were a few wry smiles around the table.

'OK then. No more bugs. No more rocks. Why don't we try for results?'

17

Bloom parked her Seat on the road alongside Jameson's sister's home. The last time she had been here their client, fifteen-year-old Jane Reid, had gone missing. Jane had been staying with Jameson's sister Claire, her husband Dan and their two young daughters, and Bloom had come to both comfort Claire and inform her that they suspected her friend Lana, Jane's mother, might be involved.

She came today for a very different reason. Claire had been insisting that Bloom join the family for dinner for months and she had finally given in. Claire wanted to thank Bloom for helping to find and return Jane, and the initial day of Seraphine's court proceedings had seemed as good a day as any. She carried a bottle of good Argentinian Malbec to the door and knocked. The sound of squealing children came from within.

Jameson's nieces burst out from behind their mother when Claire opened the door.

'Sorry, Augusta, they've been very excited about your visit.'

Bloom felt a touch bemused as the pyjamaed youngsters swirled around her, grabbing her coat and eventually taking her hands and leading her inside.

'Sophie, Holly, leave Augusta alone.'

The girls ignored their mum and skipped alongside Bloom chattering about a unicorn princess they'd had from Santa. Bloom was well versed in talking to teenagers with challenging and disturbing lives, but she felt totally thrown by these excited youngsters. Jameson spotted her discomfort as she entered the kitchen and gave her a broad smile.

'Tell Augusta about your mermaid tail, Soph, she'll love that.' He winked at Bloom.

The older girl jumped on to the kitchen chair so she was nearly the same height as Bloom and regaled her with details of a swimming costume she had with a real mermaid tail. She then jumped down to run upstairs and fetch the item for Bloom to see.

'Thank you for the invite.' Bloom handed the wine to Claire.

Dan took a look at the bottle. 'Oooh, that's a good one.' He wore a knee-length chef's apron that he dried his hands on before holding one out to Bloom. 'Welcome to the nut house, Augusta. I hope you like Italian. The girls have helped me to make fresh pasta.'

'I can't imagine you as a child,' said Jameson, coming to join her at the kitchen island. 'Were unicorns and mermaids ever your thing?'

'Absolutely not.' She smiled at him as she removed her coat. He never missed a chance to fish a little into her past. She knew her privacy drove him crazy, but she didn't do it on purpose. It was just how she was. In an effort to feed his curiosity, she said, 'I was a Sindy girl through and through.'

'Sindy?'

'She was like a less curvy Barbie, wasn't she?' chipped in Claire. 'I had a brunette one.'

'Me too, and a blonde one. They were my best friends for a good few years.' She could tell Jameson was not sure if she was being serious. 'And I love homemade pasta, Dan. Thank you. You shouldn't have gone to any trouble.'

'Of course they should. You're our hero.' Jane emerged from the lounge and greeted Bloom with a tight hug. She looked older and taller, even though it had been only six months since Bloom had seen her. She'd had her brown hair cut to shoulder length and had swapped her leggings and baggy tops for skinny jeans and a fitted Superdry shirt. Jameson had said Claire and Dan were going through the application process to become her official foster parents. Despite having found the father she had never met during the drama of last year, she had opted to live here, close to her school and friends. Bloom was impressed that Claire and Dan had kept their promise to always give the teenager a home if she wanted it. They were good people. It made sense that Jameson had retained his sunny demeanour despite the things he had seen in MI6. His family were his salvation.

Bloom and Jane chatted about the teenager's forthcoming exams, only breaking off to appreciate Sophie's fashion show with the mermaid swimwear. Once Claire had settled her daughters in bed they all took a seat around the large kitchen table. Dan poured wine into four glasses and sparkling raspberry juice into Jane's while Claire laid out pasta and salad, placed a homemade

Focaccia loaf in the centre of the table and told them all to tuck in.

'Let's get it over with then,' said Jameson as Bloom served herself some salad. 'How did she get away with it?'

'You saw the news then?' She passed the salad to Dan, sat back in her chair and picked up her wine glass. 'Her defence requested a termination of the proceedings.'

'Why? She admitted everything she'd done.'

'Lost evidence apparently. They didn't go into detail.'

'What the f—' Jameson stopped himself from swearing in front of Jane. 'I bet she looked smug,' he said, placing his fork down.

'I can't believe they let her off, after everything she did to Jane,' said Claire.

'And my mum,' said Jane. Lana Reid was still missing after leaving home to play Seraphine's game. 'What happens to her now?'

Jameson scoffed. 'Nothing happens. Nothing at all.'

'What did you expect, Marcus? That she'd simply roll over and take her punishment?'

He shook his head.

'We always knew she might wriggle her way out of things. But it's not a total loss. She knows that we know what she's been doing.'

'What does that matter if she's got the justice system in her pocket?'

'How did she do it? Pay them off?' said Dan.

'Manipulation is what she does, I'm afraid. She's good at it and she enjoys it,' said Bloom.

The group ate in silence for the rest of the main

course. Bloom might have found it awkward under other circumstances, but the fact they were all experiencing the same disappointment and resentment made it comforting.

Any further talk of Seraphine was avoided and they went on to enjoy an evening of light-hearted conversation. Bloom always enjoyed watching the banter between Jameson and his younger sister, the constant jibes and sarcastic put-downs revealed a relationship of mutual love and significant strength. It was nice to see that Dan and Jane had adopted a similar humour-based style of interacting too. Bloom wondered how differently she might have turned out had she been exposed to such a relationship. Her family mealtimes had been dominated with talk of manners and matters of the world.

Jameson walked her out to her Seat at the end of the night.

'I looked into the Artemis HQ in Edinburgh today,' he said as they reached the car. 'It's operating from a townhouse in a residential area not far from Princes Street.'

'That's a pricey part of the city.'

'It's a building converted into flats, according to the Land Registry. I also found a property in the Highlands. An old farmhouse on the outskirts of a small hamlet not far from Loch Ness. I'll let you have the details tomorrow.'

Bloom paused before climbing into her car. 'A remote farmhouse, are you serious?'

'Yeah, why?'

'It's just a bit stereotypical.'

'Stereotypical of a women's rights group?' Jameson raised his eyebrows.

'It may be nothing. There's just something worryingly familiar about how they seem to be going about things.'

'You do think there's something dodgy about them then?'

'We need to find out if the families of any other members are concerned. Artemis has been operating for nearly a decade, so if there's something dodgy about it somebody out there will already know.'

18

Nine years earlier

Scarlett sat in the hallway of the house, twiddling the strap of her handbag. A single wooden chair had been placed alongside the closed door. It reminded her of being sent to see the headmaster at school. It was a privilege, some had said. Very rare, others told her. She was lucky. She didn't feel lucky; she felt terrified.

Two pictures hung on the wall opposite. One showed the Greek goddess Artemis firing an arrow into the air with a watchful deer at her feet, the other showed Paula receiving some kind of award from a grey-haired lady in a suit.

'She's ready for you.'

Scarlett stood and brushed non-existent fluff from her skirt.

What had once been the lounge of the house, with its Victorian fireplace and ceiling rose, had been turned into an office. A desk sat in the bay window covered with neatly stacked papers, and two filing cabinets lined the wall. Above the fireplace hung another picture of Paula, this time showing her handing a scroll to another woman against a Grecian backdrop of white marble sculpted into an arch of arrow-firing cherubs.

'Scarlett, how lovely to finally meet you.' Paula reminded Scarlett of Snow White: hair as black as coal, skin as white as snow and lips of blood red. She was smaller than Scarlett expected but her energy filled the room. She strode to where Scarlett stood and took hold of both her forearms. 'I'm so glad we could find the time. Please take a seat.'

Scarlett mumbled something incoherent as she sat in one of the more comfortable-looking chairs positioned round a low table. She had not felt this intimidated since visiting the solicitor to hear her dad's will being read. At least then she'd had her mum's hand to hold.

'Don't look so afraid, Scarlett. I don't bite.' Paula's smile was warm and a little amused.

'Sorry. I'm pleased to . . . to meet you too.'

Paula sat forward on her chair and tilted her head to make sure she had eye contact with Scarlett. 'I hear great things about you, Scarlett. They tell me you are kind, and conscientious, and good with numbers.'

'I'm studying Accounting and Finance.'

'Many people study Accounting. That doesn't make them good with numbers.' Paula reached one hand out to take hold of Scarlett's left wrist. 'If God has given someone a talent I believe it should be harnessed and you, my dear, have a talent. Own it.' She squeezed Scarlett's wrist before letting go.

Scarlett felt a swell of pride. The kind she used to feel when her mum said *wow* or *well done.*

'Now, I'm not here to blow smoke up your ass.'

Scarlett felt her eyes widen. No one had ever said

anything like that to her. It sounded like a line out of a movie and she supressed the nervous giggle threatening to burst free.

'Our group is not your standard self-help variety, you get that, doncha?'

Scarlett nodded. The discussions they had been having over the weeks had become more spiritual, encouraging members to look deeply into the kind of soul they wanted to have.

'The universe is so much bigger than we can comprehend. Our perspective here on this little planet is tunnel-visioned and short-sighted. I want y'all to see you're here to do more than exist. Now I need to ask you something important. Are you ready?'

Scarlett was not, but she nodded.

Paula sat upright in the chair. 'If you could change one thing in the world what would it be?'

Bring my dad back, Scarlett thought but didn't say. That was not what Paula meant; not what she wanted to hear. But what did she want to hear? None of the girls had prepped her for this question. She wasn't good at thinking on her feet and she didn't want to get the answer wrong. The silence felt like it lasted an age as she dug about in her mind for something suitable to say. Nothing came to her. Nothing she felt brave enough to admit to anyhow. And then she remembered the picture of Artemis outside and how it had made her feel looking at that warrior woman, and she knew exactly what to say.

19

Day 7

Bloom left the consulting rooms she used in Islington for her juvenile client counselling sessions. The cold air chilled her face and she pushed her hands deep into her coat pockets. There was rain in the heavy grey sky above her and she'd omitted to bring an umbrella, so she decided to take the tube back to Russell Square instead of walking as she usually did.

Once back in the warmth of her office she made a call to her most reliable police contact in Scotland, a no-nonsense Glaswegian superintendent by the name of Ned Nesbitt. It was a name that begged for comment, but those who had tried, in jest or judgement, had soon learned the error of their ways.

'Gusta,' Nesbitt said by way of greeting. He had always struggled to pronounce her name in full.

'How's the weather up there, Ned?'

'Fine as can be. Warm and mild.' This was an ongoing opening to their conversations. Bloom had worked with Nesbitt when she had been employed by the police. He had been an inspector investigating a spate of particularly violent rapes and Bloom had been asked to advise on the rapist's motives and profile. It had been a traumatic case for all involved but after months of effort they finally caught the guy. Bloom wouldn't say she and Nesbitt were friends, but living through these things left a special kind of bond.

She explained that she was looking into the Artemis group, and that their HQ was in Edinburgh, and that another of their properties was about thirty miles out of Inverness.

'What d'ya need?'

'Intelligence at this point. Have they had any interaction with Scottish police? Any suspicious activity, et cetera.'

'What you suspecting?'

'I'm simply trying to gauge their legitimacy as this stage.'

A couple of hours later Nesbitt called back. He'd checked with the database and found no contact between Artemis and the Scottish police. He'd asked a sergeant from Inverness to call Bloom about the farmhouse. Apparently, there were a few rumours about the place, but that's all they were – rumours. Nesbitt said the sergeant would be happy to fill her in.

Bloom thanked the superintendent and sent her best wishes to his family.

Jameson joined her in the office just after lunch. 'I had a couple of hits on Artemis,' he said as he entered and removed his North Face jacket, hanging it on the back of the spare chair. Water begin to drip from its hem on to the floor. The rain had clearly set in. 'There's a journalist in Newcastle who ran a story a couple of years back on female students whose parents claimed they were targeted by Artemis and convinced to pay over their student loans. She said it was all very dodgy but there was nothing concrete for police to follow up on.' He sat in his seat facing Bloom and tapped on his phone. 'She managed to get a quote from an Artemis representative.' He began reading from the screen. 'It says: "We are a charitable foundation aimed at improving the voice of women within society and any donations given are at the discretion of our supporters."' He looked up. 'The story went nowhere but she's emailed over the article and her research notes for us to check out.'

'So perhaps Tracey was right when she said Scarlett had come into contact with the assertiveness people through Liverpool Hope. Artemis may target universities. It makes sense. They reach an ambitious population with access to funds.'

'I'm not sure you can say today's students have funds.'

'No, but they still disproportionately come from middle-class or upper-working-class backgrounds, which means they have good credit ratings. They can get loans, if not family funding.'

Jameson acknowledged her point with a side nod. 'The second hit is more worrying. One of the coppers from our intel group came back with something.' They had created a database of their various police and MOD contacts when they'd started their business; people they could call on via a carefully managed mailing list.

'Go on.'

'The inspector said he was surprised to see the group named in my query as he was recently approached by a father who claims his daughter's death was linked to Artemis.'

'Her death? What are we talking?'

'She drowned in a remote loch in Scotland last month. She lived in the Artemis house in Edinburgh, by all accounts, and according to housemates had driven out into the countryside to hike on the day in question.'

Bloom wondered why this had not come up in Superintendent Nesbitt's search for Artemis. 'Who's the inspector?'

Jameson checked his notes. 'Birch from . . .'

'Cumbria Police,' Bloom finished. 'Is that where the father lives?' Jameson checked his details and nodded. That explained it. Although the various police forces across the UK tried to communicate and keep each other updated on their investigations there was still a lot of room for improvement. 'And the father thinks it's suspicious?'

'She had rocks in her rucksack and her hands bound with an elastic band.'

'Oh no. Poor girl.' Bloom thought for a moment. 'Did the housemates raise the alarm?'

Jameson slowly shook his head. 'Water company employee found her.'

'So do we have a suicide or something more sinister?'

'Birch says suicide is most likely. Her hire car was parked not far away and the rental company said she hired it in her name the day before.'

'And what does the father think?'

'I thought we'd find out for ourselves.' He held up his mobile. 'I have his number.'

Bloom pulled up a chair as Jameson dialled.

'Mr Roberts. My name is Marcus Jameson. I've been given your number by Inspector Birch of Cumbria Police. My partner and I are investigating the Artemis group and he recommended we speak to you.'

'You police?' Linwood Roberts had a deep voice, made husky probably by years of smoking.

'We are private investigators, Mr Linwood. I'm Marcus's partner Augusta. We have a client whose niece is part of the group and he is concerned about her welfare.'

'Call me Linwood. And he should be worried. He needs to get her out, and fast. No good coming to anyone in there, let me tell you. No good at all.'

'Inspector Birch told us about your daughter, Linwood. We're sorry for your loss and we don't want to intrude on your grief,' said Jameson, his voice taking on the tenderness that always impressed Bloom. 'But he said you feel Artemis may be responsible in some way. Is that right?'

'My Shauna was a good girl. A sweet girl. We lost her mum early doors but Shauna took care of us, me and her big brother. I tell you that woman Paula Kunis has a lot to answer for. She takes these kids in, promises them the world and then sucks the life out of 'em.' His voice cracked with emotion and he took a few seconds to compose himself. 'Last time I spoke to her all she could talk about was how she was letting Paula down. How she needed to work harder to be a better person. There was nothing wrong with her but that evil' – Roberts paused again, no doubt to avoid the swear word he was about to say – 'convinced her she was broken. Paula Kunis may as well have put those rocks in my Shauna's rucksack herself. No doubt when my baby stepped off that ridge that woman's hand was on her back.' Overcome with emotion, Linwood Roberts moved the phone away from his mouth or covered it with a hand.

Jameson looked at Bloom, his eyes sad but raging.

She wrote a note on her pad for him to read: *How does he think Kunis is responsible?*

'I can't imagine how you must feel, sir,' said Jameson after allowing Roberts time to calm down. 'Do you mean Paula Kunis had a metaphorical hand on her back, or do you suspect she was there?'

Roberts answered slowly, emphasizing every word. 'I think that woman attacks their minds then steps away and lets her evil destroy them.'

Bloom felt her fears about this group step up a gear. She began to write down more questions on her pad, aware there may be too many to trouble this grieving father with, given his emotional state. *How did Shauna find Artemis? How did the group recruit her? What worried Linwood about the group's influence on Shauna's thinking? Had he ever met Paula Kunis?*

'When did you last speak to Shauna, Linwood?' said Jameson, scanning Bloom's list as she wrote it.

'She never called. We'd had no contact with her for years. It was like she was dead, but she wasn't.' His voice broke again and the sobs could be clearly heard this time.

'I'm sorry. Maybe we should speak some other time?'

'No. No,' said Roberts, controlling his voice. 'If I can

help save another lass that would be something, wouldn't it? Did you know if a person does what my Shauna did without leaving a note it's not recorded as suicide, it's classed as undetermined intent? What is that? Bureaucratic nonsense, that's what. Massaging their statistics. Denying the truth.'

Bloom underlined one of her questions and Jameson nodded.

'What appealed to Shauna about Artemis? Why did she join?' said Jameson.

'She wanted to be part of something. She wanted to have an impact on the world. That's what I mean, you see, she was a good girl and they preyed on that.'

'Had you tried to get her to leave at any point?'

'All the bloody time. Me and her brother. Even in the early days when she was all full of "they said this and they said that" we both had a bad feeling. We tried to reason with her, get her to see these people were telling her what she wanted to hear, but she was already lost to us. I see that now. When a person refuses to see the truth. When they're so far gone with their dream of a perfect life and a perfect world it's impossible to reason with 'em. Her brother, Jimmy, eventually gave up, said it was her life, let her live it. But I was always watching that group and that woman, thinking one day, one day, Shauna would pop up somewhere and I'd go and . . . grab her and not let go.'

It was clear the man was struggling to continue talking. Jameson thanked him for his time and his honesty. Perhaps they could speak again, Jameson suggested, when he and Bloom had done a little more digging. Linwood

Roberts said to call anytime because exposing Artemis was all he had left now.

'Are you hearing what I'm hearing?' Bloom said.

'Some kind of twisted pyramid scheme, do you think?'

'Pyramid scheme, political movement, religious sect, they take many forms. I think we're dealing with a cult.'

Jameson looked sceptical. 'Like Waco and Charles Manson?'

'Maybe a little more sophisticated than that. More Scientology than Heaven's Gate. And you know how dangerous a cult can be.'

'I can't say I've ever come across one outside of the media.'

'Of course you have, Marcus. The definition of a cult is a group of people having beliefs regarded by others as strange and who impose excessive control over their members. I'm sure you've come across that.'

'You're thinking of certain terrorist movements, I take it.'

'Or Jacob Bello's freedom fighters out in sub-Saharan Africa,' Bloom said, referring to the case they had worked on the previous year with naval officer Captain Harry Peterson.

'So not just hippies dancing in a field then?'

'Certainly not. In fact, rarely so, because of the types of people who start them. Such groups are often led by an extreme narcissist. Someone whose inflated ego and sense of entitlement make them as destructive as any psychopath.'

'Great,' Jameson said with a deep sigh. 'Linwood did say

this Kunis woman was evil. Is it normal for a cult member to opt out of the group like Shauna did? I thought cult suicides were all end-of-the-world-type things, where everyone does it together or has it done to them.'

'Well, for starters, it's unusual for anyone to leave a cult in any way because it's difficult. Difficult to physically escape because members are often isolated by location or financial dependence, but also mentally. You have to be incredibly strong of mind to rewire your own thinking from within the propaganda machine. Everyone around you is saying black is white. But some people do manage it. There are a number of children who grow up in cults who as young adults reject the whole thing, for instance. Shauna's way of escaping may have been the only way out in her eyes, or . . .' Bloom paused to think it through.

'Or they bumped her off?'

Bloom shook her head. 'That's not what I was thinking, although we shouldn't rule it out. She may have been about to speak out against them. But I was thinking she may have felt unworthy. Suicides are often related to a person's feelings of self-worth. Her father said the group's leader Paula Kunis breaks people. I expect he means by destroying their self-esteem in order to make them reliant.'

'Why? Why do people like Kunis do that?'

'Power, status, fame, adoration. The usual reasons.' Bloom closed her notepad and went back to her desk.

20

Bloom Skyped Professor Terry Colby at Stanford University as arranged, at 10pm her time, 2pm in California. She had looked him up earlier in the day and requested a consultation. Her knowledge of cults was out of date and Professor Colby was regarded as *the* expert in the field.

A bald man with a handlebar moustache, the professor looked like a stereotypical CIA agent, which is exactly what he had been before his academic career began. Only when he smiled did he lose the stern 'I mean business' look. His smile was broad and warm and when he spoke his voice was chocolate-thick.

'Good to see you, Dr Bloom. I read your paper on the antecedents to the narcissistic personality when I was studying. There were some great insights.'

'That's kind of you to say, Professor. My career has taken me in a more practical direction since then and I'm somewhat out of touch with the latest academic thinking, so I do appreciate your time.'

'Call me Terry, please.'

'Augusta,' she said by way of response.

'So you've got yourself a troublesome little cult over there, have ya?'

'Possibly, we're still trying to confirm the nature of

the group, but I'm concerned with its level of secrecy and the tactics they are using to attract members.'

'The Marcus Jameson you mentioned in your email, he wouldn't be ex-Secret Service, would he?'

Bloom was taken aback. 'Yes, actually, MI6. Do you know each other?' She hadn't had a chance to mention this call to Jameson yet.

'Yeah, we do. Young Fugs and his team over there worked on a couple of things with our boys.'

'Fugs?'

Terry gave a short little laugh. Controlled and abrupt. Much like the man, she thought. 'Ugly Fugly. We all had nicknames. Great guy. It was a real shame.'

'That he left?'

Terry paused for a millisecond, then said, 'Yeah, that too. Anyhow, you said the leader of this group is an American, Paula Kunis. The surname rang a bell so I had an old friend do a little digging. Turns out her dad Donald Kunis was a lowly lighting engineer in Hollywood who claimed back in the eighties that he could predict an actor's success. Reckoned he'd been given the divine power of foresight. He got quite a bit of notoriety for a while with a following of budding actresses, but it soon collapsed when he failed to predict any actual successes. Your typical fraudster.'

'What happened to him after that?'

'A dropout. Turned to drugs in the nineties and overdosed but – here's the interesting bit – not before he'd been peddling the story to anyone who'd listen that he'd sired the next Hollywood great.'

'Paula?'

'Darn right. He'd take her around the studios to show her off.'

'And did she ever do any acting?'

'Not that I'm aware. Her dad died when she was fourteen and she briefly lived with her mother before ending up in foster care.'

'What happened with the mother?'

'By all accounts she'd run out on the family when Paula was a kid, and within six months of Paula going to live with her again she'd kicked the girl out. Sounds like a total liability.'

Bloom thought about the impact of such a start on Paula. One parent idolizes her as some sort of prodigy, the other abandons her, twice, sending the message that she's irrelevant.

Terry continued. 'Classic breeding ground, hey?'

'The narcissistic personality is often a result of parents bragging about their kid to the outside world but the child failing to develop the requisite skills to live up to their claims.'

'They believe they are special but they don't know why,' said Terry.

The result was an adult with an over-inflated but fragile ego. They want everyone to agree they are special, but if people don't, their temper tantrums can be legendary.

'They set themselves up as gods, sometimes literally. Paula certainly could have the temperament. I watched a few of her speeches online.'

Bloom sighed. 'I was really hoping I was wrong about this.'

'Well, better to know and be able to act than find it's too late.' Professor Colby's words were not simply general sentiment, they were born of real tragedy. His younger brother had been a member of the Branch Davidian cult run by David Koresh. Koresh was a self-styled reincarnation of Jesus Christ who convinced followers to live on a ranch in Waco, Texas and prepare for judgement day. When stories of child abuse and the stockpiling of arms came to light the ranch was raided by the ATF and the FBI, resulting in a fifty-one-day siege and a huge fire that engulfed the ranch and killed over seventy of the cult's members, including Terry Colby's brother. It was the reason that on retiring from the CIA he had invested all his energy in becoming an expert in cults.

'Any suggestions as to what we can do?'

Professor Colby talked Bloom through a couple of cases he had worked on in the last decade and the lessons learned. He said he would send her some documentation to support his points and wished her luck. Bloom hung up and sat staring at her kitchen wall. The gist of Colby's advice had been to listen and learn, and at all costs avoid inflaming Kunis's temper. That meant getting close to the group. Closer than she'd like. Colby had commented that Jameson was particularly skilled at in-depth investigations, so could advise her well.

She had never pushed Jameson on his reasons for leaving MI6, but all the signs pointed to him having had some sort of breakdown. If she was going to ask him to talk about his time as a spy, she'd need to know more about what had happened so she wasn't in danger of triggering anything traumatic.

She also needed to go back to Gerald Porter and renegotiate terms; this assignment had just changed gear.

21

Day 8

Jameson was already at his desk and reading the BBC News report on the dismissal of Seraphine's court case when Bloom arrived. How many times had he read this over the past two days? She could see the tension in his clenched jaw and hunched shoulders. She would need to wait for him to calm down before she could have the conversation she needed to have. She patted his back as she passed by way of hello and he muttered a greeting without looking up.

'You're a piece of work,' he said to the screen as he viewed the picture of Seraphine standing meekly behind her QC in her badly fitting suit. He rubbed his face with both of his hands and then stood and snapped his laptop closed. 'I'm going for a walk. I need fresh air and food.'

Bloom read through Professor Terry Colby's case studies as she waited for Jameson. An hour later he returned and he looked a little lighter. At least he had colour in his cheeks.

'You're going back in to see Porter this aft?' he said. She had emailed him the night before to say she had requested another meeting with the detained Foreign

Secretary via DCI Mirza. She had avoided mentioning Professor Colby to Marcus, figuring that, as there was a history there, it was better to bring him up in person. 'I drew a blank on exactly why they have him detained. It's classified as Top Secret.'

'Losing your touch? I suppose it has been five years since you retired,' she teased.

'Funny.' Jameson smirked. 'I can still access some information but when it comes to the country's secrets my contacts take it very seriously and rightly so.'

'Top Secret. What would that usually relate to?'

'Material that would cause exceptionally grave damage to national security if made public, so anything related to military attacks, terrorism, crime, economic security, cyber security.'

Someone selling secrets would fit the bill, Bloom thought.

'National security is a big deal. That's why we have at least four agencies dedicated to it,' continued Jameson.

'Four?'

'MI5, MI6, Defence Intelligence, GCHQ – and that's just the big boys.' He winked.

He appeared in good humour. The walk and breakfast had done him good. But now she'd have to bring him down again. She didn't relish the idea but she knew it was necessary and long overdue. She spun her chair so she was facing him and crossed her legs.

'Can we have a chat?'

'Uh oh,' he said, leaning back in his chair. 'Am I in trouble?'

'I need to ask you something. I wouldn't normally but it's important.'

'You know you can ask me whatever you like, Augusta. I'm an open book.'

Bloom gave him her warmest smile. The smile she reserved for vulnerable clients. 'I spoke to Professor Terry Colby at Stanford University last night. He's an expert in the psychology of cults, and ex-CIA.'

'Terry Colby? I know him. Shiny head, impressive moustache? A professor, you say? Well, there's hope for us all.'

'He said you worked together.'

'Sometimes the world of espionage is a small one. Good guy.'

'He said the same about you. He also said it was a shame . . . what had happened to you.'

'He said that?'

Bloom nodded and waited in the silence, determined that Jameson speak next.

'What do you want to know?'

Bloomed softened her tone. 'What happened.'

'Why? Why do you need to know? It's in the past, dealt with.'

'You'll be OK to talk about it then.'

'I am, but not without good reason. I don't pry into your private life, do I?'

His defensiveness told her whatever it was probably hadn't been dealt with.

'I think you've had more insight than most into my demons this past year or so, Marcus. But I take your point. Terry said the critical thing with a cult is to tread softly. They are often led by volatile characters who can dramatically overreact when they perceive they're under attack. Research is the key.'

'So you do need to be a spy.'

'Possibly. At some point. I may need to get deeper into the group and Colby said you could help me do that.'

'Sure. No problem.'

'These groups are not to be underestimated. They're experts in mind control and their tactics are all about breaking the spirit and playing to a member's vulnerabilities. What would you know about that?'

'Mind control?'

'Having your spirit broken?'

A flash of irritation crossed Jameson's eyes. 'You think I'm too broken to help you?'

The ringing of his phone interrupted them. Jameson answered without hesitation. 'Hey Lucas, what you got?' he said. It was clear after a few seconds that this was going to be an in-depth discussion.

Fifteen minutes later Jameson hung up and immediately launched into updating Bloom. Deflection and distraction. Bloom had to be impressed. His tactics for avoiding conversation were practised and slick.

'Finally, we've got something tangible. Lucas managed to track down a redundant Yahoo email account of Scarlett's. It's not been used for eight years but one of the emails in the final month of activity is confirmation from Barclays bank that funds of over £2 million have been transferred to another account.'

Bloom cringed a little at the tactic of hacking into the email account. She would have preferred to have requested a warrant via the police but Porter had been clear that their investigations into Scarlett had to be under the radar. 'Please tell me it went to another savings account and not Artemis.'

'Not Artemis. Paula Kunis herself.'

Bloom felt her jaw clench as she clamped her teeth together. Scarlett had not only had her liberty stolen by this woman but also her financial security. She would have become entirely reliant on the group after handing over her savings. Bloom knew that cult members often lived in destitution with limited access to food, home comforts and the outside world while their adored leaders led a life of immense wealth and privilege.

'I need to tell Porter we'll take the case. We need to get her out of there.'

'Her and the rest. I did some digging with HMRC. Artemis are a registered charity with over fifty employees.'

Bloom collected her things. 'I don't think you're broken, Marcus,' she said before leaving, 'but I do think you're keeping things not just from me but from everybody. And that worries me. Sometimes I feel like I'm stepping around an abyss I don't know the size or depth of. And this isn't about the case or helping me to spy; this is about me wanting to protect my friend.'

Jameson gave a curt nod. She wasn't sure if that was simply to acknowledge her point or an agreement to talk. Time would tell.

22

Porter looked a little more dishevelled than he had on her previous visit. His beard had grown, and the abundance of grey hair had her wondering if it was usually dyed its striking red colour. Porter once again insisted on their speaking alone. DCI Mirza had not even attended, delegating the babysitting of Bloom to DI Bristol.

'Aren't you a sight for sore eyes,' said the Foreign Secretary as she took the seat opposite him. He wore a clean shirt and blue tie. Porter was a showman at heart; ordinary man of the people one minute, smartly dressed man of power the next. Even for a one-to-one meeting in police custody he'd dressed to impress. Perhaps the beard was due to the refusal of a razor in case he tried to harm himself.

'I'm afraid to say I haven't located Scarlett yet, but I do have a good idea what we might be dealing with when it comes to Artemis, and this tells me that getting to your niece is going to take a good deal of effort and sensitivity.'

Porter placed his hands behind his head. 'And money.'

Bloom met his eye. 'Unlike Artemis, we're not a charity.'

'And I thought you did this work to right wrongs and help people.'

'I could say the same about you, but I'm assuming you are well paid for your political efforts.'

'Touché.' Porter rocked back on the hind legs of his chair. 'What's the deal then? What's she got herself into.'

'I'm fairly certain your niece has joined a cult.'

Porter screwed his eyes into narrow slits. 'She was never a religious girl.'

'Not all cults are religious. They can be politically, financially and even family motivated. I haven't enough insight into Artemis yet to know the underlying philosophy. There's a focus on self-help and self-realization, so it could have some religious undertones; I need to research it more.'

'So Greta was right all this time,' he said, referring to his sister.

Bloom watched Porter process the news. He didn't show any particular concern in his expression or tone of voice.

'A year after joining, she transferred her entire inheritance to an account owned by the group's leader, Paula Kunis.'

This time his expression flashed anger.

'Is Paula Kunis known to you or the family?'

'Absolutely not. Never heard of her. The bloody cheek. I'm going to need you to get that back.'

'I'm not sure that's—'

Porter held his hand up and talked over her. 'I told you I need this sorting. Now. Before . . .' He didn't finish the sentence but Bloom knew from their previous conversation that whatever Porter had done to end up in the basement of the MOD had put him in danger. 'Who is she, this Kunis woman?'

'An American whose upbringing leads me to suspect she may have the kind of personality that lends itself to cult leadership.'

Porter did not hide his sneer. 'You psychologists, you always think it's the parents. She said you could be naive that way.'

His words chilled Bloom, and she met his gaze. 'Who is *she*?'

'Oops. Did I say too much?'

Bloom stood. 'I think this arrangement is over.'

'Sit down, Dr Bloom.'

She approached the door and knocked.

Porter stood too. 'I. Said. Sit. Down.'

The man Bloom now felt sure was one of Seraphine's high-functioning psychopaths stepped around the desk and stood close enough to loom over her. He was taller than he looked on TV.

'If you value your life and liberty, I suggest you sit back down and hear me out.'

Bloom faced the Foreign Secretary. She'd sensed Porter might possess some anti-social traits during their first meeting: the fake charm, the intense gaze, the wordplay were all characteristics she was familiar with, but such qualities were not uncommon in people of power. Discovering he was part of Seraphine's web was still a shock; it meant her influence reached right to the top of the British government. 'I'm not playing Seraphine's games. Her little club can sort their own problems out.'

The door unlocked and DI Bristol appeared. 'All done?'

'Yes,' said Bloom, holding Porter's gaze.

'No, not quite, thanks, Jim,' said Porter.

To Bloom's dismay DI Bristol said, 'As you say, sir,' before closing the door and engaging the lock.

Porter moved back around the desk without a word, sat in his chair again and waited.

Bloom knew she had no choice. There was no escape. She was here until he decided she could leave. And so, despite every nerve in her body urging flight, Augusta Bloom sat down.

23

Jameson tried Bloom's phone for the second time. As before it went straight to voicemail. She should have finished her meeting with Porter by now. It had been two hours and they were due to meet with the prosecution team and senior investigating officers on one of their cases in preparation for the court case the following week. Jameson saw the barrister across the lobby of 102 Petty France, the CPS headquarters in London. Bloom was the expert witness who had assessed the accused's psychological state, and Jameson knew the barrister would be wanting to prep her for the cross-examination.

He studied his phone with concentration, hoping to buy her some time. Without thinking he clicked on the BBC News app and found his fingers selecting the picture of Seraphine outside of court again. She looked rough. Her hair was lank and her skin almost translucently pale. Was that make-up? He didn't accept for one moment that the look was genuine, even though he would have taken great delight in discovering she really was broken. He felt foolish for having fallen for her. He knew Bloom must wonder how a man of his training could be so gullible, but the truth was he hadn't wanted to see. He hadn't wanted to be that version of himself again. He had left it behind for a reason. And so it had been easy for Seraphine.

Sarah Mendax had been everything he ever wanted in a partner: intelligent, independent, irreverent and irresistible. Seraphine had studied him and no doubt created her final version of Sarah with him in mind. He had been easy prey.

He'd like to see her again now though. Just one last time so he could tell her she would never fool him again. As he closed the news app down he heard Bloom's voice in his head asking, '*Who are you trying to convince, Seraphine or yourself?*' God, he hated working with that woman sometimes.

Terry Colby seemed to have fired her up about his past as well. He knew once Bloom decided to interrogate something she could be relentless. She would be on his case until he told her what she wanted to hear. But he was nowhere near ready to talk about all of that yet. He had not just closed the door behind him when he left MI6, he'd made sure it was locked tight.

Jameson raised his hand in greeting to the chief inspector and sergeant from the London Metropolitan Police who had just arrived for the meeting. He left Bloom a message telling her to catch them up ASAP then he hung up and went to join the group at reception to sign in.

An hour later he was back in reception. He had represented Bloom's insights as well as he could. Thankfully they kept each other abreast of all aspects of the cases they worked on, and he was au fait enough with the psychological models to be able to talk in an informed manner about them. He could tell the barrister was a little irritated at Bloom's absence but he was not as stroppy as some might have been.

He handed his security pass back and walked out on to the street opposite St James's Park tube station. There had been no messages from Bloom to apologize or explain her absence. He had sent a couple of texts and a WhatsApp message. He checked the latter now and saw it had not been read. This was not like Bloom. She was diligent in acknowledging her messages even if it was only to say she would respond in full later. He knew that the use of mobile phones was restricted in the MOD's headquarters. She would have had to hand it in or place it in a locker, which would explain the lack of response. But why would she be there for three hours when she knew they had an important meeting to attend?

Turning the collar of his wool coat up and tightening his scarf against the cold wind, Jameson turned left and began walking the short distance to MOD Main Building.

24

The large white neoclassical building of MOD Whitehall filled the site of the old Palace of Whitehall and had been home to the Ministry of Defence since the mid-sixties. It was a place of extreme security. Since 2007 it had been designated a criminal offence to trespass in the building under the Serious Organized Crime and Police Act. Jameson had mixed feelings about the place. He remembered the buzz and excitement of being on the inside of security matters. But he also remembered the other stuff.

Jameson saw Bloom from a distance. She was sitting on a bench staring straight ahead. He took his phone from his pocket and called her but it went to voicemail. She must not have switched her phone back on after exiting the building. He increased his pace. This was very un-Bloom-like behaviour. The woman was a stickler for professionalism and politeness.

‘’Ey up, chuck,’ he said in his best Yorkshire accent as he sat on the bench beside his business partner.

She looked his way and blinked a couple of times before saying, ‘Oh, hi.’

‘Are you OK?’

‘He’s one of them. One of Seraphine’s.’ She stared ahead again.

'Holy crap.' Jameson felt the anger swell. Would that woman never quit? He suppressed his rage and studied his partner more closely. He could never read her real feelings towards Seraphine. She should hate the woman like he did but he knew she didn't. 'Are you OK?'

'He swears he's not working with her any more.'

'Yeah right.'

'I spent the last few hours interrogating him and I'm inclined to believe that part.' She looked up at the grey sky and took in a deep breath. 'He was one of her game players, he admits that. He also says he was one of the select few invited into the inner sanctum but that he opted out because, in his words, he doesn't run in a pack, he's a lone wolf.'

'Dickhead.' Jameson puffed out his chest and spoke in a convincing imitation of the Foreign Secretary's plummy Home Counties accent: 'I do not run in a pack. I am a lone wolf.' He was surprised to hear a small laugh from Bloom. She didn't usually approve of his attempts to defuse situations with humour.

'I think on that he is telling the truth. His kind are generally not ones for teamwork.'

Jameson clenched his jaw. They had stopped Seraphine from recruiting her gang of psychos last year but he was not naive enough to think she wouldn't regroup. He suspected by the time the woman had decided to show off her game to Augusta she'd probably had all the assets she needed anyway. She wasn't the type to gamble with the success of her plans. She was precise, organized and ruthless. You didn't need to be a psychologist to spot that. She was obviously placing her psychopaths in positions of power and making herself their twisted puppet master. If Porter really had cut his ties with her, maybe he'd talk.

'But you think whatever Seraphine is up to might make it worth their while?'

Bloom acknowledged his insight with a tilt of the head. 'He wasn't giving anything away on that score, no matter how hard I tried.'

'What was he giving away?'

She held up the envelope on her knee. 'A request for his solicitor to pay us for getting Scarlett out.'

'I say we tear it up. If his niece wants to live in a cult and give them all her cash, so be it. She's not doing any harm. And I am not putting us in that bloody woman's firing line again. Enough is enough, Augusta. Walk away.'

'I tried.'

He looked at her.

Bloom dropped her head. 'I tried, but I'm afraid that's not going to be an option.'

'What the hell? What did he do?'

She looked at him and he had never seen her look so sad. 'I'd already told him about Paula taking Scarlett's money before he revealed . . .' She stopped and frowned.

'You're worried he'll go after Paula?'

'I think a man like that with his power wouldn't stop until he'd destroyed Paula and everything she'd touched. That means every one of those women could be in danger.' She looked at him more closely. 'I put them in danger. What if I'm wrong? What if they are just trying to make the world a better place?'

'Have you spoken to DCI Mirza?'

Bloom shook her head. 'Her inspector is helping Porter.'

'Even more reason to give her the heads-up.'

'Maybe. I can't decide. I need to think about it. If I tell Mirza the Foreign Secretary is a psychopath who's manipulating at least one member of her team she's likely to think I've lost my mind. Porter has a powerful mask. He's in the public eye. He'll deny it all. As will DI Bristol, I expect. No, I'm thinking DCI Mirza is more useful, not to mention safer, if we give her the leverage of us fulfilling Porter's request. He promised to cooperate if we did that.'

'Yeah, but he probably won't.'

'I don't know. He's anticipating not being around any more. I don't think that's a game. I think he's upset someone. I think the justice system is his hiding place. I think he will cooperate if we do as he asks.'

'That's a leap.'

She sat up. She'd made up her mind, he could see. 'I know. But we've got just under a week before she has to let him go or charge him. That gives us time to test my theory.'

25

Bloom's phone interrupted their conversation. She was relieved; what she had told Jameson was only part of the story. Porter had found some powerful blackmail to make sure she continued with the search for Scarlett. Blackmail which related to Jameson's past and the incident that had led to his leaving MI6. His partner had died during an operation and Jameson had blamed himself, but he didn't know the full story. If Bloom did not do as Porter asked, or if she involved DCI Mirza, Porter would make sure Jameson found out the truth. Bloom felt sure it would destroy him.

'Dr Bloom, this is Harris Marshall. I received your message about looking for my cousin Scarlett.'

Two hours later, after Bloom had dropped Porter's payment instructions into his lawyer's office, she and Jameson arrived at Greta Marshall's house. Harris greeted them at the door. He was a tall man around thirty years old with a well-groomed hipster beard and John Lennon-style round glasses.

Greta Marshall's home was neat and clean but old-fashioned in a nineties chintzy way. The floral fabric on the three-piece suite matched that of the curtains and the footstool. The walls were painted a shade of lilac that reminded Bloom of every makeover ever done on the popular TV show *Changing Rooms*, and light fittings of overly elaborate gold with smoked-glass shades adorned the walls and the ceiling.

Greta herself sat on the sofa. She wore the same high-necked white blouse and set of pearls they'd seen her in when they'd knocked on the door a few days earlier, along with a thick A-line skirt, sheer tights and a pair of velour slippers in peach. Harris took a seat alongside his aunt.

Bloom and Jameson sat on the two armchairs with a china cup and saucer in their laps. Greta had insisted she serve them tea despite their assurances that they did not need a drink. She had not made one for herself.

'You were saying that the last time Scarlett was home would have been Boxing Day, but which Christmas was that?' Bloom said.

'I'm no use with dates,' said Greta, 'but it was the one with all that snow. You remember, Harris, you and your dad helped Mr Morgan dig out his van.'

'Well, that dates it a little. Mr Morgan's been dead six years at least.'

'And you haven't had any contact by phone, email or letter in all those years?' said Bloom.

'I don't do emails. Blasted computers. I can't make my peace with them.'

'But no calls or letters, Aunt Greta?' said Harris.

Her head shook in a brisk confirmation. She was not comfortable with this reality. What mother would be?

'How about you, Harris?'

'Not for many years now. Scarlett and I used to be

incredibly close. There's only a year between us and we spent every weekend and at least a couple of nights a week together as kids. We were more like siblings, I suppose. My dad and her dad were twins and really close, so the families spent all their time together. Then when Uncle Oliver died my dad felt it was his responsibility to care for Aunt Greta and Scarlett.'

Greta took hold of her nephew's hand and gave it a quick squeeze.

'Do you know much about the group Scarlett is associating with, Artemis?' Jameson asked.

Harris said, 'She said she felt inspired. That she'd finally found the family she'd always wanted and that hurt, you know, 'cause she and I were close. Right up to the time she met these people, we called each other multiple times a week. She'd been at Liverpool Hope about six months and I was due to go and visit after Easter; we'd planned our nights out and a ferry trip on the Mersey and I remember it was a Sunday and I was in bed with a hangover when she called. She said I couldn't come and visit, that I needed to cancel my train ticket and that was pretty much it. End of chat.'

'And was this when she told you she felt inspired and had found a new family?' said Bloom.

Harris shook his head and took a sip of his tea. 'That was before, a week or two earlier in one of our late-night chats. She was full of it. She was excited about meeting the woman who had started the group.'

'Paula Kunis?'

'That's her. I've tried to speak to her over the years,

but you can't get to her. I gatecrashed a conference she was speaking at once, tried to corner her in the restaurant, but as soon as I got close I was surrounded by all these women who sort of ushered me away.'

'You never told me that!' said Greta, looking surprised.

'I didn't want to worry you. It never got me anywhere so there was nothing to say.'

'Did you ask them about Scarlett?' said Bloom.

'I tried, but they just don't communicate. It's like speaking to someone who's blank. They smile and nod and say they're sorry and wish they could help, but I don't think they actually listen.'

Bloom made a note. If this was a cult, members would not be allowed any personal opinions or independent action. They would be expected to toe the line. Such groups breed paranoia about outsiders, who are labelled as a threat, as people who do not understand or who wish to destroy the group, and in extreme cases as evil. All of which helps to keep members committed and compliant.

'It changed her when she met them,' said Greta.

'Changed her how?' asked Bloom.

Greta collected a photograph from the mantelpiece. It showed a pigtailed Scarlett in school uniform. Her skin was dotted with pimples and she was not quite looking into the camera. 'She was a delicate girl. If I told her off she'd crumple into floods of tears until I hugged them away. I worried how she would get on in the world. You've met my older brother so you know how dark some people can be.'

Bloom smiled at Greta to show she understood.

Whether or not Greta had a name like psychopath for Gerald's character, she recognized what he was.

'She surprised me, though. When her dad died she was stronger than I thought. We became a little team, her and I. We cooked together and walked together and watched TV together and she made me laugh. That's what surprised me most. I didn't think I'd be able to laugh again after my husband left us so prematurely. She was my best friend.'

Harris took hold of his aunt's hand again.

'How did that change?'

'Well, I'm not silly. I knew university would take her away and she'd probably meet some young man and have her own family.' Greta frowned deeply for a long moment as her eyes focused on the beige carpet. 'She wasn't my Scarlett any more. That's the only way I can describe it.'

'Her character had altered?' Bloom knew one of the first signs of cult involvement was a sudden shift in a person's personality. Something quickly noticed by close friends and family.

'Not so much altered as disappeared. It was like she wasn't really in the room with me. As if her head was elsewhere. I thought it was drugs if I'm honest.' She spoke to Harris. 'I asked your mum to check with her pharmacist friend.'

'She wasn't on drugs, Aunt Greta. She was stolen from us.'

'I know. I know.'

The helplessness in Greta Marshall's words fired Bloom up more than anything she had heard so far.

Who had the right to deprive a mother of her only child? It was despicable and she would not rest until she had put a stop to it.

'What makes you say she was stolen, Harris?' said Bloom.

'After that last call I badgered her and badgered her with messages and texts for weeks, and eventually a few months later she called. She was living in Edinburgh in a communal house, she said. She told me to stop worrying, she was fine and she'd come and see me soon. But it didn't sound right. *She* didn't sound right. I got the feeling someone was with her, listening in, you know. So I kept her talking, reminiscing, and then I asked if she remembered the game we used to play as kids, the one that used to stress her mum out and get us into trouble. She said she did.' Harris looked from Bloom to Jameson. 'I told her I just needed to ask her a few questions and then I'd leave her alone. I asked if she was happy and she said yes. I asked if people were making her stay away and she said of course not. I asked if she wanted me to come and pick her up and she said absolutely not. And I asked her if she felt scared and she said no.' Harris closed his eyes for a moment. 'Then she hung up and so began my years of hell.'

'I'm not sure I—' started Bloom.

'The opposites game,' interrupted Jameson. He had sat forward in his seat. 'My nieces play it all the time. Drives their parents crazy.' He looked Bloom's way. 'Every question asked is given the opposite answer to what you mean.'

Bloom understood immediately and played back

Harris's conversation with Scarlett. 'She told you she was unhappy, being controlled, felt scared and wanted you to come and get her.'

'I tried but when I got to the place she'd been staying they said she'd left of her own free will and they had no idea where she had gone.'

'How long ago was this?' said Greta, her eyes wide and frightened.

'Nine years. I'm sorry, Aunt Greta. I tried and tried and hunted and hunted, but Scarlett vanished without a trace.'

'How about the number she called you from?' said Jameson.

'It was withheld.'

'But she told Gerald she was fine,' said Greta.

It was Harris's turn to look surprised. 'She spoke to Gerald? When?' Harris didn't show any distaste when he said Gerald's name but there was a blankness to his expression. This was the other side of the family of course: Greta's family. Harris was the son of her late husband's brother.

Greta frowned and looked confused.

'Is this the email exchange from about five years ago?' said Jameson.

'I don't know why she'd contact him. They never spoke, did they?' said Harris.

'I asked him to try to get Scarlett to come home. I thought with his job he could do that.'

Harris wrinkled his nose. 'But he didn't.'

Bloom's phone began to ring. It was a blocked number.

'Excuse me a moment. Can you give Marcus the details of where Scarlett lived in Edinburgh, please? I need to take this, sorry.' She moved away towards the front door as she answered.

'Sergeant Doyle. Thanks for calling,' she said, after the Scottish police officer had introduced himself as one of Ned Nesbitt's team. 'Ned said you might have some information about the farmhouse the Artemis group own in the Inverness area.'

'Not just a farmhouse. They've taken over the whole village. Bought up all the properties one by one, including the local shop and the pub. Not that ya can blame the villagers for selling. Nothing left for them round there after the McDougal's factory closed down. Apparently they've got a fancy spa up there now.'

This was the location of the expensive-looking retreat she'd seen advertised on the Artemis pamphlet. So not a stereotypical cult commune then.

'Ned said you'd had a few odd reports?'

'Nothing to it, really. They've upset the townsfolk on occasion but it amounts to not much more than refusing to let people walk across their land or handing out a few leaflets to the youngsters.'

'What sort of leaflets?'

'They run them self-help type groups. Harmless stuff, you know. But people here are not keen on outsiders, truth be told.'

'And why don't they allow people to cross the land? If they have the whole village these days isn't that hard to stop?'

'Not now they've fenced it all off. It's their right, though. There are no public pathways through there, so long as the road is left clear, they're free to do what they like with the rest. And in my experience people get very sensitive over their land. You wouldn't believe the number of disputes you get just because someone's garden fence is a few inches too thick.'

Fencing off a whole village struck Bloom as unusual, though. 'Are they a religious group, do you know?'

'I couldn't say.'

'What do you make of those you've met?'

'They look like they need a good meal and a hot bath most of 'em. They're a bit different, but they're harmless.'

Bloom's heart sank. Was Paula Kunis living off these women, taking their money to fund her own ambitions, turning them into worker bees to feed her ego? She needed to find out and, if so, make it stop.

'We've been looking for one of their members, a young woman called Scarlett Marshall. I don't suppose you've come across her?'

'Can't say I've been introduced to any of 'em by name. Do you have a photo?'

'It's very old but I'll send it through,' she said, finding the Facebook image Lucas George had sent her and forwarding it on. 'She's the one with auburn hair on the far left of this group.'

The sergeant took a moment to check it out then came back on the line. 'I don't recognize her. Why are you looking for her? The boss said you were a forensic psychologist – is she involved in a crime?'

'I also work as a private detective, helping people to find missing loved ones.'

'Ah. I see. Well, I can keep a lookout. If she turns up I'll let you know.'

She thanked the sergeant and took details of where the Artemis village was located. There was nothing about this group that raised the alarm to the authorities. They were a law-abiding charity going about their business in private. Even if Paula Kunis convinced new members to hand over their savings as Scarlett had done, this wasn't illegal; people could do what they wished with their own money. People joined this group of their own free will and, on the surface, it appeared that they remained of their own free will. But after speaking to Linwood Roberts and Scarlett's family, Bloom suspected the crime here was not a physical one, but a psychological one.

26

Nine years earlier

Scarlett woke up screaming. Her blood pounded in her temples and sweat soaked her T-shirt. The nightmare was always the same, like a scene from a horror movie. As she watched, her hand began to disintegrate, her fingers melting like warm chocolate that dripped on to the floor in a dark pool. Her arms followed until she could feel her shoulders sagging and pulling at her neck as they turned to mush. The panic would really grip her then as her lower body melted into that dark pool and the softness reached up her neck, taking first her chin and then her lips until it finally clawed at the edges of her eyes and seeped into the sockets, leaving her with one last look at her molten, disappearing face.

Her roommate switched her bedside light on and mumbled something sleepy that could have been, 'Again?'

'I'm OK,' Scarlett said as her roommate switched off the light and curled back into sleep.

But she wasn't.

It felt like she was losing her mind.

When she was with the group she felt so alive and important. She believed so strongly in Artemis and what they were trying to achieve and she idolized Paula. But then every night the nightmares came. Why did she have to give up so much to be the person she wanted to be? Her guilt about not having seen her mum for all these months felt like a physical weight pulling on her heart – and Harris, she missed him so much. He'd been her best friend and confidant for so long, more like a brother than a cousin; but it was clear she needed to cut them out of her life. She had called him yesterday feeling alone, desperate and frightened about the choice she had to make. He knew she was upset and he must have guessed Mel was with her as he'd made her play the opposites game. They'd loved it as kids, it would make her laugh so much that tears and snot would run down her face, but yesterday was different. She'd told him she was unhappy and scared but that wasn't really true. She was just having a bad day. Paula had helped her to see that. They had talked into the night about how important their work was in Artemis and how those who didn't understand it would only serve to distract them. Paula had reassured her that anyone taking on a mission as valuable as they were had sacrifices to make. It was not going to be easy.

Paula had taken her hand and said, 'If this life is not for you, no one will judge you. We are the family who have chosen you. We love you. We want you with us but that has to be your choice.'

And that was the problem. If only Paula would tell her to leave her old life behind, commit herself fully like the others and never see her family again. But Paula would never do that because she loved her and would never force her to do something she did not want to do. It had to be her choice. But it was so, so hard.

27

Day 9

Jameson drove with one hand on the wheel and the other holding a water bottle from which he took frequent swigs.

'I need you to coach me in how to blend in,' said Bloom. On leaving Greta's house yesterday she had called Victoria and asked if the offer of attending a weekend retreat was still open. She had to get into this group and see for herself what was really going on. Victoria had been delighted, calling her back within the hour to say a place had been made available for her this very weekend. When Bloom had expressed surprise at being able to attend so soon, Victoria had told her it was because they were so very keen to have her along. Some cult researchers referred to this kind of flattery as love-bombing. Different groups did it differently but in short they made a prospective member feel special, important and loved. You didn't need to be insecure and needy to fall for flattery of this kind. It triggered a serotonin response in the brain akin to a drug hit.

'Sure thing. Just be yourself.'

She and Jameson were now driving from London to Edinburgh, where she had been asked to arrive at the Artemis headquarters at 4pm.

'Very funny, Marcus, but I'm serious. At least one woman that we know of may have lost her life because of her involvement with this group. There could be some serious dysfunction going on in Artemis. I don't know what I'm walking into here.'

'I am being serious. No one can keep up a facade for long enough in deep cover; it only takes a bit of stress or emotion and your true colours come out. The only reliable tactic you have is to be as true to yourself as possible.' He took a swig of water. 'The trick is not to lie, but to say as little as possible, to *be* as little as possible, to blend in. Watch the group, follow their norms and be more interested in them than they ever are in you. You were made for this.'

'What's that supposed to mean?'

'I was taught at MI6 that if you need to extract intel, figure out what motivates people and what their vulnerabilities are, then use that insight to play them. Your skills as a psychologist will make it a breeze.'

'I think you are simplifying. It's easy to see things as a breeze when you're a practised professional.'

'Augusta, I used to train new agents. I know how to prep spies.'

'You used to provide part of the training.'

'All right. Judgy.' He moved to catch her gaze. 'You'll be fine. If I were recruiting new agents you'd be front of the queue. You have the intelligence, the calm temperament, the knowledge of what makes people tick.'

'Makes you wonder why they ever recruited you, hey?'

Jameson's laugh was deep and genuine. 'There's more truth in that than you know.'

Bloom swallowed and looked away. His life in MI6 had damaged him and he didn't even know the worst part. She focused on the task at hand, knowing the best way to protect him was to do the best she could for Porter.

'They'll probably take my phone to isolate me so you might not hear from me until I come out.'

'*If* you come out. I'm serious,' he said, 'you said these groups are all about brainwashing, and that anyone can be susceptible. That means you too.'

'I know.'

'Hey, don't worry. I saw the brainwashing tactics carried out by the US post 9/11 in their black sites. They deprived people of sleep, starved them, locked them in boxes to break them. Those tactics were given to the military by psychologists. Did you know that? But they didn't work. The US senate investigation found that the psychological torture inflicted on prisoners failed to elicit any new intelligence about the plans of Al Qaeda or the whereabouts of Osama bin Laden.' Jameson took his eyes off the road again briefly and winked at her. 'Old-fashioned spy work won the day.'

Bloom looked out of the passenger window. They were passing Berwick-upon-Tweed in the north-east. It was a beautiful seaside town she remembered visiting with her parents as a child. They only ever took her on UK holidays as they could never coordinate their work diaries for long enough to go further afield.

'Cults are better at it than governments though,' she said.

'You think?'

'I'm not being facetious. The tactics used to break someone's spirit are not flawed in and of themselves. Sleep deprivation, change of diet, isolation – they are all effective tactics but it's a bit like the parable of the frog in hot water. If you drop it straight in, it will immediately jump out, but if you place it in cool water and slowly heat it up, the frog will stay, oblivious to the danger.'

'Turning it into torture made it too obvious?' Jameson overtook an Eddie Stobart lorry.

'Bullying the enemy into telling you everything is what they expect, isn't it? So they're mentally ready to resist it, even trained to. The genius of the cult is that members don't see it coming. They're not prepared.'

'And that's what you're banking on? You know what they're doing so you'll resist it more easily?'

'Yes.' She looked at him for a moment. 'I'll be fine. And if I'm not you'll come and get me.'

Jameson sighed. 'Without any help.'

'I didn't say no help, just no police or military; nothing official that might incite a strong reaction.'

'You really think this Paula woman would do something drastic?'

'I have no idea yet, Marcus. There are plenty of cult leaders out there who don't, they're not all Jim Jones or David Koresh. It depends how stable she is. The likes of Reverend Sun Myung Moon led the Unification Church, or Moonies, until he died in his nineties; and L. Ron Hubbard, who created Scientology, grew it successfully until his death in the mid-eighties. It's not all drama.'

'But you'd still want to get a loved one out of the Moonies or Scientology, wouldn't you, or are those groups OK?'

'If it was my niece, I'd do everything in my power to extract her. It's not just the risk of being used for some narcissist's benefit, it's the fact they take away your freedom of thought, restrict access to outside information and sell you one world view. In my eyes, that's abuse.'

'Couldn't you say that about religion in general? Doesn't that present a one-world view?'

'Or fascism, or communism, or any radicalism. The lines are blurred, you're right, and that's why I need to go in and see for myself.'

As they approached Edinburgh they discussed tactics for keeping in touch. There were limited options if her phone was taken away. It made her realize how reliant on mobiles everyone had become. There may not even be a landline at this place. There certainly wasn't a number for the retreat on their website. Or an address.

28

Gerald Porter stood from his camp bed and stretched up to his full height. He felt a deep pain radiate across his lower back; the thing was playing havoc with his posture. It had been over a week now since they had brought him to this room. He knew it was nearly finished one way or another. Detective Chief Inspector Mirza had become increasingly frustrated with his reluctance to cooperate. He could tell the fact he had elicited the assistance of Dr Augusta Bloom had infuriated her. She was desperate to know how his niece's whereabouts was relevant to his recent trip abroad. It amused Porter to see the woman trying to find links where there were none.

Truth be told, his request to Dr Bloom had been genuine. He had been remiss in helping his sister. Although Greta infuriated him with her constant ailments and anxieties, she was his blood and his responsibility. He should have acted sooner. The only link this had to his overseas excursion, mind, was a renewed sense of urgency.

He had also been curious to meet the infamous Dr Bloom. In his short time in the employ of Seraphine Walker he had heard much of the woman. Indeed, Seraphine was quite clear that without the good doctor she would never have become what she was, or more importantly had such a good idea. An idea that Porter felt irritated he had not come up with himself. It was sublime and trumped all his previous ambitions for the Prime Minister's job. But it was also flawed and in parts downright weak. And that is why he had taken the action he had.

Using Augusta Bloom to put Seraphine Walker in her place was an elegant checkmate.

He had liked Bloom. He'd not expected that. She had responded to his threat with admirable calmness, resolutely focusing on how she could stop him from telling Mr Jameson the truth about his late partner. She was clearly a woman of steely determination and it seemed entirely possible that she would succeed in the task he had set her to locate Scarlett. But from what she'd told him about the lure of a cult, that didn't mean she would be able to get his niece to return to his sister, or make this Paula Kunis woman pay the £2 million trust fund back. And that was something he was not prepared to gamble on.

By the time Detective Inspector Bristol arrived with the usual coffee and buttered toast Porter liked, he had a plan.

'I need you to call someone for me.'

Bristol took his notebook from his pocket without hesitation. He had been an easy man to turn. He clearly disliked being managed by a woman, or maybe it was the fact she was Asian – either way, the promise of making sure she failed was enough; the suggestion that Bristol would be first in line for her job, the icing on the cake.

'Speak to Clarence Roper at HMRC, tell him I want

him to look into possible tax fraud by the Artemis charity. Then call Baroness Moore of the Charity Commission and request an official investigation into the same group. Tell them both this request comes directly from my office and is urgent. And it wouldn't harm you to introduce yourself with your rank.'

Bristol frowned as he wrote that down.

'You can get my PA at the office to follow up your calls with an email.'

'If they ask, who shall I say this charity are and what have they done?'

'Tell them I don't want to colour their findings with supposition.'

'But—' Bristol paused and looked uncomfortable. 'Who are they?'

'None of your concern, Bristol. But your assistance will be rewarded.' When the inspector didn't move, Porter waved his hand at the door. 'Off you go then.'

29

Nicola Blake walked to the back of the minibus and took the seat by the window on the left-hand side. There was a buzz in the air that filled her with optimism. She watched the other women take their seats. The youngest two sat together at the front. They couldn't be much older than twenty and had latched on to each other immediately. The blonde by the window was above average height and thick-set with masculine features. Her companion could not be more different, a slight red-head with a scattering of freckles across her nose and stunning green eyes. You would never put these two together in the normal course of things and that's what made this all so refreshing. Woman of all ages, sizes, intellect and attractiveness coming together as sisters rather than catfighting in a way that no doubt aided man's dominance in the world.

Nicola smiled at the smartly dressed woman who took the seat on the other side of the aisle. She looked like a professional, probably in her forties. She had prematurely grey, neatly cut hair resting just above her shoulders. Three other women took their seats and chatted excitedly. Nicola recognized one of them from the self-realization seminar she had attended and another was Natasha, the administrator from the event. Natasha looked up and gave a warm smile and a wave.

'Hi Nicola, so pleased you're coming along. You're going to love it.'

'I have no doubt,' said Nicola, aware that the professional woman was watching her.

She had a feeling she had not experienced before and wondered if it came from finally taking control of her life. It had been a shitty year. She had been passed over for promotion in the law firm she worked for. It didn't seem to matter that her case record was better, and her client list higher, than all her colleagues'. The managing partner had told her she was the foundation to the firm but to make partner you needed to bring something else, some charisma and natural leadership. And so they had given the position to Jacob Feathers, a man who spent his time prancing around the office loudly broadcasting his successes and telling the bosses whatever they wanted to hear. But that wasn't the worst of it. The worst of it was Callum, her long-time boyfriend. They had met at university and she had fallen in love with his strong opinions and free spirit; he had promised that they would marry and have a child before she was thirty-five and yet here she was pushing thirty-eight and neither had occurred. Every Friday he headed straight from the office to The Swan to get drunk with his mates, so drunk he would not rise from his bed until Saturday lunchtime, with a head so bad he could only bear to lie on the sofa or, funnily enough, go to the football. And then on Sunday he would insist on Sunday lunch with his parents because he hadn't seen them in ages – ages being exactly seven days – never once stopping to consider how she wanted to spend her weekend, how invisible she might feel, how irritated, how impotent he was making her in her own life.

Enough was enough.

Things were changing.

Artemis was her chance to take back her life and make it her own. Ever since the seminar she had felt inspired to take up the gauntlet of living to her true potential and having a positive impact on the world. These women were kindred spirits, they would give her something she could now see Callum never would.

Bloom sat on the right at the back of the minibus opposite a woman in an expensive-looking leather jacket and black roll-neck sweater. They smiled at each other and Bloom noted the woman wore diamond stud earrings and a thin silver bangle on her wrist. The woman's dark hair hung long and limp across her shoulders and she wore only a hint of make-up. A pragmatic woman who worked in a lucrative career; accounting and finance or law, Bloom surmised.

The receptionist from the Artemis event Bloom had attended smiled warmly as she walked towards the rear of the minibus and addressed the woman opposite as Nicola.

'And so nice to see you too, Augusta. How's your mother?'

'That's so kind of you to remember. She is no better, no worse.' Jameson had said to keep things as truthful as possible and so she did.

'We are so pleased to have you with us this weekend. Have you met Nicola?' Natasha gestured to the other woman. 'I'm sure you two will get on incredibly well. The drive will be a few hours long so you have the chance to get to know each other. We'll take a stop half-way and I have plenty of refreshments if you're in need of any.'

Natasha moved back to her seat, leaving Bloom and Nicola alone at the back of the bus.

'Have you been to one of their retreats before?' asked Nicola as the bus moved away from the kerb and the freedom it represented.

'No. How about you?'

Nicola shook her head and tucked her hair behind her ear. Then she rearranged her position so she was angled towards Bloom. 'I'm so ready for it though. I think a few days of peace and quiet and fresh air will do me the world of good. Have you seen the venue on their website? It looks idyllic. I've never been to the Highlands; Edinburgh is as far as I've ever ventured into Scotland. How about you?'

Bloom expected there would be very little peace and fresh air where they were going. 'I live in London so this is quite a trip north.'

'You don't sound like a Londoner.'

'I'm from Yorkshire originally. How about you?'

'Oh, I'm a Brummie. I've tried to drop the accent but sometimes it slips out.'

They continued to chat for the next hour or so. Bloom made sure she asked more questions than she answered.

Nicola was a bright woman, a lawyer with a first-class honours degree and a successful career in a private law firm in Chester. Had she not seen anything to concern her in Artemis yet? Bloom knew she couldn't ask. She had to maintain the facade of the keen potential member but she was fascinated that Nicola had not found the extreme positivity and friendliness of everyone associated with Artemis suspicious.

She checked the Pay As You Go phone that was still in her possession. There was a message from Jameson's number offering her financial advice on her investments. She replied with a request to be taken off their mailing list. This was an agreed strategy. Jameson would continue to send marketing-style messages and so long as Bloom had her phone she would reply. This way when she failed to respond he would know she no longer could.

At the halfway point the minibus stopped at a small petrol station with a toilet round the back and a basic shop. Bloom bought herself a bottle of water and introduced herself to the other members of the group. There appeared to be four potential recruits: herself and Nicola and two students. Kimberly was a somewhat manly-looking girl from Durham University who was studying Maths but thinking of dropping out after suffering a series of stress-related conditions that had caused her to miss most of her third year. Daisy from Edinburgh University was a petite red-head in the first year of her French and German degree. She struck Bloom as a particularly vulnerable girl. She continually wrung her hands and avoided eye contact. Bloom felt a strong urge to protect both of them, and the enormity of her task began to sink in. How many more such needy souls was she going to meet? Would it be enough to simply find Scarlett? It was unlikely. What Bloom really wanted to do was to find Paula Kunis and put a stop to the whole thing.

As light rain began to fall Bloom leaned back and watched the faint outlines of the Scottish countryside pass by in the darkness. Nicola had moved forward to talk to Natasha and her colleague. She seemed highly excited about the forthcoming few days and was asking questions about the spa and mindfulness classes advertised on the Artemis website. Bloom wondered if the venue really did boast these facilities and, if so, whether they would be able to use them. Destructive cults rarely left potential new members alone with their own thoughts so it seemed unlikely they'd let you relax in a sauna or meditate for any length of time. But she could be wrong. She could be mistaken about all of it. Artemis could be a legitimate organization focused on the empowerment of women and she might leave on Monday relieved and refreshed.

Or, in the words of 'Hotel California', she might find that 'you can check out any time you like but you can never leave'.

As they drove northwards and away from civilization, smatterings of snow began to appear on the fields and hillsides. Bloom thought of Shauna Roberts walking purposefully across this very countryside to plunge into the icy water of a loch. What would drive someone to that? What had she been exposed to? Bloom closed her eyes and wondered at the futility of suicide. Would time have healed Shauna's woes if it had been afforded the chance?

When she opened her eyes the chatter at the front of the minibus had quietened to the odd whisper. Outside, the night was thick and black. Bloom stared at it. She leaned her face closer to the window. Something had changed in the air. She couldn't see but she was sure the Scottish mountains had closed in on them. She could feel their cold shadow as if some sixth sense had detected she was hemmed in and unable to escape. The air outside gave nothing away. She strained her eyes forward to see if the headlights revealed any of the landscape but all she could make out was the hazy image of tarmac rushing beneath them. She checked her watch. It was 8.39pm. They had been travelling for over three hours and should be nearing their destination soon. She ran through her tactics for the coming days. She couldn't afford to write anything down, she had to commit everything to memory. Questioning would be the key to determining the true nature of this group. If it was legitimate, they would welcome a good degree of critical thinking and be prepared to answer questions transparently. If they were a mind-control cult, some curiosity would be expected in potential new members but they would look to close it down as soon as possible and be unwilling, or even unable, to answer any truly pointed questions. Questions like, what is the ultimate purpose of your organization? What qualifications does the founder have to lead such a group? How do you feel about ex-members?

The question she had to judge most carefully was that of

Scarlett Marshall's whereabouts. If she enquired too early on it might raise suspicions about her motives, but if she left it too late she might run out of time to reach Scarlett.

A short while later the moon broke through the clouds to reveal her sixth sense had been bang on. Snow-covered monoliths towered over them, occasionally revealing a dark-grey outcrop of rock too steep and smooth for the white coating to stick to. The spiky black branches of bare shrubs and trees bordered the road as if warning travellers away from the harsh land beyond, and the tarmac beneath them was packed with snow. It truly felt like they were out in the wilderness, alone.

30

Jameson arrived at the Airbnb apartment he had rented in the centre of Edinburgh and found the key in the lockbox as instructed. It was a garden flat, with a large bedroom that had French windows opening on to a small patio complete with a wrought-iron table and two matching chairs. In the bedroom there was a double bed, two-seater sofa and large desk, with a TV attached to the wall above. Jameson moved a box of tissues and a vase of silk flowers on to the small coffee table and placed his laptop on the desk. He had set up the Find My Phone app on Bloom's Pay As You Go mobile and he logged on to the wifi now and checked her location. She was closing in on the Inverness area.

Here he was again, in another rented room, watching a partner head into the dark, unsure of what she might find. What if Bloom *had* fired up Porter to go after Paula? He might be in custody but if Bloom was right he'd turned at least one of his police guards already. What kind of revenge would a psychopathic man like him take on Paula and her comrades? Jameson wasn't sure Bloom's plan to infiltrate them had been the wisest step.

A familiar feeling of impotence came over him. The last time he'd done this his partner in MI6 had agreed to take the lead on a meeting with one of their contacts in

Latvia. He'd had food poisoning or a bug, been throwing up all night, so she'd said he should stay back and let her go in his place. It was a decision that changed the course of his life. Because it had ended hers.

Why was he thinking about this again? Bloody Terry Colby, that's why.

He stood up straight and arched his back.

He closed his eyes and for the first time in years the image of Jodie filled the darkness. She had not been attractive in the conventional sense – the bosses had lauded her plainness as particularly useful for blending in – but he thought she was beautiful. It was her fearlessness and her intelligence. He had never met a braver woman, nor one with such a passion for fighting for her beliefs. He knew aspects of Bloom reminded him of Jodie; the pursuit of truth and the determination. It gave him some comfort to still be surrounded by these qualities.

He pulled out the chair and sat. He would learn everything he could about Artemis and its location so he could keep Bloom safe.

He'd tried to suppress most of the skills MI6 had trained him in. Only occasionally did he tap into them, like last year when they had worked with Captain Harry Peterson. On that occasion he had used the hundreds of photographs people had taken at a military ball to piece together the minutes leading up to a bomb explosion that killed three people and maimed nine more. Patterns were his thing. He was a super recognizer with the ability to identify faces he had seen only once before or those in deep disguise. He was never sure how his mind did it – perhaps he should ask Bloom some time – but whether it be faces or facts, he often felt a strong intuition about something that might be important.

For the next hour he searched the internet for any local news stories related to Artemis, his current location in Edinburgh very near where their HQ was, and the region south-east of Inverness where they had their retreat. An article in the *Inverness Courier* had a headline about a runner saving a young boy from a burning car near to the latter. He flicked past it. There must be other Linwood Robertses out there if Bloom's suspicions about this group were correct. He knew if he had a relative who had been manipulated by a cult and the police were powerless to help, he'd go to the press. They were the next best means of piling on the pressure.

He couldn't decide if Bloom going to this retreat weekend was necessary or a waste of time. She seemed certain it was the best way to get to the truth about Scarlett, but Jameson couldn't help wondering if Porter's niece hadn't succumbed to the same fate as Shauna Roberts some time in the past five years. It struck him as unlikely that a woman with a loving family and a bank account full of cash would give all that up for a cause that might well be worthy but was hardly life and death. Then again she did have a psychopath for an uncle, so who knows what had really gone on in her home life.

He went back to the story about the runner. Why was he drawn to this? He scanned the article and then returned to the beginning and read it carefully. The incident had happened within a few miles of the Artemis village, and police had put out an appeal for information on the young boy. According to the report, his mother had perished in the accident and the boy had been collected by family before the hospital had a chance to gather any details about who they were. A subsequent article reported that the car involved was a stolen vehicle, taken from outside a Co-op in a nearby town while the owner was shopping.

Jameson looked up the number for Bloom's primary police contact in Scotland, Superintendent Ned Nesbitt, but then stopped. She had made it very clear that they should not involve the authorities until they knew what they were dealing with. Nearly every instance of a cult imploding had been precipitated by some official investigation or enquiry from the authorities. His priority here was finding intelligence that would help him to help Bloom. He checked the name of the runner then began searching for her online. He found her name in a list of finishers at a recent race and that led him to her running club's Facebook page, from where he found her personal page and her mobile number.

He dialled and waited. It rang for a long while and he expected voicemail but then a woman with a soft Scottish accent answered.

'Is that Lori?'

'Yes, who's this?'

'My name is Marcus Jameson, I'm a private investigator

looking for a client's missing niece up here in Scotland. I'm hoping I'm wrong but I'm wondering if the young lady from your recent car accident may be her?'

'Oh, I see. I don't think I can help. I don't know anything about her. The police would be your best bet.'

'From the description of the accident, I'm suspecting you may be the only person who saw the driver before the explosion. Is that right?'

'Err, yeah. I suppose so.'

'And someone took her son away before the hospital could take any details of who they were?'

'His aunt came, yes.'

'His aunt?'

'That's what a nurse at the hospital told me.'

'And do you know if the police have made any progress finding out who this mother and son were?'

'I don't think so. They haven't told me anyway.'

'I don't want to stir up any traumatic memories, Lori, but I'd really appreciate your telling me what you remember. Even if it's just to rule this lady out. Her family are desperate to find her. Is there any way you could do that for me, please?'

After a short pause, she said, 'I suppose.'

Lori described the lead-up to the accident, where she had been running, and how she hadn't recognized the sound of the car because it was being driven so fast up the hill in a low gear.

Jameson considered the reasons why someone might be driving like that. If the car was stolen they would be unfamiliar with it, or they might be an inexperienced driver, or they might be filled with adrenaline because they were fleeing.

Lori went on to tell him about injuring her arm and calling the police before spotting the young boy in the back of the car.

'Can you describe the boy?' he asked when she had finished telling him how she had smashed a window to get him out.

'He was about five or six, I think, with dark hair and pale skin. I remember thinking he was really light when I picked him up. I was able to carry him with one arm. If he'd been as heavy as my godson who's a similar age I don't think I'd have managed it.'

Jameson knew adrenaline could again be at play here, giving Lori a short burst of super-human strength. Or the boy could have been slight, or underweight.

'The woman had lighter hair, I think,' Lori went on to say. 'Maybe mid-brown and long, past her shoulders.'

'Did you see her face?'

Lori took a moment then said, 'I'm not sure. Her head was leaning to one side and her hair covered some of her face. She looked young, though, maybe in her twenties.'

'Anything else strike you? Anything about her clothes or jewellery?' Jameson knew this was a long shot. Witness memories were notoriously vague. Another influence of adrenaline. In MI6 he had been trained to quieten his senses in a crisis so he could take in all the critical information. The agency routinely placed him and his peers in adrenaline-fuelled situations until they mastered their stress response well enough to control its impact on perception and decision-making.

'I thought she might have been a beautician or something like that. She wore one of those tunic tops they wear. I told the police that.'

'Is that the sort of thing someone who works in a spa might wear?'

'Yes. Is that what the lady you're looking for does?'

'I'm not sure. It's just an idea.' Jameson remembered something Bloom had told him about the Artemis seminar that had struck her. 'Can you remember what colour this top was?'

'Oh, er, no, sorry.'

'OK, thank you, Lori. I really appreciate this. Is there anything else you recall that could help me?'

'Not about the woman, no.'

'But there is something else?'

'Just how quickly the aunt got to the hospital. How did she know there'd been an accident at all? The police didn't identify the car and where it had been stolen from until the next day, so how did she know to come for him?'

'Have the police shared any theories with you?'

'No.'

'What do you think?'

'I'm not sure.'

Jameson waited, sensing that Lori did have a theory. After a few moments she spoke in a quieter tone, as if she was sharing a secret or voicing something embarrassing.

'Perhaps someone was following her, chasing her, and that's why she was driving like that.'

'Did you see any other cars?'

'No. I don't think so. I can't remember. After the explosion, it's all a blur. Sorry. Do you think it's the person you're looking for?'

'It's hard to say at this stage but please don't apologize, Lori, you've been very helpful and gracious talking to me.'

'Will you let me know if it's your lady? I'd like to know who she was. I think it would help me, if you can understand that.'

'I do indeed and I'll be sure to let you know.'

31

The sound of the minibus tyres leaving the snow-covered tarmac and turning on to gravel alerted Bloom to their imminent arrival. Ahead of them she could see a large converted farmhouse with an open entrance and warm orange light flooding out of its windows. She could not see any other buildings through the darkness and had not spotted the fence Sergeant Doyle had mentioned. Maybe he was mistaken, maybe it only surrounded part of the village rather than the whole thing.

Natasha stood as the vehicle came to a stop and welcomed them all to the Artemis Lodge Retreat. She told them to head straight inside where it was warm; their bags would be brought in for them.

Bloom and Nicola exited the bus last and Bloom thanked the female driver, wondering if she too was a member. They followed the others inside to find a spacious white reception area with huge vases of white and green flowers that filled the air with the sweet smell of spring. Two women sat behind the curved reception desk with wide smiles and warm welcomes. A long table ran down the side wall topped with an urn of complimentary tea surrounded by small cups and saucers, a glass dispenser of cucumber water and a few plates with canapé-sized flapjacks and savoury pastries. Kimberly and Daisy immediately went to select a few treats to eat, so Bloom approached the receptionists. It would be good to settle into her room and freshen up before the drinks Natasha had told them about on the bus.

'Welcome, Augusta,' said the younger of the two women as Bloom came up, even though no introductions had been made. She was of oriental descent and had her black hair piled into a neat bun on the top of her head.

'Thank you, Lisa,' Bloom said, reading the woman's name from her badge. 'This is wonderful,' she said, looking around the space, and she wasn't faking. It really was an impressive room that was full of light and warmth and the faint smell of chlorine. She felt a flicker of relief. Maybe there was a spa after all.

'It only gets better,' said Lisa. 'I have your welcome pack here. There is a towel, robe and flip-flops to go with your lounge wear. You can use the changing rooms to the left behind me to change before the welcome begins.' She handed Bloom a dark-green fabric bag filled with the specified items then she took a small lockable box off a stack behind her and opened it. 'If you'd like to place your watch, phone and any other electricals in here for me, and I will keep them safe. We encourage a total retreat at Artemis Lodge.'

Bloom was momentarily distracted by the large portrait of Paula Kunis on the wall above the reception desk, then she realized what Lisa had asked.

'Oh, I have a sick mother. I explained to Natasha. I need to be contactable in case her condition changes.'

Bloom removed her watch and placed it in the box; now they would be unable to keep track of time. Clever.

Lisa held out her hand for the phone Bloom was holding. 'Not a problem, Augusta, I can leave it out here as someone always mans the desk. We will come and get you should the hospital call.'

'It's a nursing home actually,' she said, placing the phone in Lisa's hands. There was no point making a fuss so early on. She was here to watch and learn and they were clearly well prepared for handling objections.

Lisa wrote a note on an index card and placed Bloom's Pay As You Go phone in a tray on the shelf behind her. 'Do you have your charger?'

'In my overnight bag, do you want me to get it?'

'No, that's fine, we can sort that later.' She smiled. 'You can change now and hand your own clothes back to me in the bag. I'll make sure they get to your room with your luggage.'

Bloom looked up at the portrait of Paula again. It had a soft-focus appearance to it. Her skin looked smooth and almost luminescent against her dark hair.

'It'll be nice to have a few days' peace,' said Nicola as she placed her phone in a secure box and the other receptionist closed it, locked it and removed the key.

Bloom watched Nicola thank the receptionist and carry her green bag towards the changing rooms. *Are you not going to ask why they would need to lock you out of your own belongings?* she thought.

32

Jameson could see from the Find My Phone app that Augusta was now stationary in the location of the Artemis village. He had sent two further marketing-style messages and received no reply, so he knew she no longer had access to the phone. This was it then. Either she would arrive back in Edinburgh on Monday morning or she would not. He had two days to fill.

Speaking to Lori had left him with a bad feeling. He felt sure her suspicion was correct and the young woman who died was fleeing from someone who then hot-footed it to the hospital to retrieve the little boy. Was the driver someone trying to leave Artemis? Were there children in that place? Nothing in their research had suggested there were, but nothing had ruled it out either. The group was populated by women of child-bearing age, so it was possible that one of them had been pregnant on joining, or taken her children with her.

He began to think through his weekend activities. There were only five days left before their agreed deadline for DCI Mirza. If Bloom could not get out of that place on Monday he needed a plan, and a plan needed intel. Tomorrow he intended to drive up to the retreat location and scout it out. He would leave in the afternoon so he could arrive at dusk then search it in the dark. He had brought his night-vision glasses and dark clothing. The glasses had been sourced a few months after leaving the service, when he'd taken a rare independent security job with an old colleague. It was far too close to his old job for him to want to do it again, but he'd kept all the equipment just in case.

He opened up Google Earth and homed in on the Artemis village location. It was out in the hills with very little around it. A single-track road led through it, coming to a halt at a small loch a few miles further along. The surrounding land looked to be a combination of forest and rugged hillsides. It was secluded and private. No one ever needed to pass through it. When it came to the UK he couldn't think of a better hiding place.

Jameson closed his laptop and put on his coat. Time to start his stake-out of the Artemis HQ here in the city. Throwing his rucksack on his back he left the flat and put his bobble hat on as he walked. It was only quarter of a mile to their four-storey building on a curved side street behind Princes Street, the main road running through the centre. He had been to the city a few times before, once for the Edinburgh Fringe, which had seen the place transformed by street entertainers and crowds of people hoping to see the birth of the next big thing in comedy. He had been here in 2005 when Aussie Tim Minchin had won the Best Newcomer Award. Jameson had not seen Minchin perform but had always liked the idea of being here when he was discovered.

The streets were quiet now. It was late and cold and people had wisely cocooned themselves within the warmth of their homes and hotels for the night. It was no different at Artemis HQ. The building was in darkness apart from two of its curtained windows lit from within. He walked slowly past the front door. The Land Registry listed the building as flats but there was no sign of the call buttons for an entryphone system that you usually found on such residences. In fact there was no bell or buzzer at all. Just a plain door, no knocker and one keyhole.

Jameson crossed the street and looked up. He counted nine windows above him and one below in the basement. The building looked to be in good repair. There were no scuffs or knocks on the door and the window frames all looked pristinely painted. The place was in an expensive area of town and well cared for. Clearly Artemis had money.

He walked to the end of the street where there was a set of railings bordering the front gardens of the houses opposite. From his rucksack he took an old blanket, which he laid on the pavement. Much like in most other cities in the UK these days, it was no surprise to find a homeless person on a street corner. He sat and removed his Camelback flask of coffee. The flask looked battered and old because it was. It had travelled the world with him but still kept his coffee hotter than any other version he'd owned.

He knew what Bloom would say. Why didn't you bring the car so you could have sat in the warmth? But he wasn't an investigator, he was a spy. He didn't observe, he infiltrated. And that meant you had to look like you belonged; something he hoped Bloom was pulling off too.

33

Day 10

Bloom had no idea what time it was, but she knew it was late. Her eyes felt gritty and for the second time a wave of fatigue-induced nausea hit her. If she had to guess she'd say three or four am. They had been in the welcome event since arriving and those running it showed no signs of bringing it to a close anytime soon.

It had all started innocently enough. Drinks had been served and, after changing into the green lounge wear, Bloom, Nicola, Kimberly and Daisy joined half a dozen others who had arrived earlier in the day and experienced a mindfulness seminar. On entering the room Bloom had suggested to Nicola that they stick together. She knew an important way to insulate yourself from mind control was having someone to talk to who sees what you see, but within minutes of entering the room she and Nicola had been separated by existing group members keen to introduce themselves. Before Bloom knew it, Nicola was on the other side of the room. And by the time they sat down she could see that all the new arrivals had been separated, and each was now sitting with their own little minder.

Not that anyone else appeared to have noticed. The

mood was light-hearted and the chatter constant. No one looked intimidated or concerned. No one looked suspicious, and why should they? Everyone was very friendly. The surroundings were as luxurious as promised. It felt like any seminar or workshop you might attend with all manner of organizations. The only clue that something might be different here were the large photographs of Paula that hung on every wall; some of them so softly focused and artily posed it was hard to take them seriously.

The group sat in an arc of softly padded green chairs and, as in the lobby, large vases of flowers filled the room with a sweet fragrance. In front of the chairs sat their host for the evening, none other than Margaret Lowe, the speaker from Bloom's London event. She had flown up that very afternoon, she said, and was delighted to be here to welcome the group to what promised to be a life-changing weekend of talking, sharing and understanding what could be achieved together.

Bloom listened carefully to Margaret's every word. She watched her peers nodding and smiling, and at one point, when Margaret shared her experience of an abusive marriage, a number of them wiped away tears. Margaret was as eloquent as she had been at the London seminar. She talked extensively about the status of women in society through the ages. She highlighted abuses of power and injustices imposed upon women who she emphasized were 'just like us'. She talked about how the suffragette movement had faced obstacle upon obstacle in its fight to earn women the right to vote.

She listed the many women who had achieved great things in history and been overlooked or forgotten. She talked about women who day in, day out tolerate an abusive relationship or experience discrimination. She asked the group if they thought this was OK and they said no. She asked if the women present had experienced some of what she was talking about and many said yes. She asked if they were prepared to let it go on, or willing to take a stand, because if they were willing to do something about it Artemis had the answer. No longer did they need to feel frustrated, put upon or alone. In Artemis they could realize their own potential and benefit from a collective power. They could effect real change in the world, in society and, most importantly, in their own lives.

Bloom felt in part inspired, in part appalled. She knew women had pushed for equality for many years but she'd never appreciated how hard they'd had to fight to make progress or how much injustice remained around the globe.

Eventually Margaret brought the session to a close. 'I think we should let you rest and refresh,' she said, ignoring the fact that apart from the nibbles in reception no food had been provided since they had left Edinburgh at 5pm that afternoon.

'That was quite the introduction,' said Bloom to Nicola as the group were taken down a corridor towards their rooms.

'Yeah, exhausting but fascinating. I feel awake for the first time in my life, don't you?'

'It was certainly thought-provoking.' She had been listening with a sceptical ear, trying to spot holes in their argument or any sweeping generalizations that smacked of propaganda. But, as far as she could tell, Margaret had made a compelling and convincing case for change.

'It's nice to hear people finally speaking the truth, don't you think, calling out the bullshit? That stuff about how three-quarters of deaths from domestic violence are women killed by their partner or ex-partner. It has to stop. We have to stop it.'

Bloom didn't disagree, nor did she doubt the statistics Margaret had used. She had read similar numbers in police reports over the years. The only doubts she had related to the mysterious answer Margaret kept alluding to. *Artemis has the answer*, she had said numerous times. *Stick with us and we'll give you the answer* was another frequently used phrase. The promise of revealing a truth later down the line was an effective tactic for keeping people interested. It was the reason the likes of Scientology had different levels of membership, each one promising to reveal more of the 'truth'. Could that be how they hooked people in here?

'You'll find all your belongings ready and waiting for you by your beds,' said Lisa the receptionist.

Bloom was directed to a room with Daisy and a lady called Julia. There were six beds, three on either side of the room, and in between each a small side table. Bloom's overnight bag was at the end of the bed furthest into the room on the left and her toiletry bag had been removed and now sat on top of the side table. The same set-up could be seen by the nearest bed on the left and the middle bed on the right. Beside the other three beds, Bloom could see picture frames, hairbrushes and reading books laid out neatly. These beds must belong to the Artemis members who had followed them in. One was Natasha from the minibus who now chatted warmly to Daisy, another was Mary, an articulate lady of a similar age to Bloom with a background in IT analysis. She had approached Bloom at the start of the welcome event to say she'd been assigned to help her settle in. And finally they were joined by an older lady with grey hair piled on top of her head whose name Bloom had yet to learn. She had clearly been chosen to befriend Julia. They were clever pairings; someone had thought carefully about who to put with whom.

Bloom moved to her bed and removed her night clothes from the case. It irritated her that someone had opened it and removed her washbag. Had they searched it at the same time? Maybe to try to learn what they could about her.

The door to the bathroom was in between her bed and the one opposite. She checked with the group that she could use it first and closed the door behind her. What time was it? She looked at her reflection. Her eyes looked red and there were bags underneath. She had never fared well without sleep. She was an eight-hours-a-night person.

'What did you think of the welcome, Augusta?' came the voice of Mary through the door.

'I'll just be a moment,' said Bloom as a cue to be afforded some privacy, but Mary carried on talking to her, restating many of the points Margaret had made and asking if they resonated.

Bloom quickly changed and brushed her teeth. She was an introverted thinker. She relied on quiet time to process her thoughts and she was finding the constant conversation exhausting. The shared rooms were a disappointment and the lack of privacy unsettling.

She left the bathroom and climbed into bed, smiling at Mary as she passed. She had to remember most of these women were doing what they were told to in good faith. Cult members rarely see the objective truth of what they are tasked with. If indeed it was a cult. It was entirely plausible that the Artemis organization itself was professional and legitimate. Listening to Margaret speak, Bloom had the sense that the Artemis goal was not some kind of facade. They were serious about women's rights and diligent in checking their data. They didn't need to manipulate the facts to find followers; their cause was sound. Perhaps Scarlett and Shauna had had the misfortune of coming across a rogue element: an individual or clique within Artemis that was controlling or abusive in some way.

She huddled down under the covers, using them to give herself some feeling of protection and privacy.

The other occupants took their turns in the bathroom, and throughout their hosts kept up the conversation, asking question after question. Even when the lights were out and Bloom felt herself drifting off to sleep, Mary said, 'So, what did you really think of today, Augusta? You haven't said?'

'It was great,' Bloom recalled mumbling before sleep claimed her.

34

Jameson packed the blanket into his rucksack, removed his woolly hat and gloves, and ran his fingers through his hair. He needed fresh coffee but first he would check out the house. There had been no activity overnight: around midnight the remaining two lights had been switched off and the street was quiet until the break of dawn.

He removed his down jacket and rolled it as small as it would go, placing it with the blanket in his rucksack. He then put on a smarter wool coat that, folded inside his bag, had provided an effective pillow. He turned his back to the house then removed a bottle of aftershave from the front pocket of the rucksack and sprayed it liberally on himself, before popping a chewing gum in his mouth. How you look and how you smell tells people a lot about who you are, or who you want them to think you are. He stood up straight, buttoned up his coat and placed the rucksack on his back. In a few small movements he had transformed from street sleeper to businessman.

It was just past 8am and the city buzzed with morning activity. Jameson crossed the road and strode purposefully to the front door of the Artemis HQ, knocking hard three times. When nothing happened, he knocked again and stepped back to look at the windows. No curtains moved and no people appeared. Perhaps the residents couldn't hear the front door from within their rooms.

He was about to knock again when he heard something on the other side of the door. It opened a small amount and a black lady with an impressive Afro looked out.

'Good morning,' said Jameson in his poshest southern accent. 'I am trying to locate a Miss Shauna Roberts. Is this the correct residence?'

The woman stared at him blankly for a moment then shook her head.

'Oh dear. I'm terribly sorry.' He made a point of looking back out to the road. 'This is Circus Place, is it not? You can probably tell I'm not from around here.'

'Yes, but there's no Shauna here.'

'Damn it,' he said for effect under his breath. 'Any chance you could be of help to a lost fool? I need to find her quite urgently. I work for her family's solicitors and I have some important news about an inheritance. I was told this was her current address.'

'I'm sorry, I don't know her.'

'Might someone else in the building know? Is this one residence or flats?'

'One residence and none of us knew Shauna.'

The choice of tense made him raise his eyebrows. She knew she had spoken out of turn and dropped her gaze.

'So she was here at some point?'

'I'm sorry, I can't help, I have to go.'

He held the door with one hand, preventing her from shutting it. It was then he noticed she wore a tunic top, like the one Lori had described the driver of the car wearing. This one was green. 'If she's no longer here, I won't trouble you. But you don't know if anyone has a new address for her by any chance?'

A blank kind of look came into her eyes. 'I can't help you, sorry.' She pushed the door hard against his hand and he let it close.

He hadn't expected to get any intel from knocking, he just wanted to see the kind of people he was up against. Nothing beat looking a target in the eye. As he walked back to his accommodation, he assessed what he had seen. Behind the woman in the hallway there had been piles of boxes, all uniform in size and shape, stacked three high against the wall, and a large green rug with the Artemis logo in its centre covering the wooden floor; so far, so corporate HQ. But then on the back wall facing visitors as they entered hung a huge portrait of Paula Kunis. And he meant huge. It must have been three foot square with an elaborate gold frame. What was that about?

As for the woman who answered the door, her evasiveness about Shauna was odd. Why not just tell him she had passed away? The police were certain that she had most likely taken her own life, which was sad but not a secret, so why make it one? But that was not what had disturbed him most – that had been the look in the black woman's eyes. He'd seen a similar look before in his old life, a vacant sort of blankness that gave him the creeps.

He picked up a toasted bagel and take-out coffee on his walk back to the garden flat and ate while logging in to the company bank account. He had withdrawn some cash for expenses before buying breakfast as he didn't want to use his card when he scouted out the Artemis village later. He was sure no one would be checking his transactions but old habits die hard. He was surprised to see the account balance had jumped up by four grand. Looking now, he could see a deposit had been made the day before for £4,007.31. It was an odd amount, firstly because they rarely received such a large bulk payment and also because of the £7.31.

They typically invoiced for time and expenses separately on a monthly basis, with the latter provided as an itemized bill that rarely exceeded a few hundred pounds. So even if a client had paid their fees and expenses together it was unlikely that a fee of £4,000 would incur expenses of only £7.31, but the only other scenario was for expenses to have amounted to more than £1,007.31, which would be incredibly high. He checked the payer details and saw the transfer was from a company called Farr, White and Saunders. He sat back and chewed on the last of his bagel. He tended to oversee their accounts, as he enjoyed it more than Bloom, so it was unusual to have money coming in that he wasn't expecting. He checked their invoice files and couldn't find anything for Farr, White and Saunders or for an amount that totalled £4,007.31. He googled the company and found it was a firm of solicitors in central London. This must relate to Gerald Porter. Bloom had been carrying a white envelope when she came out of her meeting with him. She had said it was instructions for Porter's solicitor to pay them for extracting Scarlett. She'd dropped it into their offices while he'd fetched the car to drive them out to see Harris Marshall at Scarlett's mother's house.

But none of that explained the odd amount.

He dialled the number listed for Farr, White and Saunders and waited.

'Morning, this is Marcus Jameson from the Bloom Jameson Agency. I need to query an invoice we have recently been paid by you.'

The receptionist said she would transfer him to accounts.

He listened to some piano music for far too long and was about to hang up and dial again, assuming he'd been lost in the system, when an older female voice came on the line. 'Mr Jameson. This is Maureen, Mr Farr's PA. I understand you have a query about a payment?'

'Hello Maureen, sorry to bother you. I was hoping to speak to accounts to query a recent payment you have made to us as I have no matching invoice.'

'I can help with that. Your partner Dr Bloom delivered a payment request in person the day before yesterday. I handed it to Mr Farr myself.'

'I see. Sorry, Dr Bloom is indisposed at present. This is a rather large amount and I'd like to reconcile our records. You couldn't help me out and send a copy of the request she brought in, could you?'

'One moment. I'll check.' A few piano melodies later Maureen was back. 'Mr Farr said he did not retain the note, but he is confident the amount is correct. Is there anything else I can help you with?'

Jameson thanked her and said no. He could have

insisted on speaking to Farr himself but something told him he'd receive a similar rebuff. This was very odd. Had Bloom opened the letter or simply handed it on? He expected the latter, as he felt sure she would have mentioned the contents and the fact such a large payment was going to be made. What had she not told him? And what had Porter offered her so much money to do?

35

The sound of loud music jolted Bloom awake. She had no idea where she was, her eyes felt heavy and her head pounded. She turned to the side and saw Mary sitting on the end of her bed, dressed.

'Good morning, feeling refreshed?'

Bloom genuinely thought the woman was joking.

'Why don't you ladies take turns having a shower and then we can join the others for the morning's activities?'

Bloom sat up and looked at Julia and Daisy. They looked as disorientated as she felt as they slowly rose from their beds. The sun was shining outside, it was clearly morning. 'How long were we sleeping?'

Mary laughed and touched Bloom's upper arm. 'It's the Scottish air. It's so refreshing. It makes you feel like you've slept a whole day, don't you think?'

'No. I don't feel like I've slept at all,' said Julia.

Daisy rubbed her eyes and yawned.

'Oh dear. I'm sorry to hear that,' said Mary. 'Perhaps tonight will be better. I know some people don't rest when they're not in their own bed.'

'But how many hours have we slept for?' persisted Bloom.

'I know I slept well,' said Mary, standing and smoothing down her top.

'That's not what I asked. What time is it now and what time did the welcome event finish?' Bloom was too tired to watch her tone.

'It's time for breakfast. So I suggest a quick freshen-up and change.'

'Are you avoiding my question?'

'No. Not at all. You have all had a good night's sleep. I promise. This weekend is about refreshing and rethinking. Rest is critical.' At that point Mary walked purposefully out of the room.

'So yes, then,' said Bloom under her breath.

Julia smiled. She was an older lady, maybe mid-sixties, with naturally grey hair in a shoulder-length bob. 'They're an incessantly cheery bunch, aren't they?'

'Sorry. I don't mean to be a mood hoover.'

'Mood hoover. I like that. You do right to question them, though. I don't think we've had more than a few hours in bed. I'm a bad sleeper. I tend to notice the hours. I think they maybe got a little carried away last night and kept us all talking too long.' Julia gestured to the bathroom. 'Do you mind if I . . . ?'

Bloom nodded for her to go ahead. Daisy had curled up in a foetal position on the bed again.

'And I tell you what, I'm ready for that breakfast,' said Julia before closing the bathroom door.

Keep us up late, wake us up early, don't feed us, don't leave us alone with our thoughts. She knew these were the things to watch out for and, despite her hope last night that the group might not be a cult after all, they had all happened within the first twenty-four hours. She needed a way to track time. She cursed herself for not asking Jameson about that. She expected he had ways.

Moving to the window behind the beds opposite hers, she looked for the sun, hoping it might give her a clue. It sat just above the horizon, a large orange ball against the clear blue sky – but her interest in it was quickly forgotten; instead, she stared at the metal fence that rose in between. It must have been eight or nine feet high. She tracked it left and right. There were no breaks, no gates, and around the top ran three strings of barbed wire.

Bloom stepped back and took a few breaths to calm her racing heart. This place was everything she had feared and more. She hoped she had the willpower to fight it.

36

Around an hour north of Edinburgh, Jameson passed the city of Perth and left the M90 motorway to join the scenic A9. He had driven this road before and recalled the winding journey through the edge of the Cairngorms National Park and onwards to the town of Aviemore, where he'd once enjoyed the nearby ski runs. He stopped there to pick up fuel and eat a sandwich, taking a quick walk to stretch his legs and remember the place a little.

The wind was icy cold up here and he wrapped the collar of his down jacket tightly around his neck. It was approaching 4pm, and dusk was already threatening to fall. He wanted to drive by the Artemis village while there was still some light so he headed back to his car and continued on. He had set his satnav to take him to the small loch past the village and it soon directed him away from the A9 and across the winding roads of the Scottish wilderness. He wondered if he was anywhere near where Lori had her accident.

Jameson mulled over the four-grand payment. Was Augusta keeping something from him again? They'd had a rough run the past year or so as a result of her keeping secrets. He'd felt betrayed and angry that she'd not trusted him enough to share her plan for outsmarting Seraphine when they'd been investigating her game, a decision that had put his life in danger. But she'd apologized and made amends, or so he thought. Their working relationship was recovering. Would she really jeopardize that again? If so, that would be the end of them. Permanently.

Maybe the bulk of the money was for Scarlett. Her uncle may have wanted Bloom to pass on some cash after being told Artemis had taken all her trust money. The idea gave him comfort. There didn't have to be something underhand going on here. It could be entirely innocent. Until he'd had the chance to ask Bloom, he needed to give her the benefit of the doubt. After all, she was relying on him to look out for her while she willingly walked into what could be a powerful mental trap.

He slowed and pulled his car over to the side of the road. The Artemis village had come into view a quarter of a mile or so ahead in the valley below. He removed his binoculars from his rucksack and aimed them at the retreat where Bloom was staying.

Some of the village was shielded by trees but, even so, he could see it was bigger than he'd expected. There was a church spire in the middle and a scattering of stone residences surrounding a village green. The large farmhouse had a one-storey extension reaching out from the back that dwarfed the original house. He could not see any people but it was nearing dark and bitingly cold so he wasn't really surprised. What did surprise him was the fence. As Bloom's police contact had said, it surrounded the village and skirted the edge of the road he was on. It was too high to climb and made out of industrial-looking metal that did not complement the rustic buildings of the town or the idea of a spa retreat.

He zoomed in on the barbed wire around the top. How come the police officer hadn't mentioned that? It had three strands of barbs. At best this looked like security overkill, but at worst you had to consider the angle of the barbed section, slanting downwards from the top of the fence towards the village buildings.

Jameson placed the binoculars in his lap. Why would they position the barbed wire that way, angled like that of a prison: not to keep people out but to keep them in?

37

The day passed in a stream of presentations and discussions with little let-up. They were fed bowls of fruit for breakfast and the same again for lunch, all eaten while listening to Margaret talk or watching long videos of Paula. The latter comprised recordings of her conference speeches alongside to-the-camera monologues, presumably for Artemis use only. In between clips Margaret showed videos of grateful Artemis members expressing their joy at being part of such a groundbreaking movement and the life-changing impact it had made on them. Bloom had yet to hear exactly how Artemis was world-changing or groundbreaking but maybe that was the secret only shared with the chosen few. She was trying to listen with an open mind, despite the fence and the lack of sleep or sustenance. If Artemis members were being coerced and controlled, she needed to establish who was in the know and who the innocent victims were.

Paula Kunis spoke in more measured terms when addressing a conference than she did in the monologues. When talking to Artemis recruits alone she evangelized more: challenging members to take responsibility, stand up to the menfolk, start a change by changing yourself. *Commit*, she implored. *Leave your past behind. Focus on the future. Join us. Be part of something.*

Another thing Bloom noticed about Paula Kunis was that she rarely smiled. Her body language had a sort of stern, school-ma'am air about it. She used her arms to make strong frames and increase her presence. It was a technique Bloom knew the likes of Margaret Thatcher had employed to look more impactful and, ironically, given Paula's mission, masculine. And, as with many charismatic speakers, if you listened to the words, as Bloom had been doing, there was a lot of repetition. The woman's genius was in her delivery. She spoke with passion, fervour and, at times, indignant anger. It was the sort of speech that demanded you listen and take heed. Bloom could see this was a woman who took herself seriously and demanded that others do the same.

As dusk began to fall, Margaret turned off the projector.

'Congratulations on taking this first step towards a brighter future,' she said, ensuring she made eye contact with every person. 'Coming here this weekend is an action you have chosen to take because you know things aren't right. You want to change your own life or the lives of other women. Thank you. We welcome you and hope every single one of you will choose to become part of the Artemis family. We want and need you all.' She left a long silence so her words could sink in and then she smiled broadly and stood from her seat. 'And now the thing you've all been waiting for, ladies, the spa.'

A rumble of excited chatter moved around the group and the women began to make their way to the changing rooms where they were told they would find their swimwear, robes and flip-flops.

'I wonder if I could trouble you with a couple of questions, Margaret?' said Bloom when most of the others had left. Only her continual shadow Mary had remained behind with her.

A brief frown touched Margaret's brow before she said, 'How can I help?'

'Augusta is one of our more inquisitive delegates,' said Mary.

Bloom pushed aside any worry that this may give her away, remembering Jameson's advice to be as close a version of herself as she could, and she was curious.

'I wanted to ask about the group's mission. A lot of what we've heard so far speaks of changing things, breaking ground, which is appealing, and I want to know how that is being done?'

'Well, that is something that our members have a great deal of faith in.'

Bloom stayed quiet. This had not answered her question.

Margaret held her gaze for a moment. 'Well,' she said, 'we are challenging stereotypes and pushing for equality.'

'Yes. I get that. I suppose I was more intrigued about how we do that?' She used the word *we* on purpose to give the impression she was on the way to joining.

'Together. As one.' Margaret smiled as if that truly answered everything.

'You said in London you were originally a secretary and now you're a Head of Procurement.'

'Yes, I quit my career and spent two years working solely for the Artemis cause until I found my new calling.

I wouldn't be where I am without taking that time to know who I really was and what I could really achieve.'

'Did Artemis help you to retrain or gain qualifications?' If the answer was yes, this could make them more functional and constructive despite the heavy sales pitch.

'It is not about what Artemis can give to us, but about what we are prepared to give to it.'

'So did you retrain off your own back then?' Bloom knew that traditionally cults did not like members going outside of the group to study as they could not control what they learned. If they were encouraging that, it would be a good sign.

'What is it you would like, Augusta? What frustrates you about your life?'

'Oh, many things. Life never turns out how you'd like, does it?' She purposefully kept her response as vague as Margaret's. 'How about your family, did they support you taking such a long career break?'

'Ah, come, sit.' Margaret gestured for Bloom to follow her to the now-empty seats in the middle of the room. Once seated, she turned to Bloom with her hands clasped on her knee and her posture leaning forward in a sign of care and concern. 'Many of us find that those not in the Artemis fold don't always understand or accept how important and valuable our work is. Members often find it easier to put a little distance between themselves and any of that negativity.'

'Are you saying people give up their families for your cause?'

Margaret's laugh was low and patronizing. She placed

a hand on Bloom's. 'We have families here. We have a school with ten lovely children on site. We are not against families, we *are* a family, a family that people choose to join rather than be born into.'

Bloom was taken aback by the news that there were children on site. 'Are there husbands here too then?'

'Why? Are you married, Augusta?'

'No, but . . . I thought Artemis was exclusively female.'

'It is. But families come in all shapes and sizes these days. Love is not the exclusive right of heterosexual couples. We provide an environment where women can be whatever they desire, and that includes being a mother. How could it not? It is one of our most essential contributions, raising the next generation. Does that answer your questions?'

Bloom wondered if Margaret knew she had been evasive and vague or if she was so indoctrinated she thought she'd been open and honest. There was one question Bloom really wanted the answer to, as she knew it was a good indication of how dysfunctional a group might be. She quickly ran through different ways she might ask it without being too pointed.

'Before coming, I tried to speak to some previous Artemis members just to gauge why it might not work for some women, but I couldn't find anyone. Is there anyone you could recommend? It would really help me to weigh up the pros and cons.'

'No.'

The direct refusal was unexpected and Bloom knew Margaret saw the surprise on her face.

'For the simple reason that there aren't any.'

'No one has left. *Ever?*'

'No. Not one. This is a community that empowers and enables. Why would anyone leave?'

'Changing personal circumstances maybe?'

Margaret smiled and shook her head.

'In nearly a decade, no members have ever left?'

'None.'

Shauna Roberts, Bloom thought. Could she mention her? Had the news reports said anything about her involvement in Artemis? She hadn't checked. She couldn't risk bringing her up in case not.

'We welcome curiosity, Augusta. It is healthy. But there comes a time when trust and faith must step in. You will not get all your answers from questioning. You will only get them from living and experiencing.' Margaret stood. 'Please do go and enjoy the spa with your friends.'

Professor Colby had told her that his research identified two key characteristics that dysfunctional cults have in common. Firstly, they create a 'them and us' philosophy where non-members are seen as negative and leavers are disparaged or denied, and secondly, they shut down questions as early as possible. Bloom had detected some of this in the sessions so far but the conversation with Margaret confirmed it. No group of nearly ten years' standing has no leavers. That had to be a lie. And that threw into doubt everything else that had been said.

38

The auditorium hummed with conversation. People occupied every one of the 1,500 seats. It was the largest crowd she had ever addressed and anticipation buzzed in her veins. The previous speaker had been professional but lacked pizzazz or chutzpah or whatever you wanted to call it. There was no drama, no punch and, therefore, in Paula's view no point. Here was a captive audience. Once you began, they had to listen, and if they were listening that was half the battle won. She had learned that from her father. He could stand up in the cheap diners they used to go to for soggy pancakes and limp bacon and take the room. People tutted at first, catcalled for him to sit down. Americans were not like Brits. They had no problem telling an asshole to shut the hell up. But before long they fell silent as they all looked his way and started to listen. Really listen. Long story short, her father had never paid for a meal anywhere they went.

And while all those strangers had been listening she had been listening too, not only to his words of hell fire and damnation but to his every breath, his tone, his silence, his volume – until she could mimic it to perfection.

Once again it was time to use what he had taught her.

Before the conference chairwoman had a chance to introduce her, Paula walked to the centre of the stage and spoke in a loud voice that made the most of her American accent.

'Are you women God-fearing?'

Silence fell instantly; every pair of eyes was on her.

'Do you know your place?' she said a little more quietly before dropping her voice to as close to a whisper as she could get away with and still have the microphone pick it up. 'Are you the weaker sex?'

She surveyed the room slowly and then stood to her full height and spread her arms. 'You are allowed to answer. You can say no.'

A ripple of laughter passed through the crowd and a large number of the 1,500 women called out, 'No!'

Paula entered her hotel room looking forward to opening the bottle of Shiraz she had stashed in her case. The healthy-living ethos of Artemis was something she had no interest in personally, but found it worked extraordinarily well for the members. They appeared to love the self-denial and feeling of improving themselves, so she went along with it when she was in their eyeline.

'Paula Kunis, how delightful to meet you.' An attractive woman with long blonde hair and piercing blue eyes sat at the dressing table.

Paula paused in the doorway. *Should she call for security?*

'Don't worry, I'm not stalking you. I'm not one of your groupies. Come in, come in. I have a business proposition for you.'

Paula wasn't sure how to respond but she was intrigued, so she closed the door.

The blonde stood and held out her hand. 'Seraphine Walker.'

'How can I help you, Seraphine?'

'People usually call me Miss Walker, but don't worry, I'll let it go for now. Please take a seat.'

Paula felt her hackles rise. Who did this woman think she was, breaking into her hotel room and treating it like home?

'I'm good standing, thank you. What do you want?'

'You may have heard about me on the news recently – the psychopath accused of recruiting other psychopaths?'

'I can't say that I have. I'm a very busy woman.'

'One who's not fazed by a self-confessed psychopath. Good for you. Naive, but god for you.' Seraphine sat again and crossed one long leg over the other. She wore what looked to be an Armani trouser suit with red-soled Louboutin heels.

'Make it quick, I have to change. I'm the special guest at the conference dinner.'

'Of course you are. I've been reading all about you. Very impressive work, and all so' – Seraphine waved her hand in the air, showing off her elegant fingers and professionally painted nails – 'well meaning,' she finished.

'You said you had a business proposition?' Paula removed her suit jacket and laid it on the bed. This woman was clearly very wealthy but Paula suspected also a touch eccentric. Why did she attract such people? It was as if the crazies were out there waiting for someone to latch on to, someone who would tell them what to do and how to live.

'You have charitable status, I believe?'

'What has that to do with anything?'

'I'm just hoping it's legitimate and able to withstand scrutiny.'

Paula looked at her sharply.

'Now, that got your attention, didn't it?'

'Are you threatening me?'

Seraphine laughed lightly. 'Not at all. But I do know someone who's taking a close look at your organization. I'd be happy to tell you their name, if you can give me something in return.'

Paula's patience ran out. How dare this woman come in here and interrogate her? She was Paula Kunis. No one got to speak to her without a full vetting.

'I'm going to have to ask you to leave and make an appointment with my assistant. I haven't time for your theatre. Like I say, I'm a very busy woman.'

'Oh. I see.' Seraphine held eye contact until Paula felt uncomfortable and looked away. 'I'm only trying to help you.'

'Like I said, if you really wish to help' – Paula paused and looked the other woman in the eye again – 'if you can indeed *be* of any help. Make. An. Appointment.'

Seraphine Walker stood up and left without another word. Paula removed the wine from her case and took a swig from the bottle, closing her eyes as she did. Whatever that woman wanted, Paula wasn't interested. People loved her. She could do no wrong and she could talk herself into and out of anything. *Bring it on, disgruntled member of the public. Do your best. Because I'll be one step ahead.*

39

Jameson drove past the village and out to the other side. The fence bordered the buildings all the way along, providing no access apart from one entrance. He slowed just a touch so he could take in the detail. The gates were as high as the fence, electronically operated with a keypad entry system. The only upside was that they were not topped with barbed wire.

A few miles along the road he parked the hire car on the grassy verge and reached into the back for his equipment. He fitted the small night camera to the lapel of his jacket and turned it on. It linked to an app on his phone and he checked it was working before climbing out and covering his head with a black balaclava. He then jogged back across the field towards the village. At first he used his head torch to navigate but as he came closer to the fence he switched to the night goggles.

His induction into the secret service had included a period of commando training with the Royal Marines. They covered everything from navigation and weapons training to scoping out a target location. The general principle was not to approach from the front but to take a wide arc around the target so you could check out the perimeter for alternative entrances, exits and, of course, the enemy.

He used this approach now, circling the village away from the road and tracking the perimeter fence. The ground under his feet was marshy and rocky, meaning he had to watch his step. Breaking an ankle out here would not be helpful.

There were no other gates, and he found it odd to look through the industrial-style fence and see the small stone church and a village shop. He paused when he came alongside a playground with a painted hopscotch game and small climbing frame; so there were children here. How awful to have to play next to this fence. He imagined they took it for granted though. He remembered speaking to kids out in Afghanistan who thought that everyone lived in a war zone. That had been one of the saddest moments in his MI6 career. He had been there to find intelligence sources and turn Taliban commanders, but it was all taking too long and a whole generation was growing up thinking conflict was normal.

When he had made it all the way around and back to the road he walked to the entrance, hunkered down to one side and waited. Beyond the gates a smaller road curved left into the village and towards the church. Two hundred metres or so along on the right, a gravel driveway led to the farmhouse, opening out into a large circle in front of the entrance. The double-width wooden door had no glass in it but a warm orange glow came from the surrounding windows.

He scanned the gates. The vertical metal posts extended out of the top but as luck would have it there were no spiked tips. On the fence post nearest to him sat a CCTV camera, again angled inwards rather than out: to spy on those leaving rather than those entering. He was pretty confident if he climbed here he could stay in the CCTV's blind spot. He took one last look around to make sure no one was watching then braced one foot against a vertical post, took hold of the post above with both hands and slowly walked himself up, hand over hand, foot over foot. At the top he used the horizontal bar to swing himself over and then he slid down the other side. On landing he kept his back to the gate and moved slowly along the fence to the right, away from the CCTV camera watching the farmhouse door.

40

By the time Bloom made it to the spa area, a group of women was already settled in the bubbling Jacuzzi at the far end of the infinity-style swimming pool. As expected, she could see that three of the women in the Jacuzzi were Artemis hosts, stuck like glue to their delegates. She assumed the rest of the group must be in the sauna or steam room. She could see doors for both along the side wall. Her own shadow, Mary, had popped to the toilet, so Bloom took the chance to come through to the pool by herself and swim a few lengths. She was craving the thinking space and time alone. She'd read how cults often break people down by talking to them constantly but she'd never imagined how exhausting it would be.

She had felt a little uncomfortable finding her own bathing costume and goggles set out for her in the changing room. This habit of going through her things was intrusive. She planned to sound the others out on how they felt about it if she had the chance.

Cool water washed over her head as she pushed away from the wall and began her swim. It felt refreshing and comforting all in one go, like diving into a cocoon of peace and tranquillity. She really had not expected Artemis would actually have a spa here, or that they would be able to use it, so this was a pleasant surprise. It made her feel another tingle of doubt. She didn't want to simply see what she was expecting to see. Shauna Roberts' father had been convinced there was something troubling going on in Artemis, and Scarlett's cousin seemed to concur, but what evidence was there really? What had she seen? Sure, they had kept them occupied and accompanied since their arrival but the content had been innocuous enough – just a lot of bluster about improving your life and your situation. What was wrong with that? Then there had been the lack of sleep and food. She had worried about this before arriving, but was that worry colouring her perception? Had they been deprived of sleep or, as Mary said, had they slept for longer than she thought? And if she was honest, was the provision of fruit for breakfast and lunch so unusual in a women's health spa? Wouldn't that be a desirable thing for many who wanted a healthy weekend away?

She approached the pool wall for the third time and somersaulted before pushing herself into her fourth length. The fence was the most worrying aspect, and the assertion that no one had ever left the group. These were the things to interrogate. A pair of legs stood at the other end of the pool. On her next breath Bloom glanced forward and confirmed that Mary had climbed in to join her. *Thinking time over.*

'You're a strong swimmer, Augusta.'

Bloom stood and removed her goggles. 'I find exercise relaxing.'

'Isn't that an oxymoron?'

Bloom smiled. 'I suppose it is, but it clears my head, especially if I'm stressed.'

'You're not stressed here, are you? We don't want you to feel like that.'

'I mean in general. How long have you been with Artemis, Mary?' Bloom pushed her hair back from her face, feeling the water run down the back of her neck.

'Oh, four years now. I couldn't be happier. It changed my life.'

'How so?'

'They are my world, my family. There is nowhere I'd prefer to be.'

'Is it true what Margaret said about people never leaving?'

'Of course.'

Bloom decided to push. 'Don't you find that odd?'

'What I find odd is that women choose not to leave a violent marriage, not that they choose to stay in a loving and supportive home like ours.'

'Do you live up here then?'

'Yes. I have a son in school here, Patrick. He's eight.'

'I didn't realize some of you had children. How does that work with Patrick's father, does he visit?'

'He was not a nice man. Pat is better off away from him. That's one of the ways Artemis really helped me. Do you have children?'

Bloom shook her head.

'A lot of women decide that motherhood is not for them. It's a perfectly legitimate decision.'

'A lot of women also don't have a choice.' Bloom could not help the small challenge. Her instincts told her there was a naivety about Mary's world view despite her age.

'Is that the case for you?'

'I'm just observing that choice is not the only reason women don't become mothers. Does Patrick like it here, does he have friends?'

'He has family. He loves it.' Before Bloom could enquire how she felt about her son being fenced in, Mary said, 'There's space in the Jacuzzi, let's join the others.' She lifted herself out of the pool without waiting for a response.

Bloom knew she could ignore the suggestion and continue to swim, but politeness and social norms exerted a strong pull. Mary had already clocked Bloom's questioning nature, perhaps that was enough for now. No need to set herself any further apart. Everyone else was joining in, she should too. 'I'll swim up to it,' she said by way of a compromise.

She pushed away from the wall and once more submerged her head. Every interaction she had with an Artemis member sounded rehearsed, like they had been fed the lines to say and the questions to ask. She was struggling to work out the truth; it was infuriating and exhausting. She wished she had Jameson here to sound out ideas on her best next step. So far she had no strong sense of who she should speak to about Scarlett. Who could she trust to give her an honest answer? She simply didn't know.

Maybe her whole strategy was flawed. It might have been better to have simply asked about Scarlett at the start, at the seminar or in her meeting with Melanie and Victoria. Why hadn't she done that? She was finding it hard to remember now.

In the Jacuzzi, the discussion was animated and excitable. Nicola from the minibus was one of those present, along with her Artemis shadow, Patrice, and Julia from Bloom's dorm room with her Artemis shadow, a quiet lady called Vera who all but blended into the background. They appeared fired up by what they had heard from Paula and were comparing notes on the injustices against women they had witnessed. Nicola talked openly about her relationship and how disappointed she had become with her partner, Callum. Julia talked about the fractured relationship she'd had with her father, who sounded like a harsh disciplinarian, and how this had affected her relationships with men throughout her adult life. Bloom liked how Julia talked. It was obvious she was an intelligent woman who was thinking hard about the information they were being given. She qualified her opinions with statements like, 'This might just be me,' or, 'Correct me if I'm wrong,' which spoke of a woman secure enough in her own skin to be challenged. That could be useful.

Overall, there was something a touch clichéd about the conversation. Not that Bloom would discount either woman's experiences, or the impact on their lives, but she also knew that if you look for the bad in any experience you will tend to find it. She'd had a supportive and loving relationship with her father. He wasn't a tactile man, but he was interested and interesting. However, if called upon to criticize him, she could find many an anecdote of bad temper, impatience and over-reaction to recount. She could make him sound unreasonable and even uncaring should she be so inclined. Every person was flawed, so you could make every person sound bad if you only described their flaws. Her worry about the discussions Paula and her team were inspiring was that they were skewing these women's perspectives on the men in their lives.

One fact that was coming over loud and clear was that, in the Artemis battleground, men were most definitely the enemy.

41

Jameson kept his distance from the windows of the main building as he moved slowly around it. There was not much to be seen inside other than a long corridor that ran the length of the extension. Its plain walls were lined with photographs of Paula Kunis, and occasionally there was an internal door on the opposite side, always closed.

He continued around to the other side, where it was a different story. Here he could see into a series of small dorm rooms. There were six beds in each, some with belongings stacked neatly on the bedside tables, others unmade and clearly unoccupied. Next to the window of each room was another frosted one indicating an en suite of some kind. He counted at least a dozen beds that were made up and ready to be slept in. He carefully scanned each of the rooms for any sign of Augusta's belongings, but saw nothing he recognized. He wasn't sure he would know her personal items if he saw them anyway. He had stayed at her family home once, a year earlier when they were investigating Seraphine's game, but he'd had his own en suite so had never seen what shampoo, face cream or even toothpaste his business partner might use.

He checked the time. It was nearing 9pm.

The next section of the extension had no windows except for a domed glass roof, and a strong smell of chlorine pumped out of an extractor fan. The spa. Is that where Augusta was, sitting in some sauna relaxing while he crept about in the freezing darkness? He realized he hoped so. Better that than her being subjected to any of the mind-control tactics they had discussed on their drive up.

He moved carefully away from the main house, making sure to stay out of sight of the CCTV camera on the gate. So far he hadn't seen any further cameras, which made sense, seeing as there was clearly only one way out of this place, thanks to the height of the fence and its barbed wire. Moving slowly and low to the ground, he reached the school, which was locked and in darkness. With the aid of his night vision goggles he could see small tables and chairs inside and walls decorated with large alphabet letters. There were clearly young children here then, like the boy Lori had described. He looked over at the houses spaced at regular intervals away from the main building. Could the little boy from the accident be in one of those, wondering where his mother was?

Using the trees for cover he approached the nearest terrace of four houses, all with their curtains closed and little sign of life. Only the end one had a light on downstairs. Jameson moved close to the window. There was one more CCTV camera on the main building but it was not pointing in this direction. It was watching the road and the only exit out of the place. He could hear voices. He strained to listen. It sounded like two women but he couldn't make out the words.

As he concentrated, he scanned the surrounding area

for anyone who might catch him snooping. On the far left of the church, he spotted a row of garages. They looked dilapidated and unused and yet the central one was secured with three large padlocks. What did they have in there to warrant such security?

Having no luck with the eavesdropping, he decided to go and investigate the garage. Keeping low, he moved quickly across the street, stopping outside the middle garage and removing a small set of bolt cutters from his rucksack. If he used them, they would know someone had been on site. He knelt to where the bolts were fastened to the bottom of the garage door and spun the first padlock's digits to 0000. He tried to release it. Nothing. He tried 1234 but that didn't work either and then he tried 0123. In his experience, people often found such combinations easiest to remember. Still no luck. He was about to resort to the bolt cutters when he decided to try one more time but reversing the order so it read 1234 from the bottom to the top instead of the top to the bottom. On his final try of doing the same with 0123 he felt the lock release.

The same code unlocked the other two padlocks. Jameson marvelled at the fact such a clever lock design could be so easily undermined by human laziness.

With the locks undone, he lifted the garage door just far enough to roll underneath. Once inside he closed the door behind him and turned to see what in this room was so important.

42

Nicola followed Patrice into the cosy side room and sat in one of two low armchairs. Despite having showered she could still smell the faint scent of chlorine on her skin; her face felt flushed from the heat of the sauna and her fingertips were wrinkled and puffy.

It had been an exhilarating twenty-four hours. She felt exhausted by it but also full of hope. Patrice had suggested a personal mindfulness session and Nicola had jumped at the chance. She was a little in awe of the woman. Despite being a couple of decades older than Nicola, her skin was luminous and in no need of any make-up to enhance it. She also talked with a wisdom that Nicola had never come across. It felt almost spiritual. And Nicola felt humble and ordinary in her company.

They had met at the welcome event and struck up an instant rapport. Patrice had joined Artemis on the back of a long relationship that had failed to bring the children she desired. She described feeling lost and without purpose, which was exactly how Nicola had been feeling. And then she said something that resonated so clearly: 'In Artemis we believe a woman can never truly shine while she remains in the shadow of a man.' In that moment Nicola saw that professionally and personally she had let herself live in the shadow of men: her boyfriend, her boss, even her elder brother, who insisted on being successful at every damn thing he turned his hand to.

Patrice took her seat opposite. How was she making the lounge wear look glamorous? Nicola tugged at the V-neck collar which had hitched up around her collar bones, resulting in an unattractive flap of material over her chest.

'How are you feeling right now?' said Patrice, her gaze intense and interested.

'I think content best describes it. I feel calmer than I have for a long time.'

'Good. You have emerged from your cocoon of life like a colourful butterfly, I think.'

Nicola laughed with embarrassment. 'Oh I don't know about that. I don't think I've ever been described as colourful.'

'Why ever not? You are one of the most colourful people I've ever met. You're full of bright vitality. I'm in awe of it.'

Hearing Patrice describe her in the same terms as she had been viewing this impressive woman was a surprise. It took her a moment or two to process it.

'You don't believe that about yourself, do you?'

Nicola shrugged and averted her gaze.

'You are a beautiful woman, Nicola. Do you see that?'

Nicola continued to keep her eyes on the ground as she shook her head. She knew from the brutality of secondary school that she was not one of the pretty girls. They had mocked her high forehead and chunky ankles mercilessly.

Then at university she had received no interest from the opposite sex at all in her first year, despite her fellow students bringing a stream of boys home. Only when she met Callum did she feel attractive for the first time. But even he would make fun of her flaws. It was just teasing, he'd say, but she remembered their first holiday together when she'd emerged from the pool hoping to look sexy in her new bikini only to have him say, 'Blimey, Nic, the sun shining off your forehead is blinding me,' and then he'd laughed for far too long as she'd brushed her fringe forward. It was true to say that whenever she looked in a mirror all she really saw was whether or not her hairstyle was effectively covering her forehead.

'That is very sad, Nicola. You are beautiful inside and out and the world should have shown you this already. How old are you now?'

'Thirty-seven.'

'Don't you think it's time you opened your mind to the truth?'

'Not everyone is perfect, are they? You have to accept the cards you've been dealt.'

'Do you? Do you really believe that?'

She thought so. It's what she'd always believed.

'What if there's another way? A way to channel all that vitality and energy into making yourself a better person. Would you be open to that?'

'Of course.'

'At Artemis we believe everyone has the potential to be more, you only have to be willing to work hard.'

'I definitely have that ability.'

'Good. Good.' Patrice leaned forward, her eyes full of affection. 'I am so happy you came to us. We are going to do great things together. You are special, Nicola, and I'm going to make it my business to make sure you know this.'

Nicola curled her feet under her and picked at a thread on her sleeve as she said, 'Thanks.' Inside, she was glowing.

43

Jameson had hoped to find something more exciting in the garage than a stack of luggage. He'd wanted there to be something he could use to justify the irritation he was feeling towards this group. Ever since they'd started looking into Artemis, the 'man-hating' tone had riled him. Not all men were hell bent on keeping the little woman in her place. Many celebrated the opposite sex with genuine admiration and affection. He had watched a few videos of Paula Kunis and been distinctly unimpressed. To him she looked like a bitter drama queen angry about not getting her way.

He steadily moved around the space so the camera could take in all the stacked cases. Each bag had a label with a name written on it. Halfway around he paused on reading the name Shauna Roberts. He knelt beside the hard-backed wheelie case, laid it on its side and carefully unzipped it.

Inside he found clothes, shoes, a chick-lit novel and a mug with 'Best Sister in the World' written on it. Jameson carefully checked the internal pockets for any other items. Maybe there would be a diary or a notebook that might give him some insight into Shauna and her experiences here, but there was nothing. He rezipped the case and replaced it in position, feeling angry that these possessions had not been returned to Shauna's father, Linwood. There was nothing particularly personal or sentimental inside, aside from maybe the mug, but still, the case now belonged to her next of kin.

He continued to move through the garage scanning the labels, but saw no further names he recognized, including Bloom's. He wondered how long these cases had sat here – from the point at which women decided to move in? Not wanting to invade anyone's privacy too much, he gently opened a few more to confirm the contents were similar to those of Shauna's.

After exiting and relocking the garage, he carefully retraced his steps back across to the main building, then kept as close to the wall as possible as he moved around it. As before, the bedrooms were empty. He paused before rounding to the other side to check no one was out by the gate. When he was sure it was clear he began to move towards it, staying close to the fence to avoid the CCTV as before. A movement in his peripheral vision made him stop then step back to ensure he was fully in the shadows. An internal door on to the corridor had opened and two women now walked towards the front of the farmhouse. Both women were dressed in identical green outfits. The taller woman was in her late fifties and the younger dark-haired woman he recognized as Bloom's companion in the back of the minibus. He had followed Bloom to the Artemis HQ, where she had been asked to assemble yesterday for their journey here. Watching from a safe distance, he had seen the various women arrive and take their seats, noting that three of them arrived independently, making them new recruits like Bloom, and the rest exited the HQ building together so he took them to be Artemis staff.

The younger dark-haired woman had arrived by taxi with a small wheelie case not too dissimilar to that owned by Shauna Roberts. Jameson studied her, knowing this might be the closest he would get to seeing how Augusta was doing. Whatever they had been subjected to here, this woman had experienced it too.

As luck would have it, the woman glanced out of the window towards where he stood. Her expression surprised him; she looked calm and happy, laughing at something her companion said before looking away again.

Jameson stood for a few minutes after the two women had passed through another doorway. He should be pleased that one of Augusta's peers looked happy, shouldn't he? That meant nothing too sinister could be going on, and that his partner was probably fine.

The problem was he couldn't get Bloom's warning about a cult's tactics out of his head. 'It's a bit like the parable of the frog in hot water,' she'd said. 'If you drop it straight in, it will immediately jump out, but if you place it in cool water and slowly heat it up, the frog will stay, oblivious to the danger.'

44

Everyone crowded into the reception area, some dressed for bed, others still in their spa robes and flip-flops.

'Ladies, ladies, I have wonderful news. Gather around, please.' Margaret had stood on a chair in front of the reception desk as if addressing a large crowd rather than a dozen women. 'This is unprecedented for people at our retreat events and we are so excited for you. It is a great privilege.' She took a deep breath and smiled.

Bloom had an idea of what was coming and glanced quickly around her fellow recruits. Every one of them looked wide-eyed and attentive. She was beginning to wish she'd attended with at least one other sceptical soul.

Margaret continued. 'Our venerable leader, Ms Paula Kunis, is to join you all here on Monday. It is such an honour. Many Artemis members have yet to meet her in such intimate circumstances so you should feel very special.'

Bloom waited for someone to point out the obvious but when no one did she put her hand up. 'Are we not leaving on Monday morning?'

Margaret clapped her hands together. 'Not any more,' she said, jumping down from the seat and beginning to circulate through the attendees, shaking hands and hugging people as she went.

'Anyone would think the queen is paying us a visit,' said Bloom under her breath.

The Artemis member next to her must have heard. Their eyes met for a moment, and there was something in the woman's gaze that caused Bloom to place a hand on her arm as the younger woman turned to move away.

'It's Lisa, isn't it? You were on reception when I arrived yesterday. I'm Augusta.'

The woman paused for a second then pushed her shoulders back and faced Bloom with a wider than necessary smile. 'Are you enjoying your stay, Augusta?'

'What's not to like?' Bloom let the comment hang in the air and watched a small frown crease Lisa's brow. Her jet-black hair was tied in a neat ponytail and she was probably in her mid-twenties. 'Have you been with Artemis long?'

'Since university.'

'What made you join?'

'Fate. It was meant to be,' said Lisa. When Bloom made no response, she continued. 'I had just lost someone very close to me and no one understood how I felt. Then I met Kirsty. She was handing out leaflets about Paula's TED Talk, we started chatting and she told me all about how Artemis had helped her when she was going through a bad time with her parents.'

'She empathized with you?'

'More than that, she educated me. She told me that the goddess Artemis was a protector of women, that she had the power to relieve their pain and make them stronger than any man, as strong as a bear even. The idea that women could be equal to men was something the ancient Greeks believed, but society has forgotten this or chosen to ignore it. I wanted to be part of righting that wrong.'

'And you also liked the idea of Artemis taking away your pain, I expect.'

'Yes,' Lisa said in a small voice.

Bloom had looked up the Greek goddess Artemis last week to see if there were any clues to the group in its choice of name. Lisa was correct in saying Artemis had been a protector of women, specifically women in childbirth, hence her power over pain. She had also been a skilful warrior, defeating many an attacker and potential rapist, according to the legends. The ability to make women as strong as a bear was a little twisted, however. From what Bloom had read, Artemis took young girls into servitude for a year and made them act like bears as some kind of punishment for her rivals having killed a bear she'd kept as a pet.

Lisa struck Bloom as particularly genuine. Perhaps she was a good source of intel. 'It sounds like you were fortunate to meet Kirsty when you did. Another of your members said the same about meeting' – she hesitated as if trying to remember the name – 'Scarlett, is it?'

'Oh, Scarlett is lovely. We'd all love to be like Scarlett.'

Bloom was taken aback at how easy that had been. 'What's so special about Scarlett?'

'She's been with Paula since the beginning. She's very close to her. If you need any advice from Paula, you go to Scarlett.'

This was not what Bloom had expected. She had foolishly assumed Scarlett would have blended into the ranks, given what they'd heard about her timid nature from her friend and her cousin. She'd missed the fact Scarlett had joined Artemis fairly close to its inception and that typically meant as things grow you move up the pyramid.

They could be talking about a different Scarlett, of course.

Bloom went on, 'Your colleague said Scarlett had lost her father young and had to care for her mother, is that right?'

'Yes, I believe so. But Paula says one of the reasons Scarlett is so pure of spirit is that she didn't have a dominant male colouring her view of the world when she was growing up.'

This not only confirmed they were talking about the same Scarlett but also demonstrated how effectively Paula could twist facts to suit her narrative. From what Harris had said, Scarlett had not grown up devoid of male input; her father's twin brother, Harris's father, had been around, as had Harris himself.

'Is becoming pure of spirit a goal for those in Artemis?' It was the first pseudo-religious term Bloom had heard, other than Melanie's statement in London that Artemis was a source of purpose and truth.

Lisa took a long intake of breath. 'Paula says realizing your potential relies on the purity of your spirit. If you know your core values and use them to dictate your decisions in life you cannot fail.'

And yet, if Bloom was right, here stood a woman who felt like a failure. 'Would you say you are now pure of spirit after all your years in Artemis?'

'I'm working on it. It's a long journey but a worthwhile one.' The haunted look that had been in Lisa's eyes when Bloom compared Paula's visit to the queen coming returned.

'What were you studying at university?' said Bloom, feeling a strong urge to help Lisa. It was well known within the psychological community that cults encourage members to repress their true selves in favour of a more compliant and vanilla character. Bloom decided to try to draw out Lisa's pre-Artemis identity. Remembering who you were before joining could often plant an important seed of doubt.

'English Literature.'

'A fellow book lover. Have you read anything good recently?'

Lisa shook her head. 'I'm too busy to read. There's more important things to do with my time.'

Bloom took a different tack. 'What was your favourite book growing up?'

Lisa's eyes lit up a touch as she said, 'Oh, that's easy, *Alice in Wonderland*. I loved it. My grandma used to read sections of it to me before bed every night.'

'She sounds like a wonderful grandma. Were you close?'

'Yes, very, she pretty much raised me, as my parents were useless.' Lisa blinked a couple of times and looked away. 'She's the person I lost. She died in my first year of university. Cancer.'

'Oh, I'm sorry. That's very sad.'

Lisa swallowed and nodded.

'Did she read many books to you?'

'So many, from Shakespeare to Stephen King. She had eclectic tastes.' Lisa's smile was a million miles away from the fake version she had put on earlier.

'Good for her. I had a similar thing with my grandfather. He used to read *The Lord of the Rings* and *The Hobbit* to me. I had no idea what was going on as I couldn't understand much of it, but I loved the idea of this other world.'

'Like with Alice's wonderland.'

'Yes. It's a shame we lose all that imagination when we grow up, don't you think?'

'Totally.'

'Would your grandma have approved of your work with Artemis?' Bloom said, deciding to test Lisa's thinking.

'I don't know. I hope so.'

Bloom glanced over to where Margaret was still chatting excitedly to people about Paula's visit. 'What did she hope for you, do you think? What kind of life did she want for you?'

'She never said.'

Bloom stayed quiet and let the silence pressure Lisa to speak.

'What did you grandfather want for you?' Lisa finally asked.

She looked genuinely interested so Bloom took a punt that this wasn't a tactic to move the focus of the conversation on to Bloom. 'He wanted me to be brave and explore. He used to say, "There isn't enough time to see it all, Augusta, not even half of it, so get moving."'

'And did you?'

'Not as much as he wanted me to, no.'

Lisa brushed her hands down the front of her top a few times as if trying to wipe something off. 'I don't think Grandma would like how I turned out.'

'Why would you think that?'

'I'm not living up to my potential. I have this amazing opportunity to be part of something she would have been proud of.'

When Lisa did not expand, Bloom said, 'But?'

The young woman squared her shoulders. 'I need to work harder.'

'Would your grandma have preferred that you work hard or that you be happy?'

'I can't be happy unless I work hard.'

'Says who?'

'Paula. She's so impressive. So intelligent and insightful. Did you know she used to work with Hollywood movie stars? It's a very male-dominated industry and she helped women stand up for themselves and negotiate fairer deals.' Bloom watched Lisa regain her Artemis facade as she spoke. The fake smile returned and her eyes took on a distant blankness.

'Is that so? I hadn't heard that.' She had read nothing of this in her research, but Paula may be inclined to embellish her past if, as Professor Colby had suggested, she had narcissistic tendencies.

'Does Paula make you feel good about yourself?'

'She's a wonderful woman. She opens your mind to your true potential.'

The line sounded rehearsed. Bloom dropped the volume of her voice so only Lisa would hear. 'Hmmm, that doesn't always feel good though, does it, when someone points out you're not living up to the person you could be?'

Lisa frowned and glanced at Bloom.

'Being told you *could* be great is sort of like being told you're not great right now, isn't it?' As Margaret approached, Bloom quickly added, 'For what it's worth, I'm sure your grandma would think you're great just the way you are.' Something told her this young woman needed a boost of self-esteem. Having your confidence and peace of mind chipped away at was at the core of coercive control, as any abusive partner knows. Was this the change Linwood Roberts had witnessed in Shauna?

More importantly, how many more women in Artemis felt the same?

Before Margaret could begin raving about Paula's visit, Bloom said, 'I can't stay here until Tuesday, I'm afraid. I have to see my mother.'

'Oh, yes, I heard she was unwell. We can call the hospital and check on her if you'd like?'

'I'd rather call myself, thank you, and she's in a care home not hospital.'

'Well, that's good, she can't be at death's door then.'

The dismissal was galling even though Bloom was exaggerating her mother's condition. 'She's still in a vulnerable state and she needs me.'

'I understand. The problem is we have no transport now until Tuesday morning but we can get you away first thing.'

'What about the minibus?'

'It won't be back until Paula arrives.'

'I'll make my way to Inverness then and catch the train.'

'That would be a long walk, Augusta. Why don't you stay and meet Paula? Take another day or so for yourself. You deserve it.'

'Others here must need to leave on Monday too.'

'Everyone seems happy to stay.'

Because you're giving them no choice, thought Bloom. 'I'll call a taxi.'

'As you wish.' Margaret touched Bloom's upper arm. 'But you should know you are one of the reasons Paula is coming. Melanie spoke very highly of you. She thought you were incredibly professional and intelligent. Paula would like to meet you specifically.'

Was this the line she'd been peddling around the room? Is that why they were all happy to stay, because they'd been told they were being singled out as special? If so, Paula's visit was a tactic and something they did on every one of these retreats. She could see how effective it would be to orchestrate a surprise visit from the woman they'd been building up over the past few days; a visit that required women to stay just a little longer so they could be worked on and worked on.

There was some basic-level psychology going on here. By setting Paula up as such a high-status person they were making the women feel they ought to stay. Margaret had also told Bloom everyone else was happy to remain, putting pressure on her to stay because most people feel compelled to conform to a group consensus even when they privately disagree. No doubt this was the reason behind them all being dressed the same. A uniform is an effective tool for ensuring people behave a certain way; it is why the military, emergency services and schools use them. But most worryingly they were breeding a feeling of helplessness. When people are exposed to a negative experience – such as being trapped and having no access to the outside world – they start to feel helpless, even when the negative conditions they face become escapable. It is a state of mind that means once a cult has broken you down and made you reliant they can release you into the world again knowing you won't leave.

Bloom knew these human factors could come into play incredibly quickly given the right set-up. She could see it happening in the group around her already and that scared her because making members so compliant inevitably led to abuses of power. What was to stop the group's elite from taking advantage of the obedient and the helpless?

Every cult she had read about, even those with the premise of bringing peace and religious righteousness to the world, was dogged with rumours of physical or sexual abuse. Because power does corrupt and no one has more power than a person with a legion of adoring followers.

Bloom knew that if she really wanted to leave she could find a way to go, but she could not pass up the opportunity to meet Paula Kunis. And if Lisa was right about Scarlett Marshall being close to Paula, it could be the quickest way to reach Scarlett too.

45

Day 11

Jameson had considered wild camping near the Artemis village or trying to find digs in the nearest town, but in the end he knew there was little extra he could see in the daylight so he'd got on the long road back to Edinburgh. The last thing he wanted was to be spotted spying on them when he'd gone to all that trouble to scope out the place under the cover of darkness. Plus if all went to plan, Bloom would be leaving tomorrow so they could compare notes. Hopefully she'd had some luck locating Scarlett.

Before getting his head down for a few hours' sleep, he had uploaded the video he had taken inside the garage at the Artemis lodge and sent the file to Lucas George. Perhaps Lucas could find some background on the other names and give them a lead on some more people to talk to. There had been no luggage label for Scarlett Marshall so she may not be on that site. She could still be living in the HQ building, despite what her cousin Harris had been told about her leaving. Or she may be at another location they had yet to uncover.

It didn't feel like he'd achieved much over the last thirty-six hours and he hoped Bloom had fared better. At least he'd kept busy enough to work up sufficient fatigue to enable him to sleep. He didn't even remember closing his eyes.

The ringing phone woke him and, half asleep, he grabbed the mobile and rushed to quieten the noise that hurt his head. Fortunately, at the last moment he spotted the call divert notification.

He swung his legs over the side of the bed and sat up straight. Then he coughed to clear his throat and answered in his best Yorkshire accent.

'Good morning, Forrest Glade Residential Home, Brian speaking.'

Bloom's voice was a relief to hear. 'Morning, Brian. This is Mrs Webb's daughter, Augusta. I'm away for the weekend and wanted to check on how she's doing, please?'

'Certainly, give me a mo, I'll check the notes.' He walked to his dormant laptop and tapped on the keyboard so to anyone listening it would sound like he was accessing files. Her mother's delicate condition provided a useful reason to insist on making a call if Augusta lost access to her own phone. They had agreed she should divert the landline of her Harrogate house to his mobile so that if Artemis checked the number she had dialled it would look as if she was calling a residence in that location. To add extra weight to this, Lucas had posted a temporary website for the fictitious Forrest Glade Residential Home, just a holding page announcing that the website was under construction, with Bloom's landline listed as the contact number. 'And how are you, Augusta? I haven't seen you here for a while.'

'I was very much hoping to come in to see Mum

tomorrow, but I'm afraid I've been held up here so won't be able to make it.'

Jameson's heart sank, but he kept his tone chirpy. 'OK, well, the notes say she had a restless night and was asking after you at lunchtime. When do you think you can get in to see her?'

'Hopefully no later than Tuesday.'

'I'll make a note. Do we call you on this number if anything changes?' If Bloom wasn't out of that place by Tuesday, Jameson suspected Mum might be taking a dramatic turn for the worse.

'Yes. Please do.'

'Anything else I can help you with?'

'Could you give Mum a message for me, please? Tell her I'm meeting a very important woman tomorrow, someone she would have admired. Hopefully that will make up for my not coming in.'

'Anyone I'd know?'

'I'm not sure you'd have heard of her, Brian, but Paula Kunis is a bit of a rockstar.'

'Well, you enjoy it, love. I'll pass on your message personally.'

Bloom said thank you and hung up. Jameson sat back in his chair. What he couldn't glean from that call was whether Bloom had decided to stay longer so she could meet Paula, or if she was unable to leave. She'd been so set on the importance of leaving that place on Monday. She'd said if they kept to their word of a three-night retreat it would absolve them in some way, but if they made her stay longer that was a bad sign.

So why had she sounded happy? That worried him.

It had to be useful though, meeting Kunis first hand.

He was about to contact the landlord of his Airbnb to request a few further nights when his phone rang again. Call divert as before.

'Good morning, Forrest Glade Residential Home, Brian speaking.'

The line went dead.

So they were checking up on her. Either they suspected she was up to something or they systematically disbelieved the women who came into contact with them. Neither of which was a good scenario.

An hour later he was sitting in a lavender-walled café that specialized in homemade buttermilk pancakes. He had ordered scrambled eggs with a coffee and was reviewing the Artemis case notes on his iPad when he came across the payment from Gerald Porter again. Taking a pen from his rucksack he jotted it down on a napkin. £4,007.31. What was he missing here? Why would Porter pay them so much up front and what was the significance of the £7.31?

If he'd been savvy enough he could have quizzed Augusta when she called earlier – made up something about querying a payment for her mother's care. Then again, what could she have said that wouldn't have given them away?

Thinking of their coded call gave him an idea. He circled the number on the napkin. Was this a code? If so, had it been a message to Bloom or to someone else? He considered who else would have sight of the amount;

certainly Porter's lawyer, who had made the payment on his behalf, but anyone else? Someone at the bank maybe?

Breakfast arrived and he ate it too quickly to appreciate it. He'd had no food since yesterday afternoon and was famished. He wiped his mouth with the napkin and pushed aside his plate, wondering whether to order some of the amazing-looking pancakes. An email pinged on his iPad from Lucas George and he opened it while finishing his coffee.

From: Lucas George 09.34
Subject: Call me when you get this

Marcus,

I checked out the names on the luggage and found something weird. Three of the names came up as deceased after a fire at a house in Liverpool six years ago. Twelve people died in total but many of the bodies could not be identified, even against dental records. I've sent you a link below and will continue digging.

Lucas

Jameson dialled Lucas's number. He answered on the first ring.

'What are we looking at here, Lucas? Are you thinking the other nine bodies could be names from that luggage too?' Jameson opened the *Liverpool Echo* article and began to scan it.

'The only way to be sure is to find some of the other women from your luggage labels alive and well, which up to this point I haven't. I've managed to confirm that six of the names from the luggage are on the police Missing Persons database so I have a few extra details and photographs to go on. I'm starting with those names and looking for anyone who has turned up alive since.'

'It says here there was evidence the people in this house might have been locked in?'

'Some padlocks on the internal doors. Yeah. It was all very odd.'

'What did the police say?' Jameson read to the end of the article but there was no police comment.

'I've emailed one of my contacts. He says he'll look into it. I'll let you know as soon as I hear.'

'It doesn't say how the fire started in the article. See if he can tell you that too? Are there any other articles?'

'Yeah a few. I'll ping 'em over.' As he said that the forwarded emails began to arrive.

Jameson studied the other four articles Lucas had sent, including one in the *Daily Mail*. The latter suggested these women may have been part of a trafficking ring similar to the child sex abuse ring uncovered in Rochdale in 2010. In that case young girls had been locked in rooms and drugged so they could be passed around more than nineteen men. Another *Liverpool Echo* article claimed that petrol-soaked rags may have been posted through the front door of the building which housed the two flats.

Jameson ran his hands through his hair. Twelve women sharing two flats; flats like those in the Artemis HQ here. And six women per flat like the six-bed dorm rooms he had seen at the lodge. His mind often picked up on such patterns and over the years it had served him well; people really were creatures of habit.

He opened Google Maps and searched for the area of Liverpool where the fire had occurred. It was south of the city centre not far from Liverpool Cathedral. He used Street View to look at the exact road. This was not your sex trafficker's typical haunt. They were large residences, well looked after and in an affluent area of the city centre just like the Artemis HQ building here in Edinburgh. Whoever owned the building that burned down had a bit of cash behind them. Jameson made a note to find out who that was.

He knew he couldn't tell the police. Not only had Bloom made it very clear that they should not be involved until she was out of that place, he had nothing but a hunch. But it was a strong hunch. On top of Shauna Roberts and the driver of the car that hit Lori, Jameson feared Artemis may have had a hand in twelve further deaths.

And Bloom was in there, possibly unable to get out.

He sat back in his seat and looked at the napkin with Porter's payment scribbled on it. Did Porter have a hand in this? Had he known exactly what his niece was caught up in and specifically chosen Bloom to spy for him for a reason? She'd said herself after that first meeting that his asking for her made no sense. But now they knew he'd been associated with Seraphine, who was a clear link to Bloom. Maybe he had an axe to grind. Putting Bloom in harm's way would not go down well with Seraphine, he felt sure. He should do a bit more digging into the Foreign Secretary, try again to find out why he was being hidden in the basement of MOD Main Building.

'Crap,' he said under his breath. He knew what that number meant. Taking the phone out of his pocket he looked for DCI Mirza's contact details and called. It went to voicemail and he left a message for her to call him urgently.

46

Bloom felt light-headed and sluggish. She had eaten nothing of substance since a sandwich on Friday; only fruit, crackers and a few small bowls of thin vegetable soup. She had also experienced little to no sleep. She was convinced that on the first night they had sent them to bed just before dawn and woken them an hour or so later. Last night the excitement about Paula's surprise arrival, fuelled by the Artemis members, had the group discussing how to make her visit special until the early hours. Then when they finally retired to their rooms, Bloom's companions continued to chat for what seemed like an age. Eventually she had said, 'I think if we want to make the best impression possible on Paula we should all get some rest.'

It was now Sunday. She had managed to call Jameson using the excuse of checking up on her mother. It had taken some firm negotiations with Natasha on reception to make the call herself. '*Please carry on with your discussions,*' Natasha had said, '*I'll call the home for you myself and let you know what they say.*' But Bloom stood her ground, saying to not speak to the home personally would cause her a great deal of anxiety, and so the other woman relented and said Bloom could call from the Artemis mobile. Bloom considered pushing for the use of her own phone on the basis she could not recall the number. It hadn't escaped her notice that her mobile was no longer in a tray behind reception. It had been locked away like the others. But she worried it would only delay contact with Jameson and might cause Natasha to start googling the home. Although Lucas had posted a holding page for the home's website with her Harrogate number listed under Contact, she didn't want to risk them digging any further.

Hearing Jameson's voice had made her feel giddy with joy. It was the tiredness, she knew, inhibiting her ability to control her emotions. She wondered what progress he might have made since Friday. He wasn't the type to sit in his rented accommodation and wait. He had no doubt scouted out the Artemis HQ in Edinburgh and she wouldn't be surprised if he'd driven up to take a look at this place. It may even be that when she called him this morning he was nearby. The idea gave her an unexpected feeling of comfort. Despite being surrounded by overtly friendly women in this place, she realized she was feeling quite isolated and vulnerable. She had attempted to strike up a friendship with Julia, the older lady from her dorm room, but every time she approached her an Artemis member magically appeared to whisk one of them away. Bloom wondered if this was because they saw what she saw: that Julia was similarly sceptical of mind. Without an ally she could feel a sense of helplessness creeping in. She couldn't let that take hold. She'd only been with them for two days, for goodness sake, she was more resilient than that.

Margaret had asked for a private chat at the end of

this morning's workshop, in which they had been sharing ideas on how to raise awareness of gender equality in their various communities. Bloom had struggled in the session, feeling fidgety and uncomfortable. It was a relief to move away from the full group.

The two of them entered a small side room with large comfy chairs and a window out on to the gardens. Bloom walked to the window and took a good look around. She had not seen outside this part of the building, as the only windows she'd had access to were those in their bedroom, which looked out on the opposite side. From this window she could see a large landscaped garden with thick borders of evergreen shrubs and three bare fruit trees planted in a wide triangle in the centre of the lawn. Between the trees was a green metal bench with the Artemis logo sculpted into its back. It might have been a pleasant and serene view were it not for the barbed wire fence beyond.

'I wanted to check in with you after our conversation last night,' Margaret said as she sat in one of the chairs. 'I sense you have some reservations that it might be useful for you to unpick.'

You mean useful for you to break down, thought Bloom, but she sat anyway. She was exhausted with the constant talking and wanted nothing more than to get this over with. 'I'm fine really. I was simply concerned about my mother but I called the home earlier and she will be fine until I can get there on Tuesday. What time do you think we can set off? I'm happy to be dropped at the nearest train station.'

'I'm glad to hear that. Augusta, I've been wondering . . . Tell me what appealed to you about my talk in London.'

Bloom was not at all surprised that Margaret dodged her question, but she was too tired to fight it. Her head pounded with a low-level headache.

'I've always been curious as to why people join groups and societies such as this. I've always been self-reliant, you see.' She knew most people joined organizations such as Artemis because they wanted a sense of purpose or the chance to make a difference, and had considered using one of those reasons, but she didn't have the energy to pretend.

'Curiosity is an admirable quality, Augusta. If only there were more curious people in the world, perhaps we would have more open-mindedness.'

'Perhaps.'

'Don't shy away from your assets, Augusta. Curiosity and self-reliance are strong qualities. Qualities we value highly in Artemis, despite being a group of like-minded ladies.'

'I wasn't shying away from them. I'm very proud of them.' She shuffled in her seat, unable to find a comfortable position.

Bloom's words threw Margaret for a second; her eyebrows rose a touch and then her eyes narrowed. Bloom guessed she was not used to counselling the confident. Groups like Artemis prey on those in need of something. They would rarely attract the content.

Bloom said, 'Why do you need such a high level of

security here in the middle of nowhere?' She leaned forward in her chair and looked out at the external fence.

'Oh I know. I felt the same when I came here. It's a bit crazy when you first see it, isn't it? Apparently when we were buying the last few buildings here, the previous residents became quite troublesome and began vandalizing the properties and stealing the materials the builders were using to create this place. They couldn't afford to live here any more but they didn't want lots of women moving in. Paula said the men became very aggressive and those living here felt scared. The fence acted to reassure as much as keep out.'

Bloom watched Margaret speak. She sounded genuine and her explanation made sense on some level. Bloom struggled to think of an objection; her mind felt foggy with tiredness.

'Doesn't it make the women feel weak, having to fence them in to protect them from men?' she said after a long delay.

'Maybe you think too deeply about some of this, Augusta. I'm sure your training in behavioural insights is to blame. Things don't have to be so negatively interrogated in my experience. The fence is not a symbol of oppression or suppression, it is simply there to keep us safe and protect our premises. Full stop.'

Bloom tried to concentrate. Was it significant that Margaret had used the terms 'oppression' and 'suppression' to describe the fence? Was the other woman leaking the truth with her choice of words? Bloom's usually sharp mind failed to reach a conclusion.

'What is the real reason for your reticence, Augusta? Why are you holding back?'

Because I think you're a mind-control cult that's trying to manipulate me, she thought, but said, 'I'm not.'

'You said you were curious as to why people join groups like Artemis. Do you not see the value in our cause?'

'I respect that you see the value.'

'You don't personally see the value in improving your own opportunities and those of other women?'

Bloom moved position again, crossing and then uncrossing her legs.

'Of course, I just don't know if I need to be in a group to do that.'

Margaret's smile was starting to look forced. 'And how might you do that alone?'

Bloom closed her eyes momentarily to try to relieve the regular pulse of pain in her head. 'By being good at what I do.' Her words were becoming harder to get out.

'And you being good at what you do, is that enough to change the world?'

Closing her eyes had been a bad decision. She was now struggling to keep them open. The tiredness felt like a weight pulling on her eyelids. All she wanted to do was rest her aching head against a soft pillow and let sleep take away the pain.

'It shows I should be judged on merit rather than gender,' she said with some effort.

'But surely you see that if we all do those things collectively our voice is louder and our progress quicker.'

'I suppose.'

'You're an intelligent woman, Augusta, can you give me a good reason why you shouldn't help to change things?'

She probably could on another day, but right now no reply came to mind.

'Not everybody is so self-reliant. So many women struggle to stand up for themselves. They need people like you and me to be stronger and to fight for them. Are you really prepared to turn your back on that responsibility?'

Bloom began to shake her head and then stopped. *What was she doing? What was the question?*

Margaret leaned forward in her chair, quickening her pace. 'Paula has taught us that the world is not ready to listen to one strong woman, frustrating though that may be. The unconscious bias too firmly favours the male. Across the globe men are allowed to be free in ways we are not, powerful in ways we are not, even flawed in ways we are not. When we show empathy we are labelled as weak, if we show strength we're called bossy. When we use our sexuality we are labelled as loose, but if we don't we're deemed frigid and in need of a good seeing to. How do we defeat that alone?'

'I – I don't know.'

'Consider this, Augusta. Maybe you were given all that curiosity and self-reliance for a reason. A reason that then brought you to Artemis. Perhaps there's a higher purpose to serve here.'

Bloom closed her eyes again. She wanted this conversation to be over.

'Join us. Let's change things.'

Bloom looked around the room feeling disorientated. *What were they talking about?* She suspected she may be experiencing micro sleeps.

'You know there's no good reason not to help, don't you?'

'Sure,' she said wanting to get out of here now.

'So you will help?'

Bloom blinked a few times fighting to keep her eyes open.

'Augusta?'

'Yes?'

Margaret reached out and touched her hand. 'Will you help me to help others?'

47

DCI Mirza called as Jameson was paying for breakfast.

'Mr Jameson, if you called with an update on Dr Bloom's progress, I'm afraid it's going to be too little too late.'

'Is Porter not in your custody any more?' Jameson took his receipt from the lady behind the counter and mouthed a thank you.

The line fell quiet as he stepped on to the pavement.

'What makes you ask that?' Mirza said eventually.

'He made a payment to us last week for the work he's asked Dr Bloom to do—'

'Excuse me?' she interrupted. 'How did he make a payment? He's had no ability to do so since he met Dr Bloom.'

'He gave her a letter of instruction to take to his lawyer.'

'That's not possible.'

'Well, it happened. I saw the envelope myself after she visited last. Do you want to know the amount he paid?'

'I want to know how he got his hands on paper and an envelope, not to mention a pen.'

'I'd ask your inspector about that,' Jameson said. 'But, more importantly, Porter's lawyer deposited four thousand, seven pounds and thirty-one pence into our account.'

'Are you ringing to show off about your lucrative careers in private practice or do you have a point?'

'Were you holding him in room 7.31 by any chance, four floors down in MOD Main Building?'

'Wait one second,' said the DCI.

Jameson heard a door close and the background noise drop away.

'Right. You have my attention, Mr Jameson.'

'I couldn't work out why he paid us so much in advance and such an odd number, particularly the £7.31. But then if you look at it as code it tells you—'

'Go down four floors to zone seven, room thirty-one. Are you telling me Dr Bloom helped Porter to escape?'

'So he did get out? That's pretty much impossible, you know.' The Ministry of Defence Main Building was a fortress of security.

'I am aware.'

'It had to be an inside job. How did it happen?'

'That's classified.'

'No shit. Someone breaks out of one of the UK's most secure sites, heads are going to roll, yours included. I'm not sure if you know my background but I can help if you let me.'

'I'm more interested in Dr Bloom's role in all of this. From where I'm standing it seems to me she colluded with a prisoner and aided their escape.'

'No. Augusta is straight as a die. I don't even think she saw the amount. It was a sealed envelope and she simply passed it on as requested.'

'Well, she's either stupid or corrupt in my book. She

should have told me the second Porter gave her something to take out.'

Jameson didn't disagree. Why had Bloom not done that? It was out of character. 'Maybe she should, but she's not your concern, the person the coded message was for is who you want.'

'And how do I know that's not Dr Bloom?'

'Why would she need to hand over the instructions to the lawyer if the message was for her?'

'OK, so who was this lawyer?'

'I'll text you the details. But it won't be him either – well, not entirely anyway.'

'How do you work that out?'

'Because they transferred the money.'

It only took Mirza a moment to cotton on. 'Which means they needed someone else on that money trail to see the message about Porter's location.'

'I'm thinking someone at the bank.'

'Send me the lawyer's details and email the bank transaction information too. I'll take it from there. And if I find out you or Dr Bloom had any hand in this . . .' She let the point hang.

'If I thought for one minute that my partner and friend had helped Porter get out, rest assured I wouldn't have alerted you to the possibility.'

'How very public spirited, Mr Jameson. You're an inspiration.'

Jameson hung up and tapped the phone against the palm of his hand. Gerald Porter had been arrested and held for having done something so serious it was classified

Top Secret. He was being held for fourteen days, which implied terrorist activity. Then he had managed to alert someone to his exact whereabouts, someone capable of breaking him out of possibly the most secure building in the country. Using force was against the question, you wouldn't get past the entrance; that kind of scenario was planned for and practised. It had to be more subtle, especially with a figure as recognizable as Porter. If Jameson had to take a bet he'd say the Foreign Secretary left the building by the front door and in a manner that appeared entirely legitimate. That meant with the police or the security staff themselves.

As Jameson picked up his pace to get back to his room and send the agreed details to the DCI, he realized the other person who may be able to walk you out of the door legitimately was your lawyer.

48

Day 12

The reception area was bustling with activity. Fresh flowers were being placed in the large vases, even though the outgoing flowers still looked fine, the windows and floors were being cleaned and what looked to be a roll of carpet stood by the entrance.

'Are they actually rolling out the red carpet?' said Bloom as she joined Nicola, who was polishing the top of the reception desk. Her headache was less intense today, but she still felt groggy and uncomfortable. Her eyes felt gritty and her skin was itchy and dry, probably from the chlorine.

'I think it's green but yeah. Fab, isn't it?'

'Why are you polishing, Nicola? You're a guest here. We paid for this.' It was true. They had been relieved of over £300 for the retreat experience and Bloom knew this would only be the start of the expected monetary contributions. Scarlett had handed over her entire trust fund of £2 million to Paula within a year of joining.

'I like to keep busy. I offered to help. It's good to finally feel part of something special. I was so bored with my life. Being here has helped me see how trapped I was by my choices. I feel liberated, don't you?'

'You're thinking of joining, then?'

'It's a no-brainer. As soon as I'm out of here I'm handing in my notice, which gives me a month to sort things out with Callum. I expect we'll put the house up for sale. I can't see him having the wherewithal or the motivation to buy me out, unless Mummy and Daddy step in, of course. Another example of how spoiled your typical male is in this world.'

'Not all men are the enemy, Nicola. You know that, don't you?' She was worried that the woman appeared a touch manic.

Nicola stopped polishing to crouch down and look across the glass to check the quality of her work. 'I don't think they mean to be, but the world is designed that way. I'm no longer prepared to be undervalued and overlooked. I want to change things and I can do that with Artemis.' She stood and smiled at her work. 'How about you? Are you with us?'

'I haven't decided yet. We've known these people for less than a week, and we've heard nothing but their version of the truth.'

'What are you afraid of, Augusta, really?'

It was a good question. Although she had strong reservations about how Artemis was trying to influence them she could find little to argue about when it came to the content of their statements. Their mission was so credible she couldn't help thinking that with the right leadership Artemis really could be a powerful force for change.

The activity in the room increased as women rushed to roll out the long green carpet and everyone was told to get into position to meet Paula.

'She's coming. She's nearly here.' Margaret looked a little hysterical with excitement. Her face was flushed and her movements jerky as if she'd taken something.

'I'm afraid of that,' Bloom said in a low voice.

Nicola followed Bloom's eyeline. 'Margaret? She's great.'

'Why is she so excited? Paula's just one of us, isn't she? Just another woman trying to bring about a better world.'

'No. She's more. So much more.' Nicola spoke with real conviction. 'She started this. She saw things for what they are and called it out. That makes her different. She's special and she needs our help.'

'Or she's running a cult.'

Nicola blinked a couple of times, then laughed. 'You're funny, Augusta.' She folded her duster and placed it behind the reception desk. Then she went to join Patrice at the front of the green carpet.

Bloom held back and kept her distance from the door. She wanted to get as full and clear a view of Paula Kunis as possible.

A shiny black limousine pulled up outside the entrance. Bloom shook her head. Margaret had given the impression Paula would be arriving by the same minibus they had; that was why it wasn't available to take Bloom to town. But of course that was not the case. Characters like Kunis expected the height of luxury and special treatment. No doubt she had flown to Inverness from wherever she had been peddling her message and now she was arriving in style.

The door to the limo opened and a slender woman

with auburn hair tied in a neat French plait climbed out. She walked to the door with purpose, her smart black skirt suit and green blouse in stark contrast to the group's lounge wear. Bloom noted how all the Artemis members had straightened to their full height. This was not Paula but it was someone of status. The woman's eyes briefly landed on Bloom as she scanned the waiting audience.

The photograph Bloom had seen of a shy teenager posing at the edge of her friendship group bore little resemblance to the woman who stood in front of her now. This woman had presence, looking comfortable and composed in the limelight. Clearly the cult of Artemis had served Scarlett well.

49

Jameson paced outside his Airbnb. Artemis was bad. Worse than they'd thought and Augusta had no idea of that. She didn't know about Lori's accident and the woman who might have been running away with her son. She didn't know about the women who had died locked in their rooms in a house in Liverpool. Women whose luggage was still in a garage at the Artemis lodge.

And she didn't know Gerald Porter was out and free to take Artemis matters into his own hands.

Her call yesterday telling him she would be staying an extra night had set him on edge. Not only because she'd previously warned that cults try to keep new members as long as possible so they can break them down, but because she'd sounded happy. On their drive up to Edinburgh, he'd sensed her nervousness. She'd asked for tips from his past life – not only on how to spy without being exposed, but also how to cope with interrogation techniques. He'd told her that when you're sleep deprived you feel restless and find it hard to focus, so lazy thinking takes over, which is when you make mistakes. But if he was honest, he'd not briefed her as fully as he could have done because he really didn't believe this group could be all that bad. They were running self-help sessions and a spa, after all. The worst he'd thought they might be guilty of was conning people out of their money. How wrong he had been.

He suspected if Augusta had known his views, she'd have chastised him for his stereotypical thinking and male prejudice.

The run had done nothing to calm his nerves. He couldn't shake the memory of sitting in his hotel room waiting for Jodie. How long had his gut told him something was wrong, and yet he'd let logic tell him it was irrational; she was well trained and highly experienced, and it was a low-risk meeting. By the time he got there she was already succumbing to her injuries; a fact that haunted him. If he had acted sooner she'd still be alive.

He was not willing to make the same mistake again.

On his run an idea had occurred to him. It was a very bad one. Really bad. But unless he came up with something else quickly, it may be the only option he had.

He checked his watch. It was nearly midday on day twelve. Since Porter's escape from custody their deadline with DCI Mirza was no longer relevant but Augusta didn't know that. She would still be operating with a sense of urgency. What if she had not been as immune as she'd hoped? What if she'd become distracted by the Artemis propaganda? What if the decision to stay had been because she wanted to and that's why she sounded happy?

He realized this was the thing he was most afraid of.

He'd thought about trying to get on site himself by posing as an official of some kind; a gas man come to read the meter or a health and safety officer there to test the air conditioners for legionnaires' disease. But it was a risky strategy. He may not be allowed in, they may insist on checking his credentials, and even if successful there was no guarantee he could be on site long enough to locate and talk to Augusta, never mind convince her to leave if she didn't want to.

If he were a woman it would be different. He could con his way in there as a keen new member, he felt sure. What he needed was a woman who could do that on his behalf, but one who would not be susceptible to their mind games.

And he knew only one such person. Which brought him back to his bad idea.

He had brought her number up on his phone half a dozen times and then talked himself out of it. The thought of asking for her help made his skin crawl, but he also felt sure she was his best option.

He took a long deep intake of breath and dialled.

Seraphine answered almost immediately. 'I can't tell you how long I've been waiting for you to see sense and call, my darling Marcus. You certainly know how to keep a girl dangling.'

'This is not a social call. Augusta's in trouble.'

'With you and me, baby, it's always a social call. And Augusta will be fine. She's a big girl.'

'Look, we've been working on a case for someone looking for his niece. Turns out she'd joined a cult. Augusta went in to try to get her out and now I've lost contact.'

'A cult? Gosh. How very Middle America.'

As she laughed Jameson felt the usual bile in his throat. This was a mistake.

'I'm sorry I called,' he said.

'Don't get stroppy and hang up. You made the call so see it through.'

He took another deep breath. He hated how she could make him feel like a petulant child. 'I wondered if you'd—' *What was he doing? This was a wrong.*

'I'd what? Spit it out, Marcus, no need to be coy.'

'Fine,' he said. 'Here's the deal. I figured if cults play on people's emotions an emotional vacuum like you might make a good asset to send in.'

'Oh, you do say the sweetest things and with such a cute topping of venom.'

'Well, I'm not your biggest fan.'

'And yet you're asking me to be your asset. Are you a man just a touch in denial, do we think?'

'Seraphine. Stop trying to make out this is some sort of banter. This is business.'

'Say it again?'

'What?'

'My name, silly. Say it again. I liked it.'

'We know Gerald Porter is one of your minions. Are you involved in why he's asked us to investigate Artemis? Or were you behind his escape?'

The line was quiet long enough for Jameson to check the call was still connected. It was. 'You still there?'

'I'm here.' In those two words Jameson could hear that something had changed. The mask had dropped.

'You didn't know he was out?'

'I know everything, Marcus.'

'No. Not this. I can hear it in your voice. You've gone all psychopathic and cold. The news surprised you.'

'Augusta thinks Artemis is a cult and Porter is involved.' She didn't ask this as a question.

'Did you even know he was being held in MOD Main Building? Oh! Oh! I just worked it out. Of course you didn't. He was hiding himself from you. That's why they held him there for so long. It wasn't to keep him in, it was to keep you out. Oh man, you're losing your touch, Seraphine. Your own little gang is outwitting you. Had to happen sooner or later.' Jameson could not help the laugh that escaped his lips. 'Now *this* is banter.'

'There's no way Augusta has succumbed to a cult, you know that as well as I do, because you know she is closer to being like me than like you.'

'That's not what she says. What if you're wrong?'

'I'm never wrong.'

'Except about the Foreign Secretary, it would seem.'

'Sometimes I feel like you really get me, Marcus, and then other times I just feel disappointed.' The playful tone had returned. The mask was back.

'Good. I don't want to *get* you.'

'But you do want me to help you?'

He was unsure. She had a point about Bloom being unlikely to succumb.

'Well, if you change your mind,' she said in response to his silence, 'you should know it comes with a condition.'

Seraphine hung up and redialled.

The day after she'd been told Porter's office had recommended investigations into Artemis with the tax office and Charity Commission, she had paid the Artemis woman a visit. It was the only instruction Porter had given the whole time since he'd gone incommunicado so she wanted to check it out. But the woman had seemed insignificant at best, rude at worst, and she'd concluded that Paula Kunis was nothing more than Porter's latest plaything; someone who'd crossed him and was now receiving payback. What had she missed? Why was Augusta investigating them?

'Joshua?' she said when her assistant answered. 'I've received some intelligence to suggest our friend Gerald has been in some kind of custody in the Ministry of Defence Main Building in Whitehall. Can you confirm which groups have the authority to hold someone there?'

Her team had found no sign of Porter despite hunting for him all week. She had people everywhere: in government, in the police, in the armed forces, not to mention every powerful old boys' club going. And not just in the UK. Her network was global and of a scale that would make any country's secret service salivate. It had made no sense that the man had simply disappeared.

Half an hour later Joshua called back.

'Any of the ministry's agencies can use the building's rooms on application, but we had interrogated all of them already. But then buried in some of the paperwork I found the sign-off on a new covert police team with a remit to investigate crime within the government and specifically the cabinet.'

Seraphine had known Joshua would be a wise recruit. 'Who signed off on this team?'

'That's the interesting bit. That's how I found it. It was signed off by the Home Secretary but proposed by—'

'Don't tell me. The Foreign Secretary's office.'

Gerald Porter had been planning his betrayal for longer than she'd realized. He had instigated this covert police unit with the express purpose of using it to hide from her. He had outwitted her and that was not something she was prepared to live with.

50

'Ladies, how lovely to see you all,' said Scarlett. 'Thank you for this welcome, I know Paula will be very pleased.' She placed clasped hands over her chest and looked from one face to another with a broad smile. 'Now, if you will please give a very, very warm welcome to Ms Paula Kunis.'

The clapping began before Scarlett had finished saying the words 'warm welcome' and Paula's name could barely be heard over the whooping and cheering. Bloom joined in with a light clap as she watched her peers working themselves into a frenzied state. It was the sort of group behaviour common to sporting events or rock concerts but rare in a room of fewer than twenty people. It felt like a hoax. As if at any moment some prankster TV crew might jump out from behind the scenes in the spirit of good old-fashioned entertainment like *Beadle's About!* or *Candid Camera*.

By the time Paula Kunis walked through the door, a number of the women were crying, including Nicola. Paula moved down the line, clasping hands in both of hers and looking women in the eye as she shared words of welcome or thanks. Bloom stood at the end of the carpet to one side, watching. The interactions looked genuine and warm. Paula was one of those people with a charisma that demanded you look at her. She was not particularly attractive, but she had presence and an energy that people clearly found intoxicating.

'This is Augusta, the lady Melanie talked to you about,' Margaret said, appearing from behind Bloom as Paula approached.

Paula's hands took hold of Bloom's. 'A benefit to our cause, she told me, if we can convince you to embrace the Artemis way. It's not for everyone, but from what I've been told you could really make a difference.' She squeezed Bloom's hands. 'Welcome. It's lovely to meet you.'

Bloom watched Paula walk away with Scarlett at her side. She had expected something different: somebody more smarmy or obviously manipulative. But the woman came over as professional and sincere. If it was an act, it was a good one.

She felt another twinge of doubt. According to what Professor Colby said, Paula had experienced the kind of childhood that could breed a self-obsessed personality, but that didn't mean it was inevitable, or that she didn't genuinely believe in her cause. Was it intentional that she made the likes of Lisa or Shauna feel like they weren't good enough, or simply the unfortunate by-product of a leader with high standards?

'If you could all take your seats in the auditorium, Ms Kunis will speak to us all collectively,' said Natasha, whose role as receptionist and administrator also stretched to crowd control, it seemed.

The group moved as instructed, the excited chatter and laughter continuing as they went. Bloom entered last. She had tried to mentally distance herself from the others since arriving on Friday but was struggling to keep it up. She'd expected the whole experience to be more overt, but each time she felt sure they were a cult, her next interaction left her with doubts. Maybe it was the tiredness, or the inability to have a moment to yourself to think, but the underlying sensation was one of a strong magnet pulling you in a direction of travel you weren't sure you wanted.

51

The alerts pinged continually on his phone as he showered. Jameson switched off the water and grabbed the towel from the rail, drying his face and arms as he scanned his phone screen. Every message related to Artemis. He had put a Google alert on them a few days earlier and there had been little activity in the interim. Quickly drying off, he dressed in a T-shirt and jeans and sat on the end of the bed to read them properly. It appeared the hashtag #LostToArtemis was trending on Twitter. He opened the app.

'Ha,' he said to the room when he realized they were all attacks on Paula Kunis.

Who is this witch @PaulaKunis? She makes a mockery of #METOO, said one, *she should be ashamed. This does not help equality. It breeds hate.* Then a whole string of pretty vile messages from male users along the lines of, *Who does this c**t @PaulaKunis think she is?* And, *If @PaulaKunis wants a war, bring it on, we're ready.*

Jameson couldn't work out where this was all coming from and it was hitting faster than he could follow it. The main theme that had captured people's imagination appeared to be the trending hashtag, which had set off a whole stream of tweets asking, *Where are these women @PaulaKunis?* These were accompanied by image after image of young girls who were missing, and families wanting to know if Artemis was to blame.

Jameson called Lucas George, hoping their technical wizard could identify what had sparked this.

'The original tweet looks to be from an ex-employee at the Charity Commission, someone calling themselves @thecharitychampion,' Lucas said. 'He claims he flagged Artemis as suspicious to bosses years ago but was ignored. They announced an official investigation this morning so he took his chance to speak out.'

'And say what? People are furious for some reason.' Jameson was still trawling back through the tweets to try to find the original post.

'I'll read you his tweet. *Fake charity Artemis is about to be exposed. Watch your back @PaulaKunis. Your man-hating methods will steal our daughters and their money no more.* He then mentions a number of usernames, one of which is @LinwoodRoberts5.'

'Shauna Roberts' father?'

'Yep. And he also attached a clip of Paula Kunis. I'm assuming it's been heavily edited but it makes powerful viewing. I'll send it over.'

Jameson followed the link to the video. It showed spliced clips of Paula Kunis speaking at various events. 'Women need to stick together, men will always do us wrong,' she said in one, and then, 'Don't let them oppress you and control you. They won't think twice about abusing you mentally, physically and sexually because they don't need to think twice. The world permits them to have the power they have.' There were more statements along the same lines, with Kunis looking more evangelical in each. It was followed by pictures of her with arms spread wide and messiah-like. Lots of pictures. Then a scrolling list of names with the hashtags #LostToArtemis and #HowManyMore.

Lucas said, 'Linwood Roberts then posted a video of himself blaming Kunis for his daughter's suicide. That one's been trending too.'

'This is bad.' Jameson paused as he read a tweet. Somehow, someone had reached the same conclusion as him about the female driver in Lori's car accident. *Was this poor woman trying to escape Artemis? And did @PaulaKunis steal her child?* someone had tweeted, with a link to the newspaper article.

Lucas said, 'Seems like it's about time, if all this is true. Sometimes the public need to step up and call out the truth.'

'No. I mean this is bad for Augusta and the women in there. I need to go, Lucas. I'm heading up to the retreat. Let me know if things change or get worse for Kunis. All this could be a trigger for violence.'

52

Paula changed into a smart cream wrap dress and nude court shoes that she knew would be in stark contrast to the loose-fitting leisure wear her ladies were in. It was her favourite outfit to wear when greeting the newbies. It made her feel ethereal. Or at least it usually did. Today she was too incandescent with rage to be otherworldly.

The Walker woman had been right. Someone was out to get her and had triggered multiple investigations of her organization. The tax office and the Charity Commission were on her case and she had railed at Scarlett all the way from Cardiff, where she had attended the International Women's Conference event. She wanted these investigations shut down and she wanted to know who the hell thought they could take her on and not feel her wrath. She had money and power and would not hesitate to destroy them.

'They're ready for you.' Scarlett had also changed into a fitted jumpsuit in Artemis green. Paula envied the woman's leanness and ability to look good in such an outfit. Maybe she should be a bit stricter on what her second in command could wear; level the playing field a bit.

At least she had Scarlett, her most loyal and committed of followers. She had been there pretty much from the start. There had been some shaky moments in the early days when Paula thought she may have to take her in hand and teach her the error of her ways, but then Scarlett came good. From that point on she had never wavered. Paula had entrusted her with some of Artemis's most sensitive incidents.

'Any progress?' she asked as they walked to the main room.

'Not yet, but we'll sort it. I've asked Denise to come up from Edinburgh to help me. Don't let it distract you. Not now. Enjoy this. It's your favourite thing to do.'

Scarlett was right; Paula revelled in her retreat sessions. But today something felt off. There was a tension in her neck and an anger in her veins that she just couldn't shake. She needed to protect her empire. This was her house. She wasn't about to sit back and let men and lesser women come in here and judge her.

'Get some security here. Call the same guys who helped with the villagers.'

'Are you sure? I think we can probably—'

'Just do it, Scarlett. I don't need your questions, only your actions.'

As she took to the stage she knew what she had to do. She wasn't just recruiting, she was rallying. If the fight was coming they would be ready.

53

'Fugly! How the devil are ya?'

Jameson had been driving for over an hour when Professor Terry Colby returned his call. 'Thanks for coming back to me so quickly.'

'Hey, no worries. I'm always available to the old boys' network.'

'There were women in it too, you know?' Jameson said, surprising himself with the sharpness in his tone.

'Sure, sure. Some of the best. I didn't mean any offence.'

'Sorry. This Artemis group have even got me jumpy about gender equality.'

'This is Little Miss Kunis's cult, yeah?'

'I'm driving up to their retreat location now. Augusta, who you spoke to last week, is there and things have started to kick off, big style. I'd appreciate your take.' Jameson filled Colby in on the social media attack that Paula Kunis was currently undergoing, as well as the fact an investigation into Artemis's legitimacy as a charity was afoot.

'That's often where these groups get caught out, trying to dodge taxes. Augusta said they weren't a religious group as such, is that right?'

'Correct. They appear to be all about women's rights with a bit of self-help stuff on top.'

'That'll be their recruitment angle, the self-help. If Augusta is right about this being a cult, they'll be using that to tempt people in. A counselling service is a good way to deliver the love-bombing that coaxes people to join, followed by the character assassination that weakens their ability to leave. We've had a few groups like that over here.'

'How did they turn out?'

'It varies. Some of 'em run outta steam, some of 'em evolve into a legitimate organization.'

'And the others?'

'They end messy with arrests and scandals. You just hope that's as bad as it gets. At least if there's no religious angle you ain't got the whole apocalyptic, end-of-the-world-is-nigh nonsense to worry about.'

Jameson knew Colby's background and how his younger brother had died at Waco as a member of David Koresh's Branch Davidian cult.

'It's all women as far as I know, so I'm banking on a low level of aggression in their response to this attack on their leader. Plus access to arms over here is much tougher so less chance of a shootout.'

'You guys feel so smug about that, doncha? Anyhow, did Augusta get my email about Paula's juvenile record?'

'When did you send it?'

'Close of business on Friday, my time.'

That would have made it after midnight in the UK. 'I expect not. She went into this retreat on Friday evening and I think they took away her phone. Is it relevant?'

'Possibly. I found out Paula has a sealed juvenile

record from the short time she lived with her mother after her dad died. The charges were for theft of her stepfather's credit card and vandalizing his car but it's the reason she gave that jumped out at me. She said the stepfather had sexually assaulted her, but no charges were brought against the guy and within a month Paula was in foster care.'

'Wow, if that's true that could explain her hatred of men.'

'Sure could.'

'Look, my plan was to go up there, knock on the door and get to see Augusta by feigning some family emergency, but we now have all these fathers threatening to head that way too.' Lucas had called half an hour earlier to say social media was now alive with a rallying call for the fathers of any missing girls to make their way to Artemis sites and demand to know if their daughters were inside. The addresses for the HQ in Edinburgh and the Inverness retreat had been posted. Jameson explained all this to Colby then said, 'I don't know how many will turn up but . . .'

'If you were a father who'd lost contact with his daughter wouldn't you wanna go see, just in case?'

'That's a lot of families.'

'You betcha. That's also a lot of desperation and in my book desperation breeds recklessness. You might wanna let the authorities know if they haven't picked up on it already. A site full of women being picketed by an angry mob of men. That could go downhill fast.'

'That's what I wanted to check. Augusta said no police

until she knew the status of the group, as it might inflame things. But my instincts tell me the time for worrying about that has passed.'

'Your police may be able to calm the parents and negotiate some communication that hopefully answers their questions.'

It was a relief to hear such decisive advice. 'There's something else. A few years ago twelve women were killed in a house fire, three of whom were linked to Artemis, the rest were unidentifiable. It's believed an accelerant was used and I fear Kunis may have had a hand in that.'

Colby whistled. 'You got yerself a hot one there. Excuse the pun. You know what . . .' There was a pause before he said, 'What happened to her as a kid, if the stepdad did assault her, that could mean she places very high expectations on women not to let her down like her mother did.'

'You think she might have killed those women because they let her down?'

'If she perceived they weren't living up to what she wanted, she might. It depends how much repressed hatred she has towards her mother. From what I've seen, leaders of these kinda groups usually have a big chip on their shoulder about something.'

Jameson knew he needed to get this intel to Bloom somehow. It might help her to manage Paula. 'So I'm thinking: call the authorities, fully brief them on what I know and then let them do their job.'

'Sure. That's sound thinking. I don't believe you'll leave it there, mind.'

Jameson smiled to himself. He and Colby were cut from the same cloth.

'Alls I'll say on the matter, Fugs, is if I had the chance to go back and be there in Waco, I would not have stood behind that line. I'd have got in there somehow, tried to affect things from within and changed that outcome.'

54

Bloom felt alert and on edge all of a sudden. Paula Kunis had been agitated in her speech to the group. Having watched the many videos they had been force-fed over recent days, Bloom had become cognizant of Paula's style of delivery; how she used gestures and volume to emphasize her points, and how she ordered her content to build slowly towards her more controversial views. This evening the delivery had been less polished and at times bordered on a rambling rant. Her basic premise of 'all women good, all men bad' was overt to the point of distasteful. She had referred to men as weak, corrupt and bastards, shouting that they could not be allowed to suppress her voice. She called for the women to stand up and fight for what was right. The time was coming, she said, when words would not do any more, when action was called for. The whole thing worried Bloom. She wanted to ask if this was normal for Paula's talks to members, but was unsure who might answer her honestly. Margaret was too sycophantic and Natasha far too subservient, but Lisa might be a good source.

She found her standing with Natasha and the two students from Friday's minibus: Daisy and Kimberly. Bloom quietly asked Lisa if she had a second. Lisa looked surprised and the other three women looked curious.

'It'll only take a moment.' She glanced at the other three. 'Just something personal following our chat the other day.'

The use of one-to-one counselling between existing and new members had been actively encouraged over the second half of the stay, so this explanation satisfied the other three. Lisa and Bloom took a couple of steps away.

'I hope you don't mind my asking you, Lisa, but I feel I can trust your opinion,' Bloom said, hoping to warm the girl up with a bit of flattery. 'I know you said the other day you felt you weren't working hard enough to fulfil your potential, and well, I can relate, I've been feeling that way since I arrived, and then hearing Paula speak just now, well it . . .' She made a point of looking around nervously as if she felt embarrassed.

Lisa placed a hand on Bloom's upper arm: the Artemis hold, as Bloom had come to think of it. 'What do you need?'

'Is she always so . . . I don't know . . . demanding of us?' Bloom held Lisa's gaze, hoping to see something in her eyes even if she didn't answer candidly.

'Paula is a perfectionist, she's very driven and rightly so.'

The response was disappointingly 'on script'. Bloom bit her lip and tried again. 'She seemed angry with us though. Is that normal?'

'I . . . I don't think she was angry with us.'

'Have you heard that before? Is that usually how she speaks to new members?'

Lisa looked at her blankly. There was a possibility she

had become so indoctrinated that she was immune to changes in the tone of things.

'Sorry. It probably is. That's probably Paula's manner. I don't know the lady yet. I thought maybe she'd had a bad day.'

'Yeah, maybe that's it.' Lisa spoke slowly as if thinking about every word.

'So, she was different today?'

Lisa's frown deepened to form long creases in her forehead.

It occurred to Bloom that Lisa may well have seen this side of Paula before, but she would put money on the fact that potential new recruits were never exposed to it. Earlier in reception Paula had come over so sincerely it made Bloom question her assumption that this woman might be exploiting her members. But of course that was only one version of Paula: the public version. Behind the scenes, her character could be much darker and much more demanding.

What interested Bloom was why Paula had shown a hint of her true colours now. Something was going on and she needed to investigate. But that was easier said than done.

It was impossible to move around the building alone. An Artemis member was always watching and ready to reel you in. But she had discovered some ways to create space around herself. From the start she'd habitually taken her time leaving any room they were in, feigning deep thought or even a daydream to stay seated until everyone was nearly out. At first the Artemis gang had hustled her along, but they soon became accustomed to the behaviour, seeing it as just Augusta being Augusta. They let her follow at her own pace, meaning she not only stole a few moments here and there for private thought, but she could also view the group from the back and assess the dynamic.

Following Paula's speech, they had been instructed to form action-planning teams to look at tactical ways to defeat the enemy. Intriguingly, the enemy had been extended beyond any male of the species to also include any females who 'do not hear our call'. This escalation frightened Bloom and she wanted to know what Paula meant by action now being needed.

She also needed to find a way to speak to Scarlett. It was day twelve in Gerald Porter's detention. He would be released on Wednesday. And unless Bloom could get a message to him about his niece, he would leave without speaking to DCI Mirza about whatever it was she needed to know. She was tantalizingly close to securing some insight into Scarlett that might convince Porter to talk. From what she had seen, the chances of convincing Scarlett to leave Artemis were low. But if she could at least convince the woman to contact her mother and let her know she was safe and well that would be something.

She picked up a leaflet from the bookcase by the door as she followed the main pack towards their break-out rooms. Her own personal shadow, Mary, had been asked to accompany Paula and Scarlett at the end of the presentation so Bloom knew this was her one chance to slip away from the group. As she walked behind them she noted that anyone arriving today would not be able to pick out the new members from the longstanding ones. At some point the group had become homogeneous; not only did they dress the same, they were now behaving the same. There was a comfort in it, she knew. The security of being part of a collective and the familiarity of knowing 'how we do things around here'.

Bloom slowed her pace and opened the leaflet, reading it as she walked. The group was streamed into three smaller rooms. She walked even more slowly, with her nose buried in the leaflet. If spotted she would claim to have been distracted. But no one came back out and a few moments later she heard the doors click shut one by one. Each sub-group would now assume she was with another. She picked up her pace but kept her eyes on the leaflet. Her heart pounded in her chest and at any moment she expected to hear her name being called, but it never was.

The darkness outside was absolute. There was no moonlight because she could not even see the outline of the trees or the external fence through the windows running the length of the corridor. She could hear voices ahead, and light came from an open doorway a few metres further along. Bloom shifted closer to the internal wall and kept her footsteps as quiet as possible.

'It's everywhere. We don't know how to stop it.'

'Well, find out!' Paula's angry voice was unmistakable.

'We're trying. I had hoped it would calm down by now but it appears to be spiralling. There's threads on Twitter, Facebook, Instagram—'

'I don't *care* where it is. Shut. It. Down.'

'We can't shut down social media. I could put out our own statement, talk about the good work—'

'No! No.' Paula cut the other voice off. 'I will not explain or apologize. I want you to find out who started this . . . *this* witch-hunt . . . and then I want you to find the first ten people who supported it.'

Bloom had reached the edge of the doorway now. In the reflection in the darkened glass of the window opposite she could see into the room. The second voice belonged to Scarlett. She stood sideways on to the door, facing the part of the room Bloom could not see and from where Paula's increasingly frustrated voice came. Alongside her stood a black woman with a large Afro, who Bloom had not seen before. Unlike Scarlett, this new arrival wore the same green Artemis lounge wear Bloom did.

'When you've found those ten people,' continued Paula, 'we expose them for the evil misogynists that they are. Go after their families, their jobs, their reputations. I don't care what it takes.'

Another door on the opposite side of the room opened and Bloom saw Mary enter with another woman she had not seen before.

Paula immediately set upon this girl. 'Do you want to tell me why? Why you think it's OK to betray me?'

'I . . . I . . .' The woman tried to stammer out a response. She had tightly curled mousy hair cut close to her scalp and looked to be in her late twenties.

'I . . . I . . .' Paula mimicked. 'Do you know what you've started by failing to stop that pathetic traitor? By causing an accident that has everyone looking our way?

It's all over the internet.' Paula spat the last sentence with fury.

Scarlett quietly said something to the black lady, who nodded and left via the door Mary and this young woman had arrived through.

'I'm sorry. I tried to stop her,' said the young woman. 'I went after her but then she crashed and—' Without warning, Paula came into view and hit the crying woman across the face with the back of her hand.

Bloom placed her hands over her mouth to stop any noise escaping.

The curly-haired woman spoke again, saying something about a hospital and a boy but her words made no sense to Bloom.

Paula hit her again, harder. The sound of flesh on flesh turned Bloom's stomach. The young woman cried out and Paula hit her again and again. When the woman dropped to her knees and tried to curl into a ball, Paula kicked at her with her high-heeled shoes.

All the while Scarlett and Mary stood side by side, showing no reaction at all. A fact that disturbed Bloom even more than the beating.

55

'I want her isolated for seven days,' said Paula when she had finished kicking the whimpering woman on the floor. 'See to it, Scarlett. Put her in the usual place. No contact, you hear me. None. And let that be a lesson to every woman who thinks they can fail me. Mary, with me.' Paula left by the opposite door, followed by Bloom's shadow.

Bloom was still rooted to the spot in shock. Knowing cult leaders could be sadistic and vicious had not prepared her for seeing it. She knew she should have stepped in and stopped it but everything had happened so fast.

'It will pass,' Scarlett said, placing a hand on the shoulder of the young woman who was rising slowly to her feet.

Bloom wondered if Scarlett referred to the pain the woman was no doubt in, or the seven days of isolation she was about to endure. Either way, at least she was showing some sensitivity to the younger woman's plight. Better late than never.

Scarlett and the young woman began to move Bloom's way. She hadn't considered they might exit through this door. She looked back down the corridor towards the rooms where the other women were. There was no way she would make it that far and get inside before being seen. In between here and there, there were no other exits or hiding places. There was nothing she could do. She was going to be caught spying. What would the penalty be for that from Paula, she wondered? One thing was for sure, she would not stand and take it like this poor woman. Paula was of no consequence to Bloom at all. She neither admired nor feared her.

At the last moment, she remembered Jameson's advice about hiding in plain sight. With only seconds to spare she took a number of large strides back down the corridor, travelling as far as she could. When Scarlett and her charge came into view, Bloom changed direction and walked purposefully towards them.

'Is everything OK?' Bloom said to Scarlett's surprised expression. 'I heard someone cry out. Has there been an accident?'

'What are you doing here?'

'I heard a cry. I thought someone was hurt.'

'No. I mean where should you be?' Scarlett was taking care with her words.

'I felt unwell. I was heading for the Ladies.'

The two women looked at each other for a long moment. They both knew there was no way anyone would be allowed to walk around unaccompanied just yet, but Scarlett was bright enough to know she couldn't admit to this. If for some reason Bloom *had* innocently escaped the group, pointing out that it was not allowed would raise alarm bells if Bloom was not yet fully indoctrinated.

'Oh my goodness, are you OK?' said Bloom, stepping

closer to Scarlett's companion. The younger woman kept her eyes on the floor and did not react.

'Rose is feeling under the weather. I'm taking her home to rest,' said Scarlett quickly.

'Let me help,' said Bloom moving to the other side of Rose and hooking her arm over her shoulder before Scarlett could protest.

'That's not necessary. We'll be fine.'

'Don't be silly. I'm here now. Where are we going?'

Eventually Scarlett began moving again and Bloom moved with her. Rose was clearly struggling to walk and occasionally winced in pain. 'Should we call a doctor?'

'She'll be fine. A few hours' sleep will do the trick.'

'I don't know, she seems in pain. Are you in pain, Rose?'

The woman did not reply but gave a small shake of her head.

'She has a condition. It's manageable.'

The lie sounded so genuine that Bloom could not help looking at Scarlett. At what stage had she decided this kind of thing was OK? Or was she more than an observer? Was she sometimes the aggressor? It wasn't unheard of for the upper echelons of such groups to become abusive over time, either to please or appease their leader, or simply to exert their own status. Scarlett appeared composed and professional, but this in itself was a shift from the compliant and shy personality her cousin Harris had described. In the past nine years, she had undergone quite the transformation; did that change also extend to cruelty?

They exited through the front door and the fresh air tasted glorious to Bloom. She had forgotten how it felt against her skin and in her nostrils. She took a large breath of it and savoured the coldness as it sank down her throat and into her chest. She wondered if this was how prisoners felt on their visits to the exercise yard, sensing freedom in their grasp even though they remained behind barbed wire.

The walk to the isolation building was not far. It was a single-storey detached box opposite a terrace of four traditional stone houses with neat square gardens. The door to the box was a solid grey slab of metal and the windows were high up and small, like those you might find in old-fashioned toilet blocks. Bloom had expected something more subtle, but this actually looked like a prison.

'This is her home?'

'Wait here,' said Scarlett, and there was a firmness to her tone. She took a key from her pocket, unlocked the door and guided Rose inside. The door shut behind them and Bloom was left alone. She had seen nothing but an empty hallway. Hopefully there was a bed and food in the place. Seven days on your own with nothing to do, that was enough to break anyone's spirit. This was the flip side to all the love-bombing going on around Bloom and her fellow initiates. It no doubt started with small attacks on your character to chip away at your self-esteem, then the punishments would kick in. Punishments for not working hard enough, for not committing yourself enough, for defying the many rules of the leader. How many of the women had been isolated like Rose? She guessed Shauna Roberts was one.

No more than a minute later Scarlett came back out.

'Don't you think you should have checked her injuries in case it's something serious?'

'Like I said, she has a condition, no injuries.' Scarlett began to walk away.

'Really? She hasn't been beaten?' Bloom had seen enough in this place. Spying was not her forte. How Jameson had kept it up for months at a time she'd never know.

Scarlett stopped. 'No. Why would you say that?'

'She looked like she'd been beaten, it sounded like she was being beaten.' Bloom decided to shy away from saying she'd actually seen it. She didn't want to end up locked in that building with Rose.

Scarlett huffed and walked on. 'What a crazy idea. Who would beat Rose? You have a keen imagination – sorry, I didn't catch your name.'

'Augusta,' Bloom said, hurrying to catch up. 'You've been with Artemis since the start, I was told. Are you one of its leaders?'

'Goodness no. I just support Paula where I can.'

'She trusts you.'

'Yes.'

'What has that entailed?'

They reached the entrance to the main building and Scarlett held the door for Bloom. 'You should rejoin the group. You're missing out.'

'Are you happy in Artemis?'

'Yes.'

'Has it lived up to everything you hoped for when you joined?'

'Yes. Now I must be getting on.'

'Just one last question.' Bloom paused and then asked softly, 'Do you miss your family?'

Scarlett blanched. 'Excuse me?'

'How do you all do it? Walk away from everything and everyone you've known on a whim.'

'There is no need to walk away from anything, Augusta. You are free to choose the level of your involvement.'

'Really? Is that why I'm still here on Monday evening when I only paid to attend for the weekend?'

'I was under the impression everyone here had requested to stay and meet Paula.'

'Were you? And who told you that?'

Scarlett placed a hand on Bloom's upper arm. 'You are free to leave at any time, but I would encourage you to discuss it with your group first. They may be relying on you more than you think.'

'They miss you.'

Scarlett frowned and took her hand back.

'Your mum, your cousin Harris, your friends.'

'I'm sorry. You'll have to excuse me. Please go back to your group.' She walked away briskly. The comments had shaken her, Bloom could see, but for someone who'd been deep in this for years there would be no shortcuts to snapping out of it. Nine years ago Scarlett had asked her cousin to rescue her. What had happened after that? Had she thought about running, tried to escape and been punished? Or in defence of her own mental health had she succumbed to the Artemis world view and chosen to stay?

Finding herself alone in the entrance, Bloom

considered walking out of the door and away from the place. Surely there must be a release button for the gate on reception. But then what? How far could she get on foot? Margaret had said it was miles into the nearest town. She had no phone, no money, no coat. The realization explained why Scarlett had left her here without concern.

She was considering hunting behind the reception desk for the locked box with her phone inside when she heard the groups breaking up and voices moving her way. Changing tack, she joined them all as they filed back into the main room and sought out Lisa.

'I need your help. Something's going on. Something bad. I overheard a conversation between Paula and Scarlett.' She spoke quietly so the others wouldn't hear. 'Do you have a phone?'

Lisa's eyes were wide as she shook her head.

'This is really important, Lisa. We might be in danger.'

'What do you mean? What sort of—'

Bloom grasped Lisa's wrist to quieten her. 'I don't want to start a panic. I just need to find out what's happened.'

'What did you hear?' Lisa looked scared now. That was good. Nothing motivated action like a touch of fear.

'I need you to get me a phone. Can you do that?'

'I don't have one.'

'But you work on reception so you can get mine from the box.'

'That's not allowed.'

'It's my phone, Lisa.'

'I know, but I could get in trouble. We are supposed to leave them there until the retreat is done.'

'Ladies, ladies,' said Margaret loudly. 'Come join in.'

'The retreat *is* done. It was technically over this morning. Please, Lisa.'

'Lisa? Augusta? We're ready to start.' Margaret's tone sounded impatient.

Bloom looked up and smiled at Margaret. 'Sorry, one moment.' She leaned closer to Lisa. 'Do you know Rose?'

Lisa nodded.

'I just saw her beaten and thrown in isolation. That ever happened to you?' The look that crossed Lisa's eyes was not one of surprise, so Bloom knew it probably had. That's why Lisa felt so defeated. 'I can help. If you get me that phone.'

Time was up. Margaret was moving their way.

'Ask yourself, what would your grandma tell you to do?' Bloom squeezed Lisa's wrist gently as a final plea and went to join the group.

56

Paula flicked from Twitter to Facebook, reading the posts with increasing anger. Bloody Linwood Roberts. Of course he'd be front and centre in this. He'd been on her case incessantly since his waste-of-space daughter jumped in that loch. The man kept turning up at the various events she was attending and shouting abuse. It wasn't her fault he'd raised a weakling. Paula had done her best to improve the girl but she was a lost cause.

Where the hell was Scarlett? How long did it take to throw someone in isolation?

There were some pretty abusive posts from cowardly men who talked big when they were hiding behind their computer screens. She knew those same men would never have the balls to question her to her face. Most didn't have the smarts to win an argument with her. She was better than all of them. Every person shouting their abuse through their phones, every father planning to turn up at her door and demand their daughter back. She didn't recognize the majority of the names, which meant their daughters weren't even here. They were idiots, the lot of them. And she would not let them pull down everything she'd built.

Artemis wasn't a charity. The tax office was right to be suspicious. It wasn't there to help others and improve the world. It was her empire: a testament to her superiority. Every day she looked out at these women and saw that they needed her to lead them, to teach and improve them. No angry group of assholes was taking that away from her.

A text beeped on her phone and she checked the message. It was from the Edinburgh HQ, saying a crowd had gathered outside and the women were feeling scared.

When Scarlett walked in, Paula was on her feet and her blood was boiling. 'Is that security here yet?'

'On their way, but I really think we should handle this ourselves. I think I've identified who started the social media storm. It's no one we know. Someone from the charity world but as requested we're now compiling a list of the first ten to support it.'

'Linwood Roberts will be one. He's posted a video crying over his pathetic child and blaming me.'

'I saw.'

'You know we can't stand for this, Scarlett. We have to stamp it out. I can't continue our good work if I don't have room to breathe. Get me that security. If these idiots think they can come here and bully me, we'll make sure they don't get past the gate. Is that understood?'

'Of course. But I think we may have a problem on site too.'

'Who?'

'One of the newbies, Augusta Webb. I don't think she's who she says she is.'

57

Day 13

Back in the main room, the ladies were sharing their ideas for improving equality in their own communities when Mary entered and whispered something in Margaret's ear. Margaret suggested a comfort break and the group moved to congregate around the refreshments area to take some fruit or a glass of lemon-infused water. None of them seemed aware of the building tension in the air. Bloom watched Mary and Margaret work the room. They spoke to each Artemis member in turn: Patrice, Natasha, Lisa and the rest.

'Ladies, it's getting late. I suggest we retire for the night.' Margaret gave nothing away as she moved through the group, smiling warmly and touching people's hands.

Bloom had no intention of sleeping tonight. The exhaustion she had felt earlier had been eradicated by adrenaline. She had a bad feeling about Paula's behaviour and finding out what was riling the woman was her new goal.

'Everything OK?' she said to Mary as they walked towards their dorm room.

'Absolutely.'

'You and Margaret seemed distracted just now.'

'It's Artemis business, nothing to worry about.'

'Anything I can help with?'

Someone collided with Bloom from behind, causing her to miss Mary's reply.

'So sorry,' said Lisa as Bloom felt something heavy drop into the pocket of her trousers.

'No harm done.' Bloom avoided looking at Lisa in case someone saw something odd in their exchange. She walked to her bed and watched Daisy and Julia retrieve their night clothes and begin to change. Mary and Natasha stood in the doorway sharing hushed words and Lisa hovered near them. 'Would anyone mind if I took a quick shower?'

Mary and Natasha glanced her way then went back to their conversation. Whatever was happening was engrossing them. Daisy asked to use the toilet first so Bloom busied herself collecting her towel and washbag as she waited and avoided looking at Lisa.

Once locked in the bathroom she set the shower going and shut the lid of the toilet. Taking the phone from her pocket she sat and pressed the home button. She was relieved to see a small amount of charge still remained even after three days in a box. Thankfully she'd had the foresight to switch off all her data before handing it over.

It was 3.23am: proof these people had been manipulating time.

She turned on her data hoping for a signal but found none. *Dammit.* She accessed the wifi options. A password was needed for RetreatWifi but then she saw Artemis2iPhone listed. Could she steal some wifi from that? She clicked on it and waited. A few seconds later the iPhone moved to the top of the list with a tick.

She'd had four missed calls from Jameson's number and a few texts. Most were from Jameson using their marketing ruse to check if she could respond, one was from a number she didn't recognize and the last one turned her stomach. She opened it.

> **Seraphine** **Monday**
> You really shouldn't stress Marcus out this way, Augusta. You know how much he worries.

She exhaled a long breath. She had no time to worry about that now. She closed the text and opened the one belonging to the unknown number.

> **+44 7800 001010** **Friday**
> Dr Bloom, I must express my deepest gratitude. Your assistance will not go unrewarded. GP.

Bloom sat back against the toilet. GP, Gerald Porter. If he was texting her, he was out and from the date stamp on his text, early. That couldn't be good and why was he thanking her? What had she done to help him?

Her phone alerted her to the need for low power mode. Quickly, Bloom opened the internet browser and typed in Artemis. The response made her jerk forward. Paula Kunis and her charity were trending on Twitter, according to the *Daily Mail*, and not in a good way.

Bloom opened up her Twitter app and typed Artemis

into the search function. When she had read enough, she sent a quick text to Jameson, turned off her phone to conserve battery and hid it in the inside zip pocket of her washbag. She then opened the shower door, wet her hair and switched off the water.

When she exited the bathroom with a towel wrapped around her head, Mary was sitting on the end of her own bed alongside Bloom's. Julia's shadow Vera smiled shyly as she passed and took Bloom's place in the bathroom.

Bloom had not changed into her night clothes. She had no intention of sleeping. She sat facing Mary. 'Can I ask you something about Artemis?'

'Of course, anything.' Mary smiled but she looked agitated. Her eyes kept flicking to the hallway through the open door as if she expected someone to appear.

'When did you start thinking it was OK for Paula to beat women?'

Daisy and Julia were already in bed but Bloom's words made them both sit up and look over. Natasha and Lisa also looked her way from the doorway where they still stood. Bloom guessed that Lisa was hovering to see what Bloom was up to.

'I don't know what you mean.'

'Well, you were there today in Paula's office with Scarlett. I saw the whole thing.' She took the towel from her head and rubbed her hair.

'What do you mean, she beat someone?' said Julia.

'I don't know how Mary here might define a beating but I think hitting someone until they curl up on the floor and then kicking them falls into that category,' said

Bloom. She didn't take her eyes off Mary. 'The young lady in question has now been locked in an isolation building for seven days. Isn't that right, Mary?'

'Is that true?' said Julia. She looked incensed. Hopefully that meant she still had her wits about her sufficiently to see the truth behind the Artemis facade.

'I don't understand. What's going on?' said Daisy.

Mary looked even more agitated and Natasha had moved to the foot of her own bed. Lisa remained by the doorway, biting her lip.

'Sometimes it's necessary to chastise those who step out of line,' said Natasha.

'Who told you that? Paula?' Bloom said. 'Well, this is all going to stop. I don't know how many of you she has hurt physically, or mentally, but what I do know is the world out there is getting suspicious. I'm not the only one asking questions.'

'What's going on?' said Daisy again.

Bloom looked from one of her roommates to another and asked, 'Do you know what this group is?'

'It's an organization fighting for the empowerment and equality of women,' said Natasha.

'I don't mean its purpose. I mean its tactics. Bringing you here. Keeping you here. Preventing you from contacting your families, from hearing the news, from thinking for yourselves.'

'Because outsiders don't get it,' said Natasha. She sounded frustrated. 'Our families are part of the problem. They believe in a man's world, they're naive about the truth and will try to undermine it.'

'And why does that give your leader the right to beat you?'

'She helps us,' Mary said quietly.

'You think you deserve it?'

'Sometimes.'

'But not all the time?'

Julia had moved out of her bed. 'Is it really true that Paula beat this young girl?' she said to Bloom.

'I'm afraid so. I think it's one of her tactics for keeping members in their place. Artemis is not what you think it is.'

'So what is it?' said Daisy, looking younger than her age.

'It's a cult.'

'Don't be silly,' said Julia. 'You don't get cults any more. That was a Swinging Sixties thing.'

'It is estimated that there may be up to a thousand cults operating in the UK at any one time, goodness knows how many across the globe. They masquerade as yoga groups, stop-smoking clinics and wellness retreats.' Bloom paused to let that sink in. 'They can be a religious, political or – like Artemis – social movement. They always have a charismatic leader, a desire to make the world a better place and a fierce code of conduct for how members live and interact with the rest of society.'

'How do you know all this?' said Daisy.

'Because, like Artemis, I'm not what I seem.' She focused on Mary, Natasha and Lisa. 'Have you ever suspected this might be the case?'

None of them replied.

'Ever questioned how people are treated? How *you* are treated? Because I think Shauna Roberts did.'

Mary's eyes widened. 'How do you know Shauna?'

'Yes, Dr Augusta Bloom,' said Margaret, who now stood in the open doorway. 'How do you know Shauna?'

58

Bloom 03.32

Marcus, come to the retreat and
bring transport. I'm going to get
as many of these women out as I can. A

Jameson read the message again as he waited at a T-junction for a lorry to pass then typed a reply.

Tuesday 03.51

On my way. Check your email from Terry Colby.
You were right about Paula being unstable.
Be careful. I think she's dangerous. M

His car could fit in five adults, max. He'd need something bigger. He diverted off course and drove towards Inverness. It was early but he reckoned within an hour or so he could find someone to hire him a bus.

He'd called the local police and alerted them to the potential public order issue brewing at the Artemis site. They did not seem terribly interested so he'd texted Bloom's contact in Edinburgh, Superintendent Ned Nesbitt, with a request that someone look into it as a favour to Augusta. He knew she had a lot of strong relationships with members of the police force. He hoped this was one of them.

By 6am he was driving back out of Inverness in a seventeen-seater Ford Transit Minibus. Vic, the owner of a private hire company in the city, had been very accommodating given the hour of the call. Jameson had spun a line about needing to get to a family wedding, how the previous hire company had let his group down the night before and how they needed to be on the road for six. Vic was sympathetic. Some of the competition are jokers, he had said, and make sure you come to me first next time. Jameson had tipped him an extra £20 for his trouble.

The sun was up by the time he arrived at the retreat village, and he was dismayed to see others had beaten him to it. Jameson parked at the side of the road behind five cars and sent another message to Bloom to say he was outside with a minibus. His last message was still marked as unread. What did that mean? Did she have access to her phone or not?

He walked up to join the handful of men at the gate.

'Linwood?' he said, moving to one man's side. He recognized Linwood Roberts from the video the man had posted about Paula driving his daughter to suicide. 'Marcus Jameson, we spoke on the phone.'

'The investigator, yes. Hello.' The man shook Jameson's hand with a strong grip. He was at least six foot two and looked fit and strong. The whites of his eyes were a little wild-looking.

'What are you guys hoping to achieve here?'

'We intend to get in there and see if they have our girls,'

said a small, muscular man with a heavy Liverpudlian accent.

The other men voiced their agreement and even though there were only six of them here, including Jameson, there was too much testosterone in the air for his liking. He had been around gangs of men filled with bravado enough to know things could get out of hand quickly.

'Have you had any luck getting a response?' he asked, gesturing to the call button on the gate.

'Not yet. But they know we're here. The camera was moving earlier,' said Linwood. 'Have you found out if the girl you're looking for is involved in this?'

'We're pretty sure she is, yes.'

'So you want someone out too?' said the Liverpudlian. 'Well, stick with us. We're staying here until they let us in. They'll have to open these gates at some point.'

Jameson nodded but didn't respond. He was not going to let on that his partner was in there. Not until he'd gauged more about these men and how far they were willing to go.

He checked his phone again to see if Bloom had read his message. She still hadn't. His eyes moved to last night's text exchange with Seraphine. He had contacted her after speaking to Lucas about the Twitter storm. He'd worried this was exactly the kind of inflammatory pressure that could spark a cult leader's fury and he wanted Augusta out of there. He hadn't anticipated all the fathers pitching up quite so quickly, nor that this would legitimize calling in the police. When he'd messaged Seraphine he'd expected to be up here alone and had wanted someone else inside to see what was going on.

He reread Seraphine's final message – *Leave it with me* – and it made him queasy. In the clear light of day he feared he'd messed up by contacting her but it was too late now. There would be no standing her down. She was like a vampire; once invited in there would be no keeping her out.

His phone began to ring and he walked back towards his bus to answer it. It was Superintendent Nesbitt.

'What's our Gusta got herself into?' he said by way of greeting.

'This Artemis group she asked you about is looking like a cult that recruits young women and brings them to this village near Inverness. Like I said in my message, some of the fathers have decided to take matters into their own hands. I'm here now and there's a handful already congregating outside the Artemis compound. I fear more are on their way. You might want to get some guys up here.' Jameson watched a transit van drive down the road and pull in behind his minibus. 'And I'm afraid the local press just arrived too.'

Nesbitt agreed to send over some patrol cars with a light-touch remit to see if they could calm things down.

'I have no hard evidence of this, but you should also know I suspect a house fire that killed twelve women in Liverpool six years ago might have been a previous Artemis site. It was a residential property near the cathedral.'

'I see. Well, let me get someone over to you to check things out and then we can see what we're dealing with.'

The men said their goodbyes and hung up.

'You really have brought a crowd then,' said a young man in trainers and a baseball cap. He was accompanied by an older guy carrying video equipment.

Jameson realized he was standing next to the minibus and it must look like he'd brought people here. 'Not me,' he said holding his hands up. 'I'm a lone traveller.'

'Do you suspect your daughter is in there?'

Jameson shook his head. 'Just an interested observer. I don't have kids.'

The journalist narrowed his eyes and his expression read *weirdo alert*, which is exactly what Jameson wanted. The two men moved on without saying anything else.

Over the next couple of hours more and more cars arrived until the grass verge alongside the compound's fence was lined with them. The two journalists moved through the group, interviewing anyone who was willing to talk, which was most of them. Like Terry Colby had said, these were desperate people looking for answers. It wasn't only fathers who had come either, there were mothers and a few teenage siblings also dotted through the group. Jameson did a quick headcount as the two police cars arrived. Twenty-seven people and it wasn't even 9am.

He walked towards the first patrol car and introduced himself to the two officers, one male, the other female.

'We've been looking at the stuff online. It's a pretty crazy claim. Do you buy it?' said the male officer.

'I think you have to ask yourself why the barbed wire

on this fence is angled to keep people in rather than out,' Jameson said.

Both the officers looked up as two older male colleagues joined them.

'I never spotted that,' said the female officer.

'Have you had dealings with them before?' asked Jameson.

'Sorry, who are you?' asked one of the older officers with sergeant epaulettes on his jacket.

Jameson introduced himself and explained that Bloom was inside the retreat looking into the whereabouts of Scarlett Marshall. 'Dr Bloom is an old colleague of Superintendent Nesbitt, so I gave him a call when I arrived to find this going on.'

'Thank you for that,' said the sergeant, adjusting his utility belt. 'Joanne, you come with me. We'll go in and speak to the ladies,' he said to his female officer. 'Graham, Todd, you keep your eye on this lot.' He gestured to the crowd with a nod of his head. 'Light touch, the boss said.'

'Sir,' said both officers together.

Jameson walked a little behind them as the police headed to the gate. He saw the female officer, Joanne, press the call button and speak into the box. Should he mention that he'd called in the services of a power-crazed psychopath, just to add to the day's complexities, he wondered.

'When this gate opens,' said the sergeant in a loud voice that quietened the crowd, 'I'm going to need you all to be across on the other side of the road.'

There were grumbles of protest from the families.

'We will do our best to help you, but only if you help us.'

As their boss spoke, Graham and Todd took their places between the gates and the crowd with arms outstretched and started to slowly usher the group back.

But it was all in vain. The gates never opened.

59

Bloom had spent the last few hours locked in a small side room and was pretty livid. Margaret had brought her here after confronting her in the bedroom. 'Save your answers for Paula,' she'd said. 'I'll be back in a minute.'

Minutes turned into hours as Bloom waited. She expected it was Scarlett who had looked into her. As soon as she mentioned the woman's family she had shown her hand – but she had no regrets. Her patience for pretending that what this group of women was doing was normal had run out.

The room was bare, other than a large whiteboard where the notes from a recent meeting remained. A printed spreadsheet was tacked in the middle and around it a web of ideas and actions had been written in green marker pen. Bloom stood in front of the board and tried to make sense of what she could see.

When Margaret eventually came back and escorted her to Paula's office, Bloom was surprised to see a man emerge from the doorway. He glanced their way, nodded and then stood to attention with his back against the wall.

'I thought this was a female-only organization,' said Bloom as they passed him. His eyes stared straight ahead and he did not react when she looked into them. 'Who is that?' she asked Margaret as they entered the office.

'I think who are you is the most critical question, don't you?' Paula Kunis was now dressed in a black polo-neck jumper and black jeans. 'Thank you, Margaret. That will be all for now.'

'I'm Dr Augusta Bloom. I'd like to say it's nice to meet you, but it really isn't.'

The muscles in Paula's face twitched. 'And what exactly are you doing in my house, Dr Bloom?'

'I was sent to find Scarlett.'

Scarlett was standing by Paula's desk and a look of irritation crossed her face, but she remained silent.

'By who?'

'Her family. They're worried about her. They love her. Much like the fathers who are threatening to turn up and demand to see if their missing daughters are here.'

'How do you know about that? Have you seen them?' She threw an angry look Scarlett's way.

'They're here already? Is that why GI Joe is standing guard?' When Paula did not respond Bloom said, 'I haven't seen them but I have seen Twitter, who hasn't?' She felt like she had channelled Jameson for a moment and it felt good.

'How would you know that?' Paula looked at Scarlett again. 'How does she know that?'

'I retrieved my phone. Your security really isn't that hot.' She had no intention of landing Lisa in trouble with a woman who systematically beat her members.

Paula paced to the other side of her desk and began moving papers around. Her movements were agitated and repetitive. 'I understand you are associated with a woman called Seraphine Walker.'

Bloom was confused. 'Not when I can help it. Why are you asking about her?'

'She came to see me in Cardiff. Warned me someone was out to get me. Is that person you?' Paula met her gaze.

Bloom's heart sank, as it always did when she realized Seraphine was lurking somewhere in the shadows.

'I assure you I am simply here to pass the message to Scarlett that her family would like her to make contact and reassure them she is well.' Bloom turned to Scarlett, who refused to look her in the eye.

Paula scoffed. 'If Scarlett wanted to speak to her family she would. If any of my girls wanted to see or speak to their families they would. If they choose not to that's not on me. I don't deserve to be labelled the devil for helping women escape from the clutches of men.'

'If that's true you have nothing to worry about.'

'It is true. Everything I do is for these women. I've made their lives better. I make *them* better.'

'By beating them and locking them in isolation?'

Paula looked furious. 'I don't know who is giving you your information—'

'My own eyes. I was here last night. Watching from outside the door. Pretty much the same place GI Joe is now, only on the other side.' She pointed at the now closed door on the opposite side of the office. 'So you can't deny it to me.'

Paula looked momentarily uncomfortable before her eyes narrowed and she shrugged. 'Rose deserved it.'

'Excuse me?' said Bloom.

'You can't understand how things work here. Discipline is imperative. I can't let standards drop.' She came back around her desk to point a finger in Bloom's face. 'And I do not answer to you.'

Margaret appeared in the doorway. 'Ma'am, the police are here. They want to come in and speak to you.'

'Absolutely not!' Paula shouted in Margaret's direction. 'No one comes in here. NO ONE!'

Margaret retreated back a little into the corridor.

'Green?' Paula shouted and GI Joe came to the door with his back straight and his chin up. 'I want everyone inside this building. Everyone from their houses and the school. Get them in here now.'

GI Joe nodded once and left.

Paula scowled at Bloom and Scarlett. Her face was flushed and her pupils dilated. 'If these men want war, they've got it.'

60

As it turned 9.30am two significant things occurred. A BBC Scotland van complete with satellite dishes on its roof drove slowly down the road and parted the crowd as it looked for somewhere to park, and someone shouted, 'There's a fella in there.'

Jameson watched from his place on the edge of the crowd. There was indeed a man inside the compound and he was walking from building to building speaking briefly to the occupants and then moving on. A few moments after that, women began coming out and walking to the farmhouse. There were many of them, all dressed in shades of green and all paying no attention to the mass of people shouting to them from the other side of the fence.

'Rebecca!'

'Sally!'

'Isobel!'

'Ella!'

'Catherine!'

At first Jameson thought people had spotted their daughters, but if that's how it started, it soon descended into people just shouting their loved one's name in a cacophony of overlapping sounds he could make no sense of. And all the while the BBC Scotland crew filmed away. It would make dramatic TV. Desperate parents calling to blank-faced women who walked on as if they hadn't heard.

And then came the children.

Jameson counted ten of them walking in a long line with one woman leading and one following behind. The youngest was no more than a toddler, the eldest maybe eight or nine.

Good lord. Who would bring their child to live like this? Where were the fathers?

The crowd was bouncing with energy as mothers and fathers jumped and waved to get the attention of the women inside. Many of them reached out towards the fence as if they may be able to stretch just far enough to touch their loved one.

More women streamed out of the village and into the farmhouse. The lone man walked with them, guiding and pointing. Jameson studied him. He knew special forces training when he saw it. This was no cult member. His posture was too military. This was hired help: a private security group. Which meant he would be armed and ready.

The danger facing Augusta increased another notch. He had not seen this man arrive, which meant he'd been on site from before the crowd began to gather. For what possible purpose would this group of women need special forces protection?

Moving swiftly, Jameson weaved past people with a hand on their arm or their back and an 'Excuse me', 'Mind your back' and 'Thank you' spoken assertively and loudly. There must have been in excess of forty people present now. Once through to the other side, he headed up the road to the edge of the village from where he'd approached a few nights earlier. This time when he looked through the fence to the corridor of the farmhouse extension it was filled with women filing into a central room. One of the children spotted him and waved. She was a cute little girl a similar age to his youngest niece, Holly. He waved back and she smiled. The woman with her grabbed her arm and forced it down to her side before throwing him a dirty look. Jameson waved at her too.

They were pretty sure Paula Kunis was on site now. Not only had the police confirmed she'd been on a flight from Bristol to Inverness yesterday afternoon, a member of the public had tweeted a picture of her walking through arrivals. The photograph had been accompanied by the tweet, *Is this crazy Kunis the kidnapper?* to which some wit had replied, *Or #TheRealLochNessMonster.*

He widened his stride and followed the fence as he'd done before. He needed to see what level of security detail Kunis had brought in. He doubted that one guy was working alone.

'Hey? Where are you going?'

Jameson turned to see three men following in his footsteps.

'Is there another way in?' said the taller of the three. He was wearing work boots, paint-splattered jeans and a hoody. His companions were more smartly dressed, one in a Berghaus coat and Merrell walking shoes, the other in a wool overcoat and brogues. Not a group of men who would normally hang out together, Jameson suspected.

He waited for them to reach him. 'As far as I know the gate's the only way in but I thought I'd take a walk around, see what I can see.'

'We'll take a walk with you then,' said the tall guy.

'It's a free country.' Jameson continued on, thinking it might not be so bad to have some company. 'Who've you got in here?'

'Lisa, my daughter,' said Berghaus Coat.

'Did you see her earlier?'

'No, but I know she's in there and I need to get her out.'

'Has she told you she's here then?'

Berghaus paused before saying, 'We haven't spoken since she left home.'

Jameson nodded, feeling bad for the guy.

'We need to get them all out. That witch needs taking down.' Tall Guy took hold of the fence and gave it a shake. 'I reckon we could climb this.'

Jameson knew three angry fathers busting down the doors would not help negotiations.

'I understand you're worried, chaps, but are any of you certain your daughters are here? It may be best to leave it to the professionals,' he said.

'Oh yeah, and who are you here for?' said Tall Guy.

'My partner, Augusta. She came here for a spa retreat on Friday.'

'Tough break,' said Berghaus.

'What's your name?' said the overcoat guy, who had stayed quiet until now.

'Marcus.'

'Well, Marcus, my name is Sean Hill and my daughter

Georgina and her boy Eddie have been missing for three years. I don't know if they are here, but I do know she was involved with Artemis. I hear what you say about the authorities but if they can't resolve this I'm not averse to taking matters into my own hands.' The man stopped walking and said in a low voice. 'Is that a school?'

Jameson recalled his own shock at seeing the school playground bordering the barbed wire fence. He patted Sean Hill's arm and the man began walking again. Behind the fence they saw no other people. Jameson suspected everyone was inside the main building now. And there was no sign of the hired help or any of his friends.

Before they turned the corner to walk back towards the road they passed a young woman walking the other way. She smiled and said hi to their group but gave no eye contact.

Jameson was good with faces and he knew hers but it took him a moment or two to place it. The men were talking about how they needed to put pressure on the police to get the gates open.

'I'll catch you later, chaps,' he said.

'Where are you going?' said Tall Guy.

'Nature calls.'

His reply satisfied the small group and they continued on without him. Jameson doubled back to follow the woman. He found her looking in at the school yard. She wore running shoes and sportswear. He slowed a little, not wanting to spook her. She must have sensed his presence because she looked his way, jumped and then apologized.

'Lori?' he said. 'I'm Marcus. We spoke on the phone the other day.'

'How did you know it was me?'

'I'm good with faces. Yours was in the paper. Are you OK?'

'Yeah. I heard about this place on the news and I had to come and see if he was here. The boy I saved.'

'The children have been taken into the main building.'

'Did you see them?'

'Yeah, from a distance. There were a couple of boys around five or six I'd say.'

'I can't stop thinking about him, and who took him, and why they haven't contacted the hospital or the press about who his mum was.'

'If he is here, I may be able to explain that. They are a very private group who appear to live pretty reclusively here.'

'Like a weird cult or something?'

'Maybe.'

'That's bizarre.'

'Isn't it?'

'Do you still think his mum might be the lady you're looking for? Is that why you're here?'

Jameson was distracted for a second thinking of Sean Hill's daughter and grandson.

'I don't think so—' he began to say but his words were drowned out by a loud explosion that had him running back towards the gate.

61

Bloom stood in the corner of the main room trying to work out her next move. She had been allowed to join the others congregating here on the understanding that Paula was watching her. Things would have played out differently, she sensed, if the chaos outside was not occurring.

She cast her eyes around the auditorium. In addition to the women who had been at the retreat with her for the past four days, they had been joined by a further thirty-four women and ten children, if her count was correct. It was alarming. It wasn't just the large number but also the condition of these women. Sergeant Doyle had told her the women he'd seen near here needed a good meal and a bath, something that didn't tally with those she had met on arrival: Patrice, Natasha, Lisa, Mary, Vera, Margaret; these women all looked healthy and professional. But Bloom understood now. She had taken their hosts for worker bees but they were not. They were elevated members in the Artemis power structure. The women she was looking at now were the workers. They all wore green, but not the pristinely laundered spa attire she and her peers were in. Their clothes were washed out, tattered and shapeless.

Halfway along the left-hand wall the woman Scarlett

had taken to the isolation house sat on the floor with her head back and her eyes closed. Bloom was concerned to see her here. Paula didn't seem the type to back down on a punishment unless there was a very good reason.

'Can I join you, Rose?' Bloom said, taking a seat on the floor next to the young woman. 'I'm Augusta, we met yesterday.' Rose opened her eyes and looked her way. 'I saw what Paula did to you. How are you feeling?'

'I have a medical condition.'

'You also have injuries from taking a beating. The bruises are coming out on your face.'

Rose touched her cheek and winced a little.

'I'm not trying to interrogate you, Rose. I just want to check you're OK.'

Tears welled in the corners of Rose's eyes and she gave a small shake of her head. 'I deserved it.'

'That's not what you said at the time.' Rose didn't comment, and Bloom placed a hand over Rose's on the floor and gave it a squeeze. 'No one ever deserves that, you hear me. How long have you lived here?'

Rose swallowed and looked across the room to where the children all sat in a circle on the floor with a woman Bloom assumed to be a teacher of some kind.

'Is one of those yours?'

Rose shook her head. 'I've been looking after Edward since his mum . . .'

Bloom waited but Rose did not expand. 'Which one is Edward?'

'The dark-haired boy with the freckles,' said Rose,

pointing. The boy in question spotted her looking at him and waved. He was a small boy with a big smile, despite having no front teeth. Rose blew him a kiss.

'Where's his mum?'

'There was an accident. She died.'

Bloom's stomach heaved. 'Did Paula—'

'No.' Rose interrupted. 'It was my fault. She was my best friend. I tried to stop them leaving.' Large tears now rolled freely down Rose's purpling cheeks.

'It's OK. It's OK,' said Bloom, squeezing Rose's hand again.

'No, it's not. It's never going to be OK for Edward.'

Bloom said nothing. What was there to say? Rose was right. Losing a mother was the cruellest of fates. In a way, it was a blessing he was so young and may not remember the accident. But she also knew from working with traumatized teens that such losses could leave indelible scars if not handled well. Plus he lived in a commune of women who held some pretty damming views on his gender. She couldn't help wondering how these boys would fare once they became young men. They may already be experiencing some prejudice, like girls do when, born into cultures that value boys more highly.

Bloom was about to enquire again how long Rose had been here when Nicola, Daisy and Julia walked purposefully over to where she sat. Nicola looked confused, Daisy looked terrified and Julia livid. Bloom stood to greet them.

Nicola spoke first. 'Julia says you know what's going on here. That there's something wrong with these people.' She looked around at the new arrivals. 'I mean, who are all these women? Where did they come from?'

'What are we doing in here?' said Daisy. 'Why won't they let us out?'

'Because they're a bunch of nutters. Tell them, Augusta. Tell Nicola what you told us,' Julia said.

'I want to go home. I want my mum,' said Daisy, beginning to cry.

Bloom glanced at Rose, who was hugging her knees to her chest. 'Most of the women here, including everyone in this room, pose no danger to us. Like you, they came here in good faith and thought they'd found something meaningful.'

Nicola concentrated on her words. 'But some of the women not in this room *are* of danger to us?'

'Maybe. They certainly have ulterior motives.'

'Who are we talking about? Not Paula?'

'Why not Paula?' said Bloom.

'Because she's—'

'Good?' finished Bloom. 'Honest? Trustworthy? How do you know?'

'How do you know she's not?'

Bloom did not want to get into an argument. She didn't have time. She needed to do something to get them all out of here.

'They're saying the men outside were shouting out some of the women's names,' said Julia. 'Who are they?'

'Fathers looking for their daughters.'

'How do you know that?' said Nicola.

'I read it on the internet. There's a campaign on social

media for fathers who think their daughters have been taken by Artemis to come here.' She had not had long enough with her phone to determine who had started it all off but she had seen that a video of Shauna Roberts' father was doing the rounds. He had not only been devastated by the loss of his daughter when they spoke to him but also incensed at Artemis and in particular Paula Kunis for taking her away. Had their call inspired him in some way? Because all of this starting now while she was in here felt far too much of a coincidence to be unrelated.

'What do you mean, taken? I don't want to be taken. I want to go home.' Daisy was becoming hysterical and a few of the Artemis women had started to take an interest.

'I think we need to stay calm and—' Bloom's words were cut short by the sound of an explosion.

Daisy grabbed hold of Julia.

'What was that?' said Nicola as the women around them started to shout and scream. A number of them ran to the doors and tried to leave but Bloom knew all the doors were locked. She had tried them herself on being brought in here.

'I don't know but I intend to find out,' said Bloom. She looked at Nicola and then Julia. 'Stick together and don't do anything you feel uncomfortable with.'

'Where are you going?' said Nicola.

'To see Paula.' She walked through the panicking women to where Lisa stood. She realized she knew who was behind all of this. She'd always known. She'd simply been too tired and distracted by the nature of Artemis to pay attention to it. 'I know who might be behind all of this. I need to speak to Paula.'

'Why do you keep coming to me? Leave me out of it.'

'Lisa, I did not tell Paula who had given me my phone back. I said I'd managed to find it myself, but . . .' She left the point hanging until Lisa scowled and began moving towards the stage. Bloom followed. Lisa walked to the doors on the left of the room, nearest the stage, where only a few women stood.

'What was that, Lisa? Why are we locked in? Where's Paula? Who are those men?' The questions came thick and fast and overlapping.

Lisa took a key from her pocket and unlocked the door. 'I'll find out. Don't worry. Wait here,' she said.

The women stepped aside and let Bloom and Lisa pass. She had been right about Lisa being of elevated status; the women raised no challenge to her command.

'Oh my,' said Lisa after locking the door and turning to look at what Bloom could see through the window.

The crowd outside extended along the fence on either side of the gate and must have been ten people deep at its thickest point. Bloom could also see at least two news vans and a few police officers. When she looked out to her right she could see the rear of the farmhouse, from where this part of the building extended, and above it a cloud of thick black smoke. Whatever had exploded was inside the village. Had one or more of these fathers brought something to throw? Would a petrol bomb have caused such a significant explosion? Whatever had caused it, she knew two things for certain: the police would now be sending in armed officers and Paula would not react well.

'Let's go,' Bloom said to Lisa, walking in the direction of Paula's office. 'We may not have much time.'

62

When Jameson reached the front of the compound again the crowd was going crazy. People were no longer waiting on the far side of the road, as requested by the police. They were now massed around the fence and the gates. He could see the police officers trying to gain control, but their shouts and directions were being ignored. The gates shook back and forth as those at the front tried to force their way on to the site. At least one man was trying to climb up the fence but only reached the halfway point before he was pulled back down by the police sergeant.

Inside the compound a thick cloud of smoke rose from an area behind the houses to the left of the main building.

Jameson took a wide arc around the group to reach where the sergeant stood. 'What happened?'

'We don't know yet.'

'Have you called for back-up?'

'Here in five.'

'What can I do to help?'

'Just let us do our job, sir. Stay calm.'

'Have you made any contact with inside yet?'

The sergeant didn't respond, turning his attention to the man who was once again trying to climb the fence.

Jameson considered revealing his background but decided the sergeant looked too much out of his depth at this stage. Let him focus on crowd control until someone more senior arrived.

He jogged in the direction of the smoke and tried Bloom's phone as he went. As before, it went to voicemail.

The fence left the road and tracked across the fields; Jameson followed it for a few hundred yards until he could see where the smoke was coming from. It was the garages where he'd found the luggage belonging to at least three of the women who'd died in the Liverpool house fire.

'Shit,' Jameson said out loud. Paula Kunis was destroying evidence. This was getting out of hand too quickly for the local police. They had military-grade help in there.

He called Superintendent Nesbitt.

'Are you telling me they have weapons on site?' said Nesbitt when Jameson had filled him in.

'I'd say from the overly loose jacket the guy was wearing, he has a handgun on his person. And I can smell an accelerant from this garage fire. This is no accident. You need to get specialists here, plus firearms and a negotiator. A good one.'

His next call was to Terry Colby to ask if he knew of anyone who had experience of negotiating with cult leaders in the UK.

'You know what, Fugs, if you'd asked me that a few weeks back, do ya know who I'd have said?'

'Dr Augusta Bloom, by any chance?'

'She understands these extreme personalities better than most of us. I say having her in there is a huge bonus.'

Jameson thanked him and hung up.

'Come on, Augusta,' he said under his breath. Not that he had any intention of leaving her to deal with this alone.

63

Bloom followed Lisa into Paula's office and found Scarlett and Margaret standing to attention by her desk like the good foot soldiers they were. Paula sat in a relaxed position, leaning back in her chair, but her eyes told a different story. Bloom had seen the look before during her time as a police psychologist. It was the kind of blazing anger that a person with their back against the wall displays not long before they lose it. She needed to tread carefully.

'What's the meaning of this?' Paula said to Lisa.

'I think I may know who's behind all of this,' said Bloom.

'Well, fancy that. Little Miss *I only came to find Scarlett* suddenly has another story to tell.'

Bloom ignored the goading tone. 'I did come here to find Scarlett. That's the truth. But before coming I spoke to her uncle Gerald and informed him that I had some concerns about Artemis and I think—'

'What sort of concerns?' Paula held her hand up then leaned forward, placing her forearms on the desk.

Bloom took a second to collect her thoughts. She needed to avoid being too inflammatory if she were to stand any chance of influencing this woman. 'Merely that the strength of views within Artemis may estrange members from loved ones who do not share their beliefs.'

Paula pointed to the door. 'Every single father out there should hang their head in shame because their daughters would never have left them had they been up to the job.'

Bloom knew a good proportion of the crowd outside were here on false hopes. Their daughters running off to join a cult was the best-case scenario for many. But she kept her mouth shut.

'If they came to me it's because they saw what I could do for them and that *I* will not let them down.'

'Gerald has no interest in me and never has,' said Scarlett.

'See,' said Paula, sitting back in her seat again.

'That may be true, Scarlett, but for some reason, right now, he is very interested in putting you in touch with your mother. And given the kind of man he is, I don't expect riling a group of angry fathers is Gerald Porter's only tactic.'

'Your uncle is Gerald Porter?' Paula stared at Scarlett. 'As in the Foreign Secretary? Why the hell have you never mentioned that?'

'It wasn't relevant. He's not important to me.'

'But he could be important to me. He's in the government, the cabinet in fact. He could be useful to us.'

'It would be pointless. He's not the kind to—' Scarlett stopped as she saw something change in Paula's expression.

'Are you saying I couldn't sway your strong-minded *man* of an uncle?' Paula rose to her feet.

'No, that's not—'

'I thought you of all people understood what I'm trying to achieve here, Scarlett, what I'm capable of. We could have made so much more progress with his level of influence. I thought I'd done well and now I learn I could have been influencing the cabinet.' Paula moved towards Scarlett. 'What is wrong with you?'

'I think Scarlett knows her uncle is a man of particularly selfish ambitions,' said Bloom.

'I wasn't talking to you,' Paula said without a glance Bloom's way. 'I was talking to the woman I thought was my most loyal disciple. I gave you every opportunity to be something more,' she said to Scarlett. 'But you don't get it, do you? You're still that timid little nobody scared of her own shadow. I'm appalled that all my efforts haven't even touched the sides.' She pushed Scarlett's head backwards with a hand on each temple.

Scarlett said nothing and simply straightened her head.

'If this is how you treat your most loyal disciples, I'm amazed anyone chooses to listen to you,' said Bloom. She purposefully replayed the word disciple as she suspected there might be more of a religious undertone to this group than they liked to admit to new recruits. Everything from Melanie's description of the group as a source of purpose and truth, to Margaret suggesting Bloom's curiosity and self-reliance may have been bestowed on her for a reason smacked of a belief in a higher power. And now Paula was referring to her closest allies as disciples.

Paula turned on Bloom, just as Bloom hoped she would.

'Nobody is interested in what you think. You're irrelevant. Whatever you think you're doing here, you have no say. None of this is in your control. This is all about me. It always has been.'

'I've no doubt that's how it seems to you.'

'What? What does that even mean? "I've no doubt that's how it seems to you,"' she mimicked in a childlike voice. 'You don't know what I'm capable of. I'm not a woman in a man's world, I'm *the* woman. I was sent here to change things. My mission is to teach the world where they've been going wrong.'

Sent here to change things. A mission to teach the world. Bloom knew she was getting closer to the truth of the matter now. Just one more little push.

'Sent by whom?' said Bloom.

Paula tilted her head and smiled. It reminded Bloom of Pennywise the clown from Stephen King's horror story *It.*

'Sent by whom?' Bloom asked again.

'Why don't you tell her, Scarlett,' Paula said with her smile still fixed in position.

'God sent Paula to save us because *She* is sick of men taking *Her* name in vain.'

Bloom's satisfaction at being right was tempered by her knowledge that this could make things so much worse.

64

'Marcus Jameson?'

Jameson turned to see a short man with long hair tied in a ponytail at the nape of his neck approaching. Beside him walked a police firearms officer.

'Dr Ralph Waugh.' The ponytailed man held out his hand. 'I'm to be the negotiator.'

'Have you had much experience with such groups?' Jameson shook his hand.

'Not as such. I'm the Head of Women's Studies at Glasgow University and a sociologist by background. I can see you're surprised. Most people raise an eyebrow at a man heading up Women's Studies but in these days of gender fluidity I ask that you don't judge.'

'I wasn't. I'm just hoping your negotiating experience extends wider than assignment deadlines.'

'A few of us academics have what you might call portfolio careers. And we felt I was best placed to speak to this group.'

'We?' Jameson looked at the police firearms officer.

'Inspector Burr,' the man said. He had the typical firearms-unit look: fit, short hair, steely gaze. 'What do you know about this group?'

Jameson filled them in on all they had learned about Artemis over the past two weeks.

'Superintendent Nesbitt said you suspected someone is armed in there?'

'I've only seen the one guy, but I'm guessing he's a contractor, probably ex-special forces – SAS or SBS – and I'd say he has a handgun holstered on his person.'

'You saw this handgun?'

'No, but I saw the oversized jacket on a man wearing military-issue boots in a women's spa retreat.'

Inspector Burr nodded. 'And you smelled explosives?'

'In the aftermath of the explosion there was a lingering sweet smell in the air.' The wind had blown most of the smoke away by now. Only a small fire still burned where the garage used to be. 'You should know that as part of our investigations I have intel to suggest luggage belonging to three women killed in a suspicious house fire in Liverpool was being stored in that very garage. There were more items of luggage too and, if I were a betting man, I'd put money on them belonging to the other nine unidentified women who died in that fire.'

'What kind of intel?' The inspector studied the area where the garages stood. The central one was now reduced to rubble.

'A video.' Jameson brought the recording he had made inside the garage up on his phone and played it. Thankfully he'd avoided speaking and revealing himself as the one behind the camera.

'How can you be sure that's inside this garage?'

'My source informed me this was inside the central garage and I trust my source.'

'Who is?'

'I'd rather not say at this stage. I don't want to get anyone into trouble.'

Inspector Burr studied him for a long moment before saying, 'Did you see who set off the explosive?'

'No. I was around the other side when it happened.'

'Right. We'll check with the crowd, see what people saw.'

Jameson turned his attention back to Dr Waugh. 'You think you can make any progress?'

'I'll give it my best shot.'

'Did you not think a female negotiator might be more politic?'

Dr Waugh rubbed the side of his mouth with his hand. 'We discussed it but in the end we agreed that a man carries extra gravitas. It's sad to say but society still views men as having more power to make decisions.'

Jameson watched the men walking away and wondered what Bloom would make of Waugh's assessment.

The energy in the crowd had dropped. The chanting had stopped and no one was shaking the fence or trying to climb it any more. Many of the fathers and mothers had moved on to the grass opposite the gate to sit down while others had taken refuge from the cold in their cars. The parents had cheered on seeing the police reinforcements arrive, but now Jameson could feel their collective nervousness. It was not an uncommon reaction to finding yourself surrounded by semi-automatic rifles.

It was 11.30am now and he suspected most of the people had not brought any provisions. They had probably expected to get the answers they needed pretty quickly. It was a fair assumption that you could turn up at a British building, knock on the door and ask if your daughter was inside or not. Finding a nine-foot fence with barbed wire had no doubt been a shock.

'Any joy?' he asked Dr Waugh as he reached the far side of the gate where the negotiator stood with Inspector Burr and the sergeant who'd arrived first thing.

'She will not take our call.'

Jameson was not entirely surprised. 'Do you have her personal number?'

'We have the numbers listed for Artemis but so far every one has gone to voicemail.'

'Landline or mobiles?'

'A mixture of both,' said Waugh.

'Now what?'

'We'll look into options for demanding entry,' said the inspector. 'The safety of the children may be our best bet.'

'But essentially you have a group of private citizens on private property who are not breaking the law.' The three other men looked at the site. 'Any luck moving the crowd out here along?'

'It's a peaceful protest so far,' said the sergeant.

'So, we have a stand-off.'

'Indeed we do,' said Inspector Burr. 'And so we wait.'

It was over half an hour later when Dr Waugh's phone rang.

'Thank you for calling me back. How are you?' he said after listening for a moment and then walking a short distance away from prying ears. He looked at Inspector Burr and Jameson, giving them a short nod. They walked to join him. 'It is an unusual situation, no doubt, but I'm sure we can resolve it between us.'

Jameson moved closer to see if he could hear the voice on the other end of the line, but there was too much background noise with the chattering of the crowd and the wind. 'Paula?' he mouthed to Waugh, who nodded.

'I see, well, maybe if we could—' Waugh moved the phone away from his ear. 'She hung up.'

'What did she say?' asked Inspector Burr.

'That this is private property and they are a peaceful organization. She demanded that we move people on because it's scaring the children and said if we did not she was prepared to do whatever is necessary.'

'What does that mean?' said Jameson.

'That we prepare for the worst and hope for the best,' said Inspector Burr.

'Call her back. Ask her what she means.'

The sound of Dr Waugh's answer was drowned out by the whirr of a helicopter above. Jameson looked up as it passed over them. It flew over the fence, hovered above the main building before moving towards them again and lowering itself down on to the garden.

Jameson glanced at Inspector Burr, who had clearly taken up command. 'Let's hope this isn't more hired help.'

'My thoughts exactly,' said the inspector.

The crowd began to rise to their feet or climb out of their cars to watch. When the helicopter landed Jameson sensed the whole group of spectators, now over fifty strong, lean forward.

The door opened and a single figure stepped out and closed it behind them.

'That's a relief,' said the inspector.

'Is it?' said Jameson as he watched the lone figure walk across the lawn to the building entrance before stopping and scanning the crowd, looking for someone.

And when she found who she was looking for, Seraphine Walker locked eyes with Marcus Jameson and blew him a kiss.

65

The knock on the door gave Bloom some thinking time. The revelation that Paula thought she had been sent from God was worrying. A religious calling would add toxic fuel to Paula's narcissistic personality. Not only did she think she was special and that the world should revolve around her, she believed she had been singled out by the highest power in the universe. It was a dangerous delusion. She would feel justified to do whatever occurred to her on the basis she wouldn't have thought of it unless God had wanted her to.

When Jim Jones ordered the suicide of his Jonestown followers in 1978 he had no concern for the souls of over nine hundred men, women and children who had dedicated their lives to his vision of a utopian future. He was a man with a strong god delusion who thought that if his life was over – because he had ordered the murder of a visiting US Congressman – then theirs should be too. There were recordings of him made just prior to the group drinking cyanide, telling them, if we cannot live for our cause, we should die for it. These leaders were not to be underestimated in their willingness to defend their beliefs and their way of life.

And Bloom was locked in a building with one.

Could this day get any worse?

Bloom's personal shadow Mary was at the door, telling Paula a police negotiator wanted to talk to her. These women were so ordinary. So nice. They believed in Paula. They believed she could make the world a fairer place for women and also that she could enable them to reach their own potential. They weren't stupid or suckers. They had become desensitized to how wrong things were here: the conditions people were living in, the treatments and punishments they received, and the controls placed over their freedom. It would not be possible for her to talk them out of this. They weren't going to reject their leader or turn against her, they'd invested too much of who they were. Take Scarlett. She had looked devastated when she thought she'd upset Paula. Bloom expected she would have compliantly taken a beating if required.

Paula was making a call from the mobile Mary had handed her. 'This is Paula Kunis. You wanted to speak to me.' She listened and then said, 'I'm going to stop you and make this very clear. We are on private property and we have vulnerable women and children on site who are being terrorized by that mob at the gate. I want you to do your job and move them on. If you do not, mark my words, I will do whatever is necessary to protect my ladies.' She hung up without waiting for a reply.

The sound of a helicopter could be heard above them.

'What's that?' said Paula.

'Probably press. I saw a BBC van outside,' said Margaret, who thus far had stood silently in the corner.

'I'll check it out,' said Mary and left the room.

I will do whatever is necessary. Paula's words echoed in Bloom's head. She had to get Paula out of here. That was the only way to safeguard these women in the short term. Educating them about how they had been manipulated could come later. The only problem was she had no idea how she was going to do that.

'Take her away,' said Paula to Lisa, nodding at Bloom.

Lisa opened the door behind them and gasped. On the lawn outside sat a small blue helicopter, its rotors still turning slowly.

Mary reappeared at the opposite door, an anxious look on her face. 'There's a woman here asking to see you.'

'I'm not talking to any press. And what do you mean, here? You mean at the gate?' said Paula.

'No, ma'am, in reception.'

'How?'

Bloom pointed to the helicopter on the lawn. 'That should explain it.'

Paula came to look. 'Whoever she is, tell her to get the hell off my land.'

'She said you would want to speak to her.'

'I don't care. Get rid of her.'

'She said to tell you her name is Seraphine Walker.'

Bloom and Paula looked at Mary at the same time.

It turned out today *could* get worse.

Paula's eyes slowly moved from Mary to Bloom. The rage Bloom had seen in them earlier had intensified to the point that her glare made Bloom want to look away, but she didn't.

'I knew this was you.' Paula looked truly ugly as she

pointed a finger in Bloom's face. 'I said you were behind all this. You were the one who reported me to the tax office. *You* tittle-tattled to the Charity Commission and you, *YOU*, brought these men to my house. How dare you? Who do you think you are? You don't get to judge me.'

Bloom stood very still. She knew the advice for facing a grizzly bear was to look it in the eye and make yourself as large as possible, but she also knew when faced with a gorilla you should make no eye contact at all and become as small as you could. She was unsure which tactic might work best for the beast in front of her.

'Who are you working for? Tell me. Who is it? The establishment? Corporations? The Church? They're all male-dominated institutions bent on the suppression of women. I won't let them break me. They have no power over me, no power at all. I am mighty. I am strong. I am the queen.' Paula's volume increased as her grip on her temper lessened. Her face was flushed and spittle formed around her lips.

The other women in the room grew agitated too.

'You are strong. We are strong,' said Mary.

'They won't defeat us,' said Scarlett.

'We are strong,' repeated Lisa, although she didn't sound quite so sure.

'This is the devil's work. You are his agent and you may feel powerful,' Paula shouted at Bloom, 'but you are weak of mind. There is nothing here that you can change. No influence you can have. Because you are wrong. You are ALL wrong. You do not see the truth. You will not hear it because it scares you to know how powerful She is and how badly you have let Her down. And you a woman. You should be ashamed.'

'I'm not against you, Paula,' said Bloom. She had to find a way to calm this down.

'You come here with threats to tear it all down but don't you see there is nothing here you can tear down that I won't tear down in Her name.' Paula walked to her desk and in a quieter voice said something that truly chilled Bloom. 'Bringing your little friend here is not going to save you.'

66

Outside the Artemis compound the mood of the crowd had shifted once more. Impatience was now in the air as people realized that despite the presence of armed police nothing had changed. The more vocal of the men, Linwood Roberts included, had taken up their posts by the fence again and took turns shouting out demands to the police or anyone within Artemis who could hear them.

Inspector Burr was on the phone. As the most senior police officer on site he was in charge of the scene but in the Edinburgh headquarters Superintendent Ned Nesbitt had assumed Gold Command.

'That is correct, sir. In summary, we have evidence of explosives having been used on the garages and suspicions that at least one man is armed in there with ten minors.' Burr listened for a moment then said, 'Thank you, sir.' He hung up and spoke to the negotiator, Dr Waugh. 'We have the go-ahead to rescue the children by whatever means necessary. I suggest prior to doing that you text Paula Kunis and let her know. Hopefully it might be enough of a threat to move this thing on.'

Jameson watched Dr Waugh keying the text and wondered what response it might get. Like the inspector said, if they were lucky Kunis would see sense and open the gate to let the police in to mediate, but he doubted she would do this. Not only because of what Augusta had told him about such people having a skewed view of their own power and importance, but also because of the guy. You didn't bring in private security like that unless you had a plan in mind.

He tried not to think about how Seraphine's arrival might affect things. She was an incendiary device and he had sent her in there. He knew Augusta would be furious. He avoided thinking about how he might have made things worse and focused on the hope that Seraphine's obsession with Augusta would mean she'd not let anything bad happen to her.

67

Seraphine appeared in the doorway of Paula's office with an amused expression. She wore knee-high brown leather boots and a long black sweater dress buttoned down the front.

'I thought I'd let myself in.' Seraphine looked around the group. 'Am I interrupting something?'

'What are you doing here?' said Bloom.

'Don't pretend you didn't bring her here,' said Paula.

'Trouble in paradise?' Seraphine looked even more amused. 'Now, Paula, this is a nice set-up but I'm disappointed with the outfits, considering this is a place populated by ladies.' She waved a long-fingered hand at Bloom, Mary and Lisa, who all wore the standard-issue loose green tunics and trousers. She then turned to Paula. 'And I'm not sure this Milk Tray man vibe is working for you. You usually look fairly stylish, but this is confusing me.'

'Men have been using uniforms in their clubs for centuries, from the military to the Masons,' said Paula.

'Yes, but to instil pride and discipline. I saw some of your waifs and strays out there. They look like the proletariat.'

Bloom had to admit Seraphine was spot on in comparing the Artemis masses to the lowest classes of Roman society; those whose only value was their labour. That's exactly what these women had been converted into. She had not managed to establish what they did every day, but if Bloom had to guess she'd say it was all to do with fundraising.

Before Paula had a chance to react, Bloom asked again, 'What are you doing here, Seraphine?'

'I came to help.'

'What are you really doing here? Is this about your activities with Gerald Porter?'

'I *am* intrigued to meet Scarlett.' She glanced the other woman's way. 'But, honestly, Marcus asked for my help.'

Bloom hadn't been expecting that. '*Marcus* did? Why would he do that?'

'He said – let me get this right – "an emotional vacuum like you might make a good asset to send in". He does know how to flatter a woman, doesn't he?'

'Stop it! Shut up!' said Paula. 'This is my house. You don't get to come here and mock me.'

Seraphine crossed her arms and faced Paula. 'What's your deal anyway?'

'My. Deal?' Paula's top lip rose to show her upper teeth.

'She believes she was sent by God to fight for women's rights,' said Bloom.

Seraphine raised one eyebrow and continued looking at Paula. 'A god delusion. I always loved those, you know, back in the day when I was allowed to practise as a psychiatrist . . .' She left a deliberate pause, because Bloom was the reason this was no longer the case. 'When did this first occur, when did you receive your calling?'

'I didn't get a calling. I've always known.'

'It's very ingrained in your persona then. Is it

dangerous?' When Paula frowned Seraphine gave a small laugh. 'Sorry, that last question wasn't for you, Paula.' She faced Bloom.

'Not if everyone keeps their heads.'

'Are you thinking schizophrenia or bipolar? They're both associated with delusions of grandeur.'

'As are certain personality disorders,' said Bloom, referring to Seraphine's psychopathy.

Seraphine smiled her sweetest smile. 'This is true, but Paula? One of us? No.'

Paula began to say something.

'Shush now, the grown-ups are talking,' Seraphine said, holding one finger in her direction.

Bloom watched Paula's face redden to a blotchy hotness. There could not be a trickier combination of characters to handle: a temper-tantruming narcissist with a god delusion and a manipulative psychopath who liked to play with people's emotions. How was she going to get out of this?

'Green!' Paula shouted and GI Joe came to the door. 'I want these two out of here. Put them with the others but keep them apart.' The muscular man nodded and took hold of Bloom's and Seraphine's upper arms.

'Funny how you're all about the women's rights, but need a man to do the heavy lifting. Does that not sully your argument a touch?' said Seraphine.

'Seraphine. Leave it,' said Bloom.

'You really are no fun, Augusta.'

GI Joe forced them both out of the room and into the corridor before Paula could react.

'Why are you winding her up? I know you don't do empathy but surely you see how volatile that woman is?' Bloom said, as they walked either side of the man.

'You underestimate me, Augusta. I know what I'm doing.' Her voice had lost all its joviality. She sounded dead serious.

'What are you really doing here?'

GI Joe reached the door to the main room and let go of Bloom's arm to knock twice. Interestingly he kept hold of Seraphine. A man like him, with the training he'd had, would know a threat when he met one.

Patrice opened the door and the man took Bloom's arm again, steering her towards the stage and ordering her to sit.

'I told you, I came to help,' said Seraphine, as GI Joe led her away.

Paula paced in a furious circle around the office. These women should be with her not against her. They were mocking her. The rage in her veins filled her body with heat; her cheeks burned and her hands felt clammy with sweat. It was all going wrong. They were going to rip it down and take it all away. She couldn't let that happen. She couldn't be a nobody again.

'We have to get control of this situation, Scarlett. These people are laughing at us. Laughing at *me*! Look at them out there.' She stopped in front of the open office door and viewed the huge crowd. There were even more police and now two fire engines. She turned to Scarlett. 'Get Green back here. They're going to force their way in. We have to stop them.'

68

The call came as Inspector Burr and his firearms crew waited for the fire service to open the gates with cutting equipment. Two ambulances were now on site along with a fair few extra officers. A cordon had been set up in the field opposite the gate, which the public now stood behind awaiting the show. There was a feeling of anticipation and anxiety in the air.

Jameson was standing with Dr Waugh when the academic's phone rang. They had been discussing tactics for negotiating some answers from Artemis for the waiting parents should Waugh manage to get in to see Paula Kunis. It was clear a few seconds into the call that whatever was being said was far from good news. Waugh's eyes widened in shock and his pasty skin became even more pale.

A firefighter started up the hydraulic cutters and Waugh ran towards him waving his free hand. 'Stop. Stop!! I have them on the phone.'

The fireman switched off the tool and Inspector Burr and his men gathered round.

'I understand, yes. No entry at all or you'll release the gas. Thank you.' Dr Waugh hung up and looked at Jameson. 'Why did I thank her?'

'What gas?' said Jameson.

'Who was that?' said Inspector Burr at the same time.

'She didn't give her name but she was ringing on Paula's behalf. She said they knew we planned to breach the perimeter and that this was out of the question. She said they would protect themselves.' Waugh swallowed and licked his lips. 'She said they had sarin gas and they would release it without hesitation if anyone steps on their land.'

Jameson was retrieving his phone before Waugh had finished. He would let the police decide their tactics; what he wanted to know was whether this was real or a bluff. He dialled the number of Professor Helen Farrier, the go-to expert in chemical warfare for the Ministry of Defence. They had worked on a couple of assignments together and at one point he'd considered her a close friend. He quickly gave her an overview of the unfolding situation.

'Sarin gas is classified as a nerve agent. They are the most toxic of the chemical warfare agents. It works much like an insecticide,' she explained.

'How would Artemis get hold of something like this?'

'It's a long shot but they could manufacture it themselves. It would require a lab and a skilled chemist, but it can be done. The Aum Shinryko cult achieved it in Japan. They released their homemade version on the Tokyo subway in 1995, injuring thousands of people.'

Jameson returned to the inspector. 'You need to listen to this,' he said, holding his phone out on speaker.

'Sarin is a clear, tasteless liquid that evaporates quickly into a gas. People are exposed by breathing it in. It is twenty-six times deadlier than cyanide. It leads to coughing, drowsiness and confusion in low doses; loss of consciousness, paralysis and respiratory failure in high doses.'

As Farrier spoke a black woman emerged from the farmhouse carrying a black holdall. It was the same woman who had answered the door to Jameson in Edinburgh on Saturday morning. She walked to where the driveway met the internal road then placed the bag on the ground and removed three Tupperware-style boxes from within. Moving slowly and carefully she placed them across the road facing the gate.

'And how can it be administered?' said Jameson.

'In Japan the liquid was carried to public places in adapted containers – a Coke can, for example – then pierced to allow the gas to escape.'

Jameson watched as the woman sat cross-legged on the road behind the containers. Without looking up at the watching crowd, she then removed a gas mask from the bag and placed it over her head.

69

The Artemis women sat on the floor in small groups or pairs talking in whispers. Even the children who were now scattered amongst them sat quietly. Bloom looked at the stack of heavy-duty black trunks piled along the front of the stage. There were six of them, each a metre long and half as deep. They looked military in style and she had a horrible feeling there might be weapons inside.

Seraphine sat with her legs crossed studying her fingernails. She paid no attention to the fact GI Joe had been joined by two other serious-looking men. The three of them combined with the trunks could not be good news. Paula had prepared for a stand-off and that scared Bloom. How far was she prepared to go to defend her cause?

A few of the women watched one of the new men cross the room to stand next to Bloom, but no one questioned who he was or what he and his companions were doing here. Was that because they knew? Or because they knew not to make trouble?

Seraphine looked bored. There was something bigger going on here. She wouldn't have come unless she saw some personal benefit. Gerald Porter had said he no longer associated with Seraphine because being part of a gang was not in his nature. Bloom was inclined to believe him. The psychopathic personality was essentially selfish. They felt little love or empathy for others and hence no compulsion to join together. And yet Seraphine had set out to convince the most high-functioning psychopaths to do just that. Bloom knew from the game Seraphine had masterminded to recruit her psychopaths that it was a sophisticated set-up. They had money and technological know-how. She also suspected, from Seraphine's interference in Bloom and Jameson's recent cases, that her organization was not exclusive to the UK. The only thing she was not sure of was the motivation behind it. Although she had no doubt that whatever Seraphine's gang were doing it was for their own selfish benefit. Power was the most likely endgame.

But how did Artemis fit into all of that? There was nothing in the set-up or success of it that would impress Seraphine. Paula's efforts would look like small fry to someone like her. Plus Paula herself was far too emotionally driven to have any appeal. So that left only one possibility. Seraphine was here for the same reason Bloom was: Scarlett. The only difference being, Bloom wanted to save her and Seraphine wanted to use her, no doubt as leverage in whatever battle she had with Scarlett's uncle Gerald.

Bloom was not going to let that happen.

Her musings were interrupted when Paula strode into the hall, flanked by Scarlett. They walked to where GI Joe stood and spoke to him for a moment, after which he summoned over his two colleagues. Shortly after that, the three men left the room and Paula and Scarlett took to the stage.

'The time has come to stand up for what we believe in,' said Paula.

The women and children in the room began to get to their feet.

'Outside, there are men intent on forcing their way in and taking you all away from me.'

The room came alive with protests as the women took each other's hands and pulled the children closer.

'We are not going to let them do that. I always knew this day would come. I had hoped it would not but now here we are.' Paula looked at Scarlett, who stepped off the stage to stand next to the large trunks. 'I have planned for it.' She faced her people again. 'And I will protect you. Every one of you. None of us leaves this place today.'

Relieved chatter spread through the group and Bloom watched the smiles of relief with dread. Not leaving here today had more than one meaning. She looked at Seraphine, who, like her, had remained seated. Their eyes met and Seraphine shrugged then spoke up.

'How exactly do you plan to protect yourself from armed police?' she said.

Paula motioned to Scarlett, who opened the nearest trunk and took out a gas mask. The room fell silent as she held it in the air.

'We will all be protected with these,' said Paula. 'They intend to tear-gas us out but you have nothing to fear so long as you keep them on. These will protect you.'

Scarlett spoke up. 'Tear gas will sting your eyes, make you wheeze and eventually you'll cough up fluid. It's not pleasant, ladies. Please put these on. Protect yourselves.'

'I don't understand. The police wouldn't tear-gas you unless you posed some threat,' said Bloom. She watched Paula's reaction to her words carefully, expecting most would have missed the brief smile and satisfied look in her eye.

70

'We're taking advice from the fire brigade's Hazardous Material and Environmental Protection Officer, who's on his way with a hazmat team,' said Inspector Burr when Jameson enquired about progress.

'ETA?'

'They should be here within half an hour.'

'What if that's too late? Farrier said this stuff is toxic within seconds once released.'

'Which is why our priority now is moving the crowd away.'

'And what about the women and children in there?' He pointed at the building.

'We have our instructions to move the crowd away and await the hazmat team.'

'In thirty minutes everyone in that place could be dead. You have to do something to help them.'

Burr spoke assertively. 'We will. We have a plan. The experts are on their way.' He then went to join his police colleagues, who were encouraging the families to go back to their vehicles and move to a designated safe area over the hill.

Jameson knew there was no way Superintendent Nesbitt was going to authorize any action that put his officers' lives in danger. Nesbitt and Burr had discussed the possibility of preventing the woman on the drive from piercing those containers, but with no protective equipment and no expertise in chemical attacks they were left with no viable options. No British police officer was going to be comfortable using firearms against an unarmed woman on her own land, even if they did suspect she had sarin gas.

It was a clever move on Paula's part.

Jameson texted Seraphine, telling her about the sarin gas and asking her what she was doing to resolve this new danger. He received no reply.

A police officer knocked on the side of the BBC Scotland van. The journalists were all inside with the door shut. That seemed odd. Why weren't they out here watching what was going on? He got his answer a few minutes later when he received a call from Lucas George.

'Have you seen the feed Artemis have put up on social media? It's live streaming a room full of people putting gas masks on. What's going on? Is this real? The media are going crazy.'

That explained what the BBC gang were up to. Why film the outside of a building when you can look inside it online?

Jameson realized that if Paula was taking measures to protect her own people it made the threat against those outside more critical. Only about half of the parents had moved away and all the police and fire service officers were still present and working hard to convince people to move on. He looked at the black woman sitting motionless on the drive, her gas-masked face looking down at those containers. Time was running out.

'I don't know, but I'm going to find out. I'm hoping these people are bluffing, Lucas, but I don't think they are. I'll call you later.'

71

The reaction to the gas masks fell into two distinct camps. The Artemis camp compliantly took the masks and put them on, but those who had arrived on Friday, like Bloom, were more reluctant. Nicola and Julia took a mask but placed it on their laps. The others in their Friday group followed suit, including Daisy, now sobbing again.

'Instead of making us wear these, just let us go home,' Nicola said.

'Nobody leaves,' said Paula. 'The doors are locked. The gates are locked. We stay and we fight. It's the only way to show them we are serious.'

'Serious about what?' said Julia, standing up. 'Beating young girls? Does that make you feel powerful?' She walked to the stage with all eyes on her and climbed the three steps up. 'I don't know what your game is here. But I'm not in favour of being conned and lied to, so you can unlock those gates and let out anyone who wishes to leave.'

Without saying a word, Paula strode to where Julia stood at the edge of the stage and shoved her hard.

Julia stumbled backwards, her feet trying to find purchase on the wooden surface before she fell to the floor below. The sound of her body hitting the wood echoed around the room, as did her cry of pain.

'Anyone else have any objections?'

Bloom went to help Julia. The fall had obviously winded her and she gasped for breath, but it wasn't a big drop so hopefully there was no real damage.

'Please put these on,' said Scarlett, dropping two more masks at their feet. 'And I suggest soon. We don't want you to suffer.' She then placed a mask over her own head.

Nicola moved to help Julia too. 'Are you OK?'

'I'm fine,' said Julia, but there were tears in her eyes.

'I think we should put these on,' said Bloom.

'Why are you doing what she's telling you? I thought you were the one who said we shouldn't listen because she was running a cult?' said Nicola. Clearly she and Julia had been talking.

'I think we may be beyond the point of reasoning with Paula. She seems to be enjoying this battle with the authorities. I don't know what she's threatened them with but for them to retaliate with tear gas they must think she poses some serious danger.'

'Fine,' said Nicola, as Paula walked to the front of the stage. 'We're putting them on now,' she said to the woman. 'No need to cause any more bodily harm.' As she put the mask over her head, she finished in a low voice with the words, 'Once I get out of here you're going to pay for this.' She rubbed Julia's back.

Bloom placed the mask over her own head. It felt heavy and claustrophobic. As she breathed in, the suction effect made a tight seal against her skin. She passed the straps back over her head as instructed and tightened them.

A few moments later the sound of smashing glass had the women looking at each other, their eyes wide and their thoughts in sync. *The gas had arrived.*

72

It turned out that the diamond-mesh fence was easy to climb, just like the tall guy he'd met earlier had said. Jameson placed his jacket over the barbed wire so he could vault the top, then he climbed down the other side. His first thought was to circle around the back of the main building to see if he could take the woman on the drive by surprise, but when he reached the front she had been joined by two men. Neither of them was the guy he'd seen earlier; these two were shorter and stockier, but still undoubtedly ex-military. They stood on either side of the closed entrance like gas-mask-wearing sentries.

He retreated a few short strides and checked to see if Seraphine had replied to his question, but there was nothing. He had to consider that she'd had her phone taken away too, although he couldn't quite imagine her letting that happen.

His only option now was to get inside and see if he could stop things from within, just as Terry Colby had said.

Outside the first dorm room he removed his fleece and wrapped it around a rock he had picked up along the way; using his makeshift tool, he smashed the middle window as quietly as possible. Once he had a hole in the glass, he dropped the rock and used his fleece to protect his hands as he made it big enough to reach in and open the latch.

He climbed in and crept to the closed internal door to listen. When he was sure he could hear nothing, he opened it a tiny amount and peered out. The corridor was empty and the doors opposite closed. He stepped out and edged quietly down the hall towards the front of the building. He had seen the women all moving to the central room. The doors into it from the corridor were solid wood, but from within he heard muffled voices and the urgent, panicked sounds of people moving about.

Holy crap, had they released it? Was he breathing it in now?

He removed his fleece again and held it over his mouth. It wasn't an ideal barrier but it would have to do. He should have asked the professor what the first signs of sarin gas exposure were. In training he had been exposed to CS gas – the type used by the police and the military to incapacitate a person. They had been made to sit in masks as the gas was pumped around them and then told to remove their masks and breathe it in for thirty seconds. The idea was to teach them the effects so they knew when and how to use the stuff. The pain in his eyes had been indescribable, his throat had felt like it was on fire and before long a tightness began to take hold of his chest. The seconds had ticked by so slowly, each move of the watch hand seeming to drag a heavy weight behind it. He could understand why people screamed and cried and genuinely feared for their lives when exposed to it. And that stuff was non-lethal. What would sarin be like? It didn't bear thinking about.

73

Bloom watched the women scurry away from the doors on the opposite side of the room as wisps of gas began to snake underneath. Above them the air conditioning vents whirred and in the corner a video camera silently observed them.

After hearing the smashing glass, Paula and Scarlett had left the room. In a muffled voice, Paula announced something like, 'Trust me. I'm going to sort this out.'

Bloom expected the woman would let this thing run a while longer yet to milk the attention. But the situation could have been so much worse. She needed to stay calm and wait this thing out. They were all safe if they just stayed in these masks. She concentrated on her breathing. The lack of sleep was taking its toll and her eyes felt itchy and heavy.

Hopefully once this bit was over, Bloom could try to reason with Paula. She might even be able to use Seraphine for that. Together they could offer Paula something appealing enough for her to leave the premises with them and stand down GI Joe and friends. That way the police stood a good chance of getting on site and checking out the conditions these women were living in.

While waiting in the room Margaret had taken her to

this morning, she had studied the notes on the whiteboard. The web of handwritten ideas and actions were not as interesting as the printed spreadsheet tacked in the middle. It gave a clear insight into the Artemis funding model. It showed their income streams column by column. Associate membership had an annual fee of £150 for private individuals and £1,000 for corporate professionals, each providing discounted access to seminars, webinars and conference events. Then there was the retreat weekend at £300 per head and workshops open to non-members at £50 a time for non-members. The totals at the bottom of these columns showed staggering amounts for the previous year: corporate clients alone had paid Artemis nearly £10 million. But the most disturbing columns were those at the end for Artemis residents. The first column showed amounts paid for the 'buy-in dowry', the second for their monthly contributions. The Artemis women in this compound were not paid for their work; they were charged for the privilege of being here.

Faced with that kind of dedication to the cause, even if she could convince Paula to let the police in, there was no guarantee these women would have the good sense to leave. She needed to expose Paula in a way that was impossible for her followers to ignore, but she was struggling to come up with something compelling enough. After all, these women appeared to be comfortable with Paula berating and beating them. What would it take for them to accept what she really was?

It truly scared her how prepared Paula had been for this. What threat had she made to cause the police to use tear gas? Had that explosion earlier been something to do with it? Had Paula already done something to scare the police? And is that why she had these gas masks ready and waiting – because this was a stand-off she had expected or, worse, instigated?

Bloom glanced at Seraphine, who sat in a gas mask looking at her watch. She thought about going over. It galled her to ask the woman for help but perhaps she needed to bury her pride and focus on doing right by these women first.

A little girl who had been bouncing on her mum's knee began trying to remove her mask. Her mother panicked, pulling her hands away, and the other women tried to help, talking to the girl in muffled voices, no doubt trying to explain how important it was that she kept it on. Bloom couldn't imagine how frightening it must be for a mother when your child does not understand the danger. The little girl pushed and shoved and cried, fighting as hard as she could but thankfully, thankfully her mother was stronger.

Bloom realized she'd been holding her breath.

74

As the corridor opened up into the reception area, Jameson checked that the double doors to the outside were closed and the sentry guards beyond could not be seen. Keeping his breathing as shallow as possible, he moved to the side of the internal doors into the main room. They were half glazed and he needed to see if Paula and her hired help were in there. Then he needed a plan.

What he saw was unlike anything Jameson had witnessed in all his years of espionage and warfare. Every inch of the floor was taken up with women wearing large black gas masks. They were military grade, with head straps to keep the thing airtight, a visor over the eyes and two oxygen canisters attached either side of the mouth.

Even more horrifying were the children's masks. Such smaller sizes would have required a special commission, which meant Paula had long intended to put these kids in them. Jameson had personal experience of wearing the things and waiting to see if some poisonous gas was going to get you. It was an unsettling and unpleasant experience for an adult, but he imagined downright terrifying for a child. This woman was sick in the head.

He was scanning the group for Paula and her security man when his attention was caught by one of the children trying to remove her mask. There was a small scuffle as a few of the adults prevented her from taking it off before the girl gave up and slumped back to her sitting position. Something about how she hit her chest a couple of times before she sat set Jameson on edge. He pressed his fleece closer to his mouth and scanned the room, finding each child in turn. They all sat or lay leaning on their mothers. Nothing too weird about that. He looked for the littlest one, the toddler he had seen walking with the line of children into the building. There was no sign of him.

Outside earlier he'd had a clear line of sight to the woman on the drive when she had put her gas mask on. There had been no yellow dot on her mask's oxygen canisters so why were there yellow dots on every set in this room?

He needed to find that little kid.

He stepped in front of the door to get a better view, hoping Paula's hired help was not lurking in a corner.

As he scoured the room his eyes met Bloom's. She was at the far end near to a stage. She had a hand on the arm of the woman next to her, who had grey hair sticking up between the gas mask straps. It was a relief to see his partner after all these days. He could see she was trying to communicate with him, but he had something more critical to do than interpret her hand signals.

He eventually found the toddler to the left of the door. Jameson was momentarily relieved to see the child sitting upright on his mother's lap but then he noticed the boy's chest moving up and down far too rapidly.

The kid was struggling to breathe. Just like the little girl banging her chest.

Jameson took the fleece from his face and took a long deep intake of breath. Nothing felt wrong.

He tried the door. It was locked.

He took in a second deep breath. Surely if there was sarin in the air he would be feeling some effect by now.

The toddler began shaking violently in his mother's arms. The woman hugged him close to her body, possibly trying to calm him, but there would be no cuddle that could stop this. The boy was fitting.

Jameson took a few steps back and ran at the door, raising his foot and making impact to the side of the keyhole. The door lock gave way and he pretty much fell into the room as a sea of gas masks turned his way.

'Take them off! Take off the masks. Do it now. Take them off!' he shouted, righting himself and moving towards the fitting boy.

The first to try to remove their masks were the children; an adult was telling them what to do so they were doing it. Thank God.

'Don't stop them. Let the kids take them off.' He knelt by the now limp toddler and ripped the mask off his face. 'Look,' he said, turning to face the group of women and taking a third large breath in. 'I'm breathing fresh air. No gas. No poison. How are you feeling? Tired, breathless, nauseous? Take them off, ladies. NOW! The gas is in the masks.'

75

Back in her office, Paula removed her mask and sat at her desk. The situation was giving her a headache. She massaged her temples, and then took a long drink of water, but she didn't half feel smug. The moaning fathers, the vicious attackers; they had played right into her hands. She would live large off the back of the attention this was going to bring. She could imagine it now. She would travel the world telling the story of how she came under attack from men who turned up at her door and threatened her, and how she rose like a phoenix to reveal them all for the misogynistic fools they were. How the world would judge these men for their sinister attack on her innocent women and children.

'All good?' said Green, who had been waiting for her.

'More than good. This has really turned out quite well.'

'You've bought some time with the sarin gas story but you know it only means more police are coming,' Green said.

'Good. We will share our CCTV footage with the world. It will only make us look better.'

Green looked perplexed. He wasn't a bright man.

'Let me spell it out for you. It will be obvious what happened here. In a desperate attempt to move the mob away I threatened to use a gas I didn't have, and the men of power retaliated in kind, gassing us. That's the story.'

'But that's not true. The police aren't really going to use tear gas on you.'

'What does that matter in the time of Fake News. All that matters is what it looks like. Isn't that right, Scarlett?'

Scarlett understood because she'd seen the power of it when those vile women in Liverpool had tried to mutiny, claiming Paula wasn't running *her* organization in the right way. Although their end was unfortunate, it was clearly God's will. Scarlett understood that, and her genius stroke was tipping off the press about a possible paedophile ring, which ensured no attention ever came Artemis's way.

'What are we doing out here? Don't we need to go back in?' Scarlett picked up Paula's gas mask from the desk and held it out.

'I don't need that.' Paula pushed the mask away. 'I'm going to be the heroine in this. People will feel sorry for me. For what has been done to my people.'

'Paula, people are scared, they need you,' Scarlett said.

Paula was bored now. 'Seriously, Scarlett, you're killing my buzz here.'

'I'm going back in. You should come too,' said Scarlett. She had her back to the door so did not see the new arrival. Green did but had no time to react. Paula watched as Scarlett reached for her neck in surprise and dropped first to her knees and then to the floor.

76

'Do as he says,' pleaded Bloom, removing her mask. 'Do as he says. He's with me. You can trust him.'

The women started to do as she asked but many of them struggled, finding their arms weak and their fingers unresponsive. Others stumbled as they tried to stand and a few threw up.

Jameson placed the toddler on the floor and checked for a pulse. He couldn't find one. 'Do we have a doctor here?' he shouted, beginning CPR. The mother next to him started to scream. 'My baby, my baby! No. No. No.'

'Do we have a doctor?' he called again between breaths.

'Where did she go?' said Bloom, coming to kneel at his side.

'Who?'

'Seraphine. Where did she go?'

'Who cares? This boy is dying.'

'She's a psychiatrist, Marcus, that means she trained as a medic. Seraphine is a doctor.' Bloom stopped his hands working on the boy. 'Let me. Go and find her. She was here a minute ago. She must have left the way you came in.'

Jameson did as she said, checking the reception area and looking down both corridors but there was no sign of the woman. The front doors were still closed and the two men and the woman with those sarin containers were still on the other side. There was no time to play hide-and-seek. He could hear that Bloom was surrounded by crying women. That was going to attract attention.

'I can't see her. She's gone.' He knelt down again. 'If I get the chance to put one of these masks back on that Kunis woman, do not try to stop me.'

Bloom listened for the boy's breath and held his little wrist, then she looked at Jameson and gave a small shake of her head.

Shit. Why did they have to hurt children?

Jameson spoke quietly into Bloom's ear. 'There are ambulances outside the gates. But there are also two serious-looking men, probably armed, just outside the door, and a woman threatening to release sarin gas on the drive.'

Bloom looked at him wide-eyed. 'What do we do?'

'How many other security men does Paula have?' he said quietly.

'One.'

'Are you sure? This is important, Augusta.'

'Yes. I've seen three in total.'

He glanced down at the boy. 'Are you OK here?'

She nodded once. 'Don't be a hero.'

He started to stand. He didn't want to be that guy again. He'd turned his back on it all. But if they were going to hurt children, they were asking for.

77

The women around Bloom were not looking well and many were starting to call out for help. Their children were sick. They were sick. What had they been breathing in for the past five minutes? She realized how lucky she was to have been one of the last to put a mask on. Or was that wishful thinking? Would she get sick soon too?

'Don't stop, please don't stop. Come on, Bobby, breathe for Mummy,' said the mother. She was only young herself.

'What the hell?' said a man's voice.

Bloom looked up to see one of GI Joe's friends standing in reception, the front door behind him ajar. He stared into the room with a look of disgust on his face as he watched the women now crawling or lying on the sick-covered floor.

Jameson appeared from the left of reception, striding towards the man, who on seeing him reached inside his jacket. Bloom held her breath. Jameson had no gun. No way to defend himself. What was he doing? He didn't slow until he was chest-to-chest with the guy and had hit him once in the neck with the side of his hand. The man made a sort of gagging sound then began to crumple to the floor as Jameson took him out at the knee. His falling body revealed his colleague in the doorway behind, gun already unholstered. Without hesitation, Jameson dropped with the first guy, using his body as a shield as the sound of a single shot echoed off the walls. Bloom jumped and put her hands to her mouth.

Not Marcus, please no.

To her relief, the man in the doorway fell, dropping his gun as he grabbed for his wounded shoulder. Jameson removed his hand from inside the first man's jacket, unhooking the gun he had fired from its holster as he went. Then he stepped over the first guy and collected the second guy's gun from the floor, hitting him hard on the temple with it and knocking him out before placing it in the back of his waistband.

Bloom couldn't believe what she had just seen. It was like a ballet of the most violent kind. She had never seen this side of Jameson. She couldn't say she liked it but she had to be impressed. With skills like that he could no doubt have killed both men, but he had chosen not to.

She focused back on the young mother who was sobbing over her unresponsive son. Whatever they had all inhaled was highly toxic. They needed help and fresh air. She turned to the woman next to the young mum. 'Can you take over? I'll get help.'

'Please, please,' begged the mother and the large tears rolling down her young face broke Bloom's heart.

When she stood her legs felt unsteady under her and a wave of nausea took her breath away. She closed her eyes and breathed through her nose. Once she felt able to move she looked around for Lisa. She found her on her hands and knees halfway down the hall.

'Lisa, we need to open the gates and call for ambulances.'

It was clear Lisa would be of no use. She could barely lift her head and her eyes had a faraway look. Next to her a young girl lay on her side, moaning.

Bloom made her way back to the main door and into reception. Behind the desk there was a touch screen with various icons, including camera and intercom. She clicked on the camera and could see police officers at the gate. She pressed the intercom icon.

'Hello? Hello, can you hear me?'

On the camera she watched one of the officers turn and press a button.

'This is Inspector Burr. I can hear you.'

'Inspector, my name is Augusta Bloom, could I speak to the officer in charge, please?'

'That would be me.'

Another wave of nausea hit Bloom and she steadied herself against the chair. 'We need ambulances. People in here are sick and dying.'

On the camera she saw the inspector step closer to the intercom and beckon a colleague over too. 'Do you know what's making people sick, Augusta?'

'Something inside the gas masks they gave us. I'm going to open the gates and get as many people outside as possible.'

'I need you to listen carefully, Augusta. We have a woman out here on your drive threatening to release sarin gas. If you could open the gates for me, please, but then I need you to all stay in the building until we can be sure it's safe. Do you understand?'

Bloom said she did and closed down the intercom. But she could not find an icon for the gate. There was a playback icon, a light icon and that was it. She began clicking other parts of the screen but nothing happened. Her hands were shaking as she pressed each icon in turn. Behind her she was aware that the cries and moans were getting quieter, people were passing out.

She sat in the chair and closed her eyes tightly. In her head she heard the voice of her mother. '*Calm down, Augusta, don't let your emotions get the better of you. Use your brain.*' It had been a frequently heard criticism in her youth, and if her mother had been here now Bloom may well have pointed out that emotions were just as much part of the brain as rational thought, but the advice was still valid. She took two further deep breaths and opened her eyes.

When she looked back into the meeting hall there were only a few women on their feet helping others and they were the Friday arrivals: Nicola, Julia, Daisy and the rest; the very people who had resisted putting the masks on until the last moment. The others were succumbing because they had taken in too much of whatever poison had been used.

Feeling stronger, she returned to the touch screen. At the bottom left was a menu icon. She'd missed that earlier. Clicking it now, she immediately saw the option to open the gates and pressed it. On the screen she saw the inspector push them open. To her relief, behind him, an ambulance waited to drive through. But then the inspector held both his hands up and looked to be talking to someone on her side of the gate.

The woman in the drive.

Bloom stepped past the two unconscious men to reach the open front door and looked out. Sure enough, at the end of the drive the woman with the Afro hair sat in the middle of the road behind three plastic boxes. She still wore a gas mask. Bloom could hear the inspector talking to her through a loudhailer. He was asking her to put her hands up and move away from the boxes. The woman remained cross-legged and perfectly still.

Bloom knew she should leave the police to it. They would have a negotiator and she could see a firearms team flanking the inspector. The problem was, the women and children inside needed fresh air and medical attention quickly. How long would it take for the police to convince this woman to move? It could be hours if she was determined enough. Bloom guessed her gas mask was not contaminated because Paula needed her sitting there until the rest of them had passed out. Another wave of nausea hit her as she realized Paula actually needed her sitting there until they had all died.

The sound of a mother begging for someone to help her child made the decision for her. Bloom stepped outside and walked slowly towards the woman in the road.

78

Seraphine stepped over Scarlett's body and replaced the syringe in her pocket. She always carried a vial of ketamine with her. You just never knew when it would come in handy.

At the side of a rather stunned-looking Paula, her muscle man stood with his gun half lifted.

'Before you use that gun, Stephen, I suggest you take a minute and ask yourself how much you love your young nephew, Nicky.'

'How do you—?' he started to say.

'I make it my business to know your business.'

'What have you done to Scarlett?' said Paula.

'Oh, that's sweet. You actually look upset. I'm pleased. I wouldn't want you to end your days not feeling some regret for your actions.'

'What do you mean, end my days?' Paula looked to Green, who sensibly stayed quiet although he still had his gun raised. That was good.

'You should be scared. When I first met you, I said your blatant disrespect for my psychopathic nature was naive, but I never thought you'd be so brazen as to try to hurt me. You're going to have to pay for that. But before we get started, take a looky loo at this.'

Seraphine held her phone out to Paula. On the screen

was the image of women and children staggering about in the room next door.

'That's our security feed,' Paula said.

'I know. I'm streaming it live on the internet. It is quite the show. You are trending at the moment, Paula. People can't get enough of you.'

'How did you access that?'

'Oh, it's very easy when you know how. How sad that you get the fame you so desired now when you have no chance to enjoy it.'

'You can't come in here and threaten me.'

Seraphine stepped closer to the two of them.

'What am I paying you for exactly?' Paula said to Green. 'Get rid of her.'

'Careful now, Stephen. If I come to any harm, young Nicky's career in the forces will be over. If I die, well, I believe we call that tit for tat.' She held his gaze until he looked away. He might be a trained marksman but he was no match for someone like her.

He began to lower the firearm.

'Oh no, keep it up,' said Seraphine, motioning to the gun. 'I expect Paula will be more comfortable talking with that pointed at me.'

Seraphine took out the syringe again. It still had half its contents, which was plenty. She stepped close enough to smell Paula's sweat. She always liked this bit. No matter how controlled a person might be they could never stop their body from giving away the stench of fear.

'Give me the gun,' said Paula, reaching a hand out to Green as her eyes darted from one door to the other.

Seraphine knew Green would never hand over his firearm; he had been too well trained for that. He would want to keep control of the situation and the person in control was usually the one with the biggest weapon. What he was failing to consider was the size of Seraphine's.

'Out of interest, did *She* tell you to do all this? Like I said, I do find these god delusions fascinating.'

Seraphine's phone beeped in her hand and she checked the screen. It showed a still from the security feed in the corridor outside and the image of a lone figure.

Show time.

In a low voice she said to Green, 'If you don't want me to plunge this into her neck, you are going to have to shoot me.'

He raised his gun at the same time that Paula shouted, 'Shoot her!'

Dropping the phone and syringe on the floor, Seraphine raised her hands towards Green's gun. 'Please, please don't shoot.' She put a good dose of panicked emotion into her tone. 'Tell him not to shoot, Paula. I'll do anything. I'll give you anything. Please. What do you want? I'm begging you. PLEASE!'

A confused look crossed Green's face a second before Marcus Jameson's bullet hit him right between the eyes.

79

In her peripheral vision Bloom detected the firearms team tracking her movements. They wouldn't know that she wasn't a threat. She raised her hands as she walked, hoping that would buy her time.

A few yards from the sitting woman she stopped and said, 'Hi.'

The black lady slowly turned her masked head and met Bloom's gaze with a look of confusion.

'Paula wants to see you.'

'Who are you?' Her voice was muffled by the mask.

This woman had probably heard about Augusta Bloom, the investigator sent by Scarlett's family, but hopefully she didn't know what Bloom looked like. It was worth a gamble, given the situation. 'I'm Nicola.'

'Well, Nicola, I stay here until she tells me it's over herself.' She turned back to face the drive.

'She said you'd say that. She said she can't come out here because it would give these bullies what they want. But things have changed. She needs you to go and see her. She said to leave me in your place.'

'Paula said this?'

'Yes. Just now. I don't know her that well but she seemed really riled about something.' Hopefully Paula's predilection for taking her temper out on her people would sway the woman.

The woman looked past Bloom to the building beyond. She was thinking about it. Bloom needed to force the decision home.

'Sorry, I don't like to say this to you, but she said, "Tell her to get her ass in here right now. And I mean right now." ' Bloom had spent days listening to Paula's style of talking and she hoped she'd pulled off a realistic impression.

A moment passed; the other woman sat with her eyes closed and Bloom tried to think of what she could use next. But then the woman rose to her feet in one elegant movement and removed the mask, handing it to Bloom.

'You don't need to do anything except wear this and sit here until I come back. You don't move, understand?' She glanced towards the police officers with their weapons raised.

Bloom nodded, afraid that if she spoke she might spoil it.

'And avoid looking their way. It helps.'

Bloom sat as instructed. At one point the other woman looked back and Bloom pretended to be putting on the mask. But as soon as the woman was safely inside Bloom threw the mask on to the road, raised her hands and focused her gaze on the inspector.

'I'm Augusta Bloom. You can come in now,' she shouted.

Within seconds she was surrounded by firearms officers and the fire brigade. They hustled her away from the containers to where the inspector now stood a few metres outside the main building.

'We need ambulances in here,' she said.

'First we need to ensure the environment is safe,' he said. 'Thank you for your help, there.'

'You don't understand. One child has already passed away and more are very sick. There isn't time. If you don't want your ambulances in here we'll carry the children to the gate.'

The man thought for a moment then said, 'Ms Bloom, you may well have saved the day here so I'm not going to stop you from going back in, but I do strongly advise against it until we know no other gas has been released.'

Bloom was moving before he'd finished. She knew police speak for *I'm washing my hands of your decision.*

'Nicola? Julia? Get the children outside, there are ambulances. Then we'll come back for the sickest women.' Nicola and Julia immediately picked up two of the smallest children. Bloom was pleased to see they were both still conscious despite flopping in their helpers' arms as they were carried out. 'Ladies? Ladies? Anyone capable should help those most sick out into the fresh air. Take some deep breaths as you go. It helps.'

'Can they help Bobby? Please ask them to help Bobby.'

Bloom turned to the young mum cradling her son in her arms. 'Let's get you outside,' she said, fearing there was nothing that could be done now for the little boy Jameson had tried to save.

80

Paula stared wide-eyed at the dead man on the floor. His blood had speckled her face with gruesome freckles.

'Marcus, my saviour. Thanks, baby.'

Jameson ignored Seraphine and checked on Scarlett, who lay motionless on the floor. She was breathing and had a pulse. The gas mask next to her had small yellow dots on its oxygen canisters. He placed her in the recovery position then took his phone from his pocket and called Ned Nesbitt.

'Tell your men the security guards are disarmed and one is deceased. There's just the woman on the drive to deal with but I have Paula Kunis here so that should help.'

He listened as Nesbitt filled him in on Bloom's success on that score, just as the woman from the drive appeared in the doorway. She took one look at Scarlett and the dead man on the floor and started screaming.

Seraphine walked across the room and closed the door in the woman's face. 'Normals,' she said to Jameson with a wink.

Nesbitt had asked Jameson to keep Paula in her office until Burr arrived, and he'd agreed, wondering what he'd ever done to deserve being stuck in a room with these particular ladies, Scarlett excepted. He watched the unconscious woman's body for a moment to make sure she was still breathing.

'She was trying to kill me,' Paula said, looking at Seraphine, who had perched on the edge of the desk.

'Didn't try hard enough in my book,' he said. 'Sit.'

Paula did as he instructed but he could see he'd riled her. 'You can't say that. You're a police officer.'

'No, I'm not. Whatever gave you that impression?'

'You have a gun.'

He looked at the Glock in his hand. 'This thing? This belonged to one of your security men out there. No one's coming in here with the means of killing others except for you.'

'You can't hurt me. Neither of you can hurt me.'

Jameson placed both hands on his knees and leaned in to Paula's face. 'If it was up to me, you would suffer endlessly for what you did to Shauna Roberts and her family, to those women in Liverpool and their families, but most of all to the little ones. What gives you the right, hey?'

Seraphine said, 'She was sent by God.' Jameson looked her way and she shrugged. 'Apparently.'

He stood up and backed away. 'Explains a lot.'

'So can I kill her then?'

He held Seraphine's gaze as she smiled at him – long enough to freak Paula out, he hoped.

The door from the corridor opened and Inspector Burr entered with two other officers and a paramedic – all in hazmat suits. The paramedic took one look at Green's body and went to Scarlett.

Seraphine slid off the desk as she said to Paula, 'You lucked out there. I think he was about to say yes.'

81

The driveway and surrounding gardens of the Artemis retreat were alive with activity. Paramedics in hazmat suits assessed and triaged the women and children who sat or lay on the grass coughing, wheezing and crying. Above them the air ambulance moved off, containing one of the smaller children and a woman who had suffered a suspected heart attack.

The fire brigade had been swift in confirming the lack of any chemicals in the atmosphere and there had been nothing but fresh air in the three plastic boxes on the drive. If Kunis did possess any sarin gas she had not used it, but no one was taking any chances. A full search of the premises and all the buildings in the village was being undertaken by the fire service and the police.

Having informed Inspector Burr of what had occurred inside the main building, Jameson walked through the crowd. It was clear Paula's men had played a key role in the events of the day. The fact two of their number had suffered gunshot wounds, one of them fatal, was unlikely to be the main focus of the investigation. But he knew he should prepare himself for answering for his actions. He no longer had the right to take a life.

So why had he? He didn't want to think too much about the answer to that question.

He had seen Bloom earlier directing activities as the group of women were moved out into the fresh air. That had been a smart move. According to the fire brigade's Hazardous Material and Environmental Protection Officer, either chlorine powder or an aluminium phosphide agent had most likely been used to adulterate the gas mask canisters. Both of these, he said, would have reacted to any moisture present in the air – aided by the fake tear gas, which had probably been nothing more harmful than steam from a steam cleaner that was found abandoned in the corridor. They also found three glass bottles smashed on the floor outside the main hall and then swept into the corner. Probably a ruse to make the women inside think police had fired gas canisters through the windows. They would need to wait for blood tests to confirm exactly which chemical was used, but, either way, oxygen was critical to recovery and there was no better immediate source of that than being outside.

He found her now, sitting with her back to the wall next to the doors of the building. Her eyes looked puffy and bloodshot and her breathing was a touch laboured. He took a seat beside her.

'Hey partner,' he said in his best cowboy accent.

'I messed up, Marcus. I told them to put the masks on. I thought we'd be safer that way.'

'That was a fair assumption, don't beat yourself up. You couldn't have known she would do this.'

Bloom looked at him and he didn't know if the tears in her eyes were related to gas or emotion. 'Of course I could. How many times did I tell you that cult leaders often pose the most danger to their own people? I could have seen this coming. I should have.'

'Don't beat yourself up about what you did wrong. Take it from someone who knows. You can't change that now. Focus on what you did right. You were brave enough to come here and step inside the unknown and you got these people out. Think about that.'

'You were the one who saved us all.' She closed her eyes and leaned her head back against the wall. 'I know you're talking sense, but I still feel awful.'

Jameson patted her knee and sat with her in silence watching the activity. He may have clocked what was going on early enough to save most of the group. Other than the poor little boy who'd died, and the young girl and heart attack candidate in the air ambulance, most looked to be recovering well. The children were naturally being treated first. He could see three of them sitting in a line on the gurney of the nearest ambulance taking turns on the oxygen mask. More ambulances were arriving at regular intervals and it would not be long before they began taking those suffering most to hospital. But the majority of the women were now sitting up and talking to each other, which meant their breathing could not be too impaired.

On a small patch of lawn beyond the ambulances, a group of women had gathered around the mother of the dead boy. If Bloom felt bad encouraging people to put on the gas masks, how must that poor woman feel having put one on her son? It didn't bear thinking about. And despite everyone else appearing to be recovering well,

Jameson knew that the sight of the boy would stay with him. The lad would join in his head the other ghosts of people he could not save or had put in harm's way.

'Hey, did you come across a little boy called Eddie and his mum Georgina by any chance?'

Bloom opened her eyes and took a look around. 'There was a little boy called Edward, he had dark hair and . . .' She paused and then pointed. 'There.'

Jameson followed her finger and saw a boy of five or six with a mop of black hair and no front teeth stepping out of an ambulance. He held the hand of a woman with a large bruise on her face. 'Is that his mum?'

'No, that's Rose. His mum died in an accident apparently but I don't know when or how.'

'I do,' he said. Jameson watched little Eddie hug the woman called Rose. 'There was a car accident a few miles from here last week, involving Eddie and his mother. I don't know for sure but I think they might have been trying to leave this place.'

'And Rose was sent to stop them. That's why Paula was so angry with her.' Bloom sat upright. 'Where is Paula?'

'Inspector Burr has her in her office. They're trying to get her to spill the beans about the sarin gas she claimed to have.'

'How would she get hold of sarin gas?'

Jameson didn't respond. He was distracted by the sight of Seraphine walking their way. She had a mug of something in her hand and was smiling as if they'd run into each other at some garden party rather than having had a near-death experience. She sat on the other side of Bloom and handed her the mug.

'Tea, Augusta? It's good for shock, they tell me.'

'That's my cue,' said Jameson, rising to his feet. He knew Seraphine would not be able to stop herself from telling Augusta what he'd done and he did not want to be here to see the disappointment in his partner's eyes.

82

'He never even hesitated,' Seraphine said to Bloom as Jameson walked to where the little boy Edward sat with Rose.

'He has good instincts. That's his strength. He doesn't overthink, thankfully. We'd all be dead if he hadn't acted so fast.'

'True, but that's not what I meant.'

'I should have seen what Paula was planning. I was in there. I could have stopped it before that little boy—'

'She fooled us both. Are you going to drink that tea because if not I'll have it?'

Bloom looked at Seraphine for the first time since she had sat next to her. The woman didn't look dishevelled and stunned like the rest of them. The only sign that she had been in there with them was a slight reddening to her eyes.

'People never fool you. And if they do you'd never admit it.'

'I know. I was trying to be empathetic. You keep telling me it's my weakness so I thought I'd try it on, see how it fits.'

'It doesn't.'

Seraphine sighed. 'I know. It's simply not me.'

Behind Seraphine, Inspector Burr walked out of the

building, and behind him walked Paula Kunis in handcuffs with an officer holding her elbow. Burr had his hands full with Kunis. She didn't even have the good grace to hang her head in shame. She walked with her back straight and her eyes forward, an indignant expression on her face.

Bloom had met her type enough times before to know how the police interview would go. She would insist her actions were caused by others, that she'd had no choice. She might even blame someone else like GI Joe or maybe even Bloom and Seraphine. She would twist and wriggle and rage. Or she would simply refuse to speak. It would be lengthy and frustrating and Bloom did not envy Ned Nesbitt's team the task ahead of them. But she knew Nesbitt well enough to know he was like a dog with a bone. There would be no letting up or letting go until he'd exhausted every tactic open to him.

Bloom looked for Scarlett. A few moments ago she had been sitting with paramedics in their triage area, but now she was nowhere to be seen. Marcus said he'd found her passed out in Paula's office next to a gas mask with yellow dots. Interestingly, Inspector Burr had said the other mask in the room had no dots. It turned out Paula had not intended to go out with her people. It was often the case that these cult leaders chickened out at the last minute, opting for an easier route to death. Both Jim Jones and David Koresh allegedly died of self-inflicted gunshot wounds, thereby avoiding the pain of poison or fire.

Bloom needed to speak to Scarlett and apologize. She really had failed her and her family in every sense.

What had been the point? Why had she come here? She hadn't helped or made any difference to the outcome. If anything, agreeing to help Porter had triggered the whole sorry affair. She remembered something Seraphine had said.

'What did you mean when you said he never hesitated?'

'I had a little situation with Paula and her henchman. Marcus took care of it.'

'How?' Bloom stared at her.

'Shot him, right between the eyes.'

'No. Why would he do that unless—?'

'My life was in danger?'

'Your life is never in danger. You're the spider, spinning your web and catching the rest of us in your twisted plans. If he thought your life was in danger it was because you wanted him to.'

Seraphine laughed. 'Marcus and I have a connection and now we know why. I always said he was a little more like me than you'd like to admit.'

Bloom knew Seraphine was referring to the training Jameson had undertaken in MI6 to keep his actions cool and calculated. Somehow the woman thought this gave them something in common. She had completely missed the fact that Jameson's inability to remain cold and detached was exactly why he'd left the service. 'That's not love, you know?'

'Coming to my rescue. Taking a life to save my life. I'd say that's pretty good evidence he cares.'

'Manipulating him into becoming what you want him

to be is not love. There's a reason he left his past in the past. If you cared for him you wouldn't drag him back.'

'If you cared for him you wouldn't hold him back.'

'Is that why you really came, to test Marcus somehow? No. That's ridiculous. You came for Scarlett, like me. You thought she would give you leverage in whatever fight you have with Gerald Porter. He told me he'd left your little gang because he found your plans pedestrian.'

A sound much like the howl of a wounded animal erupted from the building behind them. Bloom saw a figure running out of the front door towards Paula and the police officers. She couldn't tell if Paula saw what was coming, but the officer holding her arm did. He turned his head at the last minute. But it was too late. Scarlett raised her right arm and, momentarily, the kitchen knife glinted in the sun before she plunged it deep into Paula's throat.

'Oooph,' said Seraphine beside her.

'No!' Bloom stood and moved to go and help but Seraphine grabbed her by the arm.

'It's too late. Trust me.'

Paula fell with the police officer still holding her. Blood splattered the officer's face and began to pool on the ground at an alarming rate. Paramedics rushed to help as Burr grabbed Scarlett and forced her hands behind her back. The blood-soaked knife dropped from her fingers. Her fight was done.

'Crude but effective.' Seraphine took the untouched tea from Bloom's shaking hand and had a sip. 'Look at all that blood.'

Bloom sat heavily on the floor. How had this ended so very badly?

'Looks like neither of us will be getting our mitts on young Scarlett now,' Seraphine said, before draining the tea.

83

The police cordon was now three miles back down the road. A barrier of cones had been set up, behind which the few families who had remained all sat in their respective vehicles. They could not see or hear anything from here so would have no idea if their loved ones were safe.

Jameson waited for the sergeant to park his patrol car and then climbed out of the passenger side. They walked together to the first of the cars. The sergeant had been dispatched to gather the names of the waiting families and the daughters they had come to find. Jameson had hitched a ride for his own reasons.

He found Sean Hill alone in a blue Mercedes estate. He was reading something on his phone and didn't see Jameson coming. When Jameson knocked lightly on the driver's window, Hill jumped and almost dropped his phone. He wound his window down a small amount.

'Marcus?'

'It's OK. You're safe. No toxic gas out here, you'll be happy to know.'

Hill wound his window down more. 'Did you find Georgina?'

'I think I found Eddie.' He showed Hill a photograph he had taken of the boy on his phone.

Hill placed his hands over his mouth and tears filled his eyes. He didn't say anything, simply nodding confirmation that this was his grandson.

Jameson knelt by the door so he was level with Hill. 'There was an incident in there but Edward is fine. He may have inhaled something toxic but the medics have said he should make a full recovery. But I'm afraid Georgina is not here.'

'Where is she? She wouldn't leave Eddie. He was her world.'

'My colleague who was inside the compound the whole time was told Georgina died in an accident.' He knew he had to say it quickly and plainly. There was no sugaring the pill. He watched the disbelief take hold in Hill's eyes.

'What kind of accident?'

'I don't know for sure yet, but I suspect Georgina was driving a car that crashed not far from here a week ago. I spoke to a runner who witnessed it and saved a little boy from the wreckage.'

'A week ago?' The pain on Hill's face was hard to look at. He had missed his precious daughter by a matter of days. If this had all happened before Georgina had tried to flee, she might well be recovering on that lawn. It would be a tough reality for this father to live with. Jameson could only hope that having his grandson back might soften the blow.

His phone rang in his pocket and he made his apologies to the grieving man.

'Marcus, I've found something you'll want to know about,' said Lucas.

The fact their technical whizz had not enquired how things were progressing up there, or how Augusta was, told him whatever Lucas had found must be important.

84

Day 16

Bloom sat in the windowless room on one of two chairs either side of a plastic table. She had met with others from the retreat over the past couple of days. Ned Nesbitt's team were systematically interviewing everyone who had been there so some had chosen to stay in the Edinburgh area, including herself and Jameson. She had spoken at length with Nicola and Julia over lunch in a nice Edinburgh café earlier that day. Nicola had been more shaken by things than Julia. She had really wanted to believe the Artemis story. She had felt buoyed by her time there and a strong sense of belonging, until everything changed, of course. Julia by comparison was more reflective. She had a maturity of years that made her philosophical about her near miss. 'Learn what you can and move on,' she had said.

Julia told them how she had accompanied Daisy the student to her parents' house to help explain what had happened. They had missed the whole Artemis drama and been blissfully unaware of their daughter's involvement in it.

Others had been reunited with their families in the immediate aftermath. Once the hazmat team had cleared the site, the police orchestrated the reunions for those who had gathered outside the village with a good degree of sensitivity. After all, there were a fair few parents present whose hopes were to be dashed. Their daughters were not there. The mysteries of their disappearances still to be solved.

And even for those reunited, the journey ahead would not be smooth. A significant level of trauma could be expected for the women who had dedicated their lives to a leader who turned out to be a willing executioner. All that time lost. Not to mention the effects of having been conned and manipulated out of your lives, your money and the love of your family.

Bloom had made it her priority to speak to Lisa before leaving the retreat. She had been critical to their survival by enabling Bloom to contact Jameson. Bloom wanted to thank her for that. But Lisa had been in complete denial. She couldn't accept that Paula would try to hurt any of them, insisting there must have been a mistake or the security men had acted on their own to destroy the strong women of Artemis. It was not an unexpected perspective. Many Artemis members would go through this stage of adapting to the truth. It was not Bloom's job to convince her otherwise, but she did want Lisa to see she had made a significant impact on how things turned out. That could be crucial to her recovery.

And then Bloom had to have her most difficult conversation, a Skype call with Greta and Harris Marshall. They had already heard that Scarlett had been charged with the murder of Paula Kunis and placed on remand at Edinburgh prison. Bloom tried to answer their questions as best she could, but they were confused and upset. She told them how sorry she was that she had not managed to avert this outcome but that if they were agreeable she may still be able to help Scarlett.

And so here she was.

Scarlett entered wearing prison-issue clothing. It didn't pass Bloom by that this was only one step away from the uniform used by Artemis.

It had taken some negotiating to get in the room. Superintendent Ned Nesbitt was not keen on her acting as an expert witness for the defence. He wanted her on the prosecution team. The truth of the matter was her presence at the retreat might make her testimony inadmissible anyway due to a conflict of interest, but if she was going to attend as a witness, she wanted to make sure the court understood how cult leaders like Paula Kunis coerced and controlled their members – including Scarlett.

'How are they treating you?' said Bloom, watching Scarlett sit. She looked petite and fragile. Her auburn hair was tied in a band at the back of her neck and her pale, freckled skin made her look younger than her years.

'Fine. The officers are kind.'

'Good. Thank you for speaking to me. Your family have asked me to help your defence. As you now know I'm a psychologist and frequently act as an expert witness for people accused of a crime. This meeting is not being recorded but I will be taking notes for my own report. Is that OK?' It felt weird to be reeling off such a familiar introduction to this woman. Remaining objective was going to be a challenge. Thankfully she'd managed to get a couple of good nights' rest at last, so hopefully her mind was suitably refreshed.

'Yes.'

'The evidence against you is damming, Scarlett, as I'm sure the police have told you. Everyone saw you stab Paula, but if we can explain what led up to that, it might help.'

'Thank you,' said Scarlett.

'Are you OK to begin?' Scarlett nodded. 'Scarlett, were you aware that the tactics used by Artemis are those typically associated with cult movements?'

The woman frowned and bit her bottom lip.

'Bombarding people with affection and information, removing them from their family and friends, then turning them into compliant followers.'

'We only wanted people to see the truth.'

'Which is?'

'The discrimination is so subtle now. Women are allowed to vote, to gain professional qualifications, to be promoted, but still there is no real equality. She said it didn't matter how we showed women the truth, we only needed to be sure they saw it, because she couldn't let that unfairness continue.'

'So your ends justified your means?'

'I wasn't comfortable with it at first but then she made me see it's no different to how the press or politicians like my uncle tell us what to think or believe. Everything is PR and perspective. What matters is that you are doing it for the right reasons.'

'As long as your motive is sound you can be as manipulative as you want. Is that what she told you?' Bloom could see how such a premise would free people up to use whatever tactics they could to win people over to their truth.

'She would say: show them the truth no matter the means.'

'Would she say this often?'

'Every night. Like a mantra.'

Bloom made notes. She had learned some basic shorthand early in her career to enable her to record what was said without losing focus on the person. This would be good evidence of the kind of brainwashing Scarlett had been subjected to.

'Tell me about the house in Liverpool.'

Bloom didn't think it was possible for more colour to drain from Scarlett's pale skin but it did.

'This is going to be a key part of the case against you because the police know you took out the lease for that house.' Lucas had relayed this intel to Jameson on Tuesday. As all the chaos was going on at the retreat, Lucas uncovered that although a fake address and ID had been used to lease the property, the name on the ID was Greta Porter and the photograph was of Scarlett. Jameson had rushed back from speaking to some of the fathers to tell Bloom and Burr, only to discover the aftermath of Paula's stabbing. 'You used your mother's maiden name.'

Tears began to well in Scarlett's eyes.

'What happened there? How did those twelve Artemis members die?' Bloom set her expression to show no judgement. She needed Scarlett to talk.

'Paula . . . she . . .'

'Take your time.'

'Paula told me they were disloyal and intent on destroying everything Artemis had achieved. She wanted them locked away where they couldn't do any damage.'

'And you believed her?'

Scarlett nodded. 'I'm sorry. Locking them in there was a mistake. I realize that now. It was an awful loss.' Tears ran down her cheeks as she shook her head. 'We couldn't let anyone discover a connection to Artemis. It would have looked really bad, I understood that.'

'A women's rights group locking women up. You don't say. Who set that fire?'

'We never found out.'

'But you suspect someone, don't you?'

Scarlett picked at the material of her trousers. 'It's too much of a coincidence, isn't it, the poisoned gas masks and the fire?'

Bloom felt for Scarlett. The pain of discovering this level of betrayal from someone you loved and admired would be hard to bear.

'Can I ask about Tuesday specifically? When did you realize what Paula was doing?'

'I had no idea until the paramedic told me the masks had been poisoned.'

'You weren't suspicious when Paula brought the security men in?'

'I didn't want to call them. I worried it made us look like weak women but she insisted. Paula was in one of her moods that day so I knew she wouldn't listen.' Scarlett briefly shook her head. 'Now I realize she had other reasons for them being there. We'd used them before when some of the villagers had objected to us moving in.'

'They are denying any part in it. Did you see anything suspicious?'

'I expect they saw an opportunity to put us in our place. Such men don't like it when strong women stand up for themselves.'

Nesbitt had told Bloom that Scarlett had only been able to express hypotheses about the men in her police interviews. It appeared she'd been oblivious to any negotiations they'd had with Paula. The boss of the company had been shot dead by Jameson – who had been bailed pending a charging decision once an investigation into the circumstances of the shooting had been undertaken – and the other two were taking the line that they were only following orders to pump steam into the meeting room, smash some bottles and stand guard by the door. They denied any knowledge of the poison in the masks. As far as they were aware the whole sarin gas threat was simply a ruse to disperse the crowd outside the gates, they said. But there had been no poison in their masks, so you had to ask why Paula was sparing them.

'Tell me about Denise.'

'The police said she's missing.'

This was true. The woman who had sat with the plastic containers on the drive had fled the site during the chaos. 'Were you aware of her background as a chemist?'

'I knew she'd worked for a pharmaceutical company,

but that's all. It can't be true that she helped Paula poison the masks.'

'Did you know her well?'

'Paula asked us to work together on taking care of the Artemis reputation. Denise was so sweet. I can't believe Paula would use her that way. It's cruel.'

So far there was no record of who had purchased the gas masks or the chlorine powder that had been inserted into the oxygen canisters. They were pretty sure the chemical had been placed in them on site, as traces of it had been found in one of the compound houses along with a large roll of cling film. It was thought that once the powder had been inserted, the canisters had been wrapped in film to stop any moisture activating the poison. Whoever had done this knew what they were doing and, as the group's only chemist, Denise was looking like the prime suspect. Ned's team were searching all of the Artemis computers at the farmhouse, the Edinburgh HQ and the homes of members such as Melanie and Victoria, the women who had tried to recruit Bloom in London.

For whatever reason, Paula had decided to keep Scarlett out of her plans; her most loyal disciple was an intended victim too. Bloom wondered why that would be.

'Had anything changed between you and Paula recently? Lisa told me you two were close.'

'Paula had lost her way.'

'What makes you say that?'

'A few months ago she asked me to check over a mortgage application for a property Artemis was buying. I went to check it out for myself but it wasn't like our other buildings. It was a luxury apartment near to Regent's Park in London.'

'She was buying it for herself?'

'It was beautiful, breathtaking.' Scarlett made eye contact. 'But that's not how we live, how she had told us we should live. Paula was infected by the money and the fame. It was an evil that she'd become addicted to.'

'Why do you say she was addicted to it? This is only one property.'

Scarlett shook her head and deep lines formed on her brow. 'There was more. When I dug deeper she had Artemis money going to private accounts. She had other properties in LA and Monaco. She would often take a week or so to meditate away from the group and I realized she was going to these places and living an immoral life.'

Scarlett's disapproval dripped from every word. Perhaps, like those women in Liverpool, Scarlett had been too judgemental of Paula's true motives and lifestyle. More importantly, had such discoveries contributed to Scarlett's attack on Paula?

'Tell me how you felt when you heard about the poison.'

Scarlett shuffled in her seat and averted her gaze. She didn't want to discuss this. Bloom stayed quiet and waited.

'I was horrified that Paula could try to hurt us all like that,' Scarlett said eventually.

'Is that why you stabbed her?'

She looked up at the ceiling and swallowed. 'She taught us that if the devil lives in someone's head, we should do our best to evict him. Paula had let us all down. It had to stop. I knew how convincing she could be. She would talk her way out of it and then she'd be free to carry on.'

Bloom could relate to Scarlett's assessment. She herself had feared that Paula would try to run rings around the police, blaming everyone but herself. She may have even planned to blame Denise and the hired help for the whole thing; perhaps that's why she spared them.

Time was nearly up so Bloom thanked Scarlett and said she'd come back if there were any details to check.

As she knocked to let the guard know she was ready to leave Bloom said, 'You know, it's a real pity Artemis had Paula as its leader. Your arguments were sound. Such tactics were unnecessary.' She meant this too. She had already spoken to Julia and Nicola about turning their experience into something positive. Maybe they would start a women's network of their own: a credible one, which could begin with supporting the women from Artemis in their recovery and go on to continue the women's rights movement in a legitimate manner.

'If She wills it, it will be,' said Scarlett.

The guard opened the door and Bloom held a hand up to him.

'Sorry, could I have five more minutes?' Her mind was presenting a new hypothesis: a pattern she may have missed.

She took a seat again and began skimming back through her notes.

'Is everything OK?' said Scarlett.

'Yes, sorry. I need to check one last thing.'

Bloom turned the pages and quickly read what she had written, then as she went back to the beginning and began to circle phrases she said, 'As psychologists we are told to avoid pre-judging people. You see, if we do, we see evidence of what we expect to see and the contra-evidence sort of washes by us. That's why it's drilled into us to record what we hear' – she paused – 'so we can look back and see what was said more objectively.'

When she'd finished reviewing her pages she looked at Scarlett.

'When you told me, *She would say: show them the truth no matter the means. Every night. Like a mantra*, I assumed you were talking about Paula, as if she had brainwashed you, but you weren't, were you?'

Scarlett folded her arms tightly across her body.

Bloom flicked through her notes. 'Later you said a similar thing again: *She said it didn't matter how we showed women the truth, we only needed to be sure they saw it.* And: *She couldn't let that unfairness continue.*'

Scarlett remained silent with arms folded.

'It was only at the end there when you said, *If She wills it, it will be*, that I realized what I was missing. Paula wasn't the one you were talking about, it was God, wasn't it?'

'What difference does that make?'

'Oh it makes plenty, Scarlett. Because you also said' – Bloom went back to her notes – '*She taught us that if the devil lives in someone's head, we should do our best to evict him*, and then you said you thought money and fame were an evil Paula had become addicted to. You said you felt betrayed because Paula had let you down and it had to stop.'

Scarlett blinked a few times but stayed quiet.

Bloom sat back in her chair. 'That betrayal didn't come when you heard about the poison from the paramedic, did it? You had felt that for a long time. You said about Paula's apartment that that wasn't *how she had told us we should live*, and that her trips to her other luxury houses were evidence she lived an immoral life. You'd been angry with Paula for a while, hadn't you? Did you think she was no longer worthy to lead you?'

Again there was no reply.

'And there's one other thing you said that bothers me.' Bloom read it from her notes to be sure she said it right. '*I knew how convincing she could be. She would talk her way out of it and then she'd be free to carry on.* Why were you so worried that Paula would be convincing enough to walk free? Was it because she'd had nothing at all to do with poisoning the gas masks?'

Scarlett's mouth was pressed into a thin line and her previously pale cheeks had reddened.

'I'm ashamed to say I may have misjudged Paula in this. I think her assertion that she was sent by God may have been a convenient way to convince people to give her the attention and money she desired, but would that have driven her to try to kill people? I suppose we'll never know now. But you're a different story, aren't you, Scarlett? Because you are devout in your loyalty to your God. And if She tells you to evict the devil from someone's head, well, that's what you need to do, isn't it?'

Scarlett's eyes blazed and some of her auburn hair had fallen away from its band. The woman looked like she was on fire inside, a stark contrast to the pale angelic figure who had walked into this room less than an hour ago.

'Paula asked you and Denise to protect the Artemis reputation. Is that how you came up with your plan, when you discovered Denise's background working in a chemistry lab? I saw you two together, only briefly, in Paula's office before Rose took a beating, but there was a closeness between you that I detected even in that short, whispered conversation. Was Paula even aware of what was in those gas mask canisters? When I think about the two of you making us put them on, I can't figure it out. She sounded like it was all her doing, her plan to save us from the attack, but a narcissist like that would always take the credit even if an idea wasn't their own. And you would know that, wouldn't you, Scarlett?'

Bloom closed her notepad and put down the pencil. 'How long had you been planning this attack on your own people?'

Scarlett stared unblinkingly at her with a hateful sneer.

'Had you been waiting for the perfect moment? I bet you couldn't believe your luck when all those families turned up at your door. But here's the thing, Scarlett, if God does exist, be they male or female, I'm pretty sure *Thou shalt not kill* is one of their fundamental laws.'

Scarlett rose from her chair and leapt across the table like a rabid animal. Bloom backed away, knocking her chair over as she went and stumbling out of range, but not before Scarlett had gouged a deep scratch across her face. Guards appeared from the two doorways as

Scarlett began tearing out the pages of Bloom's notepad and ripping them into shreds.

'There is no progress without sacrifice,' she spat as she fought against the men restraining her.

'Is that what you told yourself about the women in Liverpool? Because you yourself said that when it comes to who's guilty the poisoned gas masks and the Liverpool fire are too much of a coincidence.'

Scarlett's hair, now loose and wild, flamed around her head as her eyes burned into Bloom.

'Why poison everyone, Scarlett? What was there to gain? Those women gave their lives to Artemis in good faith.'

'Paula was evil and none of them could see it. They adored her. She acted like *she* was God and those fools bought it.'

'And so they *all* deserved to die?'

Bloom watched Scarlett rage and struggle as the guards dragged her away.

85

Jameson was waiting for her in the reception area of the visitors' centre.

'That was an impressive spot. Not sure I'd have clocked that. Well done, Augusta.'

'Did you pick up on my request?' she said as she joined him.

'As soon as you said it's important to record what we hear I told them to start recording.'

She had left Jameson with the prison guards watching her meeting from their office.

'Thank you. I'm not sure they'll be able to use it in evidence but at least it will give Ned some questioning tips.'

'Do you really think she burned down the Liverpool house as well?'

'Who knows, Marcus. But somebody did. If it was Paula and Scarlett knew that, or if Scarlett did it at Paula's behest or as some kind of gift, imagine how angry it would make her when years later she discovered Paula was as flawed as those women.'

'Or she's her uncle's niece and gets a kick out of killing people.'

'No. There was nothing in her history or character to suggest a personality disorder. Greta Marshall fears her brother; if her own child had shown any of the same characteristics, she'd have said.'

'Would she? A mother's love and all that.'

'You know these groups are more toxic than any nerve agent. They kill your capacity to think for yourself. Members start to believe everything they are told and that can make them do the most irrational things.'

'You think Scarlett came to believe it was OK to poison people or lock them up and burn them?' Jameson asked, looking sceptical.

'That young woman is completely radicalized. She believed every single word deep into her soul. Not even Paula could have imagined how effective her brainwashing would be. She produced a loyal follower who was so much more committed to the cause than she ever was because Scarlett truly believed they were doing God's work.'

'She did not like it when you pointed out killing people was not God's work.'

'I think she completely convinced herself they were lost souls and that their only salvation was death.'

They exited the building and walked across to the car.

'What did Nesbitt say?'

Bloom had called the superintendent as soon as she'd retrieved her phone from the prison guards.

'Not much. He wanted to see the tape. I really messed up on this one, Marcus. I got it wrong at every step.'

Her partner patted her back before he left her side to open the driver's door. 'You came good in the end. That was a win in there.'

'I'm not sure anyone is a winner in this situation.'

Jameson smiled at her but then his expression changed. Bloom turned to see what he had spotted.

'You really are intent on helping Porter's niece, aren't you?' said Seraphine, who was walking towards them from a blacked-out Range Rover. 'Why are you so willing to do that man's bidding?'

'I'm not doing anyone's bidding. This is not about Gerald Porter,' said Bloom.

'If you say so. But do you want to know a little secret about Scarlett? She's not so innocent. When they put those gas masks on us all did you notice hers didn't have any yellow dots? Paula's did but Scarlett's didn't. Why might that be?'

Bloom felt her anger rising. 'You didn't think to mention this earlier?'

Jameson shook his head. 'When I found her passed out, the mask next to her definitely had yellow dots on it. I saw it.'

'Ooooh, it's like one of those brain-teasers,' said Seraphine, clearly enjoying herself. 'A woman is found passed out in a room with two gas masks, one is full of toxic poison, the other is not, but she never inhaled any poison; how can that be?'

'What did you do?' said Bloom, realizing Seraphine was behind Scarlett's brief period of unconsciousness.

'The problem you have, Augusta, is you assume people are good until they prove you wrong. I, on the other hand, do the opposite. It helps me to see reality so much more clearly. Miss Scarlett is a prime example. She regained consciousness to be told her gas mask had poisoned her, and yet she knew that had never happened.' Seraphine looked between Bloom and Jameson. 'And she never uttered a word. That's not the behaviour of an innocent woman.'

Seraphine assumed Bloom and Jameson still viewed Scarlett as an innocent pawn. She thought she was revealing the truth to them. Bloom saw no necessity in putting her straight, all Bloom cared about was making sure Seraphine didn't try to use Scarlett in her ongoing war with Porter.

'That girl has been used and manipulated enough. Leave her alone.' Bloom knew that some day down the line Scarlett might emerge from her indoctrinated mindset to realize what she had done. She was not a psychopath who could walk away from a killing with no regrets; she was likely to be eaten up with remorse.

'Oh come on, Augusta, you know me well enough to know I don't waste helicopter fuel coming to save you from a situation that you put yourself in and that my lovely Marcus is more than capable of rescuing you from.'

'I am not your Marcus,' Jameson said.

'What use is Scarlett to you? Porter isn't really interested in her. He was only trying to appease his sister.' Bloom felt exasperated by Seraphine. Her game-playing was childish and cruel.

'You simply don't see the potential in people like I do, do you? Anyway, I didn't come here to shoot the breeze. I received a love letter yesterday.' She held an envelope out in one manicured hand.

Bloom took the note and opened it. It was handwritten on thick white paper in neat cursive script.

My Dearest Seraphine,

How I have missed our time together. It is of eternal regret to me that we are unable to put our impressive ***heads*** *together and move forward in sync, but you have made your position clear. I only hope you are ready to face the consequences.*

Don't get me wrong, I am forever indebted to you and your former mentor, Dr Bloom. She is an impressive woman. I wasn't convinced I would see what you see, but I actually found her to be insightful. She is no fan of yours, for instance. I think that, like me, she sees flaws in your ambitions, albeit of a different kind. She fears they are malevolent and harmful; I fear they are somewhat insipid.

She did me a great service in giving me time and passing my location on to my associates. I was surprised at the latter, I thought a woman of her intellect would be suspicious of my request. It turns out my efforts at distraction worked better than I could have hoped.

And my debt to you? Well, that is in the form of inspiration. Your idea is sublime and so I intend to take it: the plan, the people, the power.

I know you like your games, Seraphine, and so I have a challenge of my own.

Stop me if you can.

The game is afoot.

Dare to play?

G

Bloom began to see how effectively Porter had used her. By telling DCI Mirza he would talk only if Bloom did something for him first he had bought himself time: two weeks of it to plot his escape from Seraphine. Bloom had known his asking for her was odd, but she had pushed the worry aside because she wanted to help DCI Mirza. She could have stopped this whole thing then and there, and although part of her wished she had she knew that meant Scarlett would have put her plan into action some other day with no one there to stop her.

She had to admire Porter's skill in distracting her from that envelope with what he knew about Jameson's past. He had known she was loyal to her partner and wouldn't want him to experience any further distress, and he had used that against her. It also meant she kept that envelope a secret from DCI Mirza, which was a big betrayal of trust. Word would no doubt get around the police community and her reputation would suffer.

Jameson had told her the payment amount Porter requested was a code detailing Porter's exact location so he could be rescued. Mirza had since confirmed that the very solicitor Bloom had delivered the payment request to walked Porter out of the MOD building in broad daylight. Which meant there was no need for that money to be actually transferred, and yet it was. Now they knew why. It provided an evidence trail; one that convicted Bloom of betrayal in the eyes of Seraphine.

Bloom handed the note to Jameson. He may as well know what they were up against.

On finishing it, Jameson said, 'You're going to use Scarlett as leverage.'

'Am I? I believe she's a very capable woman. I always admire those who can hide in plain sight,' said Seraphine.

Jameson replaced the letter in its envelope and moved to hand it back.

'Keep it. I have a copy.'

'I'm not going to let you do that,' said Bloom.

'Oh I know, but that's the fun of it all, isn't it? And do you want to know the best bit?'

'Not really,' said Jameson.

Seraphine smiled and slipped her hands into the pockets of her blood-red wool coat.

'You both now owe me. And I will be coming to collect.'

As Seraphine walked away towards the prison gate, Bloom rushed to block her.

'I am not letting you get in there. I don't care how clever you think you are. You will leave that young woman alone.'

'Oh Dr Bloom, you are so very sweet. You know I have people everywhere. I can see her anytime I like, anywhere she might be. But I'll indulge you today, seeing as you've had a shock.' Seraphine blew a kiss at Jameson and walked back to the Range Rover.

'What do you owe her?' Bloom said, without looking at her partner.

'It's nothing, just biting my tongue over a drink.'

'It's never nothing with her. You know that.' She locked eyes with him. 'She'll use you. You should never have called her.' She wondered whether to enlighten him about how Seraphine had manipulated him into killing Green but decided this was not the time. If he was going to present a credible defence of his actions to the authorities he needed to believe he'd done what he had to.

As she climbed into the passenger seat she realized how different she and Seraphine really were. Although she would never admit it, she liked how some of her own traits echoed those of the psychopathic community. She felt proud of her ability to be logical and unemotional when it mattered, but on this occasion she had been distracted by the need to save people. Seraphine had seen the truth – that Scarlett was behind the poisoning, rather than Paula – because her mind was selfishly free of such emotional distractions. It may have helped her see reality better, but Bloom had no desire to be that way.

'Will this ever end?' she said when Jameson climbed in beside her. She felt weary with it all; with Seraphine's constant presence in her life over the past few years. Would things ever feel normal again? Would she ever lose that eerie sense that something untoward was coming?

'I think we have to make it end. I figure if they wanna play then we play too. Let's beat them at their own game.' He dragged the seatbelt across his jumper and plugged it in. He had thrown his jacket on the back seat.

'How do we do that?' Bloom pulled her winter coat a bit tighter. She could not get warm since leaving Inverness and they had a long drive back to London.

'Easy. We have something they don't.' He drove in a wide arc around the car park and exited through the barrier. As he pulled into the road and joined the traffic, he looked at her and winked. 'We have you.'

Acknowledgements

I have long been fascinated by cults. The idea that you might be lured away from your life and your loved ones without ever realizing what was happening is the kind of real-life nightmare that makes any fictional horror story pale into insignificance.

Much research has been done about the techniques such groups use to recruit and retain people, but I wanted to write about how it might feel from the inside. One of the most useful resources I found was the book *Combating Cult Mind Control* by Steven Hassan. As an ex-member of the Church of Unification, or Moonies, he has a wealth of personal insight into living in and leaving a cult. So huge thanks to Steven Hassan for his honesty and clarity in explaining the realities of these controlling and coercive organizations.

I must also thank two very impressive professionals who helped ensure the book has a degree of verisimilitude. A big thank-you to Chief Crown Prosecutor Siobhan Blake, for helping me with the legal elements, and to the elusive Dr Steve – an expert in all things chemical-warfare-related. Thanks for letting me put your good advice to bad!

The team at Transworld continues to be the best group of advisors and cheerleaders ever. I was faced with a change of editor for *Hunt* and was anxious about it: would the new editor like my work as much as Lizzy Goudsmit, who had discovered and championed me from the beginning; would she be as insightful? But I need not have worried. Natasha Barsby, thank you. Your feedback on my first draft had me thinking, 'Yes, yes, *that*'s the book I wanted to write!' You saw what I was trying to do and pointed me in the right direction, and I'm eternally grateful. You are a talent indeed.

Thanks also to Bella Bosworth for the copy-editing, to Hayley Barnes, Emma Burton and Sophie Bruce for your marketing and promotional support with all the Dr Bloom books, and to everyone at Transworld who works so hard to make us writers look good!

To my family. Your endless support and sarcasm keep me motivated. Thank you and please never stop! To Ella, Erica and Henry, your imaginations continue to astound me. I take great inspiration from you, but no, there will be no mermaids or pirates in my books.

And finally to Jamie. You were thousands of miles away throughout the writing of *Hunt* and yet I always felt you by my side, cheering me on, helping me think and pushing me to work harder. You're my best friend and I could not have done this without you.

If you enjoyed
HUNT
read the opening chapter of the
next book in the series:

THE FALL GUY

Coming 2022

I

Zander checked his reflection. The custom-made suit made him feel taller and slimmer. He squared his shoulders and brushed the jacket flat over his stomach before smoothing his hair down with both hands. The glass inside his thick-rimmed spectacles was clear. He didn't wear them to aid his vision.

'You look good.'

Lexi's voice sounded distant; he was consumed with what he was about to do, if he was up to it, if he could get away with it.

'I need to go alone,' he said.

She didn't reply, but he knew she understood. They had learned to respect each other's need for space over the years. The walk to the lift was short and the trip to the 36th floor swift, with just enough time to put on his gloves. He stepped out and checked his watch. 4pm. Philip had said he liked to sit in the bar in the early evenings on weekends because it was always empty then.

Zander moved to the entrance. The door glass was smoked but the window next to it had a small border of clear glazing. He angled his head so he could see the black and white room within; there was no sign of anyone there.

Perhaps Philip was late today.

Before he could type in the six-digit code that Philip

had used a few days earlier, a figure opened the door from within. Zander quickly stepped away and moved towards the lift. He couldn't risk being seen.

The suit felt heavy and hot on his body and the shirt underneath was sticking to his skin. He risked a glance back and saw a barman walking in the opposite direction. He hadn't anticipated that the bar would be staffed. That was stupid. The risks were too high. He had Lexi and AJ to think about. He reached out to the lift call button.

Then again, the barman leaving might be a sign.

He turned to watch the young man reach the end of the corridor and disappear around the corner. He felt it in every muscle and sinew. He wasn't the prey racing for cover. He was the panther.

Zander checked his watch then strode back to the door and typed in the code. If the bar was empty, he would return to his room and rethink. But if Philip was here, alone, then game on.

The door felt heavy as he pushed it wide and stepped inside the room. The interior smelled of freshly cut lilies and espresso. There were plush black and white chairs in pairs around glass tables, each set positioned far enough away from the others to afford residents the privacy they expected. Floor-to-ceiling glass ran the length of the right-hand wall, looking out over the Thames to the city beyond; a city still drenched in summer sun.

Zander placed both gloved hands into the pockets of his trousers. At a table tucked into the corner, out of sight of the door, a lone figure sat sipping whisky.

Zander was unlikely to afford his target any mercy,

and all hope was lost when Philip Berringer looked his way. His eyes widened in surprise and then narrowed as he said, 'You came back.'

'I moved in.'

'Congratulations.' The words were contradicted by the man's body language. Philip was evidently irritated that someone like Zander would live in the same building as someone like him: someone so important and sickeningly rich.

Zander's eyes scanned the room, taking in every last detail. He was hyper alert, his breath steady. He felt calm, in control, powerful. The room was empty other than the two of them but the barman could come back at any moment

'Have you seen what's going on down there?' Zander walked to the glass door and slid it open. The breeze felt cool on his face. He stepped out on to the balcony and looked back at Philip. 'Come see.'

Zander rested his arms on the balustrade, taking care to cover his gloved hands with his elbows. He glanced down at the grass, 36 floors below.

For a moment, it seemed that Philip might not move. Zander had spent hours – days even – fantasizing ways to show the smug bastard that he wasn't someone to cast aside. And, in his mind, this scenario had run without a hitch.

Make it happen, said the voice in his head.

'You'll never believe it,' Zander said.

Philip remained in his seat.

Hold your nerve.

'Seriously, man. You will not believe your eyes.'

Finally, he heard the tinkling of glass, as Philip lowered his drink to the table and slid back in his chair.

Zander smiled. No one could resist a mystery.

'I don't see anything.' Philip sounded bored as he reached the balcony.

'No,' Zander said. 'Down there.' He leaned forward as far as he could so that his torso was folded over the glass and his head hung low.

As anticipated, Philip copied him. 'I still—'

Zander stepped back, bent low and – with both hands – lifted the man so that his feet came up from the floor. Philip's body pivoted forwards. He grabbed at the glass. He tried to push backwards, but Zander kept lifting his legs higher and higher. Philip kicked and wriggled and banged but didn't scream or cry out.

Well, not until he fell.

Afterwards Zander walked back into the bar and collected one of the white chairs. He carried it onto the balcony and placed it where Philip had been standing. This had been Lexi's idea, as had the latex gloves.

'If you insist on doing it, do it right,' she had said.

Then, he removed the matchbox from his pocket. He'd bought it on a whim in the market. Bulls Eye Matches. It felt fitting. He took a single match, struck it and watched it burn. The whole thing had taken less than four minutes. He looked towards the balcony and listened to the distant sound of a woman screaming.

Smiling, he placed the matchbox on the table opposite his victim's drink then carefully laid the extinguished match on top.

'One down,' he said to the empty room.

Four strangers are missing. Left at their last-known locations are birthday cards that read:

YOUR GIFT IS THE GAME.
DARE TO PLAY?

The police aren't worried – it's just a game. But the families are frantic, and psychologist and private detective Dr Augusta Bloom is persuaded to investigate. As she delves into the lives of the missing people, she finds something that binds them all.

And that something makes them very dangerous indeed.

As more disappearances are reported and new birthday cards uncovered, Dr Bloom races to unravel the mystery and find the puppeteer. But is she playing into their hands?

There is an explosion at a military ball. The casualties are rushed to hospital in eight ambulances – but only seven vehicles arrive.

Captain Harry Peterson is missing.

His girlfriend calls upon her old friend Dr Augusta Bloom to support the investigation. But no one can work out if there is a connection between the bomb and the disappearance.

When Harry is eventually discovered three days later, they hope he holds the answers to their questions.

But he can't remember a single thing.